ONCE
UPON
A
PROJECT

Also by Bettye Griffin

THE PEOPLE NEXT DOOR

NOTHING BUT TROUBLE

IF THESE WALLS COULD TALK

Published by Kensington Publishing Corporation

ONCE UPON A PROJECT

BETTYE GRIFFIN

KENSINGTON PUBLISHING CORP.
www.kensingtonbooks.com

DAFINA BOOKS are published by

Kensington Publishing Corp.
850 Third Avenue
New York, NY 10022

All Kensington titles, imprints, and distributed lines are available at special quantity discounts for bulk purchases for sales promotion, premiums, fund-raising, educational, or institutional use.

Special book excerpts or customized printings can also be created to fit specific needs. For details, write or phone the office of the Kensington Special Sales Manager: Attn. Special Sales Department. Kensington Publishing Corp., 850 Third Avenue, New York, NY 10022. Phone: 1-800-221-2647.

Dafina and the Dafina logo Reg. U.S. Pat. & TM Off.

ISBN-13: 978-0-7582-1672-4
ISBN-10: 0-7582-1672-6

First Printing: May 2008
10 9 8 7 6 5 4 3 2 1

Printed in the United States of America

To Kim (Kimberly Rowe-Van Allen):
This one's for you!
Surprise!

Acknowledgments

Thank you to the following people:

Bernard Underwood, Mrs. Eva Mae Griffin, Elaine English, Kimberly Rowe-Van Allen. You're all the greatest! Happy 90th, Mom!

The girlfriends of longstanding: Kim White Bledsoe, Naomi Scott, Rebecca West Ogiste, Glenda Gelinas Blau, Rhonda McDaniel Tirfagnehu, Dawn Henderson Stewart, Dorothy Hicks-Terry, Sheila Tyler.

Beverly Griffin Love, my one and only sister.

My cousin Lillian Morton Walton, who inadvertently gave me the idea of how to tie this story together when she organized a reunion luncheon of former tenants of Cottage Place Gardens. Thanks, Lil!

The other cousins: Dorothy Clowers Lites, Ruth Griffin Ruff, Donna Griffin Williams, Leslie Griffin, Joanne Griffin Mc-Clain, Lynda Griffin Harvey, and Charlotte Ryer.

Bonnie Shultis and Amedee Jones, two really fun people. Working with you guys is a scream.

Pam Cowell, who keeps me smiling with those hilarious e-mails.

My author pals: Marcia King-Gamble, Gwyneth Bolton, Shelia Goss, Angie Daniels, Reon Laudat, and Roslyn Carrington.

My blog pals: Donna Deloney and Patricia Woodside.

Dorothy and the staff at Waldenbooks in the Ogilvie Transportation Center, downtown Chicago; the staff at Borders on 95th Street, Chicago; Glenn and staff at the Book Nook in Jacksonville, Florida; and the staff at Borders in Merrillville, Indiana.

The nice ladies at the Chicago Housing Authority (who assisted me with the names already used for public housing projects in the city) and at the Chicago School Board (who told me the cutoff dates for kindergarten registration in use forty-five years ago). I haven't forgotten your invaluable assistance and had planned to mention your names individually, but they went up in smoke when my computer malfunctioned. Sorry. Blame it on the geeks.

Theresa Myers, who suggested the title *Once Upon a Project* when my original title got kicked to the curb. Your complimentary copy is in the mail, with much gratitude.

Everyone who reads this book. If you're new to my work, welcome. Since my computer died, and all my extensive library of email contacts with it, I hope those of you who have read and enjoyed my earlier novels have learned that this latest one has been published! Feel free to join my website mailing list or drop me a note to help me reassemble my list: bettye@bettygriffin.com.

Prologue

The postcard invitations began arriving in mailboxes all over Chicagoland in early March.

Pat Maxwell, who'd sent them from a post office in her South Shore neighborhood, wondered about how the recipients would react to being invited to the event she'd organized. Would they be curious? Interested in attending? Ambivalent? Or would they merely toss the invitations in the trash?

The card reached Grace Corrigan in Lincoln Park the very next day. She'd known it was coming and let it lie on her console table for three days before finally affixing it to her refrigerator with a magnet. She admired Pat's determination, even if the idea struck her as silly. She'd left the projects when she was seventeen. That part of her life was long past, and as far as she was concerned, that's where it belonged.

To Susan Dillahunt, across the Wisconsin border in the town of Pleasant Prairie, the postcard presented an opportunity to escape from the unhappiness of her life and reclaim a happier time, even if only for a little while.

And to Elyse Reavis, well north of the city in Lake Forest, the postcard came as a welcome distraction after having yet another exhausting argument with her husband.

But none of these four women, friends all their lives, knew that this innocent invitation to a reunion of their childhood neighborhood would mark a turning point for them, after which their lives would never be the same.

Chapter 1

Early March
Lake Forest, Illinois

Elyse slipped into her new lace-trimmed tap pant underwear and matching bra. The underwear pinched a bit—it kept catching between her butt cheeks—but it looked so flattering and sexy with its slight A-line. Next time she'd get one a size larger, and it'd probably be as comfortable as a pair of shorts, which it resembled. Already she was planning the fun she and Franklin would have when they returned home. It was Saturday, and they'd agreed to go to the six o'clock show and have dinner afterward. She'd taken a shower and put on capri jeans and a sweater. What she wore underneath would be her own little secret, and a sweet surprise for her husband when the time was right.

It surprised her how much she looked forward to tonight. Just five months ago she'd been moping around, all dejected because Brontë, her youngest, had joined her brother Todd at the Champaign-Urbana campus of the University of Illinois. Now that Elyse had had a chance to get used to the idea of being an empty nester, she found she rather liked it. The kids came home for weekends every couple of weeks. And when they were away, she and Franklin had some private time together to enjoy the life they'd built over twenty-five years of marriage.

At least that's how it had been the first few months, when they'd taken long walks along the path that ran adjacent to the Union Pacific tracks and gone to dinner at romantic restaurants.

But lately Franklin needed to be reminded about the meaning of "couple time." He'd canceled their plans at the last minute the past two times, saying he just didn't feel like going anywhere. Well, after the show she planned to put on for him tonight, he'd never cancel again. They'd get through this rough patch they seemed to be mired in, like a car stalled in mud. She'd put on some weight in recent years, but she still had a defined waistline and her boobs had expanded to a C cup. Elyse felt she had everything all those Hollywood actresses had, only lots more.

A few minutes before five-thirty she emerged from the bedroom and headed for the coat closet, fastening the posts to her small textured-gold hoop earrings as she walked.

"Franklin! It's almost five-thirty. We'd better get going. You know how hard it is to get a seat that's not on top of the screen, now that these multiplexes have gotten so tiny."

She stopped in front of the closet, realizing he hadn't responded. Suddenly suspicious, instead of getting her coat she turned and walked to the living room, the two-inch heels of her boots clicking on the hardwood that lined the hallway floor.

The sound of soft snoring drifted up from the sofa.

She stopped in her tracks, wanting to make sure she'd heard correctly. Oh, no. He didn't. Not again.

But there he lay, sprawled on the couch, mouth open, fast asleep. "Franklin!"

His body twitched at the sudden loud noise, and his eyes flew open. He looked at her with a scowl. "What's with you startling me like that, Elyse? Can't you see I'm sleeping?"

"It's five-thirty, Franklin," she announced, her tone unapologetic. "The movie starts in thirty minutes."

"It's that late already?" He glanced at the satellite receiver on top of the television for confirmation. "Damn. Last I knew it was three o'clock."

"Well, time marches on. And so must you." Her voice held a warning, and she prayed he would heed it.

Franklin stretched, his still-buff five-eleven frame looking delectable to her. Then he looked at her sheepishly. "Elyse . . ."

She anticipated what he was about to say and had her answer ready. "No!"

"C'mon, Elyse. We can always go next week."

"No, Franklin." She crossed her arms over her chest, wanting to show him she meant business.

He swung his legs down and moved into a sitting position. "Elyse, I'm really tired. The movie will still be playing next weekend. It just opened, for Chrissake."

"Next weekend is spring break. The kids will be coming home. You know we usually stay in when they're here."

"Oh, I don't know about that. I heard Todd say something about South Padre Island."

She kept her rigid stance.

Franklin tried again. "Elyse, it's just a movie. Don't make so much out of it. Besides, I haven't been feeling so hot lately."

"You've been saying that for months, Franklin, but I don't see you going to the doctor. Nor do I hear you complaining about not feeling well when it's your bowling night, or when you go out for drinks with your coworkers, or even when it's time to get up and go to work."

"That's because I can't afford to retire until after Brontë graduates."

"That's fine, but the point I'm making"—like he didn't know it, she thought angrily—"is that you're always fine until it's time for you and I to do something together. I'm tired of it, Franklin. So, are we going to the movies and dinner, like you promised, or not?"

He hesitated, and for a moment she thought she might have won the standoff. But then he looked down for a second before meeting her gaze. "I'm too tired, baby."

Elyse let her arms fall to her sides. "Fine. I'm going out. I'll see you later." *Don't wait up,* she added silently.

"Elyse, where are you going? It's getting dark out."

"I'm old enough to be out alone in the dark," she snapped on her way out of the room.

She confidently put on her coat and left the house. Only after she got in the car and let the engine warm up did she begin to wonder what the heck she would do. She wanted to be gone for several hours, even if she had to sit through two movies alone. Let him worry . . . when he wasn't snoring his head off.

She recalled her mother cautioning her so many years ago about the perils of marrying an older man. "Franklin seems like a nice man, Elyse, but he's thirteen years older than you. Right now I know that seems exciting. Man of the world and all that. But you're only twenty-one. There's a lot you should consider. He's going to age before you do, for one. For another, he already has two children to support."

"Mom, Franklin makes good money programming computers. Plus, he has an arrangement with his ex-wife. The court isn't involved. That's when the guys get trampled, he told me."

Jeanette Hughes hadn't been swayed. "Well, friendly ex-wives tend to become a lot less friendly once they find out there's a new woman in the picture. Before he knows it, he may find himself being dragged in front of a judge and ordered to give his ex-wife half of his income. Where will that leave him? And if you marry him, where will that leave you? It'll take time for you to become a licensed physical therapist. Unless you plan on dropping out or abandoning your career plans," she hinted suspiciously.

"No, Mom. I'm definitely going to be a physical therapist. And it's too soon to talk about marrying Franklin or anybody. I've only been seeing him for a few months."

"We'll see," her mother said.

Elyse thought she saw a hint of a smile, which she immediately dismissed as her imagination.

But in the end Jeanette Hughes's instinct proved correct. Elyse married Franklin a year after college graduation, after her first year of working toward her DPT degree at the University of Illinois at Chicago. At the time she'd been twenty-three, and he thirty-six. She was the first of her close girlhood friends to be married in the traditional way—in church, with flowers and organ music and her three best friends as bridesmaids—just as she'd dreamed about so often as a kid.

The very first of the foursome to marry had been Grace Corrigan. She married her high school sweetheart, Jimmy Lucas, before high school graduation, shortly after Grace learned she was pregnant. Grace and Jimmy's drab City Hall nuptials, with only their parents as guests, were far different from the beautiful wedding and elegant reception Elyse's parents had provided for her.

Grace had been the first to have a baby, too, becoming a mother at the same age she became a wife, eighteen. Elyse used to envy her. Little Shavonne Lucas was the cutest thing, and Grace kept her dressed in pretty ruffled dresses and dainty white lace-trimmed socks, always smelling sweet.

Elyse couldn't wait to have a child of her own. But because she had her education to complete, after her marriage she limited her own experiences with children to Franklin's son and daughter from his first marriage, with whom she became friendly, almost like a big sister. Franklin suggested that she get her career off the ground before they started a family of their own. Her parents, who feared that if she left school she'd never go back, agreed. Elyse's heart used to ache whenever she saw a woman with a baby, but she dutifully went along with Franklin's wishes. She didn't get pregnant for five long years.

In hindsight, she had to admit that Franklin and her parents had been right about not having children right away. Not only did she and Franklin have plenty of couple time before taking on the responsibility of parenthood, but they were also able to build a solid financial base. And having Todd and Brontë changed Elyse's life in the best way possible. She knew that children growing up and leaving home was a normal part of life, but it didn't have to mean the end of it. She liked to think of their current stage as a nice bridge before the grandchildren came. Now she and Franklin were free to do anything they wished.

But they rarely did, because Franklin never wanted to anymore.

As Elyse drove down the slight incline from her garage to the curb, she glanced at her mailbox and realized she hadn't checked the mail today. She pulled over alongside the stone-encased box and got out to grab the contents, then threw it on the empty passenger seat beside her without looking at it. Then she flicked the remote to close the garage door and drove off.

She took a closer look at the mail when she came to a red

light. A postcard imprinted with the familiar outline of the Theodore Dreiser Homes caught her attention immediately. She frowned at the black and white image on the card addressed to Elyse Reavis. Who would send a postcard from the projects? Not exactly the garden spot of the world.

She glimpsed at the traffic light. Still red. She flipped the card over and read it.

The Theodore Dreiser Housing Project welcomed its first residents in February of 1957. In the fifty years since, thousands of families have called the projects home at one time or another.

Join us at the Soul Queen Restaurant for an anniversary luncheon, and catch up with your old friends and neighbors over a satisfying meal.

The bottom of the card listed the date, time, and fee, as well as an RSVP number. At the very bottom the card read: Organized by Patricia Maxwell.

Elyse smiled. She'd grown up with Pat. Every day they used to walk to school together, along with Grace and Susan Bennett. She couldn't remember a time when she hadn't known them; it seemed as if they were just always there. They called themselves the Twenty-Two Club, because most of them had been born on the twenty-second of the month, although in different months. Grace's birthday, the lone exception, was quite close, on the twenty-first.

Many of the girls at school envied Grace for her good looks, or Susan because of her long, straight-textured hair and because she'd captured the heart of the school's leading athlete. But Pat had been named Most Popular Girl because she was a genuinely nice person. She had something nice to say to virtually everyone, and over the years she'd retained the same winning personality. While not as pretty as Grace or Susan, Pat could never be called a slouch in the looks department, plus she had a figure to die for, all curves. Elyse always thought it odd that Pat had never married.

Elyse felt a little guilty for not keeping in touch with her old friends better than she had. She talked to Pat maybe once or twice a year, and not at all to Grace or Susan. Their contact was largely limited to the annual exchange of Christmas cards.

She abruptly pulled over into a strip mall. She'd call Pat now, right this minute. Hell, Pat wasn't married. If she had no prior plans maybe they could get together tonight, catch up over a meal. Elyse would even drive into the city, which would take a good forty minutes from here in suburban Lake Forest, and closer to an hour to get south of downtown, where Pat lived. It sure beat sitting alone at the movies on a Saturday night.

Not only would that give her the opportunity to spend time with a lifelong friend she hadn't seen in far too long, but it would give her the satisfaction of knowing that Franklin would wonder what she was up to. She'd had it with him never wanting to do anything, and then hiding behind that lame excuse of not feeling well. If her cell phone rang she wouldn't even answer it.

She pulled out her address book and reached for her phone.

"Hi, Pat!" she said when her friend answered. "Don't be shocked, but it's Elyse."

"Elyse!" Pat laughed knowingly. "You must have gotten my postcard."

"I sure did. What a great idea, having a Dreiser reunion."

"Yeah, I thought it might be fun, after all these years. Besides, it gives me an opportunity to make a point."

"A point? Do I sense the famous Patricia Maxwell activism at play?"

Pat chuckled. "Sort of. The people who live there now staged a demonstration that made the news. They're asking for all kinds of improvements that will make it more like the Ritz. They don't seem to understand that living in the projects isn't supposed to be a lifetime thing. People are supposed to progress in life, even if they're stuck in the projects for fifteen or twenty years, like our parents were."

"I agree, but are you sure they aren't just asking for decent services, like heat and hot water and maintenance, or a laundry room where half the machines aren't broken?"

"Hell, no. They want computer libraries and tennis courts and more attractive landscaping."

"Oh." Elyse thought for a moment. "If the projects had all that, nobody would ever want to leave."

"Exactly. The public library has computers. As for parents of Venus and Serena wannabees, they'll have to make other arrangements for court time. My plan is to get as many successful people as I can to attend the luncheon. I'll get the press to cover it and interview attendees—find out how many years they lived there and what they're doing now. In other words, make the point that the projects are only supposed to be a stopgap, not a permanent way of life."

Elyse thought for a moment before replying. "You have to consider that different people live in the projects nowadays. When we lived there, everyone worked, all the men and a whole lot of the women, especially those who were the head of their household. Now the population is made up of a lot of welfare recipients who don't work and have no way out. It's a lot harder to break out of poverty now than it was thirty-five years ago, but I do understand what you're trying to do."

"Good. I hope I can count on you and Franklin to come."

"Sure!" *If Franklin doesn't come with me to this, so help me, I'll crown him with a cast-iron skillet.*

"Hey, I'm just about to head up to Lincoln Park to meet Grace for dinner. Are you doing anything tonight? Would Franklin mind if you spent a few hours with some old friends?"

Elyse resisted the urge to say, *"Hah!"* Instead she said, "I'm not doing anything right now. I'd love to meet you."

She got the directions to the restaurant and hung up. Within five seconds her phone rang. It had to be Franklin.

Now that she had a definite plan for the evening, she didn't mind answering the phone. Still, that hardly meant she'd gotten over her disappointment at his letting her down yet again. "Yes, Franklin," she said into the receiver, not even looking at the caller ID.

"Elyse, I just don't want you to be mad."

"I'm sorry, but that can't be helped. You've canceled on me one too many times."

"We'll do something next weekend. I promise. Whether the kids come home or not."

"Sure." He'd stick to that promise until it was time to go, and then his convenient mystery illness would provide him an excuse. She wasn't buying it, not anymore.

He paused. "Where are you?"

"I'm still in Lake Forest, but I'm going down to Chicago."

"Chicago!"

"I'm meeting a couple of friends for dinner. Pat Maxwell and Grace Corrigan. You remember. We were all girls together in the projects. They were all at our wedding, and then you saw them again at Susan Bennett's wedding up in Kenosha."

"Yeah, I remember. Why can't they come up here? I don't want you to be driving the streets of Chicago at night. It's dangerous. You don't see your friend Susan coming down to the city from Wisconsin."

His habit of expressing that danger lurked around every corner outside of this lily-white suburb he'd moved them to always annoyed her. Anyone who heard him talk would never believe he hailed from the middle-class South suburb of Morgan Park. He sounded like someone who grew up here in pricey Lake Forest, which had maybe forty black people among its residents. They wouldn't be here themselves if their real estate agent hadn't called them about a house in less-than-stellar condition that was for sale. Franklin wanted to look at it right away because of its prime location. They made an offer the same day. That happened fifteen years ago, and it had been an excellent choice. They got a home improvement loan to make the repairs, and their house had appreciated so much that they could never afford to buy it now.

She forced herself to sound calm. "Susan doesn't even know about this, Franklin. And as far as Pat and Grace coming up to Lake County, that wouldn't be practical. Pat lives in South Shore. It would take her almost an hour to drive up here. So we're meeting at a place near Lincoln Park, where Grace lives. It's more of a central location. Plus, it's a nice neighborhood," she added, unable to hold back a touch of sarcasm.

"Yeah, Lincoln Park's not bad."

He hadn't even noticed her barb. "I'm glad I have your permission," she said caustically.

"Elyse, I didn't mean—"

"I've got to get on the highway, Franklin. Why don't we talk later?" She broke the connection as the light changed and she glided the car onto the on-ramp of I-94.

Chapter 2

Early March
Chicago

Elyse easily found the Thai restaurant on North Damen Street. Parking was a little trickier. She had to circle the block a couple of times before she slowed down by a family just getting into their car.

The restaurant was rather small, with maybe fifteen tables. Like many bistros, it had a patio for use during warmer weather, which increased the seating capacity by about thirty percent, but in early March, dining inside was the only option.

Elyse quickly spotted her friends. They squealed when they saw her, jumping out of their chairs. After a group hug, Elyse slid out of her coat and sat with them.

"I'm so glad you were able to join us," Pat said to her.

"Hell, I'm glad I came. It's been too long, girls. Not since we went up to see Susan's new baby."

"Who's probably in the first grade by now," Grace said with a smile.

Elyse smiled at her old friend. "You look great, Grace. What've you been doing, taking a de-aging potion?"

Pat laughed. "I keep trying to get her to share her secrets, but she won't."

"I don't look any better than either of you," Grace protested, if a tad insincerely.

Elyse forgave her. Grace looked good and she knew it. So what?

"Sure. Just don't count my twenty extra pounds," Pat said good-naturedly.

"In my case it's more like fifty," Elyse said with a chuckle. "And, is it me, or have all our hair colors changed?"

Grace stroked her sable-brown tresses, worn simply in a center-parted bob that curled inward a few inches past her shoulders. "My hair's still dark," she said innocently.

"Dark, yes," Pat acknowledged. "Practically black, like it used to be, no."

Like Elyse, Pat used to envy Grace and Susan their long hair. Pat still wore her hair short, but the hue had changed dramatically, from the darkest of browns to a reddish gold. "I can't even tell you how much gray I have," she said with a laugh. "I ran to the hairdresser for coloring as soon as I started noticing it, and I've been going regularly ever since, getting lighter and lighter each time. But this is as light as I get."

"I'm sure you have just a little gray," Elyse said with a smile. Her own hair was tinted a special shade of auburn that her hairstylist mixed to complement her dark skin tone. She wore it parted on the side, combed toward her face, fuller on the crown and tapering at the ends, framing her face nicely. Elyse had always had plenty of hair thicknesswise, but for reasons she never understood, it had never grown past her chin.

"I wish we could say we were too young to be gray, but I guess that hasn't been the case for a long time," Grace lamented.

Hair coloring or not, she looked splendid, Elyse thought. Grace Corrigan might be almost fifty, but she barely looked forty. She'd been one of those cute types who'd never had an awkward age. Even as a little girl Grace was adorable, with long braids framing a heart-shaped face. Not only was she pretty but she had brains, too, usually placing in the top three in her class. A lot of folks in the projects wrote her off as just another case of wasted potential when Grace got pregnant senior year, but she fooled them all. She started college at night while raising her daughter and eventually earned a bachelor's, then a master's, and now was director of public relations for a global company headquartered north of the city. Along the way Grace's marriage had capsized, but Elyse never expected it to last, anyway. Grace and Jimmy Lucas married strictly to legitimize Shavonne, in an era when most teenage parents didn't bother.

Elyse reached for a menu. "Have you guys ordered yet?"

"No. We figured we'd wait for you before we ordered dinner," Grace said. "But we brought wine. Have some." She removed a tall bottle from a tote bag on the floor and poured wine into a stemmed glass.

"You *brought* wine?" Elyse repeated.

"This is a BYOB restaurant," Pat explained.

Elyse looked around. She hadn't noticed the lack of a bar. She held the glass by its stem. "Here's to old friends."

They clicked glasses and drank.

"Too bad Susan's not here," Pat remarked.

While they waited for their food to be served, the friends talked about the upcoming reunion.

"RSVPs should start coming in next week, I hope," Pat said.

"I just realized," Elyse began. "Not only will Dreiser be fifty this year, but so will all of us."

Grace made a mock shudder. "Don't remind me. My birthday's next month."

"I never really thought about that," Pat remarked. "Probably because I feel like I just turned forty-nine." Pat was the youngest of the group. Her birthday, December 22, put her a year behind the others in a school system that in 1962 required kindergarten students to have turned five prior to December 1.

"Has anyone heard from Susan?" Elyse asked.

The others shrugged. "I had a Christmas card from her, but I haven't seen her since she had . . . I can't even remember her little girl's name," Grace said.

"Alyssa, I think," Pat said after thinking for a moment. "And that's the last time all of us were together."

"That's right," Elyse remarked. "Gee, I hope she comes to the reunion."

Their food arrived, and they sat back expectantly while the server placed steaming plates in front of them. The distinctive scents of shrimp, ginger, and pepper dominated the table.

"Oh, this looks wonderful," Elyse exclaimed. "I'm going to enjoy this."

"I'll have to do a double workout tomorrow to make up for this," Grace said with a shake of her head.

"So is that your secret, Grace?" Elyse asked. "You work out?"

"Regularly. My job has a fully equipped gym, plus I walk on the weekends."

Pat asked, "How's Franklin, Elyse? And how are the kids?"

Elyse beamed at the thought of her children. "Todd is in his junior year at U of I, and Brontë is a freshman there. So Franklin and I have the house to ourselves." She didn't add that her husband didn't seem to want to go anyplace with her anymore.

She felt a sudden urge to know about the romantic status of her friends. Maybe hearing of the struggles of single women would take her mind off her own problems . . . provided Pat and Grace were struggling at all. For all Elyse knew, they both might be in committed relationships and content not to be married. Pat had never said "I do," but Grace had been married and divorced twice. Who could blame her for not wanting to do it again? "So are either of you seeing anyone, or committed? What are my chances of being invited to another wedding?"

"My father jokes that I blew it as far as getting him to pay for my wedding. He says if I get married at this stage, I'll have to pay for it myself," Pat said. She managed a chuckle, but her limp smile hinted at the bitterness she felt. Elyse remembered all too well how Mr. Maxwell broke up the romance between Pat and Ricky Suárez after high school because he didn't approve of Pat dating a Latino.

"Well, I think you and Susan are the lucky ones, Elyse," Grace said. "All I ever wanted was a husband and a couple of kids. Instead I got them the other way around. Two husbands, one child."

Unlike Pat, Grace made no attempt to hide her disappointment, which Elyse found puzzling. The Grace she remembered never would have openly expressed wanting something someone else had. Instead she usually found something negative to say when anyone had good news to share. Elyse still remembered the year they all turned nine.

Her family was moving out of Dreiser after the New Year to a duplex a block away. She'd proudly announced the news to her friends. Pat and Susan shared her excitement, but Grace said that because they were moving so close to Christmas, it meant she probably wouldn't get many gifts "because it costs lots of money to move." Pat, her trademark consideration for others already in play, remarked that being born three days before Christmas meant she got cheated *every* year.

It started snowing the Thursday morning before Elyse's family was scheduled to move, and it snowed all day. The schools closed early, something they almost never did. Elyse did remember being sent home early on her sixth birthday, which was the day President Kennedy was assassinated, but Chicago public schools generally didn't close for snow. But no one had ever seen snow like this. Just shy of two feet fell, with drifts three times that high. There was no school on Friday, and people were stuck all over the city. They called it the storm of the century, and it went into the city's records as the Blizzard of '67. Elyse's worries about what would happen if they couldn't move were only increased when Grace said that because they had turned in their notice to the projects they would be thrown out onto the street, along with all their furniture.

That didn't happen, of course. Elyse's father postponed their move until the middle of February, clearing it with the managers of both the apartment and the duplex. But Elyse had a knot in her stomach until her parents told her that everything was settled.

Now, nearly forty years later, Elyse could still recall how crushed she'd felt. In hindsight, she realized that the ill-timed blizzard probably caused her parents quite a bit of distress themselves. Grace really hadn't meant to cause her all that anxiety; all she'd wanted to do was make the prospect of leaving the projects less desirable. Even at nine years old, they all knew that Dreiser was far from the best place to live, and Grace didn't want Elyse to leave her behind.

Funny. Elyse hadn't thought about that in years. Elyse supposed her friend had mellowed in middle age. "But look how successful you've become," she said graciously.

Grace shrugged. "Success is nice. But someone to share it with would be nicer. Preferably someone who's on the same economic rung as myself. But all the black men I meet with good jobs are married."

"What does Franklin do, Elyse?" Pat asked. "I can't remember."

"He's a software developer." Franklin had moved from writing code into development nearly twenty years ago.

Pat nodded approvingly. "Good field."

"Is he still working, or has he retired?" Grace asked.

"He's still working. He plans to work until Brontë graduates." She knew why Grace asked the question—because she remembered that Franklin was considerably older than they were. They probably wondered exactly how old he was now. She decided to volunteer. "He's sixty-two."

"Wow," Grace said. "I knew he was an older fellow, but sixty-two." She took a sip of wine and met Pat's eyes over the rim of her glass. "I know we're getting older ourselves, but that seems *really* old, doesn't it?"

Elyse merely smiled. *You don't know the half of it.*

Elyse returned home at nine-thirty to find a dark living room. Franklin had left a light on for her before moving into their bedroom. She found him there, reclining on their king-sized bed, the television tuned to a boxing match on HBO and a plate holding a crumpled-up napkin and the remnants of a slice of pizza on his nightstand. So he'd ordered out before dozing off again.

"Elyse, that you?" he murmured sleepily.

"It better be," she said, amused. "Or else you're in big trouble."

"Didja have a good time?"

"Yes, I did." She spoke confidently. The sense of wonder at how the years and separate lives melted away once she sat down to dinner with her old friends had passed during the forty-minute drive home. One thing she'd promised herself—she'd keep in closer touch with Pat and Grace from now on.

Franklin seemed more awake now. "How're your friends?"

"They're well. They both asked about you."

"And I'm sure you told them I'm an old fuddy-duddy."

She sighed. "No, Franklin, I didn't tell them that. But I did think it to myself."

"C'mere, Elyse."

She did as he requested, sitting on the edge of the bed.

He reached out and caressed her forearm through her sweater. "I promise I'll do better. Starting next week."

She slid over and reclined, her head resting in the nook where his shoulders met his neck. She loved Franklin . . . and she hated arguing with him. But she also hated the way he made her feel. If she could just make him understand how she felt.

"Franklin, you've made that promise too many times the past couple of months. Last fall, when Brontë left for school, we did things together. We went bowling, we went for walks, to dinner and the movies. We even went on a cruise for ten days. For years we've been saying that as soon as the kids were out of the house we'd really start living." Her eyes filled with tears. "Now everything's changed. What am I supposed to make of it when you don't want to spend time with me anymore?"

Chapter 3

Early March
Pleasant Prairie, Wisconsin

Susan got out of her SUV and, noticing the mail truck pulling up to the house from next door, walked to the curb to take the delivery.

"Good morning," she said to the mailman.

"Morning, Mrs. Dillahunt. Got your mail right here." He handed it to her. A circular from JCPenney, folded and rubber banded, was on the outside.

"Looks like junk," she remarked, not surprised. She paid the household bills online and received most of the bills that way as well. She loved the convenience, and the way it cut down on paperwork. What did she care about department store sales? She felt happy to be alive, happy to be able to experience the gradual warming from winter to spring.

The mailman, who delivered to her regularly unless he was ill or on vacation, began his usual response. "I don't write 'em, Mrs. Dillahunt . . ."

"I just deliver them," she concluded.

He grinned. "You have a nice day."

"Thanks."

She didn't look at the mail until she'd gotten the groceries in the house and started to put everything away. She'd bought two half-gallon containers of ice cream—actually slightly less than a half gallon, since food manufacturers had begun producing smaller packages in lieu of price increases—plus those shortbread cookies with the chocolate drops that Bruce liked.

While she and her sister Sherry were growing up in the Dreiser projects, their mother used to buy Neapolitan ice cream. Susan liked chocolate, Sherry liked strawberry, and their mother ate the vanilla. Susan didn't know whether her mother even liked vanilla—maybe she ate it just because she wanted to save the chocolate and strawberry for her two girls. Nowadays the ice-cream flavors available in the supermarket rivaled that of Baskin-Robbins. Quentin had to have Moose Tracks, while Alyssa wanted only cherry with chocolate chunks, so that meant buying them each their own containers.

Susan made room for the ice cream in the large vertical freezer. Then she sat at the built-in desk in the kitchen, pulling out the recycling bin from underneath in anticipation of throwing most of the mail inside it.

A booklet of various newsprint circulars for local stores and glossy coupon ads for fast-food restaurants made up most of the day's delivery. Also in the bundle were two postcards, one featuring a photograph of a missing child with a telephone number to call if she was spotted, and the other imprinted with a sketch of what looked like the Dreiser Homes on the South Side of Chicago, where she'd grown up.

Susan read the back of the card and broke into a smile. A reunion luncheon. What a fabulous idea! She hadn't seen Pat, Grace, and Elyse in too long, anyway. As the event's organizer, Pat was sure to be there, and Grace would definitely be an attendee. She couldn't be so sure about Elyse, who lived nearly as far away from the South Side as she did.

For thirteen years, ever since marrying Bruce Dillahunt, Susan had called the town of Pleasant Prairie, Wisconsin, home. The town's name described it perfectly. It was located on Lake Michigan, just over the Wisconsin border, and featured quaint reminders of small-town life like a drive-in theater and a Piggly Wiggly, the Southern supermarket chain that had few stores in Illinois but a strong presence in Wisconsin. The nearest small city was Kenosha, to the north, and if she wanted a big-city atmosphere she had to drive past Kenosha to Milwaukee, which was slightly closer to her than Chicago.

Susan read the card again. The luncheon would be held in just two weeks. She'd have to wear something nice. She wanted to look good. And healthy. It would defeat the whole purpose of going if she looked haggard and ill.

She tossed the rest of the mail into the recycling bin. The reunion postcard went in the zippered side compartment of her handbag.

In her bedroom she stood before her dresser, staring at her reflection in the mirror that hung above it. Slowly she turned to the left, then to the right. She looked fine. Thanks to a good-fitting bra with extra control along the upper sides, no telltale lumps gave away her secret.

Susan waited at the curb, leaning on the car. When school let out at three, she ventured only a few feet away to talk to other mothers she knew from this daily errand. She was cordial to them, if not overly friendly. At forty-nine, she felt out of place next to women fifteen years younger than she. She hadn't thought about being an older mother when she gave birth to Quentin at age thirty-nine and Alyssa at forty-two; but seeing these young mothers in their late twenties or early thirties, and the even younger nannies who picked up their charges while their employers worked at high-powered positions, never failed to remind her that more than half her life was behind her. She'd been so afraid that her illness would age her prematurely and make her look more like her children's grandmother, and felt relieved when it hadn't. She'd begun to go gray even before her diagnosis. Her facial skin felt looser these days, but it didn't sag. She looked like a woman in her late forties, which was exactly what she was.

Alyssa gave her a quick hug, but Quentin simply greeted her and climbed into the backseat. Susan knew he didn't want any of his fifth-grade friends to see him hugging his mother.

"How was school today?" she asked as she steered away from the curb.

Quentin grunted. "Same old same old," he said.

"Nothing new," Alyssa added.

"Well, I've got some news for you. Y'all are going to come along with me on a little excursion in a few weeks."

Both children immediately perked up. "Where're we going, Mom? Skiing? To the Dells?"

She chuckled. "Nowhere like that. This is just for an afternoon. I'm going to bring you to Chicago to see where I grew up."

"And then what?" Alyssa asked.

"And then . . . then we're going to have lunch with some people I grew up with."

Susan realized too late that to kids their age it sounded none too exciting, and that they probably wouldn't even want to go, but it wasn't like she could depend on Bruce to accompany her. He barely wanted to sleep with her since her lumpectomy. How could she expect him to escort her anywhere? She didn't want to go alone, even if she met up with her old friends. Besides, if the kids came along she could show them off to Ann Valentine and the rest of those old bats from Dreiser.

For a second she allowed herself to wonder if Charles Valentine would be there, but she quickly decided that was silly. Charles at a reunion luncheon? Not a chance.

Too bad. She'd love to see him again.

"Mom, you grew up in the projects," Quentin pointed out. "It probably isn't even safe for us to go there. I saw on *Good Times* when the sister got her sweater torn just going to school."

"We're not going to walk around, Quentin. I just feel you should see that everybody hasn't lived a life as privileged as yours." Susan sighed. When she and her sister were growing up, parents were doing well just to keep their children well fed and clothed. Now kids wanted trips to Florida, cruises, and the Wisconsin Dells. And many of them, hers included, got what they wanted.

"Are those the projects you lived in, Mommy?" Alyssa asked.

"No, Alyssa." The opening and closing credits of the old TV sitcom depicted the infamous Cabrini-Green projects, now being torn down. The fictional Evans family lived on the South Side of Chicago; the real Cabrini-Green had been north of downtown.

Alyssa asked another question. "Is Daddy coming, too?"

She kept her voice light. "Oh, probably not. Daddy likes to relax on the weekends. He works very hard to take care of us and to pay for all the nice things we have."

It was true that Bruce provided handsomely for them, and that his position as owner of a credit card–processing company required long hours. But in the months since her diagnosis and treatment, he'd suddenly started to say he needed to work even later. When Susan put that together with the decline in their once-vigorous sex life, it had the smell of an affair. Naturally she expressed her concerns to him, and he vigorously denied any wrongdoing.

She didn't believe it for a minute.

Relations between her and Bruce looked smooth as pudding on the outside. Even Quentin and Alyssa had no idea of any discord. Susan knew Bruce loved her. But he didn't desire her anymore, and that made her feel unattractive and sad.

Once Charles had loved her, too. She wondered what his opinion of her now would be.

Then Quentin asked the question she'd been expecting. "Do we *have* to go, Mom?"

"I'd really like you to, Quentin. I know it's an afternoon you'll never get back, but by the same token, it's only an afternoon. It's not going to scar you for life."

"Awright."

Chapter 4

Pat lounged on her living room sofa, her feet propped up on the oak coffee table, going over the list of RSVPs the restaurant staff had taken down and turned over to her. Nearly a hundred people had responded. She submitted a PSA about the event to the local radio station to announce on its Community Calendar, and also posted flyers in supermarkets and at beauty and barber shops all over the South Side. She sent postcards to anyone she had a current address for, and she also looked up telephone numbers in the phone book and online.

She grinned happily when she saw the words "Susan Bennett Dillahunt, party of three," on the list. So her old friend had decided to drive down from her home across the Wisconsin state line. Pat would be glad to see her. It had been too long.

It seemed like yesterday when the four of them walked to and from school together, wearing their Mary Janes and knee socks with pleated skirts or corduroy jumpers. Pat hated corduroy to this day; to her it would always represent a fabric only poor people or toddlers wore. They must have gone through a dozen fashion fads since grammar school: Those striped woolen caps with the extra yarn and the balls on the end that streamed down their backs, in a pallid imitation of the long hair Susan and Grace had when they were eight. Dresses with Nehru collars the year they were ten, ankle-length maxicoats at twelve, formfitting popcorn blouses at thirteen, and the platform shoes and painter's jeans and bodysuits that were popular during their high school years. Those bodysuits never rode up, which was great if you were wearing hip-hugging jeans with them, but my oh my, if you had to pee you had to be damn quick about unsnapping those crotches.

She opened her eyes, and they fell on an entry on the pad that made her gasp. *Mr. and Mrs. Enrique Suárez.*

My God. Ricky was coming. And bringing his *wife.* She'd never expected him to show up. Why had he decided to come? Did he want to rub it in her face that she'd become what used to be called an old maid?

Sure, success stories like Ricky's were what she was after, but nonetheless, Pat cursed herself for sending Miriam Suárez an invitation. Ricky must have heard about the luncheon through his mother. If she hadn't made sure Mrs. Suárez knew about it, she wouldn't be stricken with panic now to see his name on the RSVP list.

But even as Pat pretended to be indignant, she knew she wasn't being fair. She'd run into Miriam Suárez about seven years ago at the Moo and Oink on Stony Island Avenue, and she'd been shocked when Mrs. Suárez had revealed—after going on and on about how well Ricky's downtown restaurant, Nirvana, was doing—that he had recently gotten divorced.

"Ah, these women today, they're never happy," Miriam had snarled, her pretty features momentarily unattractive. "My son worked so hard in his restaurant so his wife could live in a nice home and drive a nice car and have plenty of spending money in her pockets. But instead of being grateful, she complained all the time." Her mouth twisted unbecomingly as she imitated her former daughter-in-law in a whiny voice. " 'He never spends any time with me or our daughter. He's always at work.' Hah!" she'd said, reverting to her normal manner of speaking, a youthful voice with just a faint hint of a Spanish accent. "She didn't have sense enough to realize the link between his long hours and the comfortable life she lived. I would have given anything to have a husband who loved me and took care of me instead of one who left me with two babies to support."

Miriam had moved into Dreiser as a single parent, her husband having taken off, leaving her to fend for herself and their two sons. "When Ricky found out she had a boyfriend on the side, he got his lawyer to cut her loose without a dime, plus he got custody of my granddaughter." She laughed triumphantly. "I'll bet that new man of hers can't afford to keep her in the style my son did. She's probably buying her clothes at Wal-Mart now instead of Lord & Taylor."

As Pat listened to Mrs. Suárez's contemptuous description of her former daughter-in-law, she could barely hide her delight at the news that Ricky was available again. She was convinced it was kismet for her to run into Ricky's mother. The plan came together in her head before she and Mrs. Suárez parted.

Even after seven years, Pat still remembered how hopeful she felt that day shortly after the encounter with Mrs. Suárez. Accompanied by one of the other ADAs from work, she dressed in her nicest suit and went over to Nirvana, where Ricky served a menu of steaks, chicken, and seafood with a Mexican twist. Normally she would have brought Grace, but she didn't want Grace to know how much she longed for another chance with Ricky, how her heart still ached, even after all this time. If it all worked out, *then* she'd tell her. No point in putting the cart before the horse.

She'd asked for him through their server, and he came out to say hello, looking even more handsome in middle age.

"He ought to be on a magazine cover," her friend had whispered as he approached.

Ricky closely resembled his mother, who'd been a stunner in her younger days and who even now was still quite lovely, with large dark eyes and gorgeous skin. Ricky had stayed in shape, too. His shirt was tucked into his belted pants, revealing a flat belly.

He'd been genuinely glad to see Pat and instructed the server to give them their meal on the house, but there'd been nothing in his eyes, no special spark to let her know that he still cared, or that he saw her as anyone other than a childhood friend and high school sweetheart. To him, Pat decided, she must seem like nothing more than a relic from the past.

Pat kept a smile plastered on her face for appearance's sake, but inside she felt like a fool. She thought about all the day-dreams she'd entertained ever since hatching her plan to come here. There she stood, in her mind's eye, defiantly announcing to her parents that she and Ricky were getting married, and they would just have to get used to the idea. In another imaginary scene, she explained to a stunned Grace that she'd gone to his restaurant and the old magic returned right away, with them as much in love as ever after a separation of twenty-three years.

All her dreams died when Ricky reacted the way he did. In the end Pat was glad she'd brought someone along who had no knowledge of their past history, rather than Grace. At least no one had to know how she'd tried to get Ricky back . . . and how she'd failed. It would be her own private sorrow.

Now those twenty-three years since their breakup had stretched to thirty, and learning that he'd remarried brought back all the old pain from that terrible time in her life. Not only had he made no move to rekindle their flame when they were both un-attached and available, but he'd married someone else. Again.

And Pat would have to see them together at the luncheon, be forced to smile and act pleasant, like seeing him with his wife was no big deal, if she wanted to save face, all the time feeling that *she* should have been his wife. In hindsight, she'd seen her mistake. That day at lunch she should have managed to convey to him that she no longer let her parents run her life. That was probably why he kept her at arm's length. He'd been deeply hurt by her parents' refusal to accept him, and he probably imagined her to be the same meek Pat, too afraid to disappoint her parents and go with the man she loved. Why should he put himself through all that again? What sane person would?

She could still hear his words to her when they broke up. "Pat, my mother was born in Mexico, my father in Bolivia. I was born here. That makes me an American. And I face as much prejudice as you do. I mean, look at me." He held up his golden brown hand. "Do I look white to you?

"I think it's terrible, what happened to your uncle, but it had nothing to do with me. Racism is still alive and well and living in America, but I'll tell you this—I'm going to make it. One day

I'm going to own my own restaurant. But I can't fight your parents for you all my life, Pat. It would be too exhausting. If it pains you so much to go against your parents' wishes, then I'm not the man for you. I just hope you meet someone they do approve of, or else you'll wind up an old maid."

Pat sighed as she stared at the scrawled name on the RSVP list. Ricky did just what he said he would do. Five or six years out of college, he'd opened a luncheonette in an industrial area of the South Side, catering to the workers. Then he'd ventured out and opened the more upscale Nirvana. It was successful from the start. And she, of course, became just what he'd predicted: forty-nine years old and never married. Even her parents had given up hope of ever having a grandchild. How different things could have been if only they hadn't been so unyielding . . . or if she'd permitted herself to have a backbone.

Surely she and Ricky would have stayed together if they'd gotten married, like he wanted to. Unlike his first wife, she wouldn't have felt neglected by Ricky's long hours as a restaurateur. She had her own career to keep her busy.

After law school she'd been hired by the Cook County State's Attorney's Office, and still, after twenty-four years, she loved her work. Over the years Pat had declined many offers to join lucrative private practices. She'd make better money, sure, but she didn't think she could stomach the clientele she would have to defend, like white-collar criminals who were guilty as sin or the no-good children of Chicago's wealthy. Maybe her second-floor walk-up condo in a rehabbed eighty-year-old building wasn't the fanciest place to call home, but it was hers.

It still saddened her to think of what might have been if she'd held her ground to her parents' objections. Surely her father would have come around. Would he really want to be estranged from her, his only daughter and soon-to-be only surviving child? He'd been the real holdout. Her mother felt a fear of the unknown, and history backed up her fears that black women who took up with nonblack men would only get heartbreak, fatherless babies, or both; but at least she was willing to let the relationship continue. The fact that she'd known Ricky ever since he was a toddler helped, even if Pat suspected that privately her mother hoped it was just puppy love that would eventually run its course.

But the timing had been awful. Pat's younger brother, Melvin, the real academic star of the family, had just been shot to death, caught by a bullet meant for a gang member walking a few feet in front of him. The murder broke all of their hearts, and for her parents it brought back memories of the killing of her uncle in Arkansas. This time it was poverty that had them trapped in gangland territory, not racism. But it hurt every bit as much.

She'd told Ricky that it wasn't the best time for him to ask her parents for her hand. But her father in particular began to treat Ricky with such open disdain that Ricky insisted he talk to him about his true feelings and intentions.

"I won't have your father thinking I'm only out for sex, Pat," he'd said.

Indeed, her parents had been shocked when Ricky told them he wanted to marry her. It put an end to the "He only wants one thing from you" argument she'd been hearing in recent weeks. But they quickly got over their astonishment. When Ricky promised them he would become a success and take good care of her, Pat's father pointed out that there was little money in bussing tables. A clearly frustrated Ricky replied he wouldn't be doing that sort of work after he graduated college. Before it was over there was shouting all around, and when Ricky's mother found out, she came to the Maxwell apartment and demanded to know what made them think that her son wasn't good enough for their daughter.

The two families stopped speaking as a result of all the uproar. Three months later, Miriam Suárez closed on a modest house in Bridgeport and moved her family out of the projects.

Once again, as she'd done hundreds of times before in the years since, Pat blamed herself for destroying her own future by not standing up to her parents.

Chapter 5

Late March
Chicago

Elyse fumed as she gripped the steering wheel. Franklin had canceled on her again. He'd *promised* her they would attend the reunion luncheon together; then, as she laid out his clothes, he asked if she minded terribly if they didn't go.

"My stomach really hurts," he said.

She didn't swallow that for a second. He'd just gone bowling two nights ago and hadn't said a word about tummy trouble. Now he had a hangdog look on his face like he wanted her to take him to the ER. "I'm sorry you aren't feeling well, Franklin," she said calmly. "Can I get you anything before I leave?"

She enjoyed the shock on his face. "You're going without me?" he sputtered.

"Of course. If I don't start going out by myself, I'll never go anyplace at all, not with your track record. By the way, have you made an appointment to see the doctor yet?"

"Uh, not yet. Elyse, I don't think you should go down there by yourself. It isn't safe. It's not like you're going to Lincoln Park like you did a couple of weeks ago. We're talking about the South Side, and that's not safe, even in the daytime."

"Stop acting like I'm going into a battlefield. There's nothing wrong with the South Side. I'll be fine."

He looked at her like someone had turned on an imaginary

charm button. "I wish you wouldn't go," he said in his most beguiling manner.

He gave off a sexy vibe, plus he looked devastatingly handsome, but with effort she stood her ground. "I'm going, Franklin."

Now he frowned, lines forming on his forehead. "Hey, what're you complaining about? We went to the movie and to dinner the other week, didn't we? Just like I promised."

"Just because you keep one promise to me doesn't make your canceling on me again at the last minute okay. I'm going," she repeated.

He kept trying, right up until she left, to get her to change her mind, using everything he could think of to keep her home with him. Something in her snapped when he turned to guilt tactics, asking her how she could go out when she knew he wasn't feeling well.

"Please, Franklin. Don't ask me to give up my life because of this imaginary illness of yours that doesn't require medical attention because it only arises every time you and I have plans to go somewhere. You might be in your sixties, but I'm not fifty yet. I have no intention of drying up like a raisin just because you've become an old fart."

She saw him wince and instantly feared she'd gone too far. "I'm sorry, Franklin," she said quickly. "That was mean. But you're not being fair to me. If you don't want to go anywhere it's one thing, but when you try to stop me from going anyplace because you want to stay home—it's not right. I'm going to do things with my life. I'm just hitting my stride, and I won't be made old before my time. And I'm going to this luncheon."

She half expected him to call and plead with her not to go, but her cell remained quiet. Maybe she got through to him at last. Maybe he feared that they would grow apart if she started going out without him, and that their long-term marriage would unravel. Still, she'd heard people often became more sensitive when they grew older. Could it be she was being too hard on him?

Just as Elyse felt herself softening, her resolve returned. If he thought they might grow apart, then he should do everything to fight it. Asking her to give up living so she could stay at home with him wasn't the way. He needed to get up off his ass and come along with her, at least once in a while.

Traffic was moderately heavy on this Saturday. Chicago winters were always cold, but this one had been snowier than usual. Today the mercury had climbed above fifty degrees, and everybody wanted to get out and enjoy the first glimpse of spring, knowing that it wouldn't last. Springtime tended to be iffy in Chicago, and Elyse still carried her gloves in her purse.

She found a parking spot in the lot, but before entering the landmark soul food restaurant she dialed home from her cell phone. She did want to apologize to Franklin for implying he was old and washed-up. He'd been her romantic hero when she was a young woman, and he still held her heart. She wished she could take back the words.

To her surprise, the phone was picked up by her daughter. "Brontë! I didn't know you were coming home."

"I didn't know, either, Mom. I just decided at the last minute. There wasn't really anything going on at school this weekend, so I figured I'd come home and sleep in my own bed. Maybe I'll watch some movies or read a book or something."

Elyse chuckled. "You sound restless."

"Well, you're not here, and Daddy's lying down, so I'm just kinda hanging around."

Franklin was lying down? "Is Daddy all right?"

"Yeah, he just said he was tired and he'd see me when he woke up."

"He was supposed to come with me today, but he changed his mind at the last minute. I'm down in Chicago, at a reunion of the projects I grew up in."

"The projects? Why bother?"

Elyse could picture her daughter wrinkling her nose, and it annoyed her. "Because it's a part of me, and because my friend who organized it wanted successful people to attend so she can make the point that not everyone who comes from the projects is a blight on society, that's why."

"All right, Mom. You don't have to bite my head off."

"You might find this hard to believe, Brontë, but I did have a nice childhood. My family didn't have much money. The closest we got to eating out was take-out pizza, and we sure didn't fly to Disney World for vacation like you and your brother did, but we had plenty of fun just the same."

"I get your point, Mom."

"Good. I just wanted to call to let your father know I arrived safely. You'll tell him for me, won't you?"

"Of course. Have a good time with your friends, Mom."

"I will. Call if you need me for anything."

"Sure, but I doubt I'll need to. What could go wrong?"

Brontë was right, Elyse thought. She had no reason to worry. She'd been taken aback a little when Brontë said Franklin was lying down, but he was probably just using his free afternoon to get caught up on his rest. Franklin felt the way Brontë did, that the projects were best left to distant memory. So, to get out of coming to the city with her, he'd feigned illness again—the same old excuse he'd been using for months.

Elyse dropped her phone in her purse and entered the restaurant. Pat stood at the entrance to the semiprivate room where the luncheon would take place, greeting each arrival personally and thanking the person for coming. Elyse hung back for a minute to watch her friend in action. Pat would have made a damn fine politician, Elyse thought. The woman had a real gift for people. And she looked marvelous in her red wool blazer, white collarless blouse, and black and white tweed skirt with touches of red.

After a minute or two Elyse moved forward. She peeked into the room and was pleased to see it was already more than half full. "Good turnout, Pat," she said after giving her friend a hello hug. "Congratulations."

"You don't know how hard I prayed that it wouldn't rain, or even snow."

"This late in March you're probably safe, at least from snow."

Pat glanced over Elyse's shoulder. "Where's Franklin?"

"Oh, he didn't feel so well this morning, so he decided he'd better not make the trip. He wouldn't want to cut my time here

short because he's in a hurry to get back home and lie down."
She shrugged. "You know how it is."

"Sure. I hope he feels better."

"Grace here yet?"

"Are you kidding? That girl was late to her daddy's funeral.
Held it up nearly fifteen minutes, if I recall."

Elyse became aware of new arrivals standing behind her,
waiting to speak with Pat. "I'll just go in and take a seat. I can
keep a lookout for Grace."

"Okay. See you later."

Elyse looked around the banquet room for a familiar face.
She hadn't set foot in the South Side in more than ten years, not
since her parents retired to Tennessee. Lake Forest was maybe
thirty miles north of here, but when a person no longer had ties
to a neighborhood she had no reason to go there, even if she
lived just five miles away.

"Elyse Hughes! I'd know you anywhere," said a deep female
voice.

She turned to see Minnie Johnson, who used to live on the
ground floor of the building where she and her family called
home for the first nine years of her life. Minnie was older than
the other women present, probably in her mid- or even late
eighties. An original resident of Dreiser, Minnie's younger children had been in high school when the Twenty-Two Club
trekked to grammar school.

Minnie was one of those women who'd never seemed young,
probably not even when she *was* young, but she didn't seem to
get any older, either. Elyse's mother once told her, "Dark-skinned
women like us can take years off our ages and everyone will believe us. The biggest advantage to being dark is you don't show
your age."

"Hello, Mrs. Johnson," Elyse said now. "It's nice to see you
again. How are you?"

"Oh, fair to middlin'. How do your parents like it down
there in . . . where are they again?"

"They live outside of Nashville, and they like it very much."

Elyse noticed that the women sitting with Mrs. Johnson had

stopped talking to each other and were smiling at her. This clearly was the old-timer's table. She knew Mrs. Johnson had continued to live in Dreiser until she reached the age where she could get into senior citizen housing.

"Hello, Mrs. Brooks, Mrs. Suárez, Mrs. Graham." She took a few minutes to answer their questions, which came at her like missile shots. Yes, she was still married. "It'll be twenty-six years in June." Yes, she had children—two, a boy and a girl. "Eighteen and twenty. They're both in college." And, yes, she still lived in the Greater Chicago area (which the locals knew stretched from northwest Indiana all the way to Kenosha, Wisconsin). Apparently that reply was too vague for the old ladies, for Miriam Suárez asked her outright what town she lived in. "Lake Forest." Oh, how very nice. And what did her husband do? "He's a software developer."

She tried to keep the annoyance she felt at answering one question after another out of her tone. The women's knowing nods when she named the town where she lived made her feel almost embarrassed, and she felt grateful that no one could see her four-bedroom Colonial, which looked larger on the outside than it actually was. She felt like she was still shy little Elyse Hughes, harboring insecurities about her hair, her weight, and her abilities.

In spite of her lack of confidence, the women's questions and obvious surprise to hear she had done well bothered her. She knew they saw dollar signs when she said she lived in Lake Forest, which was home to many a corporate executive. They would never know that she and Franklin bought their home through luck and circumstance. Still, did they really expect her to tell them she lived in a project someplace else?

She tried not to sigh as the rapid-fire questions continued. Yes, both her brothers were well. They lived out of state, one in Atlanta, the other in Nashville.

She let out a breath of relief when Minnie Johnson's sharp eyes caught sight of another victim, and she promptly lost interest in her. Elyse slipped away as Minnie leaned forward, her index finger bobbing up and down before she finally settled for,

"I know you. I can't remember your name, but I know you lived in Five."

Elyse turned to see whom Minnie was speaking to and broke into a smile, immediately recognizing the tall, fair-skinned woman with a liberal sprinkling of gray in her short, curly hair. Susan Bennett—her married name was Dillahunt—had actually shown up. Now, *that* was a surprise. Elyse had heard that a lot of people in the neighborhood still remembered the big fuss with Susan and the Valentine brothers, even after more than twenty years. It had been the talk of the neighborhood for months, two brothers coming to blows on a public street over Susan's affections. Their mother, Ann, had never forgiven Susan for driving a wedge between her two sons.

Elyse was happy to see her old friend for another reason: now Minnie Johnson and company had someone new to pump for information. She continued moving toward the rear of the room, far from all the appraising stares and endless questions. No wonder this group sat close to the door. That way they could question every person the moment he or she stepped inside. She'd catch up with Susan later. Right now she was just glad to get away from these women who'd been on her like vultures on a corpse.

Chapter 6

Susan answered Minnie Johnson's question. "I'm Susan. My maiden name was Bennett."

"Oh, yes, I remember," Minnie said with a nod of her head. "Your mother's name was Frances."

"Yes, that's right. Still is," she added with a laugh. She hoped that the forthright Minnie wouldn't bring up the subject of her father, David Bennett, a white man who worked occasionally, drank all the time, couldn't hold a job, and eventually was thrown out by a fed-up Frances. Susan wasn't ready for her children to know the whole story about the grandfather they adored, who'd been sober for years now.

Minnie peered at the two children hovering behind Susan's tall frame. "These your grandchildren?"

"No, Mrs. Johnson, actually they're my *children*."

She noticed that Minnie didn't look in the least embarrassed at her blunder, despite the mild rebuke Susan deliberately allowed into her tone. Instead Minnie leaned forward and peered at the youngsters over her bifocals. "Your kids, huh? How old they be?"

"I'm ten," the boy stated.

"I'm seven," his sister replied shyly, moving closer to Susan and partially hiding her face in Susan's coat.

Susan put a reassuring arm around her daughter. "I was, uh, somewhat of a late bloomer," she said with a smile.

Minnie sat back in her seat. "I'll say. What were you, forty when you had your first?"

"Thirty-nine." Susan suspected that her unfriendly tone and

the hard set to her jaw would keep all the other women from asking any more questions, although they were listening intently. They could take a hint, but Minnie Johnson was another matter. The woman didn't have a shred of decorum.

"Uh-huh. So you found somebody after all that fuss with the Valentine boys, I see. Where's your man now? He leave you?"

Now Susan could barely keep the hostility out of her voice. "He chose not to come. If you'll excuse me, Mrs. Johnson, I think we'd better find seats. It looks like they're about to start the program."

Just then Susan saw Elyse walking toward her.

"Susan, over here," Elyse called out quickly.

"Snippy little thing, ain't she? Just because her daddy's white, I suppose."

Susan turned to glare at Minnie. Quentin whispered something to her, and she said, "Don't mind her. She's rude, but she's old. Let's go sit down."

The two friends hugged each other, laughing at the silliness of it all.

Susan shook her head. "My God, that Minnie Johnson should be muzzled."

"I'm glad you came along when you did," Elyse said. "I felt like they had me on the witness stand."

"I came here to give my kids an idea of where I was raised, not to raise eyebrows," Susan declared. "My mother taught me to respect older people, and I can't say I'm surprised that someone brought up all that old stuff with Douglas and Charles, but who is Minnie Johnson to try to make me feel like I committed a crime for having children late?" She grinned sheepishly as she sat down, placing a compact black leather shoulder bag on the table. "It's good to see you, Elyse."

"Same here. I'm so happy you came. And seeing your children makes me realize how long it's been. I feel like I know them, courtesy of your annual Christmas cards with the family photo, but I haven't seen them in person since your daughter was a baby."

"Did you know my mother when she was little?" Alyssa asked shyly.

"Yes, I sure did, since we were smaller than you are today. In fact, I don't even remember when we first met each other."

Susan shook her head at Elyse's questioning glance; she couldn't remember when they'd first met, either.

"She was just always there," Elyse continued. "A group of us used to walk to school together, from the time we had to get the crossing guard to stop traffic for us to cross the street, all the way through high school."

Susan introduced Elyse to her children, who dutifully said hello.

"Mom, when do we eat?" Quentin asked.

"Soon." Susan turned to Elyse. "My son feels like I've tortured him by bringing him down here today. But I always wanted my children to see where I grew up. My husband never felt it was necessary, although he made sure they saw his old house in Kenosha, which his family owned. That's what made the difference."

"There's nothing shameful about coming from the projects," Elyse agreed, thinking of Franklin's haughty attitude. "Kids today, with all those extras they get, have no idea of how things used to be, when parents were doing good just to keep their children clothed and fed well."

"I hate the idea of being grilled like a T-bone by those nosy old women. I wanted my kids to understand just how fortunate they are. They stared like I'd brought them to another planet. Of course, Dreiser looks really raggedy now."

Elyse drew in her breath. "You actually drove through there?" Even she hadn't dared to do *that*.

"Yes. With the car windows up and the doors locked."

They laughed.

"Did you drive down by yourself, Elyse?" Susan asked.

"Yes. My husband begged off at the last minute. He really has no interest in my old neighbors."

Susan scanned the room. "I guess a lot of husbands felt that way, mine included. I only see a few men here, probably dragged by their wives. I do see Mr. and Mrs. Maxwell over there. Of course, the dragon ladies up front are all widows . . . or their husbands ran for their lives." Her eyes rested on the group briefly. Now the elderly women took up three tables, their heads bobbing as they chatted and their jewelry shining in the rays from the fluorescent lights overhead. She gasped and quickly turned away.

"Susan? You all right?"

"Um . . . yes. I just saw Ann Valentine sitting up front with the others."

Elyse instantly looked across the room. "Oh, yes. She sees you, too."

Mrs. Valentine now glared at Susan with an undisguised hostility that made Elyse's blood run cold.

"If looks could kill," Susan muttered.

"Whatever happened to Douglas and Charles, anyway?"

"Pat told me Charles is still around. Douglas has been in and out of jail."

"He still hasn't gotten clean after all this time?"

"Afraid not."

Elyse shook her head. Few things in life were more pathetic than a fifty-year-old drug addict. Douglas Valentine, unanimously considered the best high school player in all Chicago back in the early seventies, dropped out of Wake Forest University in his junior year when he'd been drafted by the Lakers. Douglas had a few shining moments in the NBA, but did not achieve superstar status in that period after Dr. J's heyday and before Michael Jordan's rise to prominence. The rumors of drug and alcohol abuse that drifted back to Chicago while Douglas was still at Wake Forest became more heated, and after a few years in the NBA Douglas found himself playing for one of the lesser teams, then an even more inferior team, and finally the European leagues, where he played until his early thirties. Upon returning to Chicago, Douglas promptly was arrested for robbing the corner store on 87th Street where he'd bought candy as a child. He'd threatened the owner with a gun and had driven all of five blocks before the police caught up with him. The presence of the gun added years to his sentence. Douglas Valentine, former NBA player, became Douglas Valentine, convicted felon.

An incident that occurred between the Valentine boys was what had Ann Valentine looking at Susan with such venom.

Douglas and Susan had gone together in high school. The relationship hit the rocks when Douglas accepted the basketball scholarship from Wake Forest. Susan would have loved to have been able to follow him there, but she couldn't afford it, so she enrolled in one of the City Colleges of Chicago. After three years of seeing each other sparingly and dating others on a casual basis—Douglas much more frequently than Susan—he signed with the Lakers. Now even farther away from Susan and suddenly wealthy, he began sleeping with many of the women who threw themselves at him. Elyse knew that most folks believed that he dropped Susan for greener pastures, but actually she quit him once she got a whiff of what was going on. Within a year she started dating Douglas's older brother, Charles. For nearly two years they kept their affair under wraps, but eventually the word spread.

When Douglas learned his brother was dating his former love, he confronted him as Charles and Susan were leaving a bar on Cottage Grove Avenue, and the siblings came to blows. The fistfight shattered their previously close relationship, and soon after Douglas was thrown out of the NBA and went to play in Italy. His drug abuse worsened, and eventually he was cut from the team, returning home in disgrace. The house he'd purchased for his parents was all that remained of his income from professional sports.

Ann Valentine told anyone who would listen that Susan Bennett ruined Douglas, as well as the lifelong camaraderie between her sons. Most people gave the first part of her rant little merit, believing that Douglas's alcohol and drug abuse lay at the core of his wasted life. Many said that Douglas's downward spiral killed his father, who died of a heart attack shortly after Douglas was sent to prison for the first time.

The two brothers fighting over Susan was a different matter entirely. The altercation occurred out in the open, by a popular bar. Many people said Susan was a whore to sleep with two brothers. But Elyse didn't see it that way—she felt that Susan had no choice but to break up with Douglas after photographs of him escorting various women were published in magazines. It wasn't as if Susan took up with Charles the next day, and Elyse doubted she had sought him out. Elyse had always suspected that Charles Valentine had a crush on Susan, but put his feelings aside when she started going with his younger brother.

In Elyse's opinion Charles made a much better match for Susan than his trifling brother, but after the brothers fought, Susan left Charles and went up to Kenosha, where her mother had settled after she left the projects. Susan never spoke about why she left Charles. Eventually she met and married business-man Bruce Dillahunt.

Elyse watched as Pat made her way to the podium. "Looks like they're about to start," she said to Susan.

"I'm surprised Grace isn't here."

"She's supposed to be coming, but Pat said she's always late. I'm sure she'll show up any minute."

Chapter 7

Grace arrived close to the end of Pat's welcome speech. Camera bulbs flashed as Pat spoke, mostly from a young man who appeared to be a professional photographer. It looked like Pat had received the media coverage she sought.

Susan held up a hand as Grace scanned the dim room. Grace nodded and waved back, then made her way to the back. Her late arrival allowed her to skip past Minnie Johnson and company, all of whom were focused on listening to Pat speak. Susan wished she'd been so lucky.

Grace looked good, Susan thought. She'd been voted Best Looking in high school, and she really hadn't changed much in thirty years. Susan's practiced eye told her Grace probably wore a size 8. None of the rest of them could say that. Elyse, who'd been on the chubby side even as a child, had put on the most weight. Pat's always curvaceous figure had become somewhat more voluptuous, but she probably wasn't much heavier than Susan herself, who managed to get into a 10 most of the time. She had to admit that despite the extra pounds they all looked pretty good for women about to turn fifty.

Too bad the Dreiser Homes hadn't held up as well. Had the fifteen-story buildings always looked so shabby? No wonder her children were so appalled at the sight of the complex. Maybe the city should just tear them down, like the other old high-rise projects they were in the process of razing.

Grace quietly leaned over to press her cheek against Susan's, then greeted Elyse the same way. "Have I missed much?" she asked in a library whisper.

Elyse shook her head. "No, not really. Pat's just saying that the buffet is ready, and that after lunch she's going to pass the mike and ask everyone to say a few words about their time in Dreiser and a little about what they're doing today."

"Perfect." Grace glanced around the room at the attendees, most of whom were rising to go over to the buffet table, then gave a dismissive shrug. "Well, I see it's mostly old folks, like I expected. I only came because Pat wanted me to make a statement after lunch." She rolled her eyes. "I hope the party tonight is more exciting than these senior citizens sitting around giving their dentures a workout."

Elyse and Susan spoke at the same time. "What party?"

"The party at Junior's Bar. When Pat posted a flyer on their bulletin board, they decided to hold a Dreiser Reunion Party tonight. They'll charge a cover and serve some chicken and spaghetti, maybe a little salad. Aren't you coming?"

"I didn't even know about it," Elyse said.

"I didn't, either," Susan added. "But it sounds like fun. If I'd known about it ahead of time, I wouldn't have brought my kids so I could go. But I'll have to bring them home after lunch."

"I wish you'd known about it," Quentin piped up.

"Be quiet, Quentin; nobody's talking to you. And say hello to Ms. Corrigan."

"Hello, Ms. Corrigan," he said obediently.

Susan then introduced Alyssa to Grace, who said, "They're so sweet, Susan. Sometimes I wish I'd had another baby, maybe while I was married to Danny, since I could afford to do more for a baby at that time in my life than I could when I was married to Jimmy." She sighed. "You girls don't know how lucky you are to still have young kids."

Elyse gave her friend a dubious stare. "What're you talkin' about, Grace? My kids are eighteen and twenty and both in college. You make it sound like they're in third grade."

"Your kids may be older than Susan's, Elyse, but they're still dependent on you to a certain degree. My Shavonne will be thirty-two in October. She's married and has two kids." A wistful look came over her pretty face. "I'm glad she got to live the dream I had. A good marriage and a couple of kids. She's at a nice age to have young children. I was too young when I had her. I was a grandmother by the time I was forty-three."

"I was forty-two when I had Alyssa, and people are always asking if she and Quentin are my grandchildren," Susan lamented. "That Minnie Johnson acts like I ought to be listed in the *Guinness Book of World Records* as the World's Oldest Mama."

Elyse chuckled. "Remember when we were kids and we used to say that our own kids would be best friends, just like us? It's ironic that none of our kids are the same age, but it's impossible to know something like that ahead of time."

"Or that Pat wouldn't have any children at all," Grace added.

Elyse stopped smiling. They all knew Pat had no children. Leave it to Grace to point it out. She probably would have said it even if Pat had been sitting with them. Although the comment couldn't be called untrue, it had been delivered with a "poor Pat" intonation to it that Elyse felt wasn't warranted. It might have been uncharacteristic of Grace to be so wistful about her life, but it was just like her to point out that other people—in this case, Pat—lacked even more.

Elyse decided to change the subject. She thought about the party tonight at Junior's Bar, and suddenly she recognized an opportunity to do something that might give Franklin the push he needed to get off his ass.

Chapter 8

"Back to tonight's party," Elyse said to Grace. "What time does it start?"

"Oh, probably around nine. Do you think you'll come? You can come home with me until it's time to go down there. We can stop and get something to eat on the way." She glanced at her watch. "It's already two-fifteen. I doubt we'll feel much like dinner before seven-thirty or eight."

Pat, who had paused to briefly talk with reporters after announcing that the buffet was open, finally joined them. "I see the late Grace Corrigan made it," she teased as she took a seat.

Grace shrugged. "A few less minutes of being bored."

Elyse put her hands on her hips. "Susan, I think we've just been insulted."

"You know that's not what I meant, Elyse."

"Grace considers any social function without eligible men present a waste of time," Pat explained with a knowing nod.

"Why shouldn't I be on the lookout for a husband? I'm almost fifty years old, and I'm by myself. I never thought *that* would happen."

"You could have had a date tonight with Judge Arterbridge," Pat said lightly.

"I didn't want to go out with him. The man turns me off. I've worked hard to keep myself in shape, Pat, and I just can't get all worked up over a man whose waistline is so big he can't even see his dick."

Susan frowned and gestured with her head toward her children, sitting at a table for two barely a foot away, certainly within hearing distance. "Grace. Language, please."

"Sorry."

"I get the feeling you two have been over this many times," Elyse guessed.

"One of the judges saw Grace and me having lunch and came over for an introduction," Pat explained. "He got me on the phone that afternoon and asked if Grace was married or involved with anyone. I gave him the number to her office."

"Without even asking me first if it was all right," Grace added, her tone suggesting it was anything but.

Pat's reply was equally indignant. "Cut me some slack, will you? It's not like I gave him your home number. He's not going to start stalking you. The man is a respected county judge, for crying out loud."

"Yeah, yeah."

"Is he all that bad, Grace?" Elyse inquired.

Grace thought carefully before replying. "He's actually rather handsome. He's in his upper fifties, I guess. He's got a commanding speaking voice, and he seems witty."

"He sounds perfect," Susan said, her forearms resting on the table and her upper body leaning forward with interest. "You can't overlook a few pounds?"

"It's more than a few pounds, Susan. It's practically a whole other person." Grace sighed. "If I can't do any better than that, I guess I'll never get married again."

"At least you've *been* married," Pat pointed out.

"Twice," Elyse noted with a smile. Pat was too tactful to point that out, but Elyse felt Grace had it coming for her pointless remark about Pat.

"Look at me," Pat continued sadly. "The only man who ever proposed to me is sitting on the other side of this room with his wife."

Grace's head jerked. "Ricky's here?"

"Yeah, he's sitting over—oh, no. They're getting up. I think they're going to the buffet line. That means they'll probably stop by and say hello."

Grace watched with trepidation, only half-aware of the

soothing remarks Elyse and Susan said to Pat, as the still-handsome Ricky accompanied his wife toward the buffet. What the hell was *he* doing here? Didn't he know that this gathering was mostly for old folks?

God, now she *really* wished she hadn't come. How was she supposed to look him in the eye after that fling they'd had back in 2000? A fling Pat knew nothing about, and would never forgive her for if she found out. A fling over which Grace had been willing to risk ending her lifelong friendship with Pat had it developed into something permanent.

For a few weeks Grace had thought she might be on track to becoming the second—and *last*, if she had anything to say about it—Mrs. Enrique Suárez. Ricky seemed captivated by her, and he couldn't get enough of her in bed. But then guilt had gotten the better of him, and suddenly it was over.

Her eyes focused on Ricky's second wife. What must Pat feel when she looked at the two of them together? Damn, why didn't the woman have thick ankles or bad skin or something? Instead she was gorgeous, a Salma Hayek lookalike with an hourglass figure to match. And she appeared young, in her late thirties at most. And here *she* was, experiencing the hot flashes of perimenopause.

It was getting hot in here now, Grace realized with dismay, as if someone had turned up the heat. Her neck felt like it was saturated inside her turtleneck sweater, and her chest was damp. Beads of sweat began to form on her upper lip and her forehead, a palpable reminder that she was about to turn fifty.

She watched helplessly as Ricky guided his wife toward their table.

"What do you know," he said jovially, "the Twenty-Two Club, together again."

Susan and Elyse eagerly stood up, clearly happy to see him again after so many years. Pat, who of course had seen him when he came in, remained seated. Grace didn't dare look at Pat, but as she reluctantly rose to her feet she wondered what her friend was thinking. However awkward Grace felt, Pat had to be feeling ten times worse. Besides, no one knew about her fling with Ricky, much less how badly it ended; but *everybody* knew how difficult it had to be for Pat to see Ricky and his wife. He'd moved on, marrying twice in the thirty years since their breakup, while Pat remained unmarried.

Ricky introduced his wife as he hugged each of his old friends. Susan took a moment to introduce the Suárezes to her children, and then suddenly it was Grace's turn to say hello.

She pasted a beauty pageant–contestant smile on her face. "Hello, Ricky."

"Grace! You look fabulous." He moved in for a hug that was over in three seconds.

"Thanks."

"Grace, this is my wife, Miranda. Miranda, Grace Corrigan."

Grace dutifully held out her hand and said hello, uncomfortably aware that Miranda Suárez looked even more stunning close up, with skin absolutely flawless and not so much as an eyebrow out of place. The wide band of her paisley-print skirt showed off her tiny waist. Grace had a good figure, too, but she worked at it seven days a week. She doubted Miranda had to do that.

"We were just about to get on the buffet line," Ricky explained. "I wanted to say hello to all of you."

"And to invite you to stop by Nirvana," Miranda said. "Ricky's introduced some new menu items that I'm sure you'll enjoy."

Wasn't that cute, Grace thought bitterly. *The little woman trying to promote the business that pays their bills.*

"My husband and I will be sure to do that the next time we come to Chicago for a weekend," Susan said.

"Good to see all of you," Ricky said with a little wave as he backed away, his palm resting on Miranda's shoulder.

The four friends suddenly became quiet, lost in their own personal memories that stemmed from seeing Ricky again.

Quentin spoke up. "Mom, can we get some food?"

"If you want to stand in line, go ahead," Susan replied. "I'm going to wait for it to die down a bit. But if you go, bring your sister with you and help keep her plate steady."

"Okay. Come on, Alyssa." The children's chairs scraped noisily against the floor as they pushed back from the table.

"And don't pile up more food than you know you can eat!" she called after them. Then she sighed. "They're bored to tears.

I guess it was a mistake for me to bring them. And because I did, I can't go to Junior's with y'all."

"I thought about telling you and Elyse about that," Pat said, "but I really didn't think either of you would be interested in coming."

The remark raised Elyse's curiosity. "Why, because we live in the suburbs?"

"I suppose. And because both of you have husbands to curl up with on a cold March night, which to me is a far sight better than going to a bar to hang out with some folks you've known all your life."

"Well, I've got a surprise for you, Pat," Elyse declared. "I'm going to Junior's."

"You are! Well, good!"

Elyse glanced at Susan. "I wish there was some way we could get you there, too. I guess you don't want to drive the kids all the way home and then come back."

Susan shook her head. "Maybe if I lived in Evanston, but not Pleasant Prairie. It's just too far, and I'd be exhausted."

Grace spoke up. "You know, Susan, Shavonne would probably agree to watch your kids for you. She and her husband don't do a whole lot on the weekends unless they can get his parents or me to babysit. My grandson is six. He'd love having some kids to play with. How about it, Susan? All I have to do is call her."

"Oh, I don't know. I know they'll be safe with Shavonne, but I don't want to intrude on her time with her family by dumping two more kids on her. And we're likely to get home late, which means I'd have to disturb her to pick them up."

"I don't think that'll be a problem. Their youngest is just four months old. I don't think anybody gets a whole lot of sleep in that house."

"That seems like all the more reason not to impose on her."

Elyse held up a hand, index finger pointing upward. "I know. My daughter came home this weekend. She said she's just going to watch some TV or read a book. I'm sure she'll watch your kids for you, Susan." When Susan opened her mouth to say something, Elyse held out a hand, palm out, like a police officer directing traffic. "It's perfect. You can follow me home, we can chill at my house for a few hours, then you ride back with me, and when we get back to Lake Forest you can spend the night. Franklin and I have plenty of room, and tomorrow morning you can be home in thirty minutes, forty at the most."

"Sounds perfect," Pat said confidently.

Elyse pulled her cell phone out of her purse. "I'm going to call Brontë right now, just to make sure she hasn't made any plans for tonight. I want to see how Franklin is feeling, anyway."

Susan watched in amazement as Elyse called Brontë and secured an agreement for her to sit with the children, giving Susan a thumbs-up. Then she heard Elyse ask to speak to Franklin. "Tell Brontë I do plan to pay her; I don't expect her to babysit my children for nothing," Susan managed to say as Elyse moved a few feet away from the table.

She could hardly believe how everything had fallen into place, thanks to Elyse. Now she could go to the party. She could imagine the surprise in Bruce's voice when she told him that she and the kids wouldn't be coming home until the next morning. He'd demand to know where she was leaving them, but he probably wouldn't say a word once she told him that Elyse's college-age daughter was keeping them, with Elyse's husband in the house as well. Their overnight absence would give Bruce an ideal opportunity to spend time with whomever he was sleeping with, but she couldn't make herself care.

Out of the corner of her eye she saw Ann Valentine's tall form waiting on the buffet line. Within seconds Ann looked her way, her smile replaced with a hostile stare.

The antagonism in Ann's eyes made Susan consider something else.

Who knew, maybe she would see Charles tonight.

Chapter 9

"Elyse, I'm not trying to get into your business, but Franklin didn't look too happy to see you leave," Susan remarked from the passenger seat as Elyse merged onto the highway.

"He wasn't. He didn't want me going to the South Side in the daytime by myself, so you can imagine his reaction when I told him I was driving back down tonight. I'm glad you decided to come with me, but if you had decided not to, I still would have gone, even if it meant hanging with Grace until it was time to head back to the South Side."

Susan smiled. While it had been sweet of Grace to try to get her daughter to babysit, she understood why Elyse would be reluctant to spend the rest of the afternoon with her. But Susan already knew all about Grace and her ways. Franklin Reavis was somewhat of a mystery man to Susan; she barely knew him. "Is Franklin the possessive type?"

"No. He's just trying to keep me in the house with him. All he wants to do is sleep on the couch all weekend, and he expects me to hang around waiting and hoping he'll want to do something." Elyse sighed. "I think his age is catching up with him, Susan. He never wants to do anything anymore, at least not with me. And that makes me wonder if he's getting tired of me."

"I'm sure he's not tired of you, Elyse. And I know he's older than you, but I doubt he's ready to sit on the front porch in a rocking chair. Didn't you say he wasn't feeling well?"

"He's sixty-two, and I think he's blowing his occasional indigestion out of proportion. He has no trouble keeping up with his golf and his bowling, that's for sure."

"Oh." Susan didn't realize Franklin was past sixty. He hadn't seemed that much older than they were when he and Elyse got married. But of course they'd still been in their early twenties back then, and he in his midthirties. It seemed weird to have a husband past sixty when you were still in your forties.

"He's always claiming to be sick," Elyse continued, "but he's taking his time going to the doctor."

Susan tried again. "Are you sure you're not taking this too lightly? I know I'd be concerned if Bruce told me repeatedly that he didn't feel well."

"Oh, Susan. If there's really something wrong with Franklin, I'm the pope. He's just making excuses for not going out with me. Not only doesn't he go to the doctor, but he hasn't missed one day at work. The only time he says he doesn't feel well is when it's time to follow through on plans he and I have made."

Susan absorbed this. So she wasn't the only one who felt hurt, even betrayed, by her husband's behavior. The moment she made that statement about dining at Ricky's place the next time she and Bruce weekended in the city, she regretted it, knowing it would never happen. They used to take weekend trips frequently, but they hadn't gone anywhere since her cancer diagnosis.

She noted that Elyse struck back against Franklin by refusing to stay in the house like an obedient little wife, and hoped that eventually he would come around and want to reclaim a social life. That seemed fair enough, but Elyse's problem was different from her own. Franklin might be slowing down some, but from what Elyse said, he wasn't cheating on her.

She could think of only one way to strike back at a cheating husband, and that was to have an affair herself, tit for tat. But that seemed childish.

Still, she couldn't help wondering how she'd react if she was to come face-to-face with Charles Valentine after all these years.

Excitement sparked the air around the nondescript corner building of dirty tan brick that was Junior's Bar. Cars jamming the street, coupled with the man just inside the door taking money and stamping the backs of hands, told onlookers a special event was taking place.

The crowd started arriving at nine o'clock. Ten dollars got a person in the door, a complimentary glass of beer or wine, and a dinner of fried chicken, spaghetti, and a roll. Susan and Elyse each paid the cover charge and entered, leaving their overcoats in the car because they knew there was nowhere to hang them up inside.

Soon the seats at the elongated bar were filled, along with the booths opposite it. Tonight the usually active jukebox stood silent and dark, with oldies music provided by a CD player and two large speakers in the back room, which was not enclosed but merely divided by the center bar. The back room had tables and chairs set up alongside the walls, and a long buffet table with chafing dishes parallel to the far wall but with about two feet of space between it and the wall.

"I'm sure Pat got here early. Do you suppose Grace is here yet?" Susan asked Elyse.

"You know Grace—no telling when she'll show up!"

Pat was standing at the bar, her right hand resting on the back of a stool while she carried on an animated conversation with its occupant and the person sitting on her left.

Pat had always been outgoing and personable, even as a child. In high school she'd been voted Most Popular. A too-strong jawline prevented her from being a classic beauty, but with her hourglass figure and attractive face she turned plenty of heads, both then and now. *The shortage of eligible black men must be a lot worse than I thought*, Elyse said to herself, *if no one has snapped up a good catch like Pat*. Elyse hoped Brontë would be able to find someone suitable when she reached marriageable age. She'd read someplace that more black women than men earned college degrees, and she knew enough about men to know that some of them didn't take kindly to women more educated than they were.

Elyse had spent a few minutes at the luncheon speaking with Pat's parents, and she recognized right away the pride Moses and Cleotha Maxwell had in their only surviving child. "She's got the best conviction record of any ADA in Chicago," Mr. Maxwell had told Elyse.

"If she wasn't so good at what she does, she probably would be presiding from the bench," Mrs. Maxwell had added.

Looking at her friend move from patron to patron, exchanging words of welcome like they were all guests in her home, Elyse wondered whether the Maxwells ever wondered if they'd made a mistake in their opposition to Pat's romance with Ricky Suárez. Had they ever considered that Pat could have achieved the same success and still provided them with a grandchild or two?

Chapter 10

Grace took advantage of the red traffic light to run a brush through her hair. She really liked the rich sable-brown color; it beat having graying near-black tresses any day. Her hairdresser had been right when she suggested that a lighter color would be softer against her face. She might be about to turn fifty, but that didn't mean she had to look matronly. People told her she looked better than a lot of forty-year-olds out there. She worked hard at it, too, spending thirty minutes in the gym at least three times a week, watching her diet carefully, and walking several miles on the weekends.

She sighed as she put the brush back inside her leather shoulder bag. She felt like she'd already wasted the afternoon by attending the luncheon, and the awkwardness of coming face-to-face with Ricky for the first time since their affair had ended and meeting his gorgeous wife truly made her regret going.

Still, it wasn't like she had anything else to do, and Pat needed people like her to make her message to the media: that children who grew up in the projects weren't necessarily destined to live their lives in abject poverty and squalor.

She knew Pat had a point. Half the high school–age kids living in Dreiser today probably had no idea that Theodore Dreiser had been a popular novelist and Chicago native in the early twentieth century. She knew from that Career Day seminar Pat had dragged her to years ago at their alma mater that many of them had no ambitions in life, other than to live in a nice "crib" and drive a nice "ride." A few did tell her they wanted to run their own businesses, but not one of them had any idea what kind of business they hoped to operate. Grace knew that merely wanting to call the shots from a corner office with a view and make a lot of money was nothing more than a pipe dream, and that ten years from now those kids would have the same dream, no better defined than it was now.

Her thoughts returned to Ricky. His forced-looking smile and stiff hug told her he felt just as uncomfortable as she did. But at least he hadn't been surprised to see her. Surely Pat knew he was coming, since she handled the RSVP list. But she'd said nothing to Grace. Why? Grace wondered. Could it be that Pat was still hung up on Ricky after all this time? My God, everything between them had ended more than half a lifetime ago.

Grace had always thought that if something serious developed between her and Ricky, like she so desperately wanted, Pat would first be upset but would come around eventually. Now she wasn't so sure.

Of course, considering the outcome, it was a moot point. Grace had been stunned when Ricky told her why he was ending their affair—just when she thought everything was progressing beautifully. She'd never heard anything so idiotic. Did he actually feel like he was cheating on Pat after being apart more than twenty years? And what about her? Pat was her best friend, yet she was willing to put that friendship in jeopardy to pursue one of the most eligible soon-to-be bachelors in Chicago. She couldn't help it that Pat had given Ricky up to please her parents.

As Grace got closer to the South Side, she wondered if going to Junior's Bar would be worthwhile. She doubted she'd see any new faces there tonight. And nobody had better mess with her Mercedes.

Two people she knew she *wouldn't* see were her ex-husbands. Danny Knight, her second husband, was happily settled in San Juan, Puerto Rico, managing the office of a worldwide accounting firm.

Nor would she be seeing Jimmy Lucas, her first husband and father of Shavonne. He'd been revered in high school for his skill at basketball, overshadowed only by his friend Douglas Valentine, whose height of six feet six made him a natural.

Grace and Jimmy had begun going together in tenth grade. She fended off his pleas for sex for over a year. Grace was afraid, of both sex itself and of getting pregnant. But by the time she got to high school it seemed like more and more girls from the neighborhood were having babies. Tanya McArdle got pregnant in tenth grade, and the word on the street was that she'd been messing with a thirty-five-year-old man.

When Jimmy started cozying up to Stacey Noe, Grace knew she'd have to take action. Rumor had it that Stacey had fucked the entire football team in the bleachers. Grace resolved to keep her man. Shortly after that she and Jimmy did it in his bed after school, when his mama was still at work. Except for one brief moment of pain, Grace loved sex, and they started having it whenever they could, with Jimmy cautioning his younger brothers not to blab to their mother. Not that Mrs. Lucas would have cared too much. To Grace, Jimmy's mother always looked bored and disinterested, puffing on an ever-present cigarette and complaining about one thing or another.

Most of the time they used condoms, but every once in a while Jimmy would forget and they couldn't turn off their sex drives. One day he didn't pull out in time, and that was how she'd conceived.

Telling her parents had been the most difficult thing she'd ever been faced with, before or since. They had such high hopes for her. She was going to be the first in her family to go to college. She wouldn't have to work at menial jobs, like stacking boxes on a forklift in a warehouse or cleaning up behind folks at a downtown hotel. Even with her being co-captain of the cheerleading squad—Susan Bennett was captain—and all the practice it entailed, she managed to keep her grades up.

Her parents were horrified at the news, as Grace had expected them to be. Lou and Helen Corrigan arranged to meet with Janie Lucas, who even back then could best be described as washed-out.

Janie, who had four children by three different men, lit a cigarette and stated in a tired tone, "I always told my son not to sleep with anybody he wouldn't marry."

For Jimmy that was the kiss of death. His mother had practically come out and said that if Lou Corrigan insisted her son do right by his daughter, she would have no objections. Her next words made her intention clear as just-washed windows: "I can't complain about having one less mouth to feed."

Parental consent was obtained, and Grace and Jimmy were married at City Hall. They had a honeymoon of one night at an inexpensive hotel on the outskirts of downtown. But Janie Lucas had spoken too soon. On Sunday afternoon Grace and Jimmy each returned to their own parents' apartments and resumed their lives as high school students. Grace managed to conceal her pregnancy through May, but word spread all over the school when, by her fifth month, in June, she could no longer conceal her growing belly as she changed for gym. Her parents spoke to the principal, showed Grace and Jimmy's marriage certificate, and asked that she be allowed to stay on a few more weeks and graduate with her class.

Grace and Jimmy each continued to live at home through July, when a cheap one-bedroom apartment was located nearby and furnished from thrift shops and stores that sold cheap balsa-wood furniture.

Teenage pregnancy among high school students in the inner cities had not yet risen to epidemic proportions back in 1975, but at the time Grace became pregnant, out-of-wedlock births were something that happened mostly to older girls, girls who'd already finished high school and who held jobs, no matter how menial, or who attended college. Occasionally some twelve-year-old shocked everyone by sprouting a big belly, but Grace, coming from a poor but moral family, caused a major scandal when she "got in trouble," as the neighbors called it.

She hated the pitying looks in the eyes of her neighbors. They'd all heard her mother brag about how she would have her pick of colleges and how she would go on to great things. Grace knew they'd all written off any future she might have, saying privately that she'd become just another welfare mother.

Fortunately, Grace never stopped believing in the bright future her parents assured her was still within her reach. She regarded her pregnancy as a temporary setback, but she always knew she would go to college one day. She wasn't about to give up her scholarship money, and she'd already met the requirement of a high school diploma. She found a reliable babysitter to leave Shavonne with, and that January she started taking classes during the day, and worked two nights a week and all day Saturday and Sunday at the customer service desk at a local supermarket. Jimmy had gotten a job in receiving at Marshall Field's. Most days they saw each other only long enough to say hello and good-bye as he came home and she went out to work.

The sex that turned them into teenage parents wasn't even as fun anymore. And Grace swallowed a birth control pill every day without fail. God forbid she have another baby. This way she was protected from another pregnancy—which would be particularly troublesome, given her affair with a fellow student in her accounting class. She already had her hands full with Shavonne without having paternity issues for a new baby.

She and Jimmy quickly learned that sex is no basis to spend a lifetime together and spent five years barreling toward the inevitable breakup. After their divorce a still-young Jimmy joined the army. He served twenty years, had another marriage along the way, and eventually got divorced a second time. Every now and again he visited Chicago.

After his mother's health began to fail, he started showing up more frequently. On one of those visits he called Grace. With her second divorce behind her and with no other plans for the evening, Grace invited him over for dinner, and they ended up in bed together for a single night of passion with no strings.

When Jimmy's mother died three years ago, Grace was going through one of her frequent dry spells in her love life and knew she wouldn't turn down any overtures Jimmy might make. But she was in for a rude surprise. Now retired from the service and with a good state-government position in Austin, Texas, Jimmy was accompanied by a woman in her midthirties with a pregnancy-swollen abdomen, whom he introduced as his new wife. Even Shavonne hadn't known that her father, who'd had no children with his second wife, had married a third time, much less was starting a second family. Grace couldn't fault him for his dismal matrimonial record, which equaled her own, but she thought it ridiculous that Jimmy would have a child younger than his grandson.

Now almost at Junior's she found a parking space a block and a half away. Before leaving the car she clicked her LoJack into place across the steering wheel. She walked down the street her sharp eyes taking in the crowd waiting to get in, which seemed to be mostly old-timers over forty. At least there were no kids in here. The last thing she wanted was to be hanging with people her daughter's age.

Grace spotted Pat making rounds. Good. That meant Pat would be able to tell her if anyone worth knowing was here. Lord knew that Pat knew half the population of the South Side, and as for the other half, well, they all knew Pat.

The crowd at the oval-shaped bar in the middle of Junior's was already two deep. Grace didn't see Susan or Elyse anywhere, which meant they probably had a table on the other side. Surely they were here by now. She moved in that direction, stopping to greet people she recognized. When she passed Stacey Noe she nodded politely. She'd never liked Stacey, mostly because of the slutty reputation she'd had in high school. If Stacey hadn't cozied up to Jimmy back then, Grace wouldn't have been so anxious to sleep with him to keep him from getting it from her.

Stacey didn't look bad, Grace thought. Still thin as a rail. She'd been blessed with a pretty face, although now it had a slightly hard edge, which even the lightening of her hair couldn't disguise. Grace knew the hardness stemmed from years of sexual indiscretions. Rumor had it that she would fuck anything— even a cucumber. She'd heard Stacey was a caseworker for Cook County. It didn't surprise Grace to see her there alone. No self-respecting man who knew her reputation would marry her. Grace found Stacey's presence at Junior's disheartening. She didn't want to be around a bunch of lowlifes.

Grace was still trying to get past the crowd at the bar when she felt a tap on her shoulder. "Well, hello there."

"Hello," she said cautiously, praying that when she turned she wouldn't see some man with a mouthful of gold teeth leering at her.

She turned, and she held her breath. Something about the good-looking, fair-skinned, mustached man struck her as familiar. Hell. Maybe she'd seen him in a movie. He was fine enough to be a star, especially now that Denzel had started to look a lot less gorgeous and more like just another man in his fifties. "Do I know you?"

He smiled, revealing even, white teeth. Her interest only increased. She couldn't get excited about a man who'd clearly gone too long without seeing a dentist.

"Eric Wade. From Building Twelve."

Grace searched her memory bank. That name sounded so familiar. Dreiser had twenty buildings, each with three stories, with five apartments to a floor. That made for a heck of a lot of people to recall.

Then it came to her. A larger-than-usual family—and many families in the projects had six or seven children—who moved in when she was in junior high. She believed they had at least ten kids. Nice-looking kids they were, too, all of them. Grace, Elyse, and Pat all had a crush on the oldest boy, Arthur, who was sixteen and didn't give any of them the time of day. Susan was the only one who didn't participate. She said Arthur Wade was full of himself.

All the Wade kids had gotten their good looks from their parents, but unfortunately both the mother and the father abused alcohol to the point where Mrs. Wade had become blowsy and Mr. Wade thin and wasted. The oldest child was a girl, who got married right out of high school and had never been seen again. Grace remembered her mother saying the poor thing had probably run for her life. One of Grace's younger brothers played with one of the Wade boys, and one day after he went to the family's apartment he came home and declared it a pigpen, with roaches running everywhere like they were listed on the lease as occupants.

Wait a minute. Didn't her brother play with this man who stood smiling at her now? Could that be possible? He'd been such a kid, maybe nine or ten years old at the most.

"Aren't you Craig Corrigan's sister?" he asked.

"Uh, yes, I am. I think I remember you, too."

"Craig and I used to be best buddies back in the day," he said.

His eyes openly roamed over her body, an action that to Grace could be handled either deftly, in a suave manner, or in a way that made her feel like a side of beef on a hook to be inspected. Eric Wade fell into the latter category, and even though his facial expression told her he liked what he saw, it made a warning bell go off in her head.

"You gonna be here for a while?" he asked.

"I just got here, so I guess so."

"Yo, Eric. Whassup?"

"Hey! I was lookin' for you, man." Eric started to step away, then looked over his shoulder. "Can I catch up with you later, Grace?"

"Sure." She shrugged easily and moved on.

Gradually she made her way to the back room. A few folks were dancing in the empty space in the room's center. Elyse caught her eye and waved to her from the table for four where she sat with Susan.

Susan looked old with all that gray in her hair, Grace thought. But Elyse looked fantastic, even with the extra weight. Hell, she could afford to carry some extra pounds. She had a husband at home, and a good one, even if he'd lost some juice. Franklin Reavis had been a handsome, fit dude of about thirty-five when Elyse married him, and the few times Grace had seen him since, he'd looked pretty good. But from the way Elyse complained about his lack of drive, she imagined him now as a big fat dude lounging in a La-Z-Boy and calling out to Elyse to bring him another beer. Grace wondered if Elyse had had the foresight when she married him to think ahead thirty years, or if his turning into an old stick-in-the-mud was more than she had bargained for.

After Grace joined her friends, she began to feel better about coming down here. She might get something out of it, something named Eric Wade. That little kid she remembered from nearly thirty years ago couldn't be called that, any more than she could. So what if he was a little younger? She could hardly be accused of robbing the cradle.

Besides, she hadn't had sex in months, and she was raring to go. It was time for a harmless diversion, and Eric looked like he'd fill that bill just fine.

Grace and her friends were exchanging the names of people they recognized in the bar when she saw Susan's expression change to one of distress. "Susan, you all right? You look like you've just seen a ghost."

"Over there," Susan hissed. "He just came in. It's Charles Valentine."

Chapter 11

Susan's throat felt dry; it actually hurt to speak. She'd allowed herself to entertain how she'd react if she saw Charles tonight after such a long time, seeing it as a harmless fantasy rather than as a reality. She never really thought there was any chance that he might actually show up. . . .

Elyse's sharp whisper stopped Susan's reverie. "Susan! Stop staring at him!"

"He's sure to notice you soon enough," Grace said. "Or some big-mouth who remembers what happened with him and Douglas—and this place is full of them tonight—is sure to fill him in, and he'll start looking for you."

"All I need now is for Douglas to come waltzing in," Susan lamented. "We can pick up right where we left off twenty-five years ago, only in a different place, and with a bigger audience."

"I wouldn't worry about that," Grace said. "Douglas is in jail."

Susan's lower lip dropped. *"Again?"*

"They got him on a DUI."

"How'd you know, Grace?" Elyse asked.

"Pat's an ADA, remember? She told me they gave him a year."

Susan didn't know what to say, but she had a mental picture of Ann Valentine's murderous expression when she looked at her this afternoon. Douglas ruined his life with his substance abuse. For Ann to blame her was so unfair. She'd paid a price, too. She'd had to give up Charles, whom she'd deeply loved, and head for an uncertain future, a future that took her years to find and now looked as dismal as the inside of a medicine cabinet.

Of the two brothers, Charles had actually been the better partner for her. When she was very young she thought she loved Douglas, but now she knew that that had been mere puppy love compared to her feelings for Charles. But she didn't see how they could possibly be happy together with the shadow of Douglas's anger hanging over them, plus the disapproval of their mother. Susan knew she'd made the right choice in refusing to marry Charles. Even her current unhappiness with Bruce didn't make her waver.

Elyse was asking a question. "All those legal troubles have to have a hefty price tag. Was Mrs. Valentine able to hold on to the house Douglas bought her?"

Douglas had bought his parents a modest home in Hyde Park after signing with the NBA. Many folks expressed surprise that he hadn't bought them a mansion up in Kenilworth or some other pricey suburb, but others understood that Douglas was on the lower end of the NBA pay scale.

"As far as I know she still lives in it. The rumor I heard was that he paid cash for it, so it had no mortgage."

"I'm so nervous," Susan said. "God. I wasn't this nervous when I went into labor with Quentin."

Grace gave her a dubious stare. "Now, *that's* nervous. I was scared to death to give birth. Of course, it didn't help that I was just eighteen."

"I think he knows you're here, Susan," Elyse said. "It looks like he's looking for somebody."

"Oh my God, here he comes." Susan practically hyperventilated as she said the words. She felt mesmerized as she watched his tall frame come around the bar, losing him momentarily every few steps as he disappeared behind this group or that. At six two, Charles did not have the exceptionally tall height of his younger brother, but he did stand tall enough to allow her to wear heels when they went out together, so she didn't have to worry about towering over him. Susan's adult height of five feet ten put her head and shoulders above most women.

He rounded the corner, and she felt the years melt away. She hadn't laid eyes on Charles Valentine in nearly half a lifetime. Normally it would be a typical bittersweet reunion of two lives that under different circumstances might have been intertwined but instead went down different paths. But she was at a vulnerable stage in her life. Not only was she living with a disease that could kill her, but she'd been rejected by her own husband because of it at a time when she needed him the most. If she had any sense she would grab her purse and make a run for her car. *But I'm riding with Elyse, and my car is parked in her driveway up in Lake Forest. Running down Cottage Grove Avenue will only bring the police.*

In the end she just sat transfixed, watching him get closer and closer. Moisture returned to her mouth, and she stood to greet him. It turned out she had no need for words. He held out his arms, and she walked into them. For a few moments they simply stood, her palms pressing into his back and his arms encircling her shoulders, their cheeks pressed against each other, oblivious to the curious stares and arm poking of most of the patrons of the bar. Then they each took a step backward to look at each other.

"You look great," he said. "I like you with your hair short."

She self-consciously fingered the short curls. "Thanks."

Charles turned his attention to the others at the table. "Looking good, Grace," he said with the ease of someone who's seen a person in the not-too-distant past. His eyes settled on Elyse and registered surprise. "Elyse Hughes? Girl, is that you?"

Elyse stood up, and Susan tactfully stepped back to allow her to give Charles a quick hug. Charles beamed down at the five-feet-four Elyse. "It's good to see you again."

"You, too."

"Join us, Charles," Grace suggested.

Because Susan had slid in the booth next to Elyse, Charles sat next to Grace. Grace felt that the way they sat benefited her. The four of them talked animatedly, and to anyone—specifically Eric Wade—who didn't know the past history and wasn't close enough to see the fondness in Charles's eyes when he looked at Susan, who sat across from him, he or she might think Charles had sat next to her because he was interested in her. The way she saw it, it could only help if Eric thought he had a little competition. She'd seen him chatting with Stacey Noe at the bar, and although her interest in Eric didn't extend beyond the carnal, it bothered her just the same.

A little while later when Eric sidled over to her while Charles and Susan were dancing, Grace suspected he'd been watching and waiting for Charles to get up. He asked her to dance.

She nodded acceptance, and at that moment she began to feel sweat form on her brow and between her breasts. Damn it, not another hot flash! She'd been noticing them for the past few months, and her gynecologist had told her she was perimenopausal, still getting regular periods but beginning to experience symptoms of the change. How was she supposed to get through ten minutes of dancing when she was sweating like a pig? Eric already knew she was older than he. She wanted to give an impression of youthful energy, not of a grandmother of two embarking on the change of life.

Oh, Lord. Were they actually playing "Got to Give It Up," that marathon number recorded by Marvin Gaye in the late seventies? Even back then she had difficulty getting all the way through it. That deejay had to know this was an older crowd. What was he trying to do, give somebody a heart attack?

To her relief, the deejay mixed a short portion of the original version by Marvin with a newer, jazzier instrumental of the same tune, then rolled into Michael McDonald singing "Ain't No Mountain High Enough." When he started mixing in another tune, she gestured to Eric that she was ready to sit down.

"Grace, would you like a drink?" Eric offered.

"Chardonnay would be nice, thanks."

Elyse was beginning to feel like somewhat of a wallflower. Susan and Charles were dancing. Grace had gone off to the bar with someone who looked like a member of the large Wade family from Dreiser, and the sociable Pat still hadn't made her way to the table where Elyse now sat alone. She wished Pat would finally get over here so she wouldn't feel so self-conscious. How much could she possibly have to say to these people?

"Elyse, is that you?"

She looked up to see Kevin Nash smiling at her. "Kevin! How are you?"

"Fit as a fiddle and ready to dance." He snapped his fingers and did some energetic steps. "Come on and dance with me, girl."

She laughed as she got to her feet. She'd known Kevin since first grade. He didn't live in Dreiser—his family owned a home a few blocks away—but he lived in the same school district, and he and Elyse shared many of the same classes straight through to high school graduation. Kevin had never been the type to tease the girls or pull their hair. He was an all-around nice kid who, she remembered, used to have some difficulty with his studies. She was delighted to see him again. Happily she fell into step opposite him.

"Oh, I'm exhausted," Susan said, fanning the neckline of her blouse. "Let's sit."

Charles followed her back to the table, which, save for half-empty drinking glasses, was deserted. "I guess everybody's dancing," she remarked as she slipped into the booth.

He sat beside her this time. "Good. It'll give us a chance to talk."

She smiled at him, her heart racing. The years had been kind to Charles. He was just as handsome at fifty-one as he'd been in his midtwenties. She wondered what he thought of *her*. . . .

"It's good to see you, Susan," he said quietly. "I'm glad you came."

"It was a last-minute decision, but I'm glad I came, too. I would have felt terrible if I'd missed the opportunity to see you again. It's . . . it's been a long time, and we didn't part under the best of circumstances."

"Ancient history," he said easily.

"How is Douglas, anyway?"

"He's hopeless," Charles said, as casually as if he were placing a lunch order. "He's broken my mother's heart. Back in jail again for the umpteenth time. It's his second damn home." He shook his head. "When he's out it gets a little awkward around the house. I live in that basement apartment in my mother's house. She likes to have me close by, now that she's gotten older and my father's gone. And every time I say I'm going to move out when Douglas is there, he gets arrested again for some petty crime and is gone again."

"That's unfortunate."

"Yeah, well, enough about him. Tell me about you."

"Well, I've been married for thirteen years, and I have two children, a boy and a girl." Susan smiled at the thought of Quentin and Alyssa. "I brought them with me to the luncheon this afternoon, and Elyse's daughter is watching them up in Lake Forest while I'm here."

"What about your husband?"

Did she imagine it, or was there a hopeful note in his tone, like he hoped she and Bruce had broken up? "He's at home, but I didn't feel like driving all the way back there to drop off the kids."

"All the way there? Where do you live, out west?" The roads leading to the Chicago's west suburbs were traditionally jammed.

She decided to have a little fun with him. "Lake Shore Drive."

"Lake Shore Drive? Life must be treating you extremely well, Susan, if you live on the Gold Coast. Wait a minute." His eyes narrowed. "You're pullin' my leg. Lake Forest is farther north than Lake Shore Drive . . . a whole lot farther."

"I live on Lake Shore Drive . . . in Pleasant Prairie, Wisconsin."

"Oh. I don't know anything about that area, but I can understand why you didn't want to drive home and then come back to the South Side." The corners of his eyes crinkled. "I guess your husband doesn't know about your great love before you met him, or else he wouldn't have let you come out alone."

No point in saying he was wrong to describe himself as her great love; that's exactly what he'd been. "We never really did a lot of talking about our past love lives. We were mature people in our thirties when we met. There didn't seem to be much point." She suspected Charles wanted to know how much time had elapsed between their breakup and her involvement with Bruce. She wanted him to know it had been quite a while, eight difficult years.

He seemed to accept her response. "Are you still an accountant?"

"No. My husband and I agreed that I would be a stay-at-home mother, at least until the kids were in middle school. So I haven't worked in about eleven years." *Here I am, a flesh-and-blood desperate housewife.*

"Nice deal, if you can swing it. I guess your husband does pretty well. I've never been to Pleasant Prairie, but anything called Lake Shore Drive is probably the better section of town."

"He owns a credit card–processing service up in Milwaukee." But she didn't want to talk about Bruce. "What about you, Charles? Are you still teaching?"

"Yeah, and a little private tutoring on the side, trying to help these kids make something of themselves."

"You aren't at our old school, are you?"

"No, I'm at Lincoln Park High. But the kids are just as wild. Sometimes I think I should have gone into the business world and made some big money instead of doing something as thankless as teaching."

Susan guessed Charles felt a little inadequate because he clearly didn't earn as much as Bruce. She sought to console him. "I think teaching is one of the most important jobs there is." A question suddenly occurred to her. "Charles, did you ever get married or have any kids?"

His gaze searched her face before breaking into a slow smile. "No. How could I? The only woman I ever wanted to marry left me."

Chapter 12

Grace downed half her Coca-Cola in one gulp. She was glad she'd asked Eric to get her a Coke in addition to her wine, which was for sipping. Maybe some cold liquid would help her stop sweating. When no one was looking she'd wipe her face, neck, and hairline. "That hit the spot," she remarked.

"Good. So, Grace, where do you work?"

She tensed. She'd known this question was coming. Instinct told her to say as little as possible. For all she knew, Eric might hold a position on a par with hers.

But even as she had the thought, she knew she was just kidding herself. Just from getting a little closer to him, she'd noticed that while undeniably good-looking, he wasn't quite as flawlessly handsome as she'd first thought. When he laughed a missing upper incisor showed. And he had a little potbelly. Plus his face held hints of that hard look of a man who liked to drink . . . a lot. His physical appeal had probably hit its peak ten years ago, and ten years from now she probably wouldn't look at him twice. Still, here and now he was reasonably good-looking, so reluctantly she named her employer.

"Oh, yeah? What shift you work?"

Grace blinked. What shift? He thought she worked in the *plant?*

At that moment any remote hopes of his being a professional faded away like General MacArthur. If Eric was accustomed to dating women who held blue-collar jobs, maybe she should cut him loose now and save herself from disappointment. She'd been through that before. The men whose eyes widened when they saw her floor-through condo, decorated with sculptures she'd picked up from her travels to Europe, Asia, and Africa, and her Mercedes parked out front. Next thing she knew, they'd ask to borrow her car, or to loan them two hundred dollars "just until payday."

Still, she abandoned the idea of excusing herself like a burning building. It had been too long since anyone who looked as good as Eric Wade had paid attention to her, even with his flaws.

"Actually, I work in their offices," she said. "I work standard daytime hours."

"Oh. Secretary, huh?"

Oh, God. She wished he'd stop asking so many questions. What difference did it make what she did? She was beginning to think he wouldn't understand it, anyway. "I work in the global relations office. I kind of . . . run things."

He winked at her. "Ah, one of those career women."

Grace made a face, her lower lip protruding slightly in a reaction that came naturally. She'd always hated that term. In her opinion it ought to be relegated to history, along with other outdated words and phrases that had no place in the vocabulary of the twenty-first century: *stewardess*, *record player*, *Betamax*, *dungarees*. The notion that any woman who didn't work behind the counter at McDonald's was consumed by her profession struck her as utter nonsense.

"The way I see it, if a woman expects to support herself nowadays and not live in abject poverty, she'd better be qualified to contribute something positive to the workplace. The days when women relied on husbands to take care of them ended forty years ago. I'd like to do something besides ring up sales at Target." Her eyes dared him to object.

Eric shrugged. "So you went to college, huh?"

"Yes." She wasn't about to volunteer that she had a master's degree.

"Where'd you go, Malcolm X?"

"No. I had a scholarship to U of I." Every muscle in her body plus every instinct in her brain told her to forget about Eric Wade, but she couldn't bring herself to do it. After all, there was nothing wrong with attending a community college. They'd grown up in the projects, not the Gold Coast. For every Deval Patrick, the gifted South Side student who earned a law degree from Harvard and ultimately became governor of Massachusetts, there were twenty who attended one of the City Colleges of Chicago.

Instead she changed the subject.

"What about you, Eric? What do you do for a living?"

"I'm a supervisor at a moving and storage outfit." He met her eyes defiantly. "I guess that sounds lame to a big shot like you."

"It sounds just fine." She raised her wineglass to her lips and took a sip.

He broke into a grin, his face softening and, under the flattering dim lights of the bar, looking more handsome than ever.

Grace began to relax. Maybe there was a chance of things working out after all.

Pat, Grace, Elyse, and Susan left Junior's at the same time, a little after one. The bar still thrived with patrons, but the four women were all tired. Charles saw them each to their car, beginning with Pat, who had parked just a few doors down from the door, and then Grace, who was the farthest away. Susan and Elyse walked with him, and after Grace drove off with a wave they turned around and walked to the opposite corner.

Elyse buttoned her checkered blazer and turned the collar up. "I think the wine I drank must be wearing off. I'm frozen."

Charles offered an arm to each of them. "It's not a bad thing about the alcohol wearing off. Are you sure you're able to drive?"

"Oh, yes, I'll be fine. There's not much traffic out at this hour, except the trucks."

He turned to Susan. "What about you? Wisconsin is a long ways away."

"Oh, I'm going to stay at Elyse's house tonight. I knew I'd be too tired to go all the way home, plus it means having to wake up my kids, who I know are asleep by now. We'll go home in the morning."

Elyse unlocked her car doors with a remote control. Charles, ever the gentleman, seated her first behind the wheel, then came around to the passenger side and did the same for Susan. As he had done with Elyse, he kissed her cheek. But he also discreetly slipped a piece of paper into her hand, saying softly, "Put this in your purse. Look at it when you're alone."

"Well, that was a heck of an evening," Elyse commented after waving good-bye to Charles.

"I'm glad we came. It was good to see Charles again, real good."

"I think it's safe to say he feels the same way."

Susan turned a suspicious eye on her friend. "Do you have something you want to say, Elyse?"

"No, Susan," she replied calmly. "I'm just making an observation. No need to get all touchy."

"I'm not touchy," Susan retorted. "I just recognize when someone's on a fishing expedition."

Elyse paused before admitting, "Okay, I'm curious about why you broke up with him. So shoot me."

"I won't shoot you, but I'm still not going to talk about it."

"Hey, can't blame me for trying."

Susan chuckled. She was glad Elyse didn't take offense at her statement. She didn't want to get into a snit with one of her oldest friends. She'd always been sketchy about her breakup with Charles. One of the important life lessons she'd learned was that the only true way to keep a secret was to not tell anyone. That was why none of her friends knew about her cancer. She didn't want them planning her funeral or even wondering about her sex life.

Which had, of course, become nonexistent.

As far as the reasons for her breakup with Charles, the truth would probably be disappointing to anyone expecting a juicy follow-up to the brothers' fistfight. Susan had told no one that Charles had proposed to her a few days before that fateful altercation, and that she'd accepted. She wanted to first make sure all was clear with Douglas, who tended to have a possessive nature, before announcing her engagement publicly. Then came the brothers' fight, which Charles won. He and Susan left the bar, with Douglas being helped up by several men who shouted epithets at their retreating backs.

That alone gave Susan second thoughts about the wisdom of marrying Charles. A few days later Ann Valentine read her the riot act for disrupting her family, and even though both Charles and his father intercepted, Susan decided she couldn't live with the shadow hovering over her of a shattered relationship between two brothers.

Charles had valiantly tried to change her mind, but she had held her guns. Blood was thicker than water, her mother always used to say. And Ann Valentine's open dislike of her would eventually lead to a showdown. She didn't want to force Charles to choose between her and his mother. Look what happened to Pat when *she* had to choose.

"I saw you talking with Kevin Nash," Susan said to Elyse. "What's he up to these days?"

"Oh, he lives up in Rogers Park. He . . . he works for a pest control company."

"Good business. People will always have bugs. What does he do?"

"Actually . . . He goes around spraying people's houses."

"Oh." Susan was taken aback. There was nothing wrong with servicing homes for pest control, but she expected Kevin would have done more with himself. His family didn't live in the projects; his father had been a policeman who owned his own home. From the viewpoint of Dreiser residents, the Nashes were well-off. In spite of that, Kevin earned a living doing something anyone coming off the street could do. And it couldn't be much of a living.

"I was surprised to hear that myself," Elyse said. "I guess he didn't exactly set the world on fire, did he?"

"No, he didn't. But he does provide a vital service." Susan felt she should say something nice.

"At least he's not without ambition. He plans on opening a Laundromat in the old neighborhood. As he said, a nice, shiny, clean place to make for a pleasant laundry experience."

"I see." But Susan *didn't* see. She had nothing against a self-made man. Bruce worked as a stockbroker for a dozen years, socking away every penny he could until he saved enough to start the credit card–processing service that made him wealthy. But he was her husband. Naturally she would defend his motives. But Elyse sounded too defensive of Kevin. Susan couldn't imagine why. Sure, Kevin had always been a nice guy, but Elyse hadn't seen him in years, and it was doubtful she'd ever see him again. She didn't understand why Elyse would want to stick up for someone she had no connection to.

Chapter 13

Susan tooted the horn as she drove off, and she and the children all waved to Elyse and Brontë. She glanced at Quentin and Alyssa in the rearview mirror. Their good-bye waves seemed genuinely affectionate. "Did you have fun, kids?" she asked.

"Yeah. Brontë's fun. She's got neat stuff, too," Quentin answered.

"Glad to hear it."

"Mom, why did we have to go home so soon?" Alyssa asked. "I'm hungry."

"And Miss Elyse invited us to stay for breakfast," Quentin added.

"Oh, I just felt that, since our staying overnight was so last minute, it would be best if we left first thing in the morning."

In truth, she wouldn't have minded lingering if it would have made Bruce worry a bit, but Franklin Reavis's demeanor, while not outright rude, wasn't exactly welcoming, either. She had the distinct impression that he was anxious for them to leave, probably so he could question—no, make that interrogate—Elyse about every detail of last night. Franklin looked pretty good for his age, still handsome and fit, with only a smattering of gray in his hair. She wondered if the old boy was having performance anxiety and feared Elyse would step out on him if she got the chance. And Elyse had spent an awful lot of time with Kevin Nash. . . .

Susan told herself that was silly. Elyse talked to Kevin because if she hadn't, she would have been sitting by herself. Grace had been off with one of the Wade brothers, Pat had circulated most of the night, and of course she'd been with Charles. She entertained that awful thought about Elyse only because of her own bad behavior. All during the ride home early this morning she allowed herself to relive the feel of Charles's warm lips against her cheek, savored what he'd said to her about his reasons for never marrying. Worst of all, she remembered how they used to burn up the sheets so many years before. She'd fallen asleep last night with the thought of his arms holding her close, of her shuddering in ecstasy and crying out in release. She scolded herself for allowing herself to dream of another man when she had a husband, but she couldn't deny that the memories made her happy.

As with any marriage, no one outside the household really knows what kind of problems a married couple has. Anyone who looked at her and Bruce would swear they were the ideal pair. The truth was, of course, quite different.

She looked forward to hearing what Bruce would have to say about her little impromptu outing when she got home.

"We're back," she called out as she followed the kids inside the house.

No one answered. "Daddy's not up yet," Quentin reported from the upstairs landing. "Your bedroom door is still closed."

For a wild moment she considered the possibility that Bruce had a woman up there with him. No, she decided, he'd never do that. If he was cheating—and there seemed little question that he was—he'd do everything possible to keep her from finding out. Besides, she'd told him they'd be back first thing in the morning.

"I'll go in and see if he's up," she said. "You guys go wash up and change your clothes. We'll go out to breakfast as soon as Daddy and I get ready."

She watched in amusement as her son and daughter raced

each other to the bathroom they shared. She waited until they were safely out of the way before slipping into her bedroom.

Bruce was stretched out in the center of their king-sized bed, snoring loudly.

He looked so sweet and innocent, and Susan couldn't help smiling at him. Memories of good times they'd spent together rushed at her like an ocean wave, wiping out the thoughts she'd had of Charles Valentine like so much sand. There were so many good things to remember about Bruce.

They met on a short flight from Detroit to Milwaukee, eight years after she broke it off with Charles and moved in with her mother and stepfather in Kenosha, Wisconsin. At first they chatted across the aisle, and then they changed seats when it became apparent the flight would not be full. After deplaning, they found an airport lounge and stopped in for a couple of drinks and some chicken wings.

They went on their first date that Saturday, and from then on they were inseparable. It amazed Susan how quickly their relationship progressed. Love had eluded her since her breakup with Charles so many years before, and she was now thirty-two. Her younger sister Sherry was already married with children, and Susan spent more and more time fearing that she'd walked away from her only shot at love and happiness, that giving up Charles Valentine meant she'd never get another chance; and then suddenly she and Bruce were madly in love.

She finally walked down the aisle at the somewhat advanced age of thirty-six, flanked by both her parents, who managed to put aside their animosity for the day and unite in pride for their firstborn. Susan felt she was too old to have a traditional bridal party and opted to have Sherry as her matron of honor, with Sherry's two daughters as her flower girls. She and Sherry, three years younger, had never gotten along particularly well—Susan disapproved of Sherry's choice to associate exclusively with white people, plus she suspected that Sherry hid her racial background. Susan tended to be a loner and hadn't formed any close friendships since her childhood. She still kept in contact with the three girls she'd grown up with, but after leaving Chicago she spoke to them only sporadically. If she had to choose just one of them to be in her wedding it would be Pat, but she didn't want to hurt Elyse or Grace's feelings, nor did she want a large number of attendants. Besides, choosing Sherry made her mother happy. She'd always wanted her two girls to be close.

Susan prayed her father would stay off the bottle long enough to come and thus make her bridal party a true family affair, and to her relief he did.

Frances and David Bennett had bravely defied the norm by getting married, a move white men rarely did with black women in the mid-1950s. They met on the job at the hospital where he worked as an X-ray technician and she as a nurse. David Bennett was about the only white man who lived in Dreiser, as Chicago's public housing was strictly segregated. Dreiser had been built specifically for blacks, although a smattering of Hispanics got in as well.

But David's drinking began to get out of hand when his two daughters were still small, and their home life consisted of loud late-night arguments between husband and wife. Eventually Frances threw him out, and life quieted down. Frances moved out of the projects after Sherry graduated from high school, settling in Kenosha, across the Wisconsin state line. A few years later she remarried, this time to a black man, Sam McMillan. David, who'd never remarried, always stayed in their lives, and even now Susan checked on him weekly and went to see him at his apartment in Libertyville every so often. Sherry, who lived closer, saw him more frequently. He still drank occasionally, but kept reasonably busy in his retirement and even had a girlfriend, a white woman in her late sixties who didn't seem fazed by his marriage to a black woman and his racially mixed offspring.

For a long time Susan and Bruce had a good marriage. A strong one, too, she believed. Then came her cancer diagnosis, her lumpectomy, and radiation treatment. It had been her plan to have plastic surgery to correct the shape of her right breast, but she was tired of doctors' offices and medications, the whole thing. She also feared that further intervention, even a fairly minor one, might spur aggressive growth of a still-hidden offshoot of her tumor. Besides, surely a little cone-shaped protrusion on the outer side of her breast couldn't come between her and Bruce.

When Susan realized the truth, she felt like she'd been floored by a punch to the belly. As she lay in bed night after night with a foot and a half between her and Bruce, she remembered newly married female celebrities who'd released interviews with statements like, "Nothing can ever break us apart," and "I've finally found my soul mate, and we'll be together forever." How embarrassing it must have been for them to have to eat their words after their marriage collapsed, admitting that they were in trouble almost from the beginning, and that their husband cheated, refused to work, or spent all their money. But those marriages usually lasted only a few years. She and Bruce had just celebrated their thirteenth anniversary last September when a routine mammogram revealed an abnormality. Thirteen years. If her husband had been so superficial all along, surely she would have noticed it before then. Maybe it was something psychological?

Susan confided in her doctor, who told her that Bruce's reaction wasn't all that uncommon, that many men had difficulty when their wives were diagnosed with female cancers. She suggested a counselor for them to see together, but Bruce refused to go. There was no need, he insisted.

"Bruce, you don't touch me anymore," Susan objected. "Of course there's a need. Our marriage is in trouble. We have to do something."

He continued to refuse, but after that he made more of an effort to resume their sex life. Every seven or ten days, and only when she was covered from the waist up.

On the surface everything seemed normal. There was no shouting, like what had gone on between her own parents. Bruce steadfastly denied having another woman in his life. He said he was merely getting older, and it was natural for their sex life to slow down a bit. He went off to work every day, she stayed home, drove the children to school and picked them up, using the hours in between to keep the house clean and well-stocked and the bills paid. But a vital part of her life was missing, and she wasn't happy.

Seeing Charles Valentine again made her more aware of that than ever.

Susan still loved Bruce, but she wasn't blind. She didn't believe his repeated claims that he wasn't having an affair. Her husband enjoyed sex too much to be satisfied with three or four times a month.

She knelt on the bed and gently shook him awake. His eyes flew open, and his handsome face looked almost comical with its wide-eyed, startled expression.

"Relax. It's not a stickup." It occurred to her that he might have been dreaming of some woman with perfectly formed breasts, and she added with a touch of sarcasm, "It's just your wife and kids."

He broke into a grin. "Hey! You're back early."

He looked and sounded glad to see her. She forced herself to keep her optimism in check; she'd been fooled too many times before by what turned out to be false hope. "I thought I'd treat everyone to breakfast. I feel I owe the kids something special for being such good sports. I had no idea when I left here yesterday that we'd be spending the night at Elyse's."

"That must have been rough for them, with no kids their age there. But I guess there's always TV."

"Actually, they both said they had a good time with Elyse's daughter, even though she's nineteen. I told them to go get washed up, but I'm going to take a quick shower. Would you—" She broke off once she realized she'd been about to ask if he wanted to join her. His being glad to see her was one thing. Taking a shower required her to be naked, and Bruce initiated sex only if her torso was covered. His actions made it abundantly clear that he had no interest in her from the waist up.

Acting on a sudden instinct, she swiftly reached below the covers for his groin. Her fingers closed around his erect penis. The muscle surged against her palm, like it had a life of its own. It hardly felt like the sex organ of a man over the hill. Hell. The way it twitched, it felt like it was about to start dancing. And why not? She and Bruce used to make love in the morning all the time. . . .

"Go on and take your shower," he murmured, his eyes closed.

She snatched her hand away like he'd slapped it.

Tears ran down her face as she washed her body in the shower. Her own husband couldn't bear for her to touch him. How pitiful was that?

She washed her face, scrubbing away all traces of tears and patting it dry. She had to put up a brave front for the sake of Quentin and Alyssa. If this is the way Bruce wanted it, then that was the way it had to be. But she did have, if not an out, at least a diversion.

She had Charles Valentine's cell phone number tucked in her wallet, behind her credit cards.

Elyse didn't have to wait long for Franklin to begin his inquisition. She had just come back into the house after waving good-bye to Susan when he said, "So, was it really worth it to drive into Chicago twice and risk your life for those people?"

"Stop exaggerating, Franklin. I hardly risked my life. You make it sound like the South Side is a war zone."

"It's a high-crime area, Elyse."

"And I'm a product of that high-crime area. I don't think it would be right for me to forget about that, just because we live in this lily-white suburb. It's part of me. That's why Susan brought her kids. She wanted them to see that plenty of kids out there don't live in mansions on the banks of Lake Michigan."

"You and your friends all did well, but it's been forty years since you lived there. I doubt that the people living in those projects now will do anything with their lives."

"That's the image Pat is trying so hard to fight. She says that the middle class and upper-middle class, and even the wealthy, view people living in the projects as caught in a hopeless web of poverty, drug use, and crime. Years ago, the projects were just a stepping stone to better things, even if you had to live there for fifteen or twenty years. You didn't stay there forever. We all made it out, but Pat lost both her brothers to the streets, Clarence to drugs and Melvin to gun crossfire."

The first funeral Elyse had ever attended had been that of Melvin Maxwell. She'd been in her first year of college at the time, and it remained the saddest function she'd ever been to. Melvin was Pat's youngest brother, just sixteen years old, a brilliant student surely destined for great things. His death resulted from one of those in-the-wrong-place-at-the-wrong-time circumstances. While walking home from school he'd been caught in gunfire from two warring gangs, and his life and promising future came to an abrupt end from a .38-caliber slug to the head.

"I guess Pat doesn't have anything else to do with her time. But you can't say that. She's not married, but you are."

Elyse smiled at him sweetly. "Yes, I'm married. I know it. But *you're* the one who seems to be forgetting your responsibilities."

Chapter 14

Pat's fingers stroked her throat as her other hand held the phone receiver. She'd been on the phone all afternoon, taking calls from attendees of yesterday's luncheon expressing thanks to her for organizing it. She knew everyone meant well and she was happy that they'd enjoyed themselves, but she was beginning to chafe at hearing the same words over and over from different people. Even listening to her own mother telling her what a good job she'd done didn't relieve her weariness. She just hoped that when the newspaper article was published next week she wouldn't get yet another rash of congratulatory phone calls.

She forced herself to concentrate on her mother's words. "Daddy and I are very proud of you, Pat. You know that, don't you?"

"Yes, Mama. Thank you." She sensed her mother wanted to say something else, and she merely waited.

"Pat . . . I saw Ricky and his wife at the restaurant yesterday."

Her shoulders slumped. Whatever her mother wanted to say about Ricky, chances were that she didn't want to hear it. Last night, the smiles and good wishes finally over with, she'd come home and cried her heart out. "Yes?"

"He looks like he's done pretty well for himself. I ran into his mother in the washroom."

In an instant Pat's upper body went from loose to tense. Nothing good could come of her mother's encounter with Miriam Suárez, who had been deeply offended by the Maxwells's opposition to a match between Pat and Ricky. An early resident of Dreiser like the Maxwells, she and Pat's mother used to sit together on playground benches while their children napped in their strollers, and later when they were old enough to play. Many a time Pat recalled going to the Suárez apartment to borrow a cup of rice, or Mrs. Suárez coming by to borrow an egg or two.

The comfortable situation of being friendly neighbors ended when a furious Miriam came to the Maxwell apartment after Ricky's talk with Moses. There'd been shouting all around. Fortunately, the Suárez family moved out of the projects shortly afterward. Rumor had it that Miriam had tracked down her ex-husband for back child support, and since her boys were now grown, she put the money down on a house.

"What did Miriam say?" Pat asked her mother now, her curiosity winning out.

"She told me that her son owns two restaurants, including a very popular place downtown. She asked if I'd ever been there. She said he has a high-rise condo overlooking the lake plus a summer cottage in Michigan."

"In other words, she drove home her point that her son was plenty good enough for your daughter," Pat said tightly.

"And she said one more thing before she left. She said that he's happily married to a Latina girl." Cleotha paused. "Then she asked about you."

"I see. She reminded you that you and Daddy didn't want me to marry a man who was both poor and Latino."

"It was a dig at your daddy and me, Pat. Miriam never had anything against you, even if she might have preferred for Ricky to marry someone Spanish. She wanted to drive home her point that Ricky is doing so well because of what Daddy said about him being a burrito boy."

"He said Ricky was just a busboy, Mama. Daddy never called

him a burrito boy to his face." Even her father shied away from making ethnic slurs, at least in the person's presence. He'd endured enough of being called a nigger down in Arkansas. "And she knows I never got married. She just wanted you to admit that I'm an old maid."

"Now, Pat—"

"It's all right, Mama. I'll talk to you later, okay?"

The conversation with her mother left Pat feeling a little sad. She tried to summon enough energy to get up and do something constructive, like vacuum. But she couldn't get the memory of yesterday's luncheon out of her head.

It seemed like she'd gone through the day in a daze. Somehow she managed to greet Ricky at the door, to be introduced to his wife, and to make her speech without looking at him. She'd even stopped at his table when she went around the room with the cordless microphone, asking attendees to tell their former neighbors a little about their current lives. Ricky and his wife shared a table with Teresa Navarro. Teresa had joined her family in Dreiser the year the Twenty-Two Club girls turned eleven. At the time she barely spoke a word of English and was placed in the fourth grade, two years behind where she should have been. Blessed with a quick mind and superior intelligence, she mastered her new language and ended up eight years later as school valedictorian. Teresa had a crush on Ricky and didn't like it when he only had eyes for Pat. But Teresa hadn't done badly. She held a PhD and worked as a medical physicist for one of the leading medical centers. She'd married a white guy, and it amused Pat to see how uncomfortable her husband looked at the Soul Queen. He had a Gold Coast "I'm the majority" look about him and had probably never been around so many people of color at one time in his life.

The phone rang again, and she reached for it languidly. "Hello."

"Hi there!"

Pat instantly recognized Grace's voice. "You sound awfully chipper this afternoon."

"Why wouldn't I? I have a date next week."

"A date? With the Wade kid?"

"Yes, Eric. And he's not exactly a kid, Pat. He's forty-five years old."

"Yes, I suppose not. I still remember him from when we were kids. But he doesn't seem to be your type, Grace."

"You know, Pat, maybe if you weren't so discriminating you wouldn't be sitting home alone most Saturday nights."

Pat wasn't deterred. "And maybe if *you* were a little more discriminating you'd have that third husband you want so badly."

"Touché." Grace took no offense, as Pat expected. Grace made no secret about wanting to give matrimony one last try and that she was actively looking for candidates.

"Honestly, Grace. What could you possibly have in common with Eric Wade other than the fact that you both lived in Dreiser? I don't know what he does for a living, but I'd bet he's nowhere near you on the success scale."

"He's a supervisor at a moving and storage company."

"And how did he react when you told him what you did?"

"Well, I didn't exactly tell him I'm director of global public relations. I don't want to scare the man, Pat. I just told him the name of the company I work for and that I'm in the public relations department."

"So he thinks you answer phones. Grace, that's so dishonest."

"Will you get off your high horse, Pat? We can't all be Dudley Do-Right."

Pat sighed. How could Grace stand to embark on yet another short-lived affair? From what she'd seen of Eric Wade, the man could barely construct a grammatically correct sentence. Yet, a successful woman like Grace was ready to start dating him. Just because he was buff. Hell, the man moved furniture for a living; he *ought* to be in shape.

Pat hardly considered herself to be a Dudley Do-Right, but she knew that she and Grace looked at life differently. Grace's entire life revolved around trying to catch a man. For Pat, there were so many other things, like community service. She practically had to drag Grace kicking and screaming to that Career Day seminar at their old high school. Grace hadn't wanted to go because there would be no marital prospects there. She knew it would always be that way, unless Grace did manage to find another husband.

"Well, have a good time. Just try not to expect too much out of it."

Grace's answer came without hesitation. "I'm expecting great sex."

After they hung up, Pat pondered Grace's outlook. Maybe she wasn't so wrong, after all, in dating these men who were less successful than she. At least she got to have sex once in a while.

Pat remembered hearing about Judge Glenn Arterbridge's divorce through the office grapevine. She'd hoped he would ask her out, even if she felt a little skeptical about that happening. In her experience the biggest men usually pursued the smallest women, and this had been no exception. The moment he stopped by the table at the bar and grill near the courthouse where she and Grace were dining, Pat knew who he was after.

That might not be the only reason. Grace was a new face to him, while she argued cases in his court three or four times a year. Perhaps he felt it improper to ask her out, although according to the grapevine, nearly as many lawyers were dating judges as lawyers dating other lawyers.

Pat sighed. Maybe she should start being a little more open when it came to the men she dated. The reunion was over. It was time to move on.

Chapter 15

Early April
Lake Forest, Illinois

"Elyse, I'll have to go to the tailor this weekend. My pants are getting loose." Franklin pinched roughly three-quarters of an inch from his waistband.

"There's someone at the dry cleaner's who's pretty good; she's done some work for me. We'll plan to drive over there Saturday morning." She smiled at him. "You don't have to have your pants taken in, you know. You can always start eating more."

"I really haven't been trying to lose, but I haven't had much of an appetite lately."

"Maybe we can go out to eat tonight and stuff you with a four-course meal," she suggested.

"I thought you might want to do that. That is, unless you've made plans with your newly rediscovered friends."

"Oh, please. Franklin, it was one dinner and one lunch."

"And one night spent at a bar."

"Yes, that, too. A perfectly respectable bar. Not the swankiest place in the world, but every place can't be The Four Seasons. But it's all over. If they have another reunion in another fifty years, I'll probably want to go to that, too."

"Elyse, we'll all be dead in fifty years."

"Exactly my point. The reunion is over, Franklin. Granted, my friends and I did make an agreement to meet for dinner every six months, starting in October. But I'll be surprised if it actually happens. We'll probably fall back into the same old habits, exchanging Christmas cards and hardly ever seeing each other." She slipped her arm through his. "So, now that you don't have an excuse, does that dinner invitation still hold?"

"Sure. It's nearly seven. We can leave now, if you're ready to eat. I'm not particularly hungry, but I probably will be in a half hour or so."

Her eyebrows jutted up. Not hungry? As far as she could tell—and Franklin wasn't one to wash out his dishes—he hadn't eaten anything since the English muffin she'd fixed him at ten that morning, over eight hours ago. An alarm went off in her head. Could something actually be wrong? She'd noticed a decrease in Franklin's food intake, but she also knew he attended many catered lunch meetings at work that left him full even by dinnertime. She just presumed he was attending meetings where food was served more often lately.

But this was a *weekend.*

She looked at him carefully. He certainly didn't appear unwell. He'd always kept fairly fit. For years he'd joked that he didn't want to get all out of shape and risk losing her to a younger man, a playful comment she noticed he hadn't made lately, since they'd had words about his lack of energy. He did have a little bit of a potbelly, but not enough to get in his way. The weight loss actually looked good on him.

Elyse had struggled with weight her whole life. As a child she'd been what was then referred to as "pleasingly plump." In her first year of college she'd packed on thirty pounds, losing it painstakingly shortly before she met Franklin at a homecoming weekend during her junior year.

Even now, with her children grown, her weight fluctuated. She kept her closet organized by clothing size—the clothing she wore regularly and the clothing for times when she picked up a few pounds.

Franklin's weight, on the other hand, had always been pretty stable. Her eyes searched for anything that suggested a change in his health. He looked pretty much as he always did, other than having lost a few pounds.

"I'm going to change. Be back in a minute."

He looked relieved and happy. She realized he'd probably worried about her intentions, thought she was about to start hanging out with her girlfriends on Saturday nights. Like she'd really want to do that. As Pat had pointed out, it was far better to snuggle at home with your husband than to be out looking for one. Her friends all had her contact information, and she'd exchanged e-mail addresses with Kevin so they, too, could keep in touch, but she had no plans to see anyone. She already had all she needed to feel happy and complete.

"Wait," she said suddenly. She moved close to him and raised her chin. "I haven't had my kiss today."

She closed her eyes dreamily as their lips met for a second or two. When she opened her eyes her smile faded as she noticed something strange.

The whites of his eyes had a yellowish tint, like he had some kind of vitamin deficiency. She hadn't noticed it until now. The first twinges that something might really be wrong wiggled through her chest.

"Franklin," she said suddenly, an underlying urgency in her tone. "I want you to promise me that you'll make an appointment with the doctor."

Chapter 16

Early April
Chicago

Pat studied the file in front of her. She'd been prosecuting the accused long enough to know when someone was holding out on her, or lying. She found that intolerable in her own witnesses. Best she find out before the defense, who would undoubtedly go for blood when they figured it out. If this witness was being evasive or outright lying, that usually meant they were protecting someone—or that they'd committed the crime themselves.

The phone at her elbow rang. She reached for it absently, her eyes fixated on the spot in the file notes that differed from what the witness had actually said on the stand. It would be easy enough to check out. She'd get her assistant on it right away.

She placed a Post-it note over the text as she reached for the phone. "Patricia Maxwell."

"Hello, Pat."

She frowned, not recognizing the male voice on the other end of the line. A look in the window panel of her phone showed that the call came from outside the building. Judging from the warmth in the man's tone, he certainly seemed happy to hear her voice.

That notwithstanding, she had no time to play guessing games. She had a full caseload. "Hello. Who is this, please?"

"It's Andrew Keindl. From Northwestern. I hope you remember me."

Her annoyance vanished like Noxzema skin cream left on too long. "Andy? Is it really you? What a surprise! What's it been, twenty-some years?"

"About that, yes. I read an article about you in the newspaper. I wouldn't have been sure if I had the right Patricia Maxwell, but there was your picture. It said you were an ADA. I figured I'd give it a shot and call the prosecutor's office."

"Are you back in Chicago?" Andy, with whom she shared numerous classes during their time in law school—they were friendly rivals for the number one spot—had taken a job in L.A. after graduation. Pat remembered good-naturedly teasing Andy about wanting to get in with the movers and shakers as she bid him farewell at graduation. She hadn't seen him since.

"Yes. My firm is opening a branch here, and I decided to come back and helm it. I'm a little tired of L.A."

His firm, she noted, not *the* firm. She wondered if he was a partner in it. Probably, she decided. He'd been a brilliant student. And here she was, toiling away as a public servant. . . .

"Am I calling at a bad time, Pat?"

Her eyes went to the file on her desk. "Uh . . . I am a little busy right now, actually."

"Well, why don't you tell me if you're free for lunch this week. I'd love to see you. We can catch up. Plus, you can give me the lowdown on the judges I'll be trying cases in front of." He chuckled.

"What's your specialty, Andy?"

"Criminal."

"That means you and I will probably be duking it out one of these days."

"I'll have to make sure I'm well prepared. You were sharp in law school, and I hear you've got a great conviction rate." He paused. "Maybe we ought to make it dinner instead. We've got over twenty years to catch up on. Hard to do in an hour."

She brought up her calendar on her computer screen. "How does Thursday look for you?"

"Thursday . . . I'm open. Six o'clock?"

"Fine. Are you familiar with the pub near the courthouse?"

"Yes, I know it. I'll see you there. And Pat—"

"Yes?"

"I'm really looking forward to it."

She looked into her closet Wednesday evening. She was no clotheshorse, like Grace, but she believed in dressing well. While she would never tell anyone, some of her very best suits had been purchased at the Salvation Army thrift store, a habit her mother had cultivated out of necessity when Pat and her brothers were growing up. Her parents, both unskilled laborers, had difficulty supporting their three children, and her mother had started making regular trips to the thrift store to purchase used winter jackets and dress clothes as well as jeans and tops, always of high quality. They used the little money they had to buy other necessities new, like underwear, shoes, and pajamas.

Pat used to pray that no one would find out where her clothing came from. Being dressed by the Salvation Army was one of the cruelest taunts that could be leveled at a child. It meant that your family was among the poorest of the poor.

They were poor, of course, even by Dreiser standards. They didn't even own a car. But the Maxwell children were among the best-dressed in the neighborhood. They wore outfits that most working-class people could never afford. Pat knew that the practiced eye of the other mothers recognized that she and her brothers wore rich people's castoffs. Indeed, many of the women who worked as maids in swanky Gold Coast households accepted the clothing of their employer's family for themselves and their children when they were discarded or outgrown. But Cleotha Maxwell instilled in her only daughter that she should never be ashamed of wearing thrift shop duds as long as they were clean.

Pat knew she would never get rich working for the prosecutor's office. Still, she wanted to look nice in court. When Pat complained to her mother about the high cost of clothing, Cleotha suggested she check out the thrift shops. Pat went browsing and found that many wealthy women donated garments they'd grown tired of, if the quality and up-to-date styles were any indication. She bought designer outfits for a song, including handbags that were usually kept in glass cases in department stores. She remembered all the attention paid to Marcia Clark's wardrobe when she prosecuted O.J. Simpson a dozen years ago. Many of Ms. Clark's ensembles had been borrowed from L.A. fashion houses glad to have the exposure. It gave Pat a strange sense of satisfaction to know that if she ever prosecuted a case that garnered nationwide attention, *she* wouldn't need to borrow any clothes. What she had in her closet would work just fine.

Even at age forty-nine, she still guarded her secret as fiercely as KFC executives safeguarded the exact mix of the Colonel's eleven herbs and spices. Grace would be appalled if she knew the origin of Pat's wardrobe. But Pat didn't make the money Grace did. She didn't earn six figures plus a hefty bonus at year-end and stock options. And Grace had only herself to spend her money on. If Pat didn't help her parents out each month, she didn't think they'd be able to live decently. As it was, her father still worked part-time bagging groceries at a supermarket, and her mother checked out books at the library to supplement their meager Social Security checks. Pat found it painful that her parents, both past seventy, still had to work, but Moses and Cleotha Maxwell never had had much money. She wished they would retire somewhere with a lower cost of living and a milder climate—like their hometown of Wabbaseka, Arkansas—but apparently her father really meant it when he said he'd never live there again.

She also suspected that her parents wanted to be close to her, their only living offspring, and she wasn't about to move to Arkansas. Even as a child, she hated going down there.

Her mother cried the first time Pat left two hundred dollars on their kitchen table, and even her father appeared a little choked up. Pat gave them that amount every month. For their golden anniversary a few years back, she'd also paid for them to go on their first real vacation, a cruise to the east and west coasts of Mexico through the Panama Canal. She and Grace sailed on the same ship—no way could Pat send her parents, inexperienced travelers, on such a complex trip alone. Both her parents marveled at the abundance of food on board, at the number of black passengers who could afford to take the expensive trip, and at how many of the ship's low-paid crew came from countries in Central America and Asia. Pat knew they'd expected to see fewer black passengers and more black crew.

It did Pat's heart good to see her parents have such a wonderful time. After dinner they danced like newlyweds, and on the formal dress nights her mother put on her new dresses, and her father looked quite dapper in the tux he'd bought from a rental shop on Cottage Grove Avenue that had gone out of business and sold its inventory at deep discounts.

In order for Pat to look good and still enjoy life—and to prepare for her own retirement, since she had no devoted children to help *her* out—she had to economize somewhere. If she didn't, she would have had to pass on that Mediterranean cruise she was taking with Grace and two other women in July. They'd planned it two years ago. Pat needed that much lead time to pay for it because of the money she gave her parents.

She decided on her brown wool suit, but instead of pairing it with a typical button-down tailored top, she chose an especially pretty high-necked yellow chiffon blouse. She hadn't seen Andy in over twenty years, but even now she still felt a faint undercurrent of competition, which had been the nature of their relationship. She'd been annoyed back in '83 when he'd received more associate offers than she, convinced that racism as well as sexism lay behind the discrepancy. He might have been ahead of her in class, but only by a hair.

Pat had felt slighted, even though she'd never wanted to be in private practice. She wanted to prosecute the drug dealers and gang members who had gotten her brother Clarence hooked on heroin and her brother Melvin shot on the street.

She remembered how Andy had said "my firm." He hadn't accentuated the first word, but he'd sounded pretty proprietary just the same. A successful criminal attorney would probably dress the part with gold cuff links, Johnston & Murphy wing-tips, the whole nine yards.

She wasn't about to show up in an ill-fitting suit and scuffed shoes.

Grace called Pat's office Thursday after lunch. "Want to have dinner after work? Someplace farther from the courthouse. I don't want to run into Judge Tubby."

"I doubt Judge Arterbridge will pester you now that you've turned him down, but sorry, I can't meet you. I've already made plans."

"Okay. I guess I'll stop by Quiznos's and pick up a salad. Have fun!"

"Thanks. Are you busy this weekend?"

"I've got a date."

"With Eric?"

"Yes."

Pat wasn't surprised. It had been far too long between dates for Grace. Still, she had to ask. "Where's he taking you?"

"To the movies." Grace sighed. "I know it's not like seeing Anita Baker at the Chicago Theater or having dinner at Brazzaz, but it's what he offered, Pat. Don't think it was my idea."

"I'll say. Do you think you'll get anything else to eat besides popcorn?" Pat smiled in amusement. She couldn't imagine Grace going on a date that didn't include a meal.

"At least I'm getting out of the house. It's not like I expect a lifetime commitment to come out of this."

"So Eric is just a diversion."

"Yes. Harmless and temporary."

Pat sighed. "There's nothing wrong with a guy like Eric. But he's not for you, Grace. I know you. You're not going to be happy with a man who can't afford to take you to the places you're used to going, the places you can afford to go yourself. And as soon as he picks you up and sees your place, he'll know you're out of his league." She didn't understand why Grace would even want to date a man when there was no future in it. It wasn't fair to the man, or to Grace, either.

"Listen, Pat, I haven't been asked out in over six months. I can't afford to be choosy anymore. Being choosy doesn't keep my bed warm at night. I plan on being nice and warm come Saturday night. And that's more than *you* can say."

Chapter 17

At five-fifteen Pat went into the ladies' room for a last check of her appearance, giving herself plenty of time to make any repairs. Sure enough, a few strands of hair just wouldn't lay right, regardless of how much she brushed. She plugged in the curling iron she kept in her desk. That would take care of it.

As she carefully wound the troublesome golden strands around the quarter-inch barrel, she wondered if Elyse had a weave. Her hair looked so thick and lustrous at the luncheon. Damn it, it seemed like her own hair got thinner every week. She probably needed to stop coloring it, or she'd end up bald.

But she didn't want to walk around with gray laced in her hair, like Susan. Okay, so there wasn't anything wrong with the way Susan looked. Pat wasn't a catty person, but she couldn't help noticing that she and Grace looked younger than their two friends. She knew how hard Grace worked at staying young looking, but she really didn't do anything special herself, just a few lackluster bends here and there and salad for dinner two or three times a week. She wondered if there was any connection to looking younger and not being married.

No, she decided, that was silly. Elyse looked a little more matronly because she was overweight, and Susan because she didn't hide her gray. Their faces looked as young as hers. Marital status had nothing to do with it. She carefully combed her hair over any sparse spots and left the restroom.

Had Andy changed much? she wondered. He'd been so handsome as a young man, with hair black as a moonless night and blue eyes a person could get lost in. She'd never told anyone, but she had had more than a little bit of a crush on him.

Pat didn't share her parents' strong beliefs against interracial dating. She knew their feelings stemmed from the lynching of her Uncle Jacob when he'd been just seventeen, back in her parents' hometown in Arkansas. With tensions already running high after the then-recent Brown ruling outlawing segregated schools, a white girl accused him of fathering her baby, and no one would listen when Jacob insisted he had nothing to do with it. It had been a nightmare for her family, and the crime remained unsolved on the books, although everyone in town knew of at least one man who'd been connected to the crime. The identity of the baby's father had never been revealed. Her father couldn't bear to continue living there after his beloved baby brother was killed. He married her mother, and the young couple made their way to Chicago.

Pat could understand how her father felt, but she'd never even known her Uncle Jacob. His murder occurred three years before her birth. Nor had she ever lived in Arkansas, although she and her brothers used to take the Greyhound every summer to spend two weeks with their grandparents and cousins. While they enjoyed running in open fields and walking to the neighborhood store for ice-cold Cokes, life there was too small-townish for them. Their cousins and the other kids seemed so . . . well, country, like a bunch of hicks. They didn't have the latest records, and they talked funny, saying "thang" for thing, "valya" for value, and "yella" for yellow. Pat and her brothers were always glad to return to the city life of the projects when the two weeks ended.

She decided to arrive a few minutes late, feeling it would be more appropriate for Andy to wait for her than for her to wait for him.

All thoughts of Wabbaseka and the murder of her uncle years ago vanished when she caught sight of the black-haired man waiting for her at the bar. She took a deep breath. Andy at nearly fifty looked ten times better than the Andy she remembered from half a lifetime ago. The long hair that had grazed his shoulders back in the day had been replaced by a more conservative haircut that looked like it could use a trim. The hair at his temples had turned gray. And his eyes were blue as ink.

He slid off the bar stool and smiled at her. "Pat. I'd know you anywhere. You look fabulous."

"So do you." He held his arms outstretched, and she happily walked into them. A pulse began beating in her throat as warm lips connected with her cheek. God help her, even after all this time, she still felt that gravitation toward him.

They separated after a prolonged friendly embrace, and she climbed on the bar stool next to him and ordered a mai tai. She looked at the handsome man sitting next to her. His hair looked as thick as it had been during their days at Northwestern. Somehow she'd known he hadn't gone bald. His blue eyes twinkled. He'd filled out since law school, but he wasn't overweight by any stretch. The man looked good enough to suck on.

Oops. Wrong word. It conjured up a highly inappropriate, if certainly not unpleasant, image. Probably just a Freudian slip. She hadn't had sex in a year and a half . . . and she now found it extremely difficult to keep her thighs still.

She'd better say something before he thought she'd gone mute. She swallowed as lightly as her carnal thoughts would allow. "Tell me what made you decide to come back to Chicago, Andy," she suggested.

He took a sip of his drink, an amber-colored liquid she guessed was Scotch. "A couple of things. For one, I've always been afraid of earthquakes."

She grinned. "After all that time out there you think The Big One is about to hit?"

"Don't knock it. I spent two weeks in Chicago a couple of years ago when all these so-called psychics were predicting a big quake in May." He chuckled. "But there are other considerations. My parents are getting up in age. They still keep their house here, even though they spend their winters on South Padre Island. I'd like to be closer. And most important of all, my ex-wife remarried and moved to Buffalo Grove."

She arched a waxed eyebrow. He wanted to return to Chicago to be close to his *ex-wife?* What was *that* about?

Andy chuckled. "I guess that didn't sound right. Let me clarify. My daughters mostly live with her. We share custody, but it's hard to do when one parent lives in Illinois and the other in California."

"How old are your daughters?"

"Fourteen and seventeen, and both beautiful. They're the lights of my life." He looked at her curiously. "I guess you use your maiden name for professional purposes only."

She shrugged. "I use it for everything, and always have. It's always been my name."

"You've never been married?"

The surprise in his eyes made her feel a little embarrassed. The "Most Popular" girl in her high school class who went on to become one of the brightest students in both college and law school had been unable to get a husband. "No." She looked him in the eye and proceeded to lie like a sleeping dog. "I guess you can say I've never met my Mr. Right."

"Mr. Keindl, your table is ready."

They both turned to face the black-vested waiter, who bowed slightly. "If you'll just follow me."

"Of course." Andy stepped down and held Pat's elbow as she moved her hanging feet to the floor, careful not to get her three-inch heels caught in the metal footrest.

On unsteady feet Pat followed the waiter. Andy was still devastatingly attractive. And better yet, he was *available*.

Her spirits lifted like an airplane at takeoff.

Their dinner lasted for two and a half hours and included much laughter and two more mai tais. "I'm wondering if I should put you in a cab," Andy remarked as he slipped a credit card in the check holder, gesturing for her to put away her wallet. "This is on me. And I don't mind telling you this has been more fun than I've had in a while."

"I enjoyed it, too. We'll have to do it again."

"Seriously, Pat, are you able to drive? You seem to be buzzed."

"Oh, I'm fine."

"It'll take you at least fifteen minutes to get to South Shore. Maybe I should follow you, make sure you get in safely."

"I don't drive to work, Andy. The traffic is unbearable, plus the parking is too expensive. I take the bus."

"Why didn't you say so? I'm not about to let you get on a bus at this hour. I'll drive you home."

"That might not be a bad idea," she heard herself saying. Her inner voice immediately began screaming at her. What was she letting herself in for, allowing him to bring her home? He was good-looking, and she was horny.

It had all the makings of a long-held dream come true.

Chapter 18

Twenty-five minutes later, Pat unlocked the door to her vestibule, Andy standing close behind her. She swung open the door. "I'm one flight up," she said over her shoulder.

She started to tell him that he didn't really have to see her to her door, but from the moment he parked, she knew he planned to do just that.

She clutched the banister for support as her legs carried her up the stairs. Andy had been right; she was feeling a little unsteady.

But she knew exactly what would happen, if she let it.

"Welcome to my humble abode," she said, flipping on the switch by the door.

"It looks real comfortable," he said, nodding approval as he looked around the neat living room with its rolltop computer desk and tan leather–and–chrome seating. "Have you lived here long?"

"Eighteen years. I got in on the ground floor, as soon as the developers announced plans to rehab this building." She slipped off her coat, draped it over a chair, and kicked off her heels. "At the time I was still up to my ass in student loans, but the idea of owning something appealed to me. Can I fix you a drink?"

He removed his coat and laid it over hers. "I'm not interested in alcohol right now."

Pat swallowed hard. She immediately understood what he meant. "This is a lot different from Northwestern, isn't it?" she asked in a whisper.

"You look sexy as hell, Pat. I thought so when we were at Northwestern, and I've been thinking about being alone with you from the moment you showed up tonight."

"I can't say I didn't think about the same thing, then and now," she admitted.

He held out his hand. "So what are we waiting for?"

Within seconds she was in his arms. The blazer she'd picked out so carefully was soon tossed to the floor. They undressed each other as they kissed, carelessly throwing garments anywhere. Something else Pat liked about Andy. The man had some lips on him. Not as full as a black person's, but nice lips all the same. Pat had dated more white men than black over the years, and one of her criteria was that the man had to have something to pucker up with. Pat had never understood why all her friends raved about Christopher Reeve being so handsome when he first played Superman in the movies some thirty years ago. The actor's tragic accident years later saddened her, but his lack of lips had always left her cold.

When Andy tugged at her skirt, she took a moment to be thankful that she'd had the foresight to wear thigh-highs and a garter belt rather than panty hose. She liked to wear these whenever she wanted to feel sexy, even if it remained her little secret. But for those increasingly rare times when she actually got to take off her clothes for a man, it felt delicious.

She felt his groping hands under her skirt, felt his surprised hesitation when he reached the bare skin at the top of her thighs. He murmured a sound of approval against her mouth, and again when her panties came down with just one tug, courtesy of her habit of fastening her stockings before she put on her underwear rather than after.

They skipped the foreplay and went at each other right there in the living room, not even bothering to turn off the lights or even to completely undress. Andy, naked from the waist up with his pants still around his ankles, scrambled inside his wallet for a condom, and Pat, her blouse unbuttoned and her skirt pushed up to her waist, leaned over the couch with her butt in the air. He took her from behind, pumping furiously while she moaned uncontrollably.

It didn't take long. Her vaginal muscles clenched his penis, and his long, drawn-out groan matched hers. He pulled out of her and straightened her up, turning her to face him. "I just have one question for you, Pat Maxwell."

"What's that?"

"Why the hell did it take us twenty-five years to get down to the real nitty-gritty?"

She laughed. "I don't know, but I'm glad we did."

"Let me look at you." He pushed her blouse off her shoulders and stared at her large breasts, overflowing from her leopard-print bra because of the leaning forward position she'd just been in. He reached behind her and unhooked the closure, and when he saw her naked breasts with their large areolae he practically salivated. "I always knew you had a good body under those jeans and sweatshirts you used to wear. I just never knew *how* good."

"I'm past my prime, Andy."

"So am I. See?" He pinched an inch of loose love handle flesh. "Hell, we're almost fifty years old, Pat."

It pleased her that her own less-than-stellar middle was concealed by her bunched-up skirt. Then she took in their half-dressed appearances and began to laugh. "We look ridiculous, don't we?"

Andy kicked off his shoes, then bent to remove his pants and socks, pulling up his blue-print boxers as he straightened up. His stomach muscles might have gotten a little loose, but she hardly had six-pack abs herself. His imperfection made her feel better about her own.

"We were in a hurry." He reached out to smooth out her skirt and then unzip it, moving it down over her hips. "But I suggest we try the bed for Round Two."

"I'm all for that. Just follow me." She led the way, swinging her hips with more gusto than usual, knowing he admired the view.

"Pat."

"Hmm?"

"It's time for me to go."

"What time *is* it?"

"Five-thirty. I want to get home and change before traffic hits. I'll call you later."

She sat up groggily. She'd forgotten how heavily she tended to sleep after a night of good sex. He was fully dressed, his tie draped around his neck. "Oh." She reached for the Asian-print cotton kimono she kept on the chair next to her bed and slipped into it. Barefoot, she plodded to the door, then stood on tiptoe when he leaned in for one more quick kiss.

In less than two minutes she had fallen back asleep.

Pat awoke to the sound of barking dogs coming from her bedside CD alarm clock. Big Mama Thornton was already halfway through her version of the old blues song "Hound Dog," the CD of which Pat used as her alarm. The blues singer's trademark growls usually had her jumping out of her skin, almost like the voice of an intruder would, but today she'd slept right through it.

She stretched lazily. Last night had been fabulous. It wasn't like her to sleep with a man on the first date, but she'd had the hots for Andy Keindl since law school. What a surprise to learn that he felt the same.

As she showered, she wondered what the future held for them. Surely it wasn't just a one-time encounter, or a one-time double encounter. The second time they had sex they'd taken it more slowly, gotten acquainted firsthand with each other's charms.

And how. She got wet just thinking about it, and she'd probably think about it all day today. She'd better put a shield in her underwear.

Pat was glad to see that her hair had held up decently through the taxing combination of vigorous sex plus a good night's sleep. If there was anything she didn't want to project, it was an Aunt Jemima image with her hair tied up. Nothing looked less sexy. At least black men knew a little about the struggles black women had with their hair, from being around their mothers and perhaps sisters, but it was a completely foreign concept to white men. She always avoided showering with them; they seemed to think that all she had to do was blow-dry her hair and it would pop into place. It took a good hour for her to dab oil on her blow-dried hair and then curl it into shape.

She didn't know whether this fling with Andy would last two weeks or ten. She just knew two things for sure: One, he wasn't going to mess up her damn hair. And two, this wouldn't be any more than a fling.

She had given up on ever finding lasting love.

Chapter 19

Grace awoke early, as she usually did. This morning she awakened with a frown on her face. Eric lay beside her on his back, ungodly snorts coming from his mouth in a regular rhythm. Had he been snoring like that all night long? It amazed her that she'd gotten any sleep at all.

She slipped out of bed and into the bathroom, where she closed the door and wiped her sweaty body with a cool cloth. These damn hot flashes were killing her. She hated waking up with her back and chest soaking wet, yet the rest of her freezing, because she'd thrown off the covers when the sweats had started.

Plus it was wreaking havoc on her hair, which was often plastered to her head when she awoke and never truly felt clean anymore unless she had just washed it. It wasn't fair. She could cope if this was her only symptom, but she still suffered from all the fatigue, cramps, and bloating she'd always had, plus these damn sweats as well. It felt like someone had turned the thermostat up to eighty degrees in here.

She brushed her hair and pinned it up. It didn't look bad, even if it was a little old-fashioned, more suited to 1947 than 2007. All she needed was a pair of wide-legged pants and fur-trimmed mules. But at least it was off her neck.

In spite of her efforts to cool off, Grace still felt sticky. She desperately wanted to take a shower, but she decided to do that after Eric left. He might hear the shower running and think she was some kind of lunatic, taking a shower at five-thirty on a Sunday morning.

She ran the wet cloth over her skin one last time before turning out the light and tiptoeing back into bed next to Eric, who continued with his incessant snoring. She lay down on her back, her head nestled against the pillows. She would eventually fall back to sleep, but it would be difficult in view of all that racket Eric was making.

She mentally laid out the things she wanted to do today. First on the list was kicking Eric out so she could get started on her weekend exercise, a vigorous three-mile walk. Not only did she begin Saturdays and Sundays with this routine as long as the weather cooperated, but it made a perfect excuse on those rare occasions when a man showed the bad taste to ask what was for breakfast, like she was going to pull out a skillet and fry up some bacon. That was a sure sign that she'd gotten involved with a real boob.

Eric stopped snoring, and the sudden silence that followed made her want to rub her ears to make sure her hearing was still intact. Then he stirred, and finally he sat up.

"Good morning, beautiful. What's for breakfast?"

Chapter 20

Late April
Lake Forest, Illinois

"It's bad, I know it."

Elyse clutched Franklin's arm. "Come on, you don't know that."

"Elyse, if I just had a touch of indigestion, Dr. Obi wouldn't request to see me in his office."

"And hasn't your workup been negative so far? The abdominal CT scan didn't show anything amiss, and neither did the MRI. He might want to speak with you personally to warn you of what could happen if you don't follow a strict medical regimen. Let's face it, Franklin, half the time you don't take your blood pressure pills. And I'm sure the doctor knows it, from the high readings you have whenever you see him."

Outwardly, Elyse sounded confident, but inside she felt as worried as Franklin was. He made a good point—why would Dr. Obi request to see him in person unless his workup showed something serious? And Franklin said that the woman who called to make the appointment suggested that his wife come along, too. Some situations simply couldn't be handled delicately, and the appointment setter's suggestion was about as subtle as those giant billboards on the Dan Ryan Expressway advertising the casinos down in Indiana. At least Dr. Obi had had the courtesy to ask that the appointment be set for tomorrow morning, so she and Franklin wouldn't have to cope with the anxiety for too long.

He pulled her close. "I know you're trying to keep my spirits up, Elyse. I love you. But my gut—the same one that years ago told me that you were the woman I would marry—tells me that Dr. Obi has bad news."

Sitting ramrod straight in Dr. Isaac Obi's elegantly furnished office, Elyse felt like she'd just been body slammed. Pancreatic cancer! She didn't understand. No one in Franklin's family had ever been diagnosed with any kind of cancer, much less one of the most difficult to pinpoint and, therefore, one of the deadliest forms of the disease.

She voiced her thoughts aloud, and her husband's doctor replied, "Mrs. Reavis, there is evidence to support that some forms of cancer—certain female cancers, for example—are more likely to occur in primary relatives in the same family, but it isn't a given by any means. And there is no evidence to support that other cancers are hereditary. Researchers are learning more all the time, but the study of genetics is still very much an ongoing science. Neither Mr. Reavis nor anyone else is protected from developing a malignant tumor simply by virtue of no one else in their family having ever been affected in the past."

Normally Elyse admired the precise speech of the Nigerian-born physician, but today she wanted to jump across his over-sized desk—made of luxurious dark brown cherry wood with no legs—and throttle him. He'd just explained that the ERCP they'd done, which involved passing a tube through the pancreatic and bile duct openings and injecting dye, came back with a reading that usually meant pancreatic cancer.

"What's my prognosis?" Franklin asked matter-of-factly.

Elyse knew instinctively that he was putting on a show of bravery for her. She wanted to put her face in her hands and weep. Instead she held her breath, waiting for the physician to reply.

"It's difficult to say at this time," Dr. Obi said. "But primary pancreatic cancer is among the most difficult to diagnose. The pancreas lies deep in the abdominal cavity. I think that the fact that we aren't able to visualize a tumor at this time is in your favor."

Elyse shook her head, unable to hold back her tears. "This can't be happening."

Franklin squeezed her hand tightly. "Elyse, we'll deal with it."

She forced herself to stop crying by thinking of him. She was supposed to be strong for her husband, and instead here she was bawling like a baby.

"Mr. Reavis, I'm going to refer you to Dr. Stephen LeBlond."

"Is he good?" A hopeful note crept into Elyse's voice. She realized that she sounded nearly childlike, but she desperately needed something positive to cling to.

"He's one of the preeminent oncologists in Chicago. He's on the staff at the University of Chicago Hospital. I've already consulted him on your case, and I asked him then if he could take you on as a new patient. He assures me he will fit you in this week, tomorrow if you like. Now that we know there is a malignancy, you'll need to have it removed, and soon."

Elyse and Franklin walked out of the office with their arms linked. "I'm sorry about the way I acted in there, Franklin," she said as he opened the passenger's-side door for her. "I didn't mean to sound hysterical."

"It was a perfectly natural reaction. That's why I tried to prepare you for possible bad news last night." He waited while she seated herself, then closed the door and walked around the back to the driver's side.

She watched him move, almost graceful in his steps, like he was gliding rather than walking. A sixth sense had told her not to offer to drive, that it would only infuriate him.

He'd always been a needy patient when he was down with a cold, asking her to make him a cup of tea or something to eat, but this was different. They both knew he would recover from a cold, and she pampered him without complaint, getting as much a kick out of it as he did. She'd even worked out a routine:

When she thought he might be feeling better and faking it just to prolong her waiting on him hand and foot, she dressed in a long white sweater that came to midthigh and beige thigh-high stockings and entered their bedroom with a thermometer in hand then bent over him to straighten his sheets so that her sweater rode up, giving him a view he couldn't resist. If he gave her ass a weak pat and did nothing else, he obviously hadn't regained his strength. On the other hand, if he grabbed her and pulled her down on the bed, he was feeling a lot better.

But there would be no recovery from this, and he wouldn't tolerate anyone treating him like an invalid. She'd have to act normally. But how long would he be able to seat her in the car and then walk around to take the wheel? she wondered. Instantly she felt a stab of guilt for such a pessimistic thought. She bit her lower lip hard to keep from succumbing to tears again.

"All right," he said as he started the engine, "we obviously have to work some things out. First of all, no one is to know about this, at least not yet. I won't be the subject of a death watch until I absolutely have to. I don't even want the kids to know, and I don't want you saying anything to your parents. Nor will I say anything to anyone at work."

Elyse realized that he'd thought this out beforehand. They'd both had a restless night last night. Had she had even an inkling of what was on his mind she wouldn't have slept for ten minutes. "What about your manager?" she asked.

"Just because I report to him doesn't mean he has a right to be privy to my health issues from the get-go. I'm taking today off, but I'll be back at work tomorrow. He'll have to be told eventually, but not right now."

Elyse felt relieved that Franklin didn't plan on going to work. It amazed her that he could get in the driver's seat and calmly drive home after being handed a possible death sentence by Dr. Obi. If he'd insisted on going to the office, it would suggest possible denial issues, which could be a huge problem in itself. Still, she didn't agree with much of what he'd said. "What about the kids? Don't you think they have a right to know?"

"Elyse, I'm not looking to keep them uninformed indefinitely. Right now, while I'm feeling okay, they don't have to know.

They'll only start falling behind in their studies because they'll be worried about me, and finals are coming up. I haven't even seen this specialist yet. We can tell them just before I go in for my surgery. A day or two before, to give them a chance to drive up here. I'll tell Frankie and Rebecca at the same time."

His son and daughter from his first marriage. Of course they would need to know about his condition, too. Elyse knew it wouldn't stop there, that they would inform their mother. She hoped that Carolyn, the first Mrs. Reavis, wouldn't call and make a scene once she learned of Franklin's illness. Carolyn had always had a flair for the dramatic, and hysterics would only serve to make an already tense situation more so.

Elyse raised her chin, her head pressed against the headrest of the Navigator, her eyes closed, asking herself for the twentieth time in fifteen minutes how such a terrible thing could happen to her Franklin. "Oh, Franklin. You have to beat this; you have to." She barely realized she'd spoken aloud.

"I hate it when people say they're going to beat cancer," he said, sounding almost angry. "It's an insult to the memories of all the folks who've died of it, implies they were weaklings."

Elyse shifted her head to its normal position. She felt like she'd been slapped in the face. "I didn't mean—"

He kept talking, as if she'd said nothing. "Long-term survivors didn't make it because they were so big and bad; they made it because they had a combination of good medical care and nonaggressive forms of disease. All the money in the world won't keep a person alive if they've got a highly aggressive cancer that spreads to vital organs. Look at Jackie Onassis . . . that billionaire businessman Reginald Lewis . . . Paul McCartney's first wife, Linda. They all had millions, but none of them lived long enough to collect Social Security."

"None of them needed it."

"That's not my point, Elyse. I'm saying that they all died, despite the best treatment money could buy. You don't think they were getting their medical care at the free clinic, do you?"

She looked at him, unsure if he really meant for her to reply to his diatribe, which she knew was more of a vent session. Still, he didn't have to jump on her, did he? She was on *his* side.

"I guess that's enough of that," he said. In an unexpected show of affection, he removed his right hand from the steering wheel to rest on top of her left. "Funny, but I'm feeling pretty good right now. Just a little tired. Not like a man with a limited lifespan." He increased the pressure on her hand when he heard the gasp she was unable to keep in. "Elyse, I love you. I'd like nothing more than to have ten or twenty more years with you. But if one of us has to leave, it's best that it be me. You know life has no guarantees. This could have happened to one of the kids. And then how would we feel?"

She shut her eyes tightly, unable to bear the thought of any harm coming to Todd or Brontë. She and Franklin were supposed to die first. But she couldn't abide imagining Franklin dying, either. Not this soon. They were supposed to live to be an old couple in their rocking chairs, playing with grandchildren.

Guilt stabbed at her like a peptic ulcer. Isn't that what she'd said to him a couple of weeks ago? That he was ready for a rocking chair? If only she'd heeded his complaints of not feeling well, noticed his diminished appetite sooner. She would have gotten him to the doctor right away. A month or two might have made a big difference in his prognosis.

Now he might not live long enough to sit in that rocking chair.

"I've lived a good life." He gave her hand a final squeeze, then returned his to the wheel. "Maybe we shouldn't talk about it anymore right now."

She nodded, opening her eyes. He wanted everything to be normal . . . at least as long as that was feasible. She choked back a sob. Franklin summed up his life just as calmly as if he'd remarked that it looked like rain.

She understood why he didn't want anyone to know about his illness just yet, but Elyse knew she was about to break her word. She couldn't put on a brave face and act like everything was normal, especially for her children and her parents, with whom she spoke regularly, unless she confided in someone. But she wouldn't talk to anyone close enough to their social circle for the news to leak out. Franklin would never forgive her.

Her old friends, the ones about whom just last week she'd

said she didn't expect to have much contact with, would help her through this.

Elyse reread Kevin Nash's e-mail once more.

> *I'm sorry your husband is sick. Let me know if there's anything I can do to help. Sometimes it's nice to just have someone to talk to. I don't work too far from you. Maybe we can have lunch together.*

That was awfully nice of him, she thought. Still, she couldn't understand why she hadn't heard from Pat. She'd left a message for her on her home phone Thursday night, three days ago, and when she didn't hear back she sent her an e-mail as well. That was when she saw the first e-mail Kevin had sent, telling her how nice it was to see her at Junior's after such a long time and asking her to keep in touch.

Elyse quickly decided that Kevin, who lived on the north end of Chicago in Rogers Park, was far enough removed for her to be able to confide in. News of Franklin's cancer wouldn't drift up and reach their friends and neighbors in Lake Forest if Kevin knew about it any more than it would if Pat did. She hit the REPLY button and typed out a brief message about Franklin's diagnosis and upcoming surgery, plus her own concerns about what the future might hold.

Kevin's caring reply immediately lifted her spirits. But she still wondered why she hadn't gotten a response from Pat.

Chapter 21

"Oh, shucks," Bruce Dillahunt said as he handed Susan a red and white plastic popcorn container. "I forgot my drink."

"I'll get it," Susan offered quickly. She was up and in the kitchen in a flash. She picked up Bruce's freshly filled glass of Dr Pepper and brought it to him in the family room, where they were about to watch the cable debut of a film they'd planned to see during its theatrical release, but hadn't gotten around to seeing.

"Thanks."

She took her place next to him on the sofa. The kids were home, but they were watching a different program in Quentin's room. It almost felt like the old days, before they had children.

Ever since that night at Junior's Bar nearly a month ago, Susan had found herself thinking continually of Charles Valentine: as she vacuumed, emptied out the dishwasher after a cycle, or folded laundry. She saw the affection in his eyes when she lay down for the night, and fell asleep with thoughts of making love to Charles.

And she felt terribly guilty. Even with things as bad as they were between her and Bruce, he was still her husband, and she couldn't justify daydreaming about another man.

The key, she thought, was to reinvigorate her marriage. She'd recapture the old magic if it was the last thing she did. This nonsense had to come to an end.

"Oops. Guess I should have brought more napkins," Bruce said.

"I'll—"

"No, I'll get them. You stay put before you spoil me so bad I won't want to wipe my own mouth." He chuckled.

It occurred to her that maybe she'd been overdoing it. She wanted to make it up to Bruce for—as Jimmy Carter so famously said—lusting in her heart, even though he had no idea of her carnal thoughts toward Charles. She'd made his favorite foods all week, even baking that chocolate pumpkin cheesecake he adored, and didn't complain once when he unfailingly announced how tired he was—which she'd come to recognize as code for "I don't want to have sex tonight."

Her hungry eyes followed him as he sprinted to the kitchen. Even the sweatpants he wore couldn't hide his sinewy thigh muscles. At fifty-two, Bruce Dillahunt kept himself in top condition, regularly lifting weights and working his abs. He could probably run a marathon if he wanted to.

When they first met seventeen years ago, their mutual attraction was intense and immediate. She still remembered the end of their first date, that almost comical look of surprise on his face when she bid him good night and coyly asked if she could have a kiss. It had been clear that he expected to stay the night with her, but she was determined to hold out, not wanting to be just another woman he got into the sack with after buying her dinner. If she gave in so quickly, they'd likely go out a couple of more times and have great sex, but then someone else would catch his eye and it would be good-bye Susan. She had to stretch out the tension, even if it meant taking cold showers and sleeping with her thighs pressed together.

In the end her strategy paid off. When she finally slept with him, they were both starved for sex. They stayed in bed all weekend, rising only to go for meals, after which they returned and went at it again, turning on the TV when they were too tired to rise. Four years later they got married, and for years afterward she felt like she had stumbled into a fairy-tale existence. A custom-built house, two healthy babies, plenty of money.

Then came the mammogram that changed everything.

Susan smiled at Bruce as he returned with the napkins and sat beside her on the sofa. It made her a little sad to realize that of the two of them, she'd changed the most physically during their years together. She didn't look bad, but she definitely looked middle-aged. When Bruce's hairline began to recede, he'd started shaving his head, which made him look younger. At the time she was still keeping her hair long, as she had worn it all her life. She'd started cutting it, a few inches at a time, some five years ago. Long gray hair might work well on that country singer Emmy-lou Harris, who was stunning; but on Susan Dillahunt it just made her look like a woman well past forty who was trying to look twenty-five. Finally she had it cut short, and was pleased to see that it curled naturally in a low-maintenance style.

Susan didn't mind growing older. She considered each day a blessing. She knew that in another day and time, before the availability of advanced medical care, she easily could have been on her deathbed by now. All she wanted, all she prayed for, was to live long enough to raise her children. If God would let her live until Alyssa graduated college, she'd be happy. If He let her live to see her grandchildren, she'd be ecstatic.

Even, she thought sadly, if it meant not ever making love again.

She went to bed first, right after the movie, but she deliberately positioned herself in the middle of the mattress so that she'd know when Bruce came in. She couldn't give up on him. He was her husband, the man she'd promised to love until she died. It would be terribly wrong for her to sneak out behind his back to see Charles. Charles belonged to her past. Her present, and her future, was with Bruce. If only he would treat her like he used to, run his hand over her breasts, squeeze and lick and gently bite them. . . .

With a smile, Susan caressed the soft, shiny fabric of the sexy nightgown she'd just bought at Carson Pirie Scott. When Bruce came to bed, she'd fling back the covers and treat him to the view. Even post–cancer surgery, she believed she still looked pretty good.

As a teenager she used to worry that her breasts were too small. She wanted big knockers, like Pat had. Time had brought acceptance and satisfaction with her bustline. She had more than enough to fill a champagne glass, and surely that was enough.

But if Bruce continued to not respond to her, she had some hard choices to make.

Eventually she dozed off, but she willed herself to sleep lightly. Her eyes flew open at the sound of the bedroom door being opened. She turned her head in time to see Bruce closing the door.

"Hey, what're you doing on my side of the bed?" he asked jokingly.

"I wanted to squeeze your pillow, since you weren't here." She propped herself up on one elbow, exposing the spaghetti straps and the lace trim of her midnight blue nightgown. A lock of curly hair fell over one eye—she was overdue for a trim. Even though it obscured her vision a little, she left it where it was, thinking it might add to the allure.

It seemed to be working, if Bruce's stare was any indication. "Uh . . . that new?"

"Just a little something I picked up the other day." She casually reached across her torso and pulled the covers all the way back. "I thought you might like it . . . and what's under it."

The light was dim, but she could still make out the smile on his face. She caught her breath as he stepped closer to where she lay.

"You are one beautiful woman, Susan," he said softly.

She lay back, relieved. It looked like her long dry spell was over. When she thought about what she'd almost done . . . !

His large hand gripped her thigh as he knelt beside the bed. He kissed the inside of her thighs, then buried his tongue where it felt the best, just long enough to leave her dripping wet. She fell back against the pillows, her breaths coming in ragged spurts.

Bruce began furiously removing his clothes, and she pulled the gown over her head. It had done its job.

Or had it?

He stood still, like a fan that had stopped midoscillation after somebody pulled the plug. "Why'd you take it off?"

"Because it'll get in the way." She searched his face, and soon realized he was staring at the small cone protruding from her right breast. "Oh, no. Not again."

"Susan—"

"Don't even say it. Your johnson is doing the talking for you." She fought back tears at the sight of his dwindling erection.

"I can't help it, Susan. If you'd kept the nightgown on—"

"So it's not your work, like you've been telling me for over six months now. I asked you what was wrong. Don't play me for a fool, Bruce. Don't you think I recognize the change in our sex life? Do you honestly believe I'm happy with it? I even suggested we go for counseling. The doctor told me your reaction isn't unusual; lots of men have a hard time when their wives have breast surgery."

"I don't need counseling."

He looked almost ridiculous, standing there naked, his penis as lifeless as a dead bird, denying he had a problem. She yanked the covers up to her shoulders. "You don't want counseling. So where does that leave us, Bruce? It's pretty obvious that you find the sight of me naked repulsive." A lone tear slipped out of her left eye, and she angrily brushed it away. "I won't let you make me feel this way anymore. I'm going to sleep in the guest room." She grabbed her nightgown and slipped it over her head while walking toward the door.

Before she left the room she turned to him. "One more thing. And don't deny it, like you think I'm stupid. If you're not getting sex from me, Bruce Dillahunt, I know you're getting it from *somebody*."

She ran to the guest room and closed the door behind her, sobbing. She'd tried so hard to make him want her. How dare he impose conditions. If you were married to someone, you were supposed to love the person no matter what, at least barring any mistreatment. If she hadn't removed her nightgown they would have had sex, the same way they had since her lumpectomy, with her breasts hidden so he could ignore them. That wasn't good enough for her anymore. She wanted to be loved completely.

She threw herself on the full-size bed. The urge to cry was nearly overpowering; her sinus system actually felt clogged. But instinct told her crying would serve no purpose.

Susan didn't know what would happen between her and Bruce, now that he'd come right out and admitted—to say nothing of the live demonstration he'd inadvertently provided—that her operative breast turned him off. Would he suggest a divorce? Did he want to marry whomever he was fucking? She had no answers, but she'd better get them quickly. She'd heard of many women who'd been left out in the cold when their husbands decided to turn them in for younger types with perfect figures. He might even want custody of the children! Hell, a live-in housekeeper could babysit, cook, and clean . . . everything she did except pay the bills. With all the money Bruce had, he could easily afford to pay for such a service. And where would she be? Would she even be able to *get* health insurance as a breast cancer patient? She made a mental note to look into it, just as a matter of protection.

It was difficult to imagine Bruce turning her out like that, but she never thought he would allow her illness to come between them, either.

She didn't respond to the soft knock at the door. It opened, and Bruce came in. She continued to lie in the same position, facing the window with her back to him.

"I'm sorry, Susan," he said. "I don't mean to hurt you."

"Then stop doing it. I'm not contagious, Bruce."

"I know that. I'm . . . I'm trying to work it out. Susan . . . Come back to bed. Please."

She continued to face the window. "Will my coming back make any difference?"

"It's a start."

"Since you're not ready to finish, I'll pass."

She didn't expect him to object. She could feel him hovering over her, and after a few moments he left, closing the door behind him.

Then she realized something.

This time he didn't deny he wasn't sleeping with someone else.

God, she felt like a fool. To think that she'd berated herself for thinking of Charles Valentine while she lay next to Bruce. That she'd been so certain she could make Bruce want her again and get their marriage back on track. She could no more make rain pour up from the streets toward the sky.

Now she knew she could call Charles and not feel guilty, even though she had doubts about the wisdom of actually seeing him.

For who was to say Charles wouldn't be as revolted by the sight of her naked body as Bruce had been?

Chapter 22

Late April
Chicago

As the wait staff serenaded Grace with a loudly performed birthday song, she felt like her smile had been painted on. How she hated these non-reservation-taking chain restaurants with all the little kids running around loose and the packed waiting areas and these noisy renditions of birthday greetings that everyone in the place could hear. All right, so the food wasn't bad, but the waiting was interminable. She could hardly believe that out of all the fine restaurants in Chicago, she was spending the evening of her fiftieth birthday at a T.G.I. Friday's. An ultraspecial day spent at an ordinary restaurant where she often had lunch.

The painful rendition over at last, the staff burst into applause. Grace hastily blew out the candles of the miniature chocolate cake they'd placed in front of her. Anything to get these people out of here.

"So my old lady really *is* my old lady," Eric said with a smile after they'd all gone off to tend to their customers.

She winced. Did he have to be so crude about her turning fifty?

"Just remember, you're not all that far behind me," she replied.

"Hey, baby, I'm only forty-five. I won't be forty-six until August. I might not be a young man anymore, but I ain't fifty." He chuckled. "But if it's any comfort, you're the hottest-looking fifty-year-old woman I've ever seen."

At least that made her feel better. "Thanks."

He leaned in and spoke in a low voice. "And I intend for you to give me a demonstration of how hot you can be when we get back to your place."

Grace shrugged. They were supposed to see a movie after dinner, but they'd had to wait nearly an hour before they could get a table, so those plans had been scratched. How could Eric choose this restaurant? He made decent money, he lived on the site of the storage facility, and he had no dependents. Would it really kill him to put three bills down for a good meal at Texas de Brazil or The Melting Pot? If those prices were too high for him, why not one of the more upscale chains, like P.F. Chang's or even the Cheesecake Factory?

Her conscience spoke to her. *I told you that you should have cut him loose after that first night, when he expected you to make him breakfast. What did you expect? The man is utterly without finesse.*

She spoke back to it silently. *But I don't want to be alone on my fiftieth birthday. This birthday is hard enough without being all by myself. My God, even* Pat *is seeing somebody.*

All right. You're fifty years old today. By tomorrow it'll be old news. Get rid of Eric Wade and find somebody more worthy of your stature.

Maybe I'll do that. But first I have to prove to him that I'm the hottest fifty-year-old on the planet!

Chapter 23

Late April
Chicago

Pat closed the front door after letting Andy out and leaned against it, hugging herself. She couldn't remember the last time she'd felt so happy. She and Andy had been seeing each other regularly since that first night when they'd had dinner. On Thursday night Andy had asked if she had any plans for the weekend. When she told him she didn't, he said, "You do now. Pack a bag for two nights. Casual stuff is all you need. We'll leave tomorrow, as early as you can get away. Let's try to make it early afternoon."

By the time she left for work Friday morning, her satchel was all packed and ready to go. She left the office at one o'clock and went straight home to change. Andy showed up just before two. He tossed her bag in the trunk of his convertible hardtop Jag and they left the city behind well ahead of rush hour, heading west on I-90.

He wouldn't tell her their destination. She teased him. "If you're planning on murdering me, I did leave a note behind that I left town with you, so you won't get away with it."

He chuckled. "I think we've got a little time to ourselves coming. For the past three weeks we've tried to spend time together whenever we could spare it. Either we're preparing for our next case, or it's my weekend to have my kids, you've got plans with your parents, or whatever. I just figured some time alone together with no other considerations would be nice."

She had to agree. As they drove farther and farther away from Chicago on a glorious spring day, with the top of the car down, she did find herself wondering where they could be going for this time alone Andy spoke of. The only place she could think of within driving distance that was west of Chicago was St. Louis, hardly the garden capital of the world. She was puzzled but decided to put her trust in Andy.

That concept alone gave her pause. She *did* trust Andy. Yes, she'd been seeing him for only a few weeks, but he was also an old friend whom she used to see every day. This allowed them to skip much of the getting-to-know-you phase of a new relationship and be comfortable right away.

After three hours of driving, they reached their destination. Pat had never even heard of the town of Galena, in the northwestern tip of Illinois near the Wisconsin and Iowa borders, but from what she could see it looked charming, with brick buildings that clearly dated back to the nineteenth century. Coming here was like stepping onto the set of an old Western. She expected to see horses and buggies going *clip-clop* down the main street . . . which, in true Old West fashion, was called Main Street.

Wait a minute. What the hell was she thinking? Andy had brought her to a small, historic town. Didn't he realize that the people here might not be as receptive to seeing an interracial couple as the people of Chicago were, who really didn't give a damn?

"Andy," she said. "Have you ever been here before?"

"No, but I'm thinking about getting a weekend place out here. It's scenic, only three hours away, and there's lots to do here."

"Do you know if there are many black people here?"

He chuckled. "My experience has been that black people are everywhere, Pat."

"I'm not joking, Andy. Sometimes you have to think about things like this. Especially here in Middle America."

"You worry too much."

She tried to relax, to remind herself that she could trust him, but the uneasiness wouldn't go away. She didn't see any Holiday Inns around; in fact, no buildings appeared taller than three stories. This was bed-and-breakfast country. She supposed that people had no business running a B&B unless they were open-minded about hosting couples of different races, but . . .

The navigation system in the dashboard spoke. "Destination . . . on the right."

The sight of the red brick Italianate mansion took her breath away, making her forget her concerns, at least for the moment. It was set back from the road with a beautifully manicured front lawn, and the windows were framed by green shutters. A narrow second-story terrace stretched across three windows, its grill-work painted white to match the window frames. Two white Adirondack chairs flanked a matching table on the left side of the lawn. "Andy . . . this is beautiful."

"This town is full of inns, but this is supposed to be one of the nicest."

They went inside and greeted the innkeepers. To Pat's relief, if they were surprised to see a mixed-race couple, they hid it well.

Andy had reserved a separate cottage a hundred yards behind the main house, where they would have plenty of privacy.

After checking in, they walked the few blocks to town, where they had a sinfully scrumptious dinner at a steak house, punctuated by a rich drink of Raspberry Stolichnaya Vodka and Crème de Cacao. Andy arranged for a horse-drawn carriage to return them to the inn.

Pat gasped when she entered the cottage for the second time. Rose petals had been strewn all across the king-sized canopied bed, with Godiva chocolates adorning their pillows, and a fire crackled in the two-sided fireplace. A bottle of a local vintage wine had been left on a tray, along with two stemmed glasses. Andy filled the oversized claw-foot tub with water and bubbles, and they eagerly stripped and relaxed in it—tuning into a show on the large television that could be seen from the sitting area, the tub, or the bed, courtesy of a swivel base—and drank most of the wine. Then they dried off, made love, and fell asleep in each other's arms.

Saturday they toured the town's historic sites and a winery, closing the afternoon by having massages. That evening they drove to the next town to an elegant restaurant overlooking the Mississippi River. They had a choice table right by the window and could see barges and riverboats floating past. The waiter informed them that a DJ spun discs in the bar downstairs, and they went down and did a little dancing before returning to the cottage for another romantic evening of rose petals, chocolate, wine, and bubbles. This time they went straight to bed, not using the tub until the next morning. They got so involved in each other that instead of going to the main house for breakfast they went back to bed.

Once home, Pat let out a dreamy sigh as she recalled the weekend full of happy memories. After leaning against the closed door for several minutes, lost in pleasant memories, Pat began the chore of unpacking. She still didn't know what would happen with her and Andy, but she was certainly enjoying it. He was her kind of man: not only did he know how to treat a woman, but he had the means to do it right.

Her thoughts automatically went to Grace and Eric. Grace had turned fifty yesterday. She'd called her friend from Galena and wished her a happy birthday, careful not to be too enthusiastic about the romantic setting Andy had brought her to. Pat knew it had been an expensive weekend. But Andy, who, as she'd initially thought, held a partnership in his law firm, could easily afford it. Eric Wade couldn't. It wouldn't be fair for her to rub salt into Grace's wounds . . . even if her intuition told her that if the situation was reversed Grace might not be so considerate.

Part of her could understand Grace's feelings about Glenn Arterbridge. The judge, while an undeniable catch, did lack sex appeal. Pat considered the irony. Two months ago she would have loved to go out with him, even with his unappealing physique. She'd actually felt disappointed when he'd showed interest in Grace. But then along came Andy, wonderful, sexy Andy, and she now couldn't care less about the judge. She'd been willing to settle. Just like Grace had settled for Eric. They weren't so different after all.

Still, if Grace wasn't so hung up on dating only black men, she'd probably go out more often, and to the types of places she could afford to go on her own. Most desirable, successful black men in their age group had been snatched up by forward-thinking, sometimes even predatory females while still in college. If they got divorced, they usually had the second wife already picked out. The same situations applied to many of their white counterparts as well, but with less frequency. Plus, there were more of them to go around.

She and Grace sought the same thing. Maybe they would never find it, but at least *she* was getting more out of her efforts.

After Pat finished unpacking, she put a load of laundry in the washer and was about to dial her parents when her phone began to ring. She wasn't surprised to hear her mother's voice on the other end of the line.

"You're back, I see."

"Hi, Mom! I just got in a few minutes ago. I was about to call you."

"Did you have a good time?"

"Oh, it was wonderful!"

"Where did you go again?"

Pat smiled. Her mother had never been good at remembering names. "Galena. It's west of here, near the borders of Wisconsin and Iowa, on the Mississippi River."

"Oh, yes, that's right. I wish you'd told us sooner that you were going. We were looking forward to seeing you this weekend."

"Like I said, Mom, it came up at the last minute." She'd given her parents a quick call once she and Andy had arrived at the inn. It wouldn't have been practical to tell them on Thursday, or even Friday morning, that she was going away for the weekend. They would want to know where, and she could hardly tell them she had no idea where she was going. They never would have understood the fun in not knowing one's destination. All they would have seen was that their only surviving child was going off for parts unknown with a man they'd never met. They would have worried themselves sick that she would never be seen or heard from again.

In a way she couldn't blame them, not after what had already happened to their family. Clarence's demise after years of heroin addiction really didn't come as a surprise, but Melvin's shooting had been the biggest shock of their lives. They frequently reminded her to be careful at work, "around all that criminal element," because she was the only one they had left.

Sometimes it amazed her to think that after she was gone, it would mark the end of this branch of the Maxwell family. None of her father's sister's children were named Maxwell. Her father's older brother had fathered two girls, and their children were not Maxwells, either. As for his younger brother, Jacob, his lynching occurred before he'd fathered any children. So although most branches of the family tree would thrive, none of the subsequent generations would carry the Maxwell name.

"I'm glad you had a nice time," her mother said. "Daddy and I didn't even know you were seeing someone. Have you known him long?"

"For nearly thirty years, although I haven't seen him since we graduated from law school. He's been out in California. The law firm he's a partner in is opening an office here in Chicago, and he decided to come home and head it up."

"Oh, a *partner*. That's impressive. Now, Pat, I don't want to tell you what to do, but I hope you aren't moving things along too fast. You know, a man won't—"

No. She's not going to quote that old line about the cow and the milk.

". . . buy the cow if he can get the milk for free."

"Mama, that's silly. I'm almost fifty years old. Any milk I put out will probably be a little sour." She giggled.

"You can still get married, Pat. I know it's too late for children . . ."

It wouldn't have been if you and Daddy hadn't raised such a stink about Ricky. The bitter thought formed before she could stop it, although she knew her resentment wasn't toward her parents but toward herself for being so weak. Her spinelessness had changed the course of her life. Even this new, thriving relationship with Andy Keindl didn't detract from her decades-old resentment, in spite of her strong bond with her parents.

". . . but I'm still hoping you'll meet a nice man to spend your twilight years with," her mother continued. "You know, your daddy and I never had much, but we always took comfort in having each other."

"That's sweet, Mama."

"But there's nothing wrong with a man with a few dollars. I gather you stayed at a nice hotel?"

"Mama, it was fantastic. We stayed at a bed-and-breakfast, and we had our own private cottage on the grounds. An—my friend spared no expense," she said proudly. "We went dancing, we took a buggy ride through town, we went bike riding. We even had side-by-side massages."

"Well, he sounds like a wonderful man." By her mother's interested tone Pat could tell she was impressed.

"I hope Daddy and I will get to meet him one day."

Pat's smile faded like ink on an old receipt. What was she thinking? Painting such an intriguing picture of a generous, successful man for whom money was no object—of *course* her parents would want to meet him! They imagined he and everyone else she went out with was black. But if they saw Andy they would probably faint dead away.

"We never get to meet any of the men you date," her mother gently chided.

"That's because I usually don't date them long, Mama, no other reason."

"How long did you say you've been seeing this fellow?"

I didn't. Aloud she said, "Since the reunion. So it really hasn't been long."

"Long enough for you to go away with him." A pause, followed by a sigh. "But I'm not going to nag you about introducing Daddy and me."

"Thanks," Pat said with a grin.

After she hung up she decided to call Grace and see how her birthday went. The staccato dial tone told her someone had left a message for her. She dialed her own home number, then entered her password.

Hearing Elyse identify herself brought a smile to her lips—maybe her friend really meant it when she said she would keep in better touch—but her expression changed to one of concern, then of distress, as she heard the halting uncertainty in her friend's tone and then the full message. Her mouth dropped open in shock and dismay. Franklin Reavis had *cancer?* How awful!

She listened to the message again, this time paying attention to the time stamp announcement at the beginning. My God. Elyse had called Thursday? Yes, now she remembered. After dinner she'd gone shopping at Carson's for new lingerie. When she got home she started packing for the weekend. She never did check her messages. What must Elyse think, leaving such a serious message and not getting a response? Her voice sounded so small on the message, like that of a little girl:

> *Franklin's just been diagnosed with cancer. He doesn't want anyone to know yet, not even the kids, but I really feel like I need someone to talk to. I'm not sure how to handle this. Please call me.*

Pat flipped the receiver and checked the caller ID. When she saw the name "Franklin Reavis" and a Lake County telephone number she hit the REDIAL button.

Andy called at 8:00. "I just wanted to see what you were doing. Thinking of me, I hope."

She managed a wan smile. "This weekend was just wonderful, Andy, but actually, my thoughts are with some friends of mine." She told him about her conversation with Elyse.

"That's a tough break," he said. "But they can do a lot with cancer treatments these days. It doesn't have to be a death sentence."

"I don't know. Elyse said it's in his pancreas, and that there's a possibility that it might have spread already."

"Oh. Yeah, I've heard that particular origin is difficult to diagnose." He paused. "Is there anything I can do, Pat?"

"No, but I appreciate your asking. I was about to call a mutual friend of ours and tell her. Our friend's husband is scheduled for surgery on Thursday. He'll be in the hospital for about a week. Maybe we can get together with her sometime next weekend, even if it's just for a little while, like between visits to his bedside."

"I'll let you go so you can make your call. Call me if I can help with anything."

"I will."

Pat held down the receiver for a few seconds, then released it and dialed Grace's home number.

Chapter 24

Grace hung up the phone, stunned. Elyse's husband was scheduled to have a cancerous tumor removed from his pancreas on Thursday? What a shock. Elyse must really be a wreck, not just because of the news itself but possibly not knowing how to handle it. The girl had practically led a charmed life, at least up till now. Grace knew such things were rare, if they existed at all, but she couldn't recall a single bad thing ever happening to Elyse. Her family had been the first one to move out of Dreiser, even if it was just to a duplex around the corner. She'd managed to get in to study physical therapy at a time when it was already difficult to get accepted. She'd had a beautiful wedding, and she'd married a successful man who loved her and who gave her a nice life.

No, that wasn't right. Elyse wasn't a housewife, totally dependent on her husband for life's comforts. That description was more fitting of Susan. No doubt Elyse's physical therapist earnings contributed significantly to that comfy suburban existence the Reavises enjoyed. Grace had been to their house once, when she and Pat drove up to see Susan's new baby girl and stopped to pick up Elyse on the way. The two-story Colonial house was rather ordinary-looking by Lake Forest standards—there were homes up there the size of small hospitals, like the one the president of Grace's company lived in—but it nonetheless had plenty of room, four large bedrooms plus a full finished basement, and it was comfortably and tastefully furnished. She couldn't believe it when Elyse said it was thirty-five years old. It looked brand new. Elyse explained that she and Franklin had just put new siding on it and had updated the kitchen.

Over the course of their marriage—hard to believe, but Pat said it was going on twenty-six years—they'd raised two children, a boy and a girl—in that order, naturally—participated actively in the lives of Franklin's children from his first marriage, and still appeared happy. Pat said that Elyse had told her how guilty she felt for not believing there was anything wrong with Franklin. Instead, she believed he was feigning illness to keep from going anywhere with her.

So what if Franklin had slowed down a little? Hell, the man was past sixty, even before his diagnosis. Naturally, he wouldn't feel like going out all the time. Elyse should have considered that he'd be ready to slow down before she would because he was so much older. Maybe instead of sulking and hanging out at Junior's Bar the night of the reunion, she should have brought her husband to the doctor. Everybody knew that the earlier the diagnosis, the longer one's chances of long-term survival.

Grace thought it odd that both Elyse and Susan had been so anxious to go to the party at Junior's the night of the Dreiser reunion. Now she knew Elyse came out of frustration with Franklin's lethargy. Susan's motives had become clearer when Grace saw her talking and dancing with Charles Valentine. Was it just curiosity to see him again after all those years, or something more?

If Grace had been impressed by Elyse's home that day seven years ago, she'd been blown away by Susan's. A gorgeous mini-mansion of tan stucco and stone, with windows and skylights everywhere, it had floor-to-ceiling fireplaces, a wraparound deck, and even its own private beach. Lake Michigan never looked so pretty, even if the water was choppy as hell and never really heated up, even in July. Of course, Susan's husband was a millionaire. Elyse and Franklin were just upper-middle class.

Grace felt a little cheated. She probably wouldn't have been interested in someone as old as Franklin, but Susan's husband had been a real catch. Sexy, good-looking, and young, and right there in Kenosha, Wisconsin, of all places; or, as it was jokingly referred to, "Ke-Nowhere." Why did Susan have all the luck? Why couldn't *she* have met him first, damn it?

Bemoaning Susan's good fortune was a moot point, and Grace knew it. When Susan announced her engagement to Bruce Dillahunt—yes, that was his name, Bruce—Grace was still married to her second husband, Danny Knight; and at the time she'd felt pretty damn lucky herself. An executive at a leading accounting firm, he'd been the man she'd always dreamed of. Together they lived a glamorous lifestyle, with a high-rise condo on Lake Shore Drive, maid service twice a week, and a boat. It started to fall apart when Danny was approached about heading up the company's office in San Juan. He expected her to give up her job, just like that. It wasn't fair. He *knew* she'd been trying to get the director position in public relations. It still angered her that he thought so little of her career aspirations. She wasn't some lowly department store clerk selling girdles, always ready to pack up on a week's notice to follow her husband all around the world.

Her mother, still alive at the time, urged her to go for the sake of her marriage. Helen Corrigan reminded her daughter that she and Grace's father had chosen Puerto Rico for their only vacation, and that he had remarked that those Puerto Ricans had to be crazy to leave that island and its beautiful climate to go settle in the northern U.S. states. Grace reminded her mother that the island might technically be part of the United States, but that most of the people there spoke Spanish, a language that she, unlike Danny, who was fluent, barely remembered from her classes back in high school.

In the end he accepted the job, and they tried a commuter marriage. It didn't work.

She shrugged. Their marriage wasn't the first to collapse under the weight of the two parties' ambitions, and she doubted it would be the last. He still kept in touch with Shavonne, the stepdaughter he'd always adored, and the last Grace heard he was still down there with his second wife, her children from her first marriage, and the one they had had together.

Yeah, Susan and Elyse didn't know how good they had it, or,

in Elyse's case, how good she *used* to have it, for life as she knew it was about to change drastically with Franklin's illness. Grace's father had died of prostate cancer around the time she and Jimmy were divorcing, and she still remembered pitching in with her siblings to help out and give her mother a break while she cared for him, which had been exhausting for her.

But neither Susan nor Elyse had to spend a Saturday night at the movies with a man who hadn't even offered her so much as a bowl of chili afterward. On the night of Grace's first date with Eric, she'd had to come right out and say she was hungry before he suggested they go to Panera Bread. Did he really think that she would fill up on that popcorn they'd shared at the movie? She'd already made up her mind to give him some—she was too horny and he looked too good—and she could tell he fully expected to get it, but that didn't mean she would be a dirt-cheap date.

Nor did Elyse have to spend the special occasion of her fiftieth birthday like she had last night. Nearly an hour waiting for a table, and then everything at accelerated speed. Everything— from the waiter's continually stopping by to see if they were ready to order, to the rather rushed singing of her birthday greeting— gave her the prickly feeling that they were supposed to hurry through their meal so they could vacate and the waiter could seat new customers at the table. It was all about the profits. Feed 'em, get their money, clean off the table the moment they left, and bring in the next party before the seats cool off.

The evening was capped with a wild session in bed—she definitely proved to him that her being fifty hardly meant she was washed-up—and her waking up to the sound of his snoring. He did surprise her by taking her to breakfast as a continued birthday celebration. She liked spontaneous actions in her men. It gave her hope that Eric had potential. Of course, her flat refusal to make him breakfast the morning after their first date might have had something to do with his decision.

Grace would trade her life for Susan's in a hot minute provided she could still get to have a daughter like Shavonne, and provided she could keep her own looks, figure, and size. Not that Susan was bad looking, if you went for the light-skinned/

good-hair type. Personally, Grace felt that if Susan was about ten shades darker and had nappy hair, no one would rave about how pretty she was. And while she had a reasonably good figure, she was so damn tall. Now that she'd put on some weight she looked positively Amazonian.

Grace had never had a weight problem in her life. She bounced right back into shape after having Shavonne, and she started paying attention to what she ate and exercising regularly while still in her twenties, during the seventies' fitness craze, when everybody from Jane Fonda to Richard Simmons had workout routines on tape. It had become a habit, one that served her well in the years to come. Every part of her body was firm, and nothing sagged. She might be fifty, but her body looked years younger.

Her eyes closed. No point in wanting to change places with Susan or anyone else. Her life was her life. Its path had probably been predetermined the moment she'd been born.

She'd go on doing what she'd been doing, looking for another husband. And in the meantime, she'd do the best she could with what she had . . . namely, Eric Wade.

Chapter 25

Elyse looked at her watch, disappointed to see that only four minutes had passed since her last time check. This surgery was taking forever. She knew from the doctor's explanation that a Whipple procedure was considered major surgery, involving removal of multiple organs and reconstruction of the GI tract. It would take some time to complete, six or seven hours, maybe more. How would she manage to get through the wait?

Brontë squeezed her hand. "Don't worry, Mom. Daddy will be fine."

"I wish I felt as confident as you do."

The kids had been wonderful. She'd called both of them and asked them to come home that weekend because their father would be undergoing surgery on Thursday morning. She refused to tell them any more until they were home.

Together, she and Franklin explained to them about his workup and diagnosis, plus his need for immediate surgery to have the tumor removed.

As Elyse expected, the news stunned them. Todd recovered first, stating that Franklin would beat this. Elyse looked on, praying that Franklin wouldn't be quite so blunt with their son about his chances for long-term survival as he'd been with her. Todd was just twenty years old and was in that invincible stage, where he felt his parents would live forever.

Franklin didn't disappoint her. He'd told the children as gently as he could that if it was meant for him to conquer this hurdle, he would, but that they had to consider the possibility that he might not.

Brontë, always a daddy's girl, had sobbed and held on to her father. Todd hadn't cried, but he looked terrified at the thought of losing Franklin.

In the end they joined hands, and Franklin led them in prayer.

Elyse was grateful for the support from her children, as well as from her friends. In addition to Kevin's e-mail, Pat had called Sunday evening, explaining she'd gone out of town over the weekend as a last-minute thing. And Grace had called last night, offering assistance and encouraging words after Pat informed her about Franklin's diagnosis.

Elyse hadn't gotten around to calling Susan yet. Maybe tomorrow. How nice it would be to be able to report that everything had gone well and that Franklin was recovering nicely.

She looked at her watch again. Exactly three minutes had passed.

This was torture.

Chapter 26

Early May
Pleasant Prairie, Wisconsin

Elyse called Susan on Wednesday and told her about Franklin. "I don't know what to say, Elyse," Susan said after an audible gasp. "I'm glad to know that Franklin came through it okay, of course. I just wish I'd known sooner. I would have, I don't know, made dinner for your family or something."

"That's sweet of you, Susan. Franklin isn't ready to tell a lot of people about his illness, but I did call Pat last week, as soon as I found out. I just felt so overwhelmed. I had to confide in somebody. I knew Pat would tell Grace, and I felt you should know, too." Elyse hoped Susan wouldn't feel left out, but the truth was that she'd always felt closest to Pat.

"I appreciate it." Susan sighed. "You know, Elyse, you and I really should see more of each other. We live closer to each other than we do to Pat and Grace. Of course, with everything that's going on, I realize this isn't a good time for us to start being girlfriends, but surely there's something I can do to help. Just tell me what I can do."

"I think I've got everything covered. Franklin will be in the hospital at least until next Thursday or Friday. I'm off today, and I'll be going down to see him as soon as I'm off the phone. The kids will see him this evening, and then again in the morning before they go back to school. They'll be back on Saturday. They're getting ready for their final exams."

"Are you off the rest of the week?"

"No, just today. I'll be working a light schedule for now, so I can see Franklin in the mornings and again after work. They'll release him to the skilled nursing center where I work in Evanston."

"Will you be his physical therapist?" To Susan that sounded like a surgeon operating on his or her spouse.

"No, that wouldn't work. But at least I won't be far away and I can speak with his therapist about his progress. He'll get daily strength training for about a week, two sessions a day. If all goes well he should be back at home by the following weekend."

"It sounds like he's had a very intense procedure."

"He did. They took out the head of his pancreas, half of his stomach, his gallbladder, some lymph nodes, and part of his digestive tract. It took over seven hours. Some patients don't even survive it."

"Oh, Elyse." The distress Susan felt carried into her tone. "How will you manage when he comes home?"

"It depends. I've thought about hiring a home health aide to care for him, but patients aren't released from rehab until they can manage their daily activities on their own. Still, I hate to think of him being home alone."

"Won't Todd and Brontë be finished with their exams by then?"

"Yes, but they both have jobs lined up for the summer, and I don't want to ask them to give them up. The sticky part will be trying to convince Franklin that he needs someone to help him. I know my husband, and he can be awfully stubborn."

"Do you think he's worried about the cost?"

"No. There's no need to. We carry supplemental insurance to help with lost income due to illness or accident. That kicked in the moment of Franklin's diagnosis, even though we don't really need it now. I spoke to the benefits specialist at his job and found out that Franklin will collect a full paycheck for up to twelve weeks. Plus, he'd bought another policy for home care so that we won't go broke if either of us ever needs a home health care aide. So it's definitely not the money. It's more of a pride thing."

"It's hard, especially for men, to be ill," Susan remarked.

"He's not going to be an easy patient. I wanted to take more time off, but Franklin insisted that he doesn't want me hovering around him like a mama bear. He wants things to be as normal as possible."

Susan nodded. She, too, had hoped for a return to normalcy after her lumpectomy, but her marriage never recovered. "I understand. But promise you'll call me if you need anything."

"I will. Maybe we can have lunch or something, like Kevin and I are going to do on Friday."

"Kevin Nash? You've spoken to him?" Susan didn't hide her surprise.

"I haven't actually spoken to him, but he dropped me an e-mail while I was waiting for Pat to respond. She didn't call me back right away. It turns out she was getting ready to go out of town for the weekend, but I didn't know that at the time. When she didn't call back I tried e-mailing her. In the meantime, there was Kevin's note. By this time I was about to bust from holding everything in, so I told him about Franklin. I e-mailed him last night to let him know everything went well, and he suggested we have lunch together. He said it might take some of the stress off. He works in Evanston like me, so it's convenient. Maybe you and I can do the same next week."

"Sure."

After they finished talking, Susan wondered how wise it was of Elyse to lunch with a handsome and virile man like Kevin Nash when Franklin would be at his weakest.

Matters between her and Bruce had barely improved over the last few weeks, since her efforts to regain his physical interest in her had gone so horribly wrong. She'd slept most of that disastrous Saturday night in their spare room, arising shortly after dawn and returning to their bed before Quentin and Alyssa got up. Relations between them were civil but not much else. She kept telling herself it would still be wrong to reach out to Charles Valentine. She was married to Bruce, and she didn't believe in cheating.

But she was desperately unhappy. She felt like she was going through each day with a twenty-pound weight around her neck.

Saturday night she and Bruce made love—no, that wasn't the right definition of what they'd done. They'd had sex, with him pushing her nightgown up to her waist and gripping her hips, satisfying himself and, much as she hated to admit it, giving her some degree of pleasure in the most basic of ways. As always since her surgery, he ignored her breasts, even the one that had been unaffected. Once more she hoped he would come around, perhaps give them a little squeeze through her nightgown; or, even afterward, grasp them in his sleep like he used to do. Once more she'd been disappointed, and she fell asleep with tears in her eyes.

Her oncologist had offered her a referral to a plastic surgeon to correct the shape of her right breast, but Susan thought the best action would be to let it be. The last thing she wanted was to undergo another surgical procedure, no matter how minor. Besides, she wasn't sure it was such a hot idea to remove the evidence of what she'd gone through. She almost liked having that small physical imperfection to remind her daily that her future was by no means guaranteed. Having cancer changed her entire outlook. She learned to view life in six-month increments, like the six-month follow-up she'd had recently, after which she was given a clean bill of health. No more planning for what she would do next year or the year after that; not until she had a damn good idea that she'd still be around. She would never be the same or feel the same . . . so why should she *look* the same?

She wished Bruce would understand that, or that he'd even talk to her about it. His face showed no revulsion the first time he saw the breast with the bandage removed and the little cone protruding from the side.

She could still see the relief on his face, could still hear him say, "Thank God you're all right, Susan. I'd be lost if anything happened to you."

She remembered how anxious she'd been that day, afraid of what she might see in his eyes. There'd been no hints of the change in his demeanor that lay just ahead, once his relief that she would survive began to wear off.

At first she'd been sure it would pass, but eight months had gone by with more of the same. And it was eating her up inside.

Susan wanted—hell, she *deserved*—full and complete happiness, not just a placid, empty existence for the benefit of their children.

She thought about how Elyse, whose husband's illness seemed much more pressing than her own, had reached out to friends, including one who happened to be a man, for support. Because when you were feeling lost and alone, it didn't really matter where your support came from, did it?—as long as it was genuine and heartfelt.

Susan considered that maybe she'd been suffering silently long enough.

She reached for her wallet and pulled out the folded paper on which Charles Valentine had written his number. Then she pulled out her cell phone.

Chapter 27

Susan sat in her parked car, asking herself what the hell she was doing. She'd just lied to Bruce, telling him she was going to spend the afternoon with Elyse in the wake of Franklin's illness. In truth, she'd just had lunch with Elyse yesterday, returning to Pleasant Prairie in time to pick up Quentin and Alyssa from school.

She believed in marriage. Her own parents' union was a disaster, but the culprit had been alcohol abuse, not infidelity. In her heart, she didn't want to do anything dishonorable. She wasn't even sure she could.

But she'd always been able to confide her deepest thoughts to Charles, and she really needed to talk to someone about the situation with Bruce. She didn't want to see a counselor, not solo. Bruce had ruled that out. What could a psychologist possibly tell her when her husband wouldn't even come with her? She didn't need to pay someone big bucks for that person to tell her that Bruce was the one who needed help dealing with her illness.

As far as nonprofessionals, Susan didn't want to talk about her unhappiness to her mother, either. Frances McMillan, in Susan's opinion, had weathered more than her share of stressful situations in her lifetime: a difficult interracial marriage long before such unions became common, single parenthood, and most recently, the death of her second husband from a sudden heart attack. Susan didn't want her mother's twilight years filled with worry about her firstborn. Frances did worry about Susan's health, but Susan knew that Frances took comfort knowing that at least Susan had a strong marriage, because Frances had said as much on more than one occasion. Susan couldn't bring herself to take away her mother's peace of mind by telling her the truth.

Then there was her sister. Sherry had decided early on that white was, if not right, at least better. She caught the eye of a good-looking finance major while at UIC and held on to him. Today he was a fund manager at a big brokerage firm, and they lived in Lake Forest, not far from Elyse. Sherry had taken off more than a dozen years to raise their children, but had returned to teaching at a private academy in town. While Sherry's husband and children knew about her mixed racial background, Susan doubted they ran around telling anyone about their black grandmother. Sherry's preference to downplay her biracial heritage had long been a source of friction between the sisters.

Susan understood why Franklin had been against telling anyone outside of the immediate family about his illness. People looked at you differently when they knew you were sick. Franklin would probably be mad as hell if he knew Elyse had told at least four people—Pat, Grace, Kevin, and her—about his condition. Susan had asked Bruce not to disclose her diagnosis to anyone, and as far as she knew he hadn't. When her neighbors asked what was wrong, or if she'd been hospitalized for anything serious, she just shrugged and said she was fine.

She also understood that women tended to be less stoic than men. Women needed to share their concerns and needed to know they could trust their friends. Men seemed to be better equipped to keep their worries to themselves. Susan knew that Elyse and Pat would be sympathetic to her, but despite their best intentions they would feel sorry for her . . . a reaction she couldn't bear.

Grace was a different story. Ever since Grace had been a little girl, she'd always had a way of downplaying the good fortune of others and emphasizing their hard luck. It still annoyed her when, after Christmas the year they turned twelve, Grace had pointed out that the bottom of her new maxicoat had gotten all wet from a puddle. Grace made no secret of the fact that she wanted one of the new-style coats for Christmas, and her disappointment at not getting one was only compounded when Susan came outside for the first time wearing the one she'd just received. Grace sounded absolutely thrilled when she pointed out how dirty street water was. Susan could tell that Grace hoped her coat was ruined. It wasn't, of course, but from that day on Susan looked at Grace with a certain degree of mistrust. Years later, when a trusted friend shared something she'd once seen, it only added to Grace's wariness.

Grace didn't like it when anyone had something she didn't. When the girls had come to see her and baby Alyssa, in the midst of oohs and aahs from Pat and Elyse, Grace managed to point out *two* downbeat facts: one, how difficult it must be for older mothers to lose pregnancy weight, and two, that it was practically impossible for women to get back into the workplace after taking off years to raise children. Susan knew that a lot of Grace's negativity stemmed from the recent bust-up of her second marriage. She was past forty and alone, and eligible men of the right age were hard to find.

At the time Susan merely laughed it off. She and Bruce were in love, their family was now complete with the birth of their daughter, and things couldn't be better. Let Grace sulk if she wanted to. Susan knew Grace would trade places with her in a second if she could.

Just like Grace had tried to take her place years ago, right after Susan broke up with Douglas Valentine. Not that that mattered anymore. Susan knew that it really hadn't mattered when it happened, even though Grace's haste to grab Douglas right after Susan broke up with him did have her reeling. Grace didn't know that Susan had found out about that fling with Douglas, and she had no intention of ever telling her.

Susan knew nothing had changed with the passing years. She'd barely been in Grace's company for fifteen minutes at the luncheon when Grace made that completely unnecessary comment about Pat never marrying, just to make herself feel better about not having a man in her life. Grace wasn't the type of person you'd want around in a time of crisis. She came off about as genuine as a McRib sandwich when it came to the problems of others.

Susan glanced down at her breast. God forbid this cancer killed her. She wouldn't put it past Grace to try to make a date with Bruce at her funeral.

No, she couldn't tell her friends about her frustration. But thank God for Charles.

She grabbed her keys and pushed open the restaurant door. She'd made a date, and it was time to keep it.

Susan spotted Charles as soon as she got inside the barbecue restaurant, which was down the street from the school where he taught. He sat at a table by the window, a tall glass of Coca-Cola in front of him, looking out on Armitage Avenue. The way he smiled at her warmed her heart. He stood as she approached. When she reached him, he took her hand and kissed her cheek with a tenderness Bruce hadn't demonstrated since the night before her surgery. "Glad you could make it."

"I hope you weren't waiting long."

"I barely had time to order a pop. I'm sorry, there's no bar."

"I don't need to drink. I've got to drive back to Wisconsin. Bottled water will be fine."

Charles left to get the beverage, returning with a laminated menu. They took time out to peruse it, and he left once more, this time to place the order in this small restaurant with a front register and no waitstaff. Susan knew that he would soon ask why she asked to see him, something he'd been too polite to ask when she called. Would she be able to tell him the truth?

"I'm glad you called me, Susan," he began, "but I have to wonder why. Was there something on your mind?"

She met his gaze head-on. "I guess I just needed a friend."

"A friend? When I saw you, you were with the girls who've been your friends all your life."

"Yes, and it was great to see them. I think seeing them again, especially Pat and Grace, reminded me of all I've been missing. At least the two of them keep in touch. Elyse is as far removed as I've been."

"So you feel like there's a hole in your life somewhere? Even living up there in Wisconsin?"

"Oh, it's a nice life. A nice house, great kids, good neighbors." She saw his quizzical look and knew he wondered why she didn't mention her husband.

Instead of asking about Bruce, he asked, "How about friends?"

"Your typical suburban street, where everyone knows each other. We're friendly, but we don't really get into each other's business. There's no one I'd feel comfortable revealing my deep, dark secrets to." She smiled at him across the table. "But with you it's different, Charles. It doesn't even seem like any time has passed since you and I were seeing each other."

Her smile faded at his next words.

"But it has, Susan. It's been half a lifetime for us. Sure, I live in the same apartment I did back then. But you're married, and you've got a whole new life, far removed from the South Side."

She hadn't the proverbial leg to stand on as far as objecting to his statement, and she knew it. But she also knew he hadn't said it to be cruel; he was merely pointing out the way things really were.

Charles leaned back into the booth. "Tell you what. We don't have to talk about it right now. Why don't we just enjoy our lunch?"

They talked about other topics as they ate. After he paid the check—Susan wanted to, saying lunch had been her idea, but he insisted—he suggested they go to the lakefront and walk off their meal.

He drove his maroon Blazer, and she followed in the M-Class Mercedes SUV that Bruce gifted her with for Christmas two years before. They parked next to each other in one of the lots.

"Nice ride," Charles commented, his hand resting on the Mercedes's waxed black exterior. "I'd like to get one of these myself. Of course, just being a teacher . . ."

"Teaching is important, too, Charles."

"Yeah, but it doesn't pay as well as your old man's field."

She sensed he was goading her. And it was working, if that

lump that suddenly formed in her throat was any indicator. "Money isn't everything, Charles."

They began walking companionably down a concrete path, their shoulders brushing every few seconds. It was a cool spring day, in the low sixties, a cloud cover keeping the temperature lower than usual and the standard crowds away. They passed no one as they walked.

"No, it isn't," he said. After a half minute of silence, he asked, "Susan, is your husband making you unhappy?"

She could delay no longer—the time had come to tell him why she'd contacted him. She found that the words tumbled out with surprising ease. "Yes, and I'll tell you why. Last year I went for my annual gynecological exam, and my doctor felt a lump in my breast. It turned out to be malignant."

"You look healthy," he said, ending with a slightly raised tone of a question. "It was probably caught in time."

She didn't miss the quick survey he did of her, looking for obvious signs of poor health, but to her relief she saw no pity in his eyes, only concern. "Yes, it looks that way. Of course, one never knows how long these things last. I had a lumpectomy and radiation treatments. I feel good, and my last exam showed no cancer."

"I feel a 'but' coming."

Susan smiled. He sounded relieved to hear she was doing okay. It meant a lot to her to know he cared. Then she looked down, knowing she had to continue. This part was difficult to say, even to Charles. "My husband has been acting like I've got a contagious disease." She stopped walking, suddenly not sure if she could go through with it. "You know, maybe this wasn't such a good idea—"

Charles grabbed her arm as she began to move in the other direction. "Uh-uh. You called me because you wanted to tell me something. I'm not letting you go until you tell me."

"And I told you, Charles. Now I'm realizing how stupid the whole thing is." She took on a deliberate falsetto, whiny tone. "'My husband doesn't think I'm attractive anymore, so I called you because I liked the way you looked at me.'" She reverted to her normal voice. "That's my deep, dark secret. Now I feel like a fool, and I'd prefer to do that in private."

"It sounds like you've been doing too much in private, Susan. Have you forgotten what you told me less than an hour ago? That you needed a friend?"

She covered her face with her hands, certain she'd made an ass of herself and feeling herself about to crumble. Charles stepped forward and embraced her, politely nodding to two young mothers pushing baby strollers with toddlers strapped inside as they passed. They glanced at Susan with curious eyes but kept walking. Displays of emotion weren't all that unusual at the lakefront, where people confronted lives as turbulent as the waters of Lake Michigan just a few dozen yards away.

Susan composed herself, and she and Charles resumed walking, his arm around her shoulder and hers around his waist. They said little, content just to be in each other's company.

After an hour, Charles said, "We should probably head back. It'll take a little time to get back to the cars from here."

"All right."

"I'm curious. What'd you tell your husband you were doing this afternoon?"

"I told him I was spending the afternoon with Elyse. Her husband just had a malignant tumor removed, and she's feeling a little frightened right now. I did see her yesterday."

"And you told Elyse not to call your house and blow your alibi."

"No, I didn't. I gave her my cell phone number yesterday and asked her to call me on that because she'll always be able to reach me. She's got too much to do to be calling me, anyway. I'm sure she's down at the hospital right now. I didn't tell her I'm meeting you. She doesn't even know I'm a cancer patient."

"She doesn't?"

"Very few people know, Charles. My husband. My mother. My sister and brother-in-law. And now you. Even my kids don't know. We thought it best that they not worry about things they don't fully understand. They know I was in the hospital for an operation, but none of the details."

"I don't get it, Susan. Your kids are too young to understand, but Elyse, Pat, Grace . . . they're certainly not."

"I didn't tell them because . . . people look at you differently when they know you have cancer, Charles. Especially breast cancer. They wonder if you'll be alive a year from now; they wonder what your boobs look like after surgery. And they feel sorry for you. I saw it in the eyes of some of the nurses at the hospital." She stopped walking to look him dead in the eye. "I didn't sense that from you, and I thank you for that."

"I don't feel sorry for you, Susan. I might be a little worried about what you've gone through, but I do believe you'll be fine. You look too good for it to be otherwise."

She gave him a rueful smile. "Thanks for your optimism." She started to walk again but stopped when he grabbed her hand. "What is it?"

"I'm glad you called me. And I know it's more than your ego needing to be stroked, to be told you still look good after your operation. You've never been a shallow person."

"Thanks . . . I think." Susan gave him a sunny smile at the backhanded compliment, but he remained serious.

"So what happens now? You've gotten that burden off your chest; you know I think you're still beautiful."

God, she couldn't stop grinning. He affected her better than any tonic on the market. "You're killing me with compliments, Charles."

"Just answer my question."

"We're friends. But I don't want this afternoon to be a one-time thing." Of that she was certain.

"So you keep lying to your husband about how you plan to spend a couple of hours."

Susan's shoulders felt like lead. "What do you want me to do, Charles? Calling you was a last-minute impulse. I haven't worked it all out in my head. For all I knew you would have pissed me off about something and I wouldn't have wanted to see you again anyway. Not that it can't still happen," she cautioned.

"Susan, we've always been friends. But we used to be a lot

more to each other than that. What if I'm not satisfied with merely being your friend?"

She didn't hesitate. "I'm afraid that's all I can offer you, Charles."

He accepted her response in silence. They walked back toward where they parked, moving faster than before, stopping to watch teenagers playing basketball at the courts.

"That kid's good," he said, his eyes on a boy in torn jeans who, when not scoring baskets, blocked attempted shots of opposing team members.

Charles moved a few feet in front of her, and for the first time Susan noticed the small bald spot on the back of his head. It would probably get larger as time went on. They really had become middle-aged, she thought with amusement.

"He reminds me of Douglas."

Her jaw went taut at the mention of Charles's brother, but she knew they had to talk about it. "How are things between you and Douglas?"

"We get on all right. We've both made a special effort for our mother's sake. He's . . . he's scheduled to be released soon. That's one reason I still live in the house. I don't trust him. I don't want him running drugs out of my mother's house, or taking her jewelry to make a buy. He knows I'm there, so he's on his best behavior. I whipped his ass twenty-five years ago, and I'll do it again if I have to."

Susan winced. She hadn't expected Charles to bring up the fight he and Douglas had had. "I guess the rumor mill put in overtime over that one."

"I'll say. I must have heard five different stories. One went that I was jealous of Douglas's success, so I went after you, the one thing Douglas had lost, just to get back at him. Then there was the one that said Douglas was keeping you in an apartment in Wisconsin, but you got tired of waiting for him and took up with me, never expecting to get caught."

"*What?*"

"Believe me, the person who told me that story almost got popped himself."

"I'm sure there were plenty more, but I'd rather not hear them, if you don't mind."

"I wouldn't have repeated the more vicious lies to you, anyway. It all happened a long time ago."

When they reached their cars, he stood behind her as she unlocked the door with her remote. She opened the door, then turned to him before getting in. "Thanks for listening, Charles. I'll be in touch."

"Don't you dare hold out your hand like you expect me to shake it," he said, practically growling.

"Charles—"

He took a step forward and embraced her, his lips claiming hers. After an initial jerk of her shoulders, she relaxed, a contented sigh escaping from her throat, and she reached out to hold him.

The kiss continued for fifteen sexy seconds. "I . . . I have to go," she said weakly, her hands clasped in front of her after she forced herself to move them from his shoulders.

"I know. I just don't want to let you go. Not again."

"I'll be back, Charles. I promise."

His arms tightened around her waist. "Make it soon."

Chapter 28

Mid-May
Lake Forest, Illinois

Elyse rolled her eyes. She'd always gotten along fairly well with her stepchildren, but now both of them were getting on her nerves, with their endless questions about the quality of care their father was receiving. Elyse knew they worried about him, but they didn't have to act like she had no stake in the matter. Franklin was *her* husband. They'd been grilling her ever since emerging from the bedroom, where he now sat in a reclining chair a good part of the day while he healed.

"I don't think Pop should be left alone while you work, Elyse," Frankie said now. "Don't you worry about him being home all by himself?"

"Of course I do, but he insisted. Kids"—it seemed odd to refer to adults in their thirties that way, but she'd always used that word when speaking to them jointly—"your father doesn't want to be treated as an invalid. As far as he's concerned, he's just like any other postsurgical patient. He wouldn't need nursing care if he just had his appendix out."

"But he *didn't* just have his appendix taken out," Frankie pointed out. "That's one of the few things they left in."

Rebecca stood with her arms crossed over her chest. "So there's no financial considerations involved, Elyse?"

"Of course not. Your daddy has excellent health insurance, plus supplemental coverage. I've been home with him since the rehab center released him last weekend. I'm convinced he'll be all right. If not, we'll get a home health aide for him."

Frankie nodded knowingly. "Yeah, I've heard about those people. They come into your house and help themselves to anything that's not bolted down while their patient is napping."

"Elyse, why would you want to have some stranger come in and take care of Pop instead of doing it yourself?" Rebecca asked. "Don't you *want* to take care of him?"

She tried not to show the frustration she felt. "Frankie, Rebecca. I know you both want your father to get the best care possible, but he and I talked all this out before we even told you about his tumor. He made it clear that he didn't want an aide unless he couldn't get out of bed. I talked to the physical therapists at the rehab center, and I happen to be one myself. I'm convinced he can manage. They wouldn't have let him come home unless they were satisfied that he could take care of his daily activities. It's important for him to have some independence. We want him to recover mentally, as well as physically.

"And as for me continuing to work, it's important to our family that I have a steady income. Your father will receive his full salary for twelve weeks, but his income will drop if he has to go on disability. Todd and Brontë are both in school, with room and board to be paid, as well as tuition. It makes solid financial sense for me to keep working. Your daddy's coverage doesn't cover the entire cost of a home health care aide, only part of it. Caretakers don't come cheap, especially with an agency surcharge tacked on."

"Well, I'm starting to wonder how clearly Pop is thinking," Frankie said. "I'm going to talk to him about it, see if I can get him to change his mind."

Elyse rolled her eyes. "You do what you think is best, Frankie."

Elyse talked to Kevin about it that night, after Franklin fell asleep, calling him from her cell phone, as she always did. She and Kevin weren't doing anything wrong, of course, but Franklin might not see it as harmless. She knew *she* wouldn't like it if some woman called the house looking for her husband.

"Honestly, they don't seem like the same kids I used to have so much fun with," Elyse complained. "They second-guess me, imply that I'm not taking care of their father . . ."

"Try not to be too hard on them, Elyse. Their father is ill, they're faced with the possibility of losing him, and they don't know how to handle it."

"*My* life has changed more than either of theirs, Kevin." She knew she sounded a little short, but it didn't seem fair for him to be so understanding of Frankie and Rebecca's behavior and show no sympathy for her.

"I know it has. I don't mean to imply otherwise."

"And being worried about their father is no excuse for treating me like someone with an agenda. I've been married to their father for nearly twenty-six years. They should know I have his best interests at heart. It isn't fair. They grill me like a sirloin steak, then go home to their own lives, and I'm left alone to monitor how much Franklin eats and drinks, dispense his medications, and check his weight."

It felt good to vent a little. She looked forward to talking with Kevin at the end of a long day. They generally spoke a few times a week, always at a little after nine at night. Kevin didn't seem to mind listening to her express her fears and annoyances, and Elyse found she rather enjoyed the attention and the sympathetic ear. Now that everyone knew about Franklin's diagnosis, she was surrounded by concerned family members, all of whom offered unsolicited advice for the best way to care for him, now that he'd been discharged from the rehabilitation center. She didn't like being told how to care for her husband, and it was getting harder and harder to keep her temper in check. Already she'd abruptly hung up on Franklin's first wife, Carolyn, when she asked the same thing her children had asked this afternoon: Why was she going back to work and leaving Franklin alone to care for himself? Elyse felt that she owed Frankie and Rebecca an explanation because Franklin was their father, but she felt no such obligation to Carolyn. As far as Elyse was concerned, Carolyn had a lot of damn nerve, questioning her like that. Who the hell was she, thinking she deserved answers?

Her other friends had been wonderful. Susan drove down last

week, when Franklin was still a patient at the rehabilitation facility, and they had a relaxing two-hour lunch at the Olive Garden. Pat and Grace came up the next day and brought a picnic lunch. Todd and Brontë came home every weekend to see Franklin, and Frankie and Rebecca drove up from Evanston on Saturdays.

Everyone anxiously awaited the pathology report, which would tell them if Franklin's cancer had spread. Elyse didn't even want to think about that possibility. The findings would be revealed to Franklin at his follow-up appointment on Wednesday.

She went back into the bedroom and saw Franklin had gotten into bed. She plumped his pillows and spread the haphazardly thrown light quilt over him evenly. "Are you comfy?" she asked.

"Yeah. Bring me a glass of juice, will you, Elyse?"

"Sure. Be right back."

As she walked to the kitchen she asked herself what he would do when he wanted something to drink tomorrow, when she was at work. Doubts filled her head, increasing with each step she took. Maybe Frankie had a point. Maybe she *should* insist they get him a home health care aide to do things like fix his breakfast and lunch and help him wash up—Franklin hadn't been given the green light to shower yet.

Thank God their bedroom was on the first floor of the house, for he'd been instructed not to climb stairs. She'd better make sure the kitchen was fully stocked with everything he might need. They kept an extra refrigerator plus a meat freezer down in the basement, and Franklin was obstinate enough to go down to get more eggs, regardless of being warned not to. Good Lord. She'd come home and find him unconscious. . . .

If only he weren't so stubborn about his care. She didn't want to bring in a caregiver against his wishes, only to have him chase her away by being obstinate and uncooperative. Franklin was old school. He equated needing a caregiver with weakness. And pointing out that he *was* weak would only infuriate him . . . which she knew was really a mask for hurt pride.

Todd came into the kitchen while she held a glass against the ice dispenser. "Mom? Is Dad all right?"

"Yes. He asked me for something to drink."

Todd leaned against the breakfast bar. "Do you really think he can manage on his own?"

She sighed. "At first I did, but now I'm not so sure. I think Frankie might have had a point. Someone should be here with him." She removed a half-gallon plastic container of a mixture of cranberry and cherry juices from the refrigerator door and filled the glass. As she put it back an idea suddenly came to her.

"Do you want me to—"

"No," she interrupted. She knew he was about to offer to take time off from school. "This is finals week, Todd. It'd be hell to reschedule your exams. But I'd like you to ride to the store with me. I want to pick up a small refrigerator for the bedroom, so Daddy won't have to do a whole lot of walking."

"Hey, Mom, that's a great idea."

"I'll bring this to him, and then we can go. Brontë can stay in case he needs anything."

That evening, after the refrigerator had gotten cold, Elyse loaded it with cold cuts, bread, deli potato salad, orange juice, cranberry juice, mustard, and mayonnaise. She would give Franklin his breakfast before she left. This way he'd have to walk no farther than a few feet to the adjoining bathroom.

She went about her work quietly, not wanting to awaken the sleeping Franklin. When she finished bringing napkins, paper plates, a couple of plastic drinking glasses and utensils, she sat on the side of the bed and simply gazed at him.

His weight loss had become noticeable. He didn't have much appetite. She hoped he would eventually gain some of the weight back, now that he was out of the hospital. He was still a handsome man, but he looked unwell.

Elyse suddenly felt a lump in her throat. She'd tried to be optimistic, telling herself there was no point in thinking about the worst when nothing had been confirmed. Sitting here watching her husband rest, she couldn't keep the thought away.

What would happen if Franklin died?

Chapter 29

Grace swung her arms as she walked the treadmill, rather than holding on to the side bars, because it burned more calories. Her feet moved in precise steps to keep up with the four-mile-an-hour speed she'd set. She kept this pace for two five-minute increments, walking two-thirds of a mile.

She'd stepped up her workout routine to twenty minutes every day after work unless she had somewhere to go. Actually, tonight she was meeting Pat, but Pat rarely left her office before six, so she had plenty of time.

The workout room at her job was kept well stocked with towels and the thermostat was kept at a cool sixty-eight degrees. Grace watched the news stories of the day unfold on CNN as she worked out. It gave her something to concentrate on, even if it was a slow news day.

She could hardly believe she was fifty years old. Fifty! Where had the time gone? She felt no older than thirty-five.

Turning forty hadn't been this traumatic. At that time she'd recently gotten her second divorce but dated regularly. She couldn't have imagined then that desirable men would become so scarce the older she got.

The moving ramp slowed to a stop, indicating she'd been on for five minutes. That meant she could rest for three, then complete her workout.

It wasn't very crowded in here tonight. She'd come down later than usual, wanting to complete the draft of a list of points she wanted to cover at a meeting tomorrow. By the time she got into her bike shorts it was after five, and a lot of people had already come in, done their thing, and taken off. Many people worked out at lunchtime or skipped working out altogether, now that it was May and they were into the loveliest time of year in Chicago. The two people who'd been on the elliptical and the stationary bikes had both wrapped up their workouts while she did the first half of her treadmill workout.

Another person was on the Bowflex, bench-pressing. Grace did a double take when she noticed a pair of muscular brown arms working it. Surely she would have recognized those arms if she'd seen them before. But he sat in a way where she could make out only two other characteristics: the shiny dome of his shaved head and, most importantly, the left hand that wore no gold band to identify him as being off limits.

Grace concentrated so hard on what little she could see of this delicious male specimen that she expanded her usual three-minute break to four and a half. She decided that she'd rested too long to get back on the treadmill. Besides, it made too much noise. Better to use a stationary bike, which would help her keep an eye on the man who seemed to be effortlessly bench-pressing substantial loads. My, how she liked a man with muscles. He could probably lift her over his head with little effort, like those male ice skaters lifted their partners.

She'd been on the bike for two minutes when she saw him get up from the Bowflex. He wasn't as tall as she preferred, maybe five ten, but she had to stop being so damn picky. Grace stood only five four and a half herself; she just liked tall men.

She forced herself to stare at the TV screen—like she really cared about the latest politician to enter the race for president—when she saw movement out of the corner of her eye. He was coming toward her.

"Hi, how's the workout going?"

Ooh, that voice. Smooth as honey.

She let her legs come to a halt, her feet still resting in the stirrups. She kept her expression impassive as she turned her face and saw his full form for the first time. It was hard to determine the age of men with shaved heads, but he appeared to be over forty. As for his looks, she certainly wouldn't turn him down if he asked her to dance at a club. Could it be that working out here at the corporate gym was about to benefit her at last?

"I feel like I'm really pushing it today. I guess we all have days when our bodies just don't want to cooperate."

"You work out every day?"

"Just about. I try to get in twenty or thirty minutes after work. Uh, I don't remember seeing you here before." That was easily possible. Thousands of people worked at this location, the company's headquarters.

"That's because I just joined. I just started work on Monday. My name's Calvin, Calvin Pendleton."

"Grace Corrigan." She held out her hand, and he grasped it firmly in a grip that didn't feel at all sweaty, probably because he'd wiped his hand on the towel he now wore draped around his neck. "I hope you'll like it here. What division are you in?"

"Hypertension. It seems to be working out so far. What about you?"

"I'm in public relations."

"I guess I'll be running into you. I was about to leave. You'll be safe working out by yourself here, won't you?"

"Oh, sure. The attendant is around somewhere. She locks up at seven, and then she mops the floors and puts out fresh towels. Some people get here right after they open at 5:00 AM. But I was about to call it a day myself."

"Okay. See you later, huh?" He disappeared into the men's locker room.

Grace watched him walk away, sorry that the length of his shirt hid his butt in the formfitting bicycle shorts he wore. She tried to pedal some more, but she couldn't get her body into it. She climbed off the bicycle and headed for the locker room, where she changed into her regulation costume after a workout: a chocolate-brown sweat suit and brown leather gym shoes that could pass for Oxfords. She always preferred to shower after she got home; there she could make sure her hair had no danger of getting wet. She hung the outfit she'd worn to work in a black nylon garment bag and stuffed it in her locker. It would keep until tomorrow night, when she would go straight home. Carrying a garment bag into downtown Chicago wasn't practical.

When she left the gym, she saw a beefy figure in gray sweatpants and a black leather jacket several yards in front of her. Apparently, Calvin Pendleton didn't believe in showering on the premises, either. What a lucky break for her.

For a moment she considered catching up to him, then dropped the idea. They'd had a nice little exchange in the gym. No point trying to press the issue. There'd be plenty of time to find out exactly what he did over in Hypertension. In the meantime, she still had Eric.

Grace smiled. Thinking of Eric usually elicited that reaction, at least for about thirty seconds, while she thought about their sex life. Just because she was fifty didn't mean she was washed-up. But while the sex was fantastic, everything else was lacking.

Damn it, why couldn't she have found someone like Andy, that white dude Pat was seeing? Most of Pat's promising relationships fizzled out after a few dates, but this one had been going on for nearly two months now, with no signs of slowing down. Last weekend they went to the dinner buffet at the casino in Joliet, then spent some time at the tables . . . traveling by limo, yet! The weekend before that they went to see *The Color Purple* at the Cadillac Palace Theater. Andy had to go out to L.A. to spend a few days at the law firm out there, and he invited Pat to go with him. And Pat said the sex was great, too. She sure *looked* happy these days.

Grace grew more jealous by the week. She told herself that Andy had some great flaw that Pat conveniently hadn't mentioned, like he had acne-scarred skin, he had a flabby body, or he wasn't nearly as handsome as Pat said. But she'd finally gotten to meet him last week at the pub, and he turned out to be every bit as fine as Pat said, with a shock of black hair with gray sprinkled through it, heavily concentrated at the temples, and sexy deep blue bedroom eyes.

Of course, even if the relationship showed the promise of becoming lengthy, it would come to an abrupt end the moment Mr. and Mrs. Maxwell laid eyes on Andy. They'd object, and

Pat would lose her nerve and break it off, just like she'd done with Ricky all those years ago. Then there was the matter of Andy's family. He shared custody of his two daughters with his ex-wife, who lived in one of those ritzy North Shore suburbs. If he knew what was good for him he wouldn't let his ex know he had a black girlfriend, or else he might not ever see his daughters again. Yes, Pat might be pampered for the moment, traveling in limos, flying to the West Coast for the weekend, but it wouldn't last.

Besides, Grace had a feeling that no matter how much Pat liked being with that guy Andy, she was secretly still in love with Ricky Suárez.

Even with Andy's great looks, Grace doubted that the sex he and Pat had was anywhere near as good as the sex she was having with Eric. He was some good in the sack, pounding her pussy with that big stick of his like it was a drum, and not needing a whole lot of time before Round Two. She tingled just thinking about it. She would have been crazy to miss out on this. Pat had been sleeping with white dudes for so long, she'd probably forgotten how good it was with the brothers.

Grace had never slept with a white man. There'd been Ricky, of course, but he'd been brown, not white. But she couldn't deny that there were more available white men than black, so when a nice-looking white guy she knew from the train asked her out a couple of years back, she'd accepted.

He'd taken her to dinner at a steak house downtown, and even before he brought her home she decided to sleep with him. But when she slipped her hands under his shirt while kissing him and felt all that hair on his back, it turned her stomach. She felt like she was kissing the Wolf Man. That curly light brown hair that she admired so much on his head was grossly out of place on his back and shoulders. The man needed a trim . . . preferably with a lawn mower. She pretended to get a crick in her back and sent him on his way, later telling him she didn't think it would work between them.

Eric might not be much, but he was better than nothing at all. Someday she'd meet someone with the right income, someone who could afford to drop close to a thousand dollars on a weekend getaway and to take her to restaurants along the Magnificent Mile instead of all those damn chains. She'd meet him, eventually, of that she was certain.

A smug smile formed on her lips. Every silver lining had a bit of tarnish. Look at poor Elyse and all she was going through. Pat had told her that Franklin still had cancer in his body, even after that massive surgery he underwent last month. The doctors were trying to arrest it with treatments, which had left Franklin drained, bald, and nauseous. Pat had suggested to Grace that the two of them drive up to Lake Forest to visit with Elyse and offer her some moral support. Grace had agreed but secretly wished she could get out of it. She really didn't like being around people in such somber circumstances. She didn't have Pat's gift for always saying something appropriate. Going to a funeral was easier; at least when it was over it was truly over. What could she possibly say to Elyse in the face of Franklin's lingering illness? There were only so many words of comfort. This time next year, Elyse would probably be among the already overcrowded ranks of single middle-aged women looking for husbands. With a house in Lake Forest that was probably worth three times as much as they'd paid for it, plus the money she would undoubtedly come into upon Franklin's passing, Elyse had better watch out for fortune hunters.

Grace checked her watch. The next company-sponsored shuttle to the North Chicago train station would be leaving in just a few minutes.

The shuttle was already parked outside when she got out front, and she climbed on, sitting on the left so she could still see Calvin. She couldn't deny her curiosity to see what kind of vehicle he drove, and sitting in a high vehicle like this shuttle bus gave her a perfect opportunity.

She followed him with her eyes as he walked out to a maroon sedan and popped the trunk then tossed his workout bag inside. From here she couldn't determine the car's make, but he had to drive closer to exit the lot.

Her face moved closer to the glass as the maroon vehicle started to move. She didn't know a whole lot about car models, but she guessed it was some kind of Honda or Toyota. Not the sleekest model for a man who looked as good as he did but not bad. It looked like a fairly recent make, maybe two or three years old at the most. And at least it wasn't a minivan.

Hmm. Maybe she'd already met her mystery Mr. Right but just didn't know it yet.

Chapter 30

Late May
Chicago

Grace rushed into the pub where she was due to meet Pat. Normally when she came into a room men's heads turned to look at her, but today no one gave her a second glance. She knew it was because of the shapeless jogging suit and plain brown lace-up shoes she wore. Usually she would have declined to meet Pat on a day she planned to work out, but the truth was that she hadn't seen much of Pat lately, and she missed her. The last time they'd seen each other was the other week, when they went up to Elyse's in Lake County to try to cheer her up in the midst of Franklin's grueling treatment regimen. They kept pretty busy, between their jobs and their love lives. Grace thought it a happy coincidence that both of them were in relationships at the same time. She didn't think it had ever happened before.

Her feet abruptly stopped moving when she recognized the person Pat was talking to at the bar. Grace used to work out with Stephanie Williams at a fitness center near her condo before she switched to the gym at her job. Stephanie was the one she'd taken with her to Ricky's restaurant. When Ricky came over to say hello Stephanie had been quite taken by him as she witnessed Grace's undisguised flirting and made a prediction that the two of them would end up in bed together before it was all over—a prediction that came true. Good Lord, what if she mentioned it in front of Pat? Grace wouldn't mind Pat knowing about her and Ricky if something had come of it. She already had her defense planned ("Well, Pat, *you* didn't want him, and it ended between you two a hundred years ago. Why shouldn't I go out with him if he asked me to?") But since it had ended badly, she saw no reason for Pat to know that she'd tried to snag the great love of her life for herself. It hadn't worked out with Ricky. Why should she lose her friendship with Pat, too?

Pat spotted her and waved, and Grace had no choice but to walk over.

Grace saw the spark of recognition in Stephanie's eyes before she squealed, "Grace! Are *you* the friend Pat's meeting? What a small world."

"Hello, Stephanie. How nice to see you."

"It's been ages, hasn't it? But I think of you often. Like every time I go to that restaurant you brought me to. Nirvana."

Pat arched an eyebrow. "Nirvana?"

"Yes, over on North Halstead. Great food. With a Mexican touch. And the owner is some sexy."

"That was a long time ago," Grace said weakly, hoping the still-hefty Stephanie would fall off her bar stool or something. For a crazy moment she considered knocking her off it herself, making it look like an accident, of course. Anything to shut her up.

She quickly decided she couldn't pull that off, so she tried another tack. She had to get Pat away from Stephanie. Already Pat had a quizzical look on her face, like she wondered why Grace had never mentioned dining at Ricky's place. "I'm famished, Pat. I always am after a workout. Why don't we get a table so we can order?"

Pat turned to Stephanie. "Stephanie, would you like to join us for dinner?"

Grace held her breath. *Say you can't make it,* she thought over and over in a silent plea.

"Thanks, but I'm kind of tired. I probably should have left with Doreen. But it was fun talking with you. I'm sure we'll see each other again."

Grace bit her lower lip. *God, I hope not.*

* * *

Grace knew Pat would bring up the matter at the first opportunity.

She'd barely picked up her menu when Pat said, "You never
told me you'd been to Ricky's restaurant."

"Oh, yes. One night Stephanie and I decided to go out to eat
after we worked out. She said she felt like something spicy, so I
suggested Ricky's place. You've always been so sensitive about
him; I thought it would be best not to mention it to you."

"So he was there."

"Yes. He stopped by our table and said hello. He even sent us
complimentary drinks and sent word through the waiter that we
could choose whatever desserts we wanted on him."

"Did he say anything about me?"

"Pat, this happened years ago," she said, not disguising her
annoyance. "I was still married to Danny." Grace deliberately
lied about the timeline. She'd actually gone to Ricky's restaurant
after her second divorce. She'd read an article in the *Tribune*
about him, an article that Pat obviously hadn't seen, and one
she didn't tell her about. Because it stated that the proprietor of
one of Chicago's hottest eateries had just gotten divorced.

"I'm sure you remember. It's okay if he didn't mention me.
I'm just curious, that's all."

*Curious, my ass. If Ricky called you tomorrow, you'd drop
Andy faster than a gambler drops fifty dollars at a blackjack
table.* "Actually, he did."

"And what did you say?"

Grace thought quickly for a suitable reply. She couldn't tell
Pat what she'd *really* said about her to Ricky that day. "I said
you were doing well. And that seemed to satisfy him."

"He didn't ask if I was married or seeing anyone or anything?"

She wished Pat would stop pressing. "No, Pat, he didn't. But
wasn't he married at that time himself?" She knew that that
hadn't been the case, but her lie about the timeline was about to
benefit her.

Pat thought a moment. "If it was before you and Danny
broke up, I guess he was. But I'm not sure exactly when that
happened. Maybe he and his wife were separated."

"I don't recall if he was wearing a wedding band or not."

"I ran into his mother after you and Danny broke up, and she told me Ricky was divorced. Maybe this was a year or two later." Pat wavered a moment, then continued talking. "I never told you this, Grace, but after Miriam told me about his divorce, I got one of my coworkers to go with me to have dinner at his restaurant. I thought we might reconnect." She grunted. "I used to daydream that he would take one look at me and fall madly in love with me all over again, and that I'd tell my parents we were getting married no matter how much that upset them. I was going to spring the happy news on you at the last minute. That's why I didn't invite you to come along with me."

Grace didn't feel too comfortable talking about Ricky to Pat, but curiosity got the better of her. "So what happened?"

"Nothing." Pat made a face. "Ricky was real nice that night, but he didn't seem interested." Her eyes took on a faraway look. "I always wondered why. I mean, he never asked if I was even *seeing* anyone."

"Maybe it's because he figured that nothing had changed, that you would still listen to your parents, and he didn't want to risk getting his heart broken again." Grace felt more at ease with the direction the conversation was taking, now that it looked like she'd gotten Pat away from Stephanie before Stephanie let the cat out of the bag. Pat would never forgive her if she knew the truth. Grace would have been sorry to see her lifelong friendship with Pat end if she and Ricky had hooked up permanently, but if she had Ricky as a husband Pat would have learned to live with it. On the other hand, if Pat found out about that brief affair now, Grace would be out of a good friend for nothing, nothing at all.

"Yeah, I thought of that, too. But it wasn't like I could come out and say I wouldn't let that happen again."

Grace saw another opportunity to get off the topic of Ricky altogether and quickly pounced on it. "Are you sure about that?"

"What do you mean, am I sure?" Pat looked miffed.

"If Andy were to call you tonight and tell you he wanted to meet your parents, what would you do?"

"That's a pointless question, Grace. You know as well as I do that men don't make those kinds of requests."

"All right, then. Say you two get really serious. Hell, say you wanted to get married. How would you handle your parents?"

"That's another pointless question. I'm never going to get married."

"You don't know that. Lots of women get married for the first time when they're past forty-five. Stop trying to avoid my question. If your parents objected to your being involved with a white guy, what would you do?"

Pat hesitated. "Well . . . I'd like to think that they've softened with time. Ricky and I wanted to get engaged just a few months after Melvin was shot."

"And if they haven't softened?"

"I'd tell them it's my life, and I'm sorry if my decision pains them, but I'm going ahead with my plans."

Grace looked at her friend across the table and tried not to giggle. Despite the defiant raise of her chin, Pat had sounded about as confident as George W. Bush had when asking members of the NAACP for their votes. She might have *wanted* to sound sure of herself, but her doubts came through as loud as a foghorn. "Admit it," she challenged. "Your parents have no idea that you've been dating mostly white men over the years. And deep down, you're worried about how they might react if they knew."

Pat looked away.

"Oh, my God," Grace moaned. "Pat, you're almost fifty years old. You were too old thirty years ago to let your folks' wishes stop you from riding off into the sunset with Ricky. And you're way too old now to let them influence you."

Pat sighed. "It's hard, Grace."

"Maybe this is mean of me, but would you rather have been happily married to Ricky now and have had those kids you always wanted, or can you honestly say you're glad you stayed single, going out less and less because the number of eligible men in the pool is dwindling as you get older?"

"All right, Grace. You made your point."

"I'm sorry if I hurt your feelings. That wasn't my intention. I just want you to understand that your life is yours to live as you please. It doesn't belong to your parents, just because they gave it to you. They can offer suggestions, of course, but they have no business dictating to you. Look at Elyse. Her parents felt Franklin was too old for her. But that didn't stop her from marrying him, did it? It looks like he did pretty well by her, too."

"That was different," Pat protested. "Mr. and Mrs. Hughes didn't lose any of their other kids, and Elyse didn't have to carry the burden of being their last chance of having a child become successful."

Grace tried to choose her words carefully. None of her own five siblings had exactly set the world on fire, but at least they were productive, law-abiding citizens . . . and they were all still alive. "Very few people can even imagine the losses your family suffered," she said. "But don't think for one minute that you haven't made a success out of yourself. That still doesn't give your parents the right to control your private life, Pat. I thought it wasn't right for them to try to manipulate you because they were grieving. They wouldn't have died if you and Ricky got married, for heaven's sake. And I wonder if they've ever considered that if they hadn't gotten in the way thirty years ago, they might have had grandchildren."

Pat rolled her eyes. "At least they've stopped asking me when I'm going to meet a nice man and settle down. Once I hit forty-five I think they realized that when I'm gone it'll be the last of our little family."

How sad, Grace thought. Hell, even *she* had two grandchildren. Moses and Cleotha Maxwell had had three children, two of whom were male, but there was no one left to carry on the name. All that promise, wasted like spilled milk.

Pat looked down toward the table. "I guess Ricky sensed all along that I'd have trouble with this again. No wonder he didn't make a move."

Grace was positive that Ricky's reluctance came from the aborted affair he'd had with her rather than any fears that Pat would still honor her parents' wishes, but of course she couldn't say that. She decided it would be best to drop both subjects— Ricky Suárez plus Mr. and Mrs. Maxwell's certain disapproval of Pat's affair with Andy Keindl. If Pat still planned to allow her parents to run her life, she'd better plan on growing old all by herself. *Completely* by herself, since her parents would probably be gone in another ten years. Of course, Grace's parents had already passed on, but at least she had a daughter and grandchildren. Pat would be completely alone in the world.

"You know I'm here if you want an ear," Grace said. "Now, let's order so I can eat already."

Chapter 31

Pat, still in her bathing suit, plopped on the bed. She never believed she'd be staying at the Beverly Wilshire Hotel, just steps away from the three-block shopping district of Rodeo Drive. This was a big thing for a girl from the Theodore Dreiser Projects. How considerate of Andy to choose a hotel where she could have something to do without venturing too far while he went to the office. She'd hate to know how much it was costing him.

She quickly remembered that this wasn't a personal expense for him, other than the cost of her airplane ticket and her meals. His firm was picking up the cost of this trip.

Her first look at the hotel came as somewhat of a disappointment. The lobby, although elegant with tiled floors and white marble, was awfully small. It looked so spacious in movies like *Pretty Woman*. But their room was lovely, all tan and olive green, with overstuffed chairs everywhere and plenty of light, overlooking the Mediterranean-style pool. She'd gone down for a dip and was pleased when a waiter offered her bottled water and a smoothie served in a shot glass.

"I hope that swimsuit is dry," Andy commented now.

"Just about." Pat quickly changed her mind. "I guess I ought to take it off." With deliberately slow movements, she crisscrossed her arms to the opposite shoulders and pushed the straps off her shoulders, then peeled off the one-piece suit. Damn it, she hated the way her breasts rolled off to the sides when she lay down, but from the gleam in his eye, it was clear he didn't mind.

She raised her hips and, sucking in her stomach, pulled the suit over her hips then tossed it carelessly on the tan carpet. Completely naked, she stretched tantalizingly on the bed. She knew Andy enjoyed looking at her, and why not? She didn't look bad for a woman almost fifty years old. Her boobs might be lacking horizontal gravity, but at least when she sat up they did, too, even if not quite as high as they used to. Her butt had no vertical challenges, either. But her thighs were starting to get a little soft, and even when she held in her stomach she looked thick around the middle. She'd have to start walking Saturday mornings with Grace. And maybe she could do a few bends to tighten up her abs.

"What kind of vacation plans do you have for this year?" he asked.

"My friend Grace and I, plus two other women, are going to cruise the Mediterranean this summer. I've been looking forward to it for a long time."

"The Riviera, huh? Sounds almost too romantic a trip to take with a couple of girlfriends."

"Probably, but it was a part of the world we all wanted to see." Pat shrugged. "If you'd come back to Chicago last year, you and I might have planned to go together."

"It shouldn't be too late to plan something together, something a little lengthier than a weekend in Galena. Maybe five days in Cancun or Jamaica."

She looked at him curiously. She'd thought he was just making conversation, but he really sounded like he wanted to go away with her.

"Something wrong?"

"Uh . . . no. I'm just a little surprised. It's only May. Do you suppose it's safe to plan anything for two or three months out?"

"Why not? You plan on dumping me?"

She didn't know what to say. Most of the affairs she embarked on petered out after a month or two. It had been years since she'd spent more time than that in a relationship. It wasn't unusual to meet families when you'd been seeing someone for six months or more.

God forbid.

"Pat? Your silence seems ominous. Do you know something I don't?"

She made a quick recovery. "No, of course not. I just find it rather flattering that you'd like to take a trip with me." At least that was the truth.

But she couldn't help thinking how her parents would react if they knew she was dating a white man.

Andy sat beside her and ran a hand over her body. "No man in his right mind would turn down a trip with you." His gaze lingered on her from her breasts to her thighs. "In the meantime, you're naked."

She grinned. "I thought you'd never notice."

"We have to do something about that."

"Give me a chance to rinse off this chlorine."

Andy was already taking off his shirt. "Do it later. Chlorine turns me on."

"*Everything* turns you on," she said playfully.

"If it's anything about you, consider me guilty."

Andy went in to his office Friday morning. Pat wandered down Rodeo Drive, browsing in the store windows, knowing she could never afford the clothing on display. She felt a little silly putting on capri pants and a knit sweater, plus heeled sandals, to go shopping, but she could hardly wear jeans and gym shoes. The only ones who could get away with that were celebrities.

Andy returned at six-thirty. "I'm sorry it took me so long," he said.

"The Friday before Memorial Day—I just knew you'd be back early."

"I thought so, too. It took longer than I expected. But I'm all yours for the rest of the weekend. What'd you do all day?"

"I went shopping on Rodeo, and then I took the trolley tour

of Beverly Hills, and then I came back for lunch, read out by the pool, and took a nap."

He took her in his arms. "You are one easygoing woman. No wonder I'm crazy about you."

She kissed him. "And don't you forget what a prize you have in me."

"No, seriously. My daughters can learn a lot from you. I'm afraid their mother is raising them to be on the high-maintenance side."

She couldn't bring herself to make a response. Was he saying what she *thought* he was saying?

His next words confirmed it. "You'll have to meet my kids one of these days."

She instantly relaxed. "One of these days" didn't exactly have an air of immediacy to it. Her curiosity got the better of her. "Do they know about me?"

"They know I'm seeing someone, yes. But I'm not in the habit of sharing details of my social life with my kids, but they asked me, and I saw no reason to lie." He shrugged, looking a bit like a bashful little boy. "Apparently they think I've been pretty cheery these days."

"As opposed to what, an ogre?"

Andy laughed. "I wouldn't say *that*. I'm an easygoing guy. But I moved back here in February, in the dead of winter. I did a lot of muttering about the windchills, about all the damn snow we had this year. I'm not complaining anymore."

"Andy. Do they know I'm black?"

"They don't even know that you used to be blonde," he joked, patting her recently restored dark hair.

"Seriously."

"No, they don't know. I saw no reason to mention it."

"Oh, you didn't? Andy, the world isn't color-blind, and neither are your daughters."

"I know that. I just don't happen to believe it'll be a big deal." He looked at her curiously. "You don't seem convinced."

"Sometimes people can fool you. I know that from my own experience."

"I'd love to hear about it."

She took a deep breath. Maybe she should just tell him now and get it over with. If she got if off her chest maybe she wouldn't feel so antsy any time the subject of family came up. "There was this boy I grew up with. His family lived down the hall from us. We played together when we were kids, but by the time we got to high school something changed."

"Sounds very sweet."

She spoke quietly. "I hope you're not being facetious, Andy."

"No, not at all. That whole high school sweetheart thing, I think it's sweet. Hell, my girlfriend from high school broke up with me the minute she got to Ohio State and took up with their star quarterback."

Pat laughed. Andy could be so funny sometimes. "Well, ours was different. My father broke it up when we were in our first year of college. He didn't like me dating Ricky because he was Latino."

Andy nodded. "Mexican? So your father doesn't like Latinos. How does he feel about German-Americans?"

"He doesn't like them, either."

Andy searched her face, his expression changing when he realized she wasn't kidding. "You're serious."

"Yes. My father grew up in a little town in Arkansas and had a little brother, Jacob. Jacob was . . . He was killed one night when the town slut, a white girl, identified him as the father of her baby. A group of punks lynched him."

"When did this happen?"

"The same year as the Brown ruling."

He nodded. "That was 1954. You and I weren't even born yet."

"Yes. Anyway, my uncle's body was found the next morning, hanging from a tree. He'd been beaten to a pulp before he was hanged. He was seventeen years old. My parents got married right after that and moved up here."

"Have they ever been back?"

"Never. My father swore he'd never set foot in Arkansas again. He did, of course, when my grandparents passed away."

"I think I might already know the answer to this, but what happened to the people who murdered your uncle?"

"They weren't even charged."

"Damn." Andy was silent for a moment. "Pat, I think that stinks, but it happened over fifty years ago. Does your father still subscribe to the all-white-people-are-devils theory after all this time? Hell, even Malcolm X softened his stance before he was killed."

He must have seen Spike Lee's movie, she thought. "I wouldn't say my father is *that* extreme. But he still doesn't like the idea of interracial dating. In a way I can't blame him. The mere implication of it cost his brother his life. And to this day no one knows who that girl's baby's daddy really was."

Andy's eyes glinted. "Listening to this, I can understand why your father feels the way he does. But in your first year of college . . . You must have been at least eighteen. That's legally an adult. I'm curious, why didn't you stand up to him?"

Tears pooled in her lower lids. "Because my younger brother had just been killed. He was the one we all had such high hopes for. He was going to be a scientist. We expected him to win the Nobel for chemistry."

Andy nodded. "The one who got hit by a stray bullet in a gang hit."

"Yes. Melvin was only sixteen. My parents were devastated. By then Clarence had already started his drug habit, and I knew they looked to me as the only one with potential to make it out of the ghetto. They said they couldn't bear it if I married my boyfriend. That I'd only end up dropping out of school because he couldn't afford to support me, and that would mean that none of their children made it in life. They were heartbroken over my brothers. I knew I could have stood up to them, but I just couldn't bring myself to do it. I was afraid they'd never recover if I did. Of course, that was foolish."

"That's a heavy load to bear, the weight of your parents' expectations, but I do believe they would have gotten over it. The way I see it they would have had no choice."

She nodded. "After a few years it occurred to me that I'd

made a terrible mistake. People learn to adapt. I believe my parents would have not only accepted my boyfriend, but loved him as well. It's not like he was a stranger to them to begin with; they'd known him most of his life." The daydreams she used to entertain regularly flashed before her: her father, who'd worked as a short-order cook, among other things, to support his family, sitting at the table with Ricky going over plans for the first restaurant Ricky opened, while her mother played with her first grandchild. "But I still didn't have the backbone to go after him and tell him," she said sadly. "Eventually he married someone else."

"His loss is my gain."

She smiled. "You really are sweet, Andy."

"So you're saying your father wouldn't approve of me, and your mother, neither."

"I'm afraid not."

He held her gaze. "And how do you feel about going against them now? You're not eighteen anymore."

"It would bother me to know I'd made them unhappy, sure, but I can't let them dictate to me any longer, Andy. It was a mistake to do it the first time."

"I guess I can't ask you for more than that."

Pat smacked her palms together, as if she could change the mood instantly. "So much for the story of my love life. Let's move on to something less boring."

"I didn't find it at all boring, Pat. I'm truly interested in the story of your life. Plus, I'm a little jealous."

"No need for that. It all ended a long, long time ago."

Chapter 32

Elyse found it difficult to stop looking at Kevin, even more at this lunch today than she had the last time. He looked so handsome, with his thick, arched brows; neat mustache and goatee; and smooth, dark skin. Handsome . . . and healthy.

She immediately felt a stab of guilt. Franklin couldn't help what had happened to him. It was her damn hormones acting overtime. She and Franklin hadn't made love in weeks, in the time between his surgical recovery and beginning his treatment regimen, which had rendered him impotent. They'd always had a healthy sex life, making love right up until she went into labor with both Todd and Brontë, despite her obstetrician's instructions not to after her seventh month. She needed to get hold of herself and be more dignified and concentrate on the menu before her . . . and remember that Kevin *wasn't* one of the selections.

"It was so good of you to suggest lunch again, Kevin," she said pleasantly.

"I didn't intend for last month to be a one-time thing. You're having a difficult time. I'd like to help if I can. I know you're about to get real busy, taking care of Franklin and with your parents visiting and all." Kevin had never met Franklin, of course, but he knew his name from their conversations.

"Yes. I'm sure my parents are going to be a huge help, and that Franklin will enjoy having them around."

"How is he, anyway?"

"Getting stronger every day," she said happily. "He's planning to go back to work after the Fourth, when his treatments are completed."

The news from the doctor hadn't been as good as she'd hoped, but nor was it as bad as it could have been. She wanted to hear that no traces of cancer remained after the removal of the tumor. The actual word was that the cancer had spread to blood vessels and lymph nodes, but not to other organs. Stage III, they called it. Dr. LeBlond, the oncologist Dr. Obi had referred Franklin to, told him he'd probably feel reasonably well for a while yet and urged him to try to live as normally as possible, although he cautioned that he didn't want him returning to work until he gave a green light. Shortly afterward, Franklin began a regimen of chemo and then radiation treatments that Elyse prayed would halt the spread of the disease. He struggled with the side effects, and it pained Elyse to see him so listless and so nauseated. She knew that people receiving chemotherapeutic agents often lost their hair, but she didn't realize the hair loss wasn't limited to their head. Franklin's legs, chest, underarms, and genital area were practically bare. It looked so odd.

Fortunately, the kids were on their summer break, so they were around more. Brontë had a temp assignment that lasted through the end of August; and Todd, who was working at the local hospital pulling and replacing patient files, asked to be put on second shift, which they did. His schedule gave him the flexibility to stay home with Franklin in the mornings, and to drive him to and from his treatments. It worked well for Franklin to accept assistance from one of his sons, more readily than he would have from one of his daughters, or even from Elyse herself. She supposed that if she was ill she would feel the same, preferring Brontë to Todd.

"Hey, that's good news," Kevin said.

"I'll say it is." She beamed, forgetting about her raging hormones at the thought of Franklin getting better. They'd just celebrated their twenty-sixth anniversary. Hopefully in another month or so, everything would be back to normal.

Franklin even joked that he was saving a fortune, both in gas—because his Navigator was parked in the garage and hardly being driven, while gas prices soared—and in shampoo, because he had no hair to wash. "And you can bet that I'm going to make every day count," Franklin had said.

It made Elyse happy to talk about Franklin's recovery, but she knew it would be wrong to show no interest in what was happening with Kevin. "So tell me," she said, "how're the plans for the Laundromat going?"

He shrugged. "It's creeping along. It's difficult to raise the funds needed to get started."

"Have you thought about the Small Business Administration? You seem to be offering a service that's needed in the community."

"Yeah, but it's practically impossible to get anything out of them. My partner and I are trying to raise the money ourselves."

Elyse found herself regretting bringing up the subject. When Kevin first told her about his plans, she'd gotten the impression that he was about to roll with them. Now he sounded uncertain that he'd be able to pull it off, which told her that he'd merely been trying to appear like he had an agenda rather than just a middle-aged exterminator. Had he done it because he felt he needed to be more than he was? Had he felt intimidated when she told him she was a physical therapist? Now Elyse understood how Grace and Pat felt when chatting with men who had less education than they and held everyday jobs—jobs which no doubt made the world go round, like delivering the mail, driving a truck, or, as in Kevin's case, providing pest control.

Worst of all, Kevin's matter-of-fact statements about being short on capital made her feel conscious of the differences between her financial situation and his. How much could start-up costs be for a consumer laundry, maybe twenty thousand dollars? Writing a check for that amount would hardly bankrupt her . . . and worst of all, Kevin had probably guessed as much. She suddenly felt guilty for being a "have" while he was a "have-not."

But the last thing she wanted to do was invest in a Laundromat miles away from where she lived. She sought to steer the conversation elsewhere before he got the idea to ask her for financial backing, if he hadn't already.

"Well, I'm sure you'll get to where you need to be eventually," she said with a smile. "Hmm . . . Those ribs really look good, don't you think?"

She felt a lot safer talking about something other than his difficulty raising money to go into business.

When the waitress discreetly brought the check Elyse took it. Kevin protested, "You paid the check last time. Let me get it this time."

She merely winked at him and said, "It's not a problem. If you want to open that business before you're sixty, you've got to watch your spending."

He walked her to her car. "I'm glad to hear that everything's going so well for you, Elyse, I really am," he said softly.

Again, she had the uncomfortable feeling that he was thinking of his own dismal situation. "I'm sure things will work out for you, too, Kevin." She gave him her sunniest smile to punctuate her words.

"Thanks for your optimism. Keep in touch, okay?"

"I'll do that. See you later." She reached out to open the car door, then gasped as he suddenly leaned forward, pinning her against the side of the vehicle. Holding her captive, he kissed her, gently at first, then suddenly thrusting his tongue inside her mouth.

Elyse stretched her back to its limit as she leaned backward, trying to get away from him. Kevin ended the kiss as abruptly as it began, and she merely stared at him, the bewilderment she felt showing on her face.

"I'm sorry," he said. "That was an impulse. I guess I should have controlled it."

"I think you should have," she said sternly. "I have to go now." She opened the door and slipped behind the wheel. Kevin still stood alongside the car, and she fumbled out of nervousness as she tried to insert the key into the ignition.

She drove off without looking at him, hoping he got the point. Inside, she couldn't wait to get home and wash her mouth.

Not because his kiss repelled her, but because she'd responded to it.

Chapter 33

Early to mid-June
Chicago

Susan backed into a parking space in front of the attractive red brick, two-story duplex in Hyde Park. She felt like a murderer trying to hide in plain sight. She hadn't killed anyone, of course, but part of her still wanted to look over her shoulder to see if anyone was watching her.

She'd spoken to Charles often since seeing him three weeks ago, but she put off seeing him out of fear. He hadn't pushed to see her, something for which she felt grateful. Charles had always been perceptive to her thoughts and feelings, and no doubt he knew what a difficult spot she was in.

He also knew that the friendship she spoke of could be maintained only over the telephone. Those sparks she felt when he kissed her and she kissed him back told her that mere friendship between them would never work. It had to be all or nothing.

When Bruce suggested they bring the kids to Lake Geneva for the Memorial Day weekend, she agreed, but did not allow herself to think anything between them would change . . . and it didn't, although they all had a good time. And when they had sex she kept her nightgown on. She'd finally learned to accept that it would always be this way.

After it was over and she laid on her side, her back to Bruce, feeling the now-familiar mix of sexual satisfaction and emotional barrenness, she knew she would see Charles again soon after the holiday weekend ended.

When she called, he said, "Something tells me you plan on coming down this way again."

It annoyed her that he knew her motives. He probably figured she'd tried to make a go of it with Bruce and failed. *That's what you get for telling him about the state of your marriage,* she told herself, although she knew her irritation had no real root. She just found it frustrating that he could read her so easily. No one wanted to be an open book.

"What else does your crystal ball tell you?" she asked.

"The signal went black. You'll have to tell me."

She chuckled, her annoyance gone. "Bruce is golfing Saturday. I thought I'd hire a babysitter for a couple of hours, if that'll work for you."

They met at the California Pizza Kitchen, where they had a leisurely lunch.

"I'm glad you called," Charles told her.

"I just felt that I had to see you," she admitted. "School's almost out. I won't have as much free time in a couple of weeks."

"School lets out here the week after next," he remarked casually. "When is your kids' last day?"

"The fifteenth, sixteenth, something like that. They had to add a few days because of the snow this winter."

"We're out on the tenth. It sounds like you'll have a free week, or at least a free couple of days, the same time I'm off."

"Good. I can come down for lunch. We can chat for a couple of hours."

"Make it breakfast, and we'll have more time. I'll even cook."

"At your apartment?" she asked incredulously. "Uh . . . Don't you think the traffic around there is rather heavy?"

"It just so happens that my mother is taking a trip with the church that week. She'll be in South Dakota, at Mount Rushmore. But in case you've forgotten, my apartment has its own entrance, so I have plenty of privacy."

She thought it odd that he didn't acknowledge that having his own entrance hadn't stopped Ann Valentine from reading her the riot act right there in the street when Ann learned she and Charles were seeing each other. Susan had never been so embarrassed, with all the neighbors looking on eagerly as Ann questioned her scruples. Had he actually forgotten? "Charles, I don't mean to sound like I'm sticking my nose into your business, but why do you still live at home in the first place? I know you lived there when Douglas first bought the house, but that was a long time ago."

"I never expected I'd still be here after all this time, but it was an ideal setup. I had my privacy, but I could still run upstairs for a home-cooked meal whenever I wanted. I planned on leaving eventually, but the price was right, for one thing."

Susan took that to mean he paid no rent. She doubted that was the case now that his mother, who'd been a court clerk, was retired and living on a fixed income, but he probably paid well below market rate.

"And after my father died, my mother asked me to stay. Said she feels better knowing I'm right downstairs. I feel better about it, too. My brother is an addict, Susan. That means he can't be trusted."

She couldn't argue with that.

Susan checked her reflection carefully. Out of habit she glanced at her right side. She saw no protrusion through her clothes, but still she felt nervous. She hadn't told Charles of Bruce's revulsion with her postsurgical figure, just that he kept his distance from her since their surgery. She didn't mean to be evasive, or to imply that she and Bruce no longer had sex at all; she just felt she had the right to preserve some dignity. It had been hard enough to confide that much to him. What self-respecting woman could admit that the sight of her naked body killed her husband's libido?

One thing for sure: if Charles insisted she keep her shirt on she would get up and leave.

She gulped as she alighted from the car. This was it. She was about to cross a border from which there'd be no return.

* * *

Charles made her feel at home from the moment he opened the door. He gave her a big bear hug that lasted just long enough and told her how glad he was to see her. Then he invited her to sit down and keep him company while he cooked.

She sat on a bar stool—a comfortable one with a padded seat and back, plus arms—on the living room side of the pass-through window. She still remembered those hard stools Charles used to have that used to make her butt sore. She hadn't been here in twenty-five years, and although the furniture had changed it was still neat and fairly bright, considering it was partially underground. Four small windows close to the ceiling helped. If she remembered correctly, it was darker in the bedroom. . . .

Uh-oh. She didn't want to think about Charles's bedroom. "What're you making?" she asked. "It smells heavenly."

"An omelet with chorizo, sautéed red and green peppers, onions, mushrooms—"

"My mouth is watering."

"—plus shredded potatoes and cheese. It's almost ready."

Susan watched him cook in the compact kitchen. He moved with the ease of a man who had prepared many a meal on his own.

She gasped when he added what looked like a homemade biscuit to her plate. "Wow," she said, lightly fingering the bumpy texture. "Charles, did you make these?"

"I cannot tell a lie," he declared in his best schoolboy voice. "They came from the supermarket. They sell them frozen."

"They look fabulous."

He turned his back to her for a moment to remove chilled stemmed glasses from the freezer, into which he poured cold pineapple juice. He placed the glasses on the counter and then carried the plates and came to sit beside her on the other stool.

"Charles, this is delicious!" she exclaimed after taking her first bite.

"Hey, you think Ricky Suárez is the only man who came out of Dreiser who can cook? All of us guys were all raised by working women."

"I just had no idea you were so talented. You never cooked for me back in the day."

"My culinary skills came later. Back when you and I were together I'd just as soon go out for some McDonald's before I picked up a pan."

After they ate she offered to do the dishes.

"You wash, I'll dry," he said.

She turned the tap to a light but steady stream of moderately hot water and rinsed each utensil, glass, and plate before placing it in the drain board. "You keep such a neat apartment, Charles. Even back in the day when you didn't really have a whole lot in here."

"I still don't have all that much, just better quality. That's the key to neatness, not having a lot of junk. That . . . and having your mother live upstairs," he added with a laugh.

"And here I was hoping you would say you did this all for me," she said with a smile. It surprised her how comfortable she felt, even with his mention of his mother. But then again, she'd always felt at ease with Charles.

He sprayed the stovetop with disinfectant cleaner and wiped it while she washed the dishes. He moved close to her to place the Teflon-coated skillet, which he'd already filled with water after he finished cooking, in the sink. "This is real easy to wash; the grease comes right off."

"No problem." Susan used the handled sponge to wash the surface of the skillet, and, as Charles said, the food particles and grease came right off. Suddenly she became aware that he was standing mere inches from her. She didn't want to look, but instinct told her he was watching her. Her earlier nervousness returned as she ran the sponge over the outer sides of the skillet. She managed to rinse it and place it atop the dishes in the drain board. "Looks like my job is done." She shut off the tap and reached for a paper towel from the hanging dispenser over the sink.

Charles took a step to the right, now standing directly behind her. She felt his palms on her upper arms. "Whatever will we do now?" he asked softly.

She swallowed hard. He certainly wasn't wasting any time. Even as she had the thought, Susan knew she wasn't being fair.

A school day was short, and it would take her over an hour to get home. It was already after ten.

Still, that didn't mean she was ready. In spite of how badly Bruce hurt her heart, that didn't change his status as her husband, and she didn't take cheating on him lightly. Even with her being all but certain that he had someone else it didn't make it any easier.

But Charles stood so close that she could feel his breath on her neck. He ran his palms down her arms until he reached her waist, then embraced her from behind, his arms encircling her middle. She caught her breath and leaned against him, suddenly feeling lightheaded. He began to nuzzle her neck, at the same time undoing the buttons of her blouse from the bottom up.

"No!" she said suddenly, clenching her shoulders, pushing his hands away from her blouse. "I can't do this, Charles. I'm sorry, I can't."

He made no attempt to step back. Instead, he stretched his fingers and pressed his palm against her chest. "I can feel your heart beating," he whispered. "It's racing. I know you want me as much as I want you."

"I'm not denying that, but I can't go through with it."

"Of course you can," he said gently, his hands sliding back to where they had been before, although not undressing her. "You're just nervous."

"You and I haven't . . . been together like this since I was in my twenties. I'm forty-nine years old now, and I've had breast cancer surgery. Plus . . . I'm married."

"Turn around and look at me."

He dropped his hands from her waist, and she did as he asked. She saw much more than mere desire in his eyes, and she wondered what he saw in hers.

He cupped her face. "Susan, when I told you that night at Junior's that the only woman I ever loved left me, I wasn't kidding. I only went there that night because I thought there was a tiny chance you might show. I couldn't let the chance to see you again go by.

"I know I jumped on you for saying the other week that too

much has changed for anything to be the same between us, but I was wrong. It hasn't changed. I loved you then, and I still do."

"Charles, don't say—"

"Do you think I don't understand how you feel? I know you're not the type of woman who steps out on her husband. I know you've never done this before. But, Susan . . . I want you. You told me he doesn't. Don't you deserve to be with a man who thinks you're beautiful . . . who'll *always* think you're beautiful?"

Tears pooled in her eyes. "Charles . . . How do I know you won't react the same way Bruce does?" She couldn't stand another rejection; she simply couldn't.

"There's only one way to find out, isn't there?"

Something in his easy grin told her not to worry, but nevertheless, she stood stock-still as he resumed unbuttoning her blouse. Then he unsnapped the front closure of her bra and pushed the cups aside. Susan held her breath. The only covering that kept her secret was gone.

She kept her eyes closed and tried not to cry when his movements stopped. She couldn't bear to see the distaste in his eyes when he saw her misshapen right breast. She'd lived through it too many times. Same shit, different man. There was nothing to do but close up her blouse and go home with what little remained of her dignity. . . .

Her eyes flew open when she felt herself being lifted. Charles placed her on the counter next to the sink, lowered his head against her chest, and began planting soft kisses on her breasts, moving from side to side as he cupped them in his hands. She gasped softly when he took her breast into his mouth. Bruce hadn't done that in so long. . . .

He stood up and spoke to her softly. "I told you, you'll always be beautiful to me."

She found her voice. "I don't think you've seen the full effect yet. You might not feel the same after you've—"

She broke off. His still-moving fingertips found the defect, and he moved his face to it. When he bent and kissed the protrusion she let out a strangled cry and began to quake, her muscles struggling to hold her eyelids shut and hold in the tears. The fingers of his other hand promptly moved to cup the side of her neck, steadying her trembling body. At last he raised his head. "Now do you believe me?"

She opened her eyes, damp with happy tears. She threw her arms around his neck and hung on like he alone could extend her life. "Yes. I believe you. I didn't mean to have no faith in you, Charles. It's just that—"

He pressed his index finger against her lips. "You don't have to tell me. I don't want you to think about anything unpleasant while we're together. Now, let's get the hell out of this kitchen." He gripped her hips and pulled them forward. Susan's arms instinctively went around his neck, and she wrapped her long legs around his waist. He lifted her and crossed the hall to his bedroom. The set of weights in a corner told her where he got the strength to lift her no-longer svelte hundred-and-seventy-pound body.

The combination of the basement location plus heavy curtains covering the small windows made it look more like early evening than midmorning. She was glad when he made no move to turn on the light.

He laid her gently on the bed, and in a playful motion she pulled him down with her. She felt so vital, so alive . . . And she couldn't wait to feel him inside her.

As her orgasm built, her guilt dissolved. Instead she thanked God for the snow last winter that kept the Pleasant Prairie schools open a few extra days. Her body exploded in wave after wave of pleasure, and she collapsed into the pillows, sobbing as she shook.

"I can't tell you how happy I feel right now," she said softly after her body was still and her sobs ceased. "I wish it could last forever."

On his elbows next to her, Charles stroked her curls. "I know it can't. So the question becomes, what happens now?"

Sadness flowed through her at the forced return to reality. "I don't know, Charles."

"You know I wasn't just trying to get you into bed when I told you I love you."

She nodded. "But everything is moving so fast. I've barely had time to adjust to our making love."

"It's not going to be easy for me to watch you leave me to go back home to Bruce."

"What else can I do, Charles?"

"I want you to think about leaving him."

Her mouth fell open. "*Leave?*"

"You can't say you haven't thought about it, even before we saw each other at Junior's. You said you'd been unhappy for months."

"Of *course* I thought about it . . . for about a minute. Charles, as you know, I'm almost fifty years old, I haven't worked in about eleven years, plus I'm a cancer patient. How the hell am I supposed to support myself and my children if I walk out on Bruce?" She looked away. Why couldn't she simply savor the feeling of being loved and desired after being denied for so long? Why did Charles have to bring up all this complicated stuff? Did she get no reprieve at all? It wasn't fair, damn it.

"I'll take care of you, Susan."

She had no response. This made no sense. Was he proposing that she and her two children move in with him? He had a one-bedroom apartment, for heaven's sake!

"It's complicated," she said finally, still not looking at him.

He reached out and rolled her back toward him. "I know. We won't talk about it anymore. Just remember that I love you."

Susan could think of nothing else.

She felt strangely calm as she got behind the wheel and drove to the kids' school. She'd gone home first and taken a quick shower. It would be just her luck that Bruce would decide to give her a treat when he got home from work, and she couldn't risk that any more than she could risk the kids mentioning that she'd taken a shower in the afternoon. That would raise a red flag.

Bruce might not want her himself, but she had a feeling he'd be out for the blood of any man she might be sleeping with.

When she got home for the second time that day, she checked her phone messages. "Hey," Bruce's voice said cheerfully. "Just wanted to let you know I'll be late tonight. I'll be home about eight, eight-thirty. Don't worry about holding dinner for me; I'll pick something up here."

Susan smiled. So he'd be late again tonight. That was just fine with her. It would give her more time to savor her day with Charles.

It beat sitting around wondering what the girlfriend he swore he didn't have looked like.

Chapter 34

Mid-June
Milwaukee

Bruce Dillahunt groaned in ecstasy as a stream of semen filled the condom he wore. He gripped Shay's hips and fell forward. That one took everything out of him.

They fell against the mattress together, his groin against her backside. It took several seconds for Shay's body to be still, even with him holding her tightly against him. He slid off her and onto his side, pulling her close.

"That was fantastic," he said when he caught his breath. He lifted long strands of her hair and threaded his fingers through them. Shay Johnson was one fine woman. She reminded him of Susan in her younger days. The two women in his life didn't resemble each other, but they shared a similar body type. They were both tall—Shay came in at an inch or two less than Susan's five ten—they both had wide hips, small breasts, and legs as long as a week that locked him in ecstasy.

"It always is," she said softly.

He couldn't argue with that. He'd met Shay in the parking lot of his office building. She worked as a supervisor in customer service for a medical claims service. That particular October afternoon her car had a dead battery and needed a jump.

Right away he'd noticed how lovely she was. Susan had undergone her lumpectomy just six weeks before, and he found that he couldn't stand to look at that damn cone shape sticking out of her breast. It was like making love to Death. He'd told her it didn't matter when she reluctantly considered plastic surgery, and while he could readily understand her not wishing to undergo another surgical procedure—and even agreeing that it would probably be better for her health in the long run to leave the area alone—he'd been unable to reconcile his desire for her with his fear of her disease recurring. Nor could he bring himself to consult a counselor, as Susan suggested. Psychologists were for the confused, for the uncertain. He had no doubts about himself. It was Susan's cancer he hated, not her. It had driven a wedge between them, invaded their marriage at the same time it invaded her body and marred her figure.

He couldn't bring himself to tell her the truth. It would be like knocking down a cripple. Because he had a lot to lose in a divorce—like half of what he'd amassed—he forced himself to make love to her occasionally in a halfhearted attempt to keep her satisfied. *He* wasn't satisfied, and he suspected she wasn't, either. Prior to her diagnosis they'd enjoyed an active, healthy sex life. He had no excuse for his diminished passion, at least none that wouldn't hurt her feelings. Bruce loved Susan. He simply couldn't reconcile his fears.

He hadn't meant for anything to happen with Shay. She'd been so grateful that day; she said she had an appointment she couldn't miss. She asked him for his card, and he gave it to her. That Friday she called and invited him to lunch as a way to say thank you.

Bruce held no illusions about her motives. She was, after all, probably fifteen years his junior. She'd seen his name and the title, president and CEO, on his business card and decided to invite him to lunch and flirt with him a little just to see where it went. If his card said he was a sales rep he knew he'd never have heard from her again.

With that in mind, from the very beginning he made no secret of the fact that he had a wife and two children.

But he found Shay enchanting and had been unable to stay away. He called her less than a week later. Within two weeks he brought her to dinner at the restaurant inside the InterContinental Hotel, and afterward brought her upstairs to the room he'd reserved and made love to her. At last he had an outlet for all the pent-up sexual frustration that had been building inside him.

They started their affair in December, and now it was June. After six months, he knew she was getting restless. Her next action proved it.

Shay sat up, the sheet covering her breasts. "How's your wife feeling these days, Bruce?"

He knew what she meant. He'd been wrong to make it sound like Susan was at death's door when she was thriving, but it gave him much-needed sympathy in Shay's eyes. He didn't want to be ruled out because he had a wife at home. But questions like this from Shay told him she was getting tired.

"She's doing pretty well," he replied cautiously.

"I'm glad to hear that, Bruce, I really am. I don't wish bad things upon people. But I'm not comfortable with sleeping with a man who's married, even if his wife is ill."

"I understand that, Shay. But what do you want me to do?"

"If she's doing well, why not file for divorce?"

"Divorce?"

"Yes. It happens all the time. You know, the flame goes out between husbands and wives and they decide it's best to start over with someone new."

"Well, that's complicated, Shay. First of all, my wife isn't well."

"You've been saying that for six months now. I'm beginning to think she's a lot healthier than you're letting on."

She was right, of course, but he didn't dare avert his gaze. That was tantamount to admitting he'd lied. "She's holding her own. But that's not the only consideration. This is a community property state. I'd stand to lose half of everything I have in a divorce."

Shay got up, yanking the sheet and remaining draped in it. "Bruce, I'm thirty-five years old and I've never had a family of my own. Both my parents were drug addicts. I grew up in foster care. I made sure I didn't get pregnant in tenth or eleventh grade like most of my girlfriends did, or afterward, either. I wanted a complete family, not to be another woman with kids and no husband. I did everything the right way. But I'm starting to run out of time. And I'm telling you now, Bruce, I'm not going to waste the best years of my life on a man who uses his sick wife as an excuse not to commit to me."

He sat up, the wood headboard hard against his upper back. He knew about her difficult childhood, about how she'd managed to get a college degree through the tuition-reimbursement plan at work. And she had a point. The fact that she had no family made her more accessible to him. It would be awfully difficult to carry on an affair if Shay had family obligations equal to his. She'd never be able to accompany him to conventions and other out-of-town business functions. He could call her at a moment's notice, like he had when Susan stayed at her friend's house overnight when she went to that tenants' reunion. Susan didn't know it, but he spent that night with Shay, arising at 6 AM to drive home so he'd be there before she and the children got back.

Yes, he understood Shay's position. But he wasn't ready to give her up. "Shay . . . I need you to be patient."

"It's been six months, Bruce. You *say* you care for me."

"I do." Bruce spoke the truth. He loved Susan, yes. She was the mother of his children, and she'd been a damn good wife to him. It pained him to know he was causing her such anguish. Bad enough that his body betrayed him that night when she took off her nightgown. All his excuses about getting older had gone out the window when his erection dwindled before her eyes. That night she hinted that he had to be sleeping with someone. She'd accused him before, but she had no hard proof. He'd been careful, flying Shay out on different flights to meet him and arranging for her airport transfers himself. Susan had said nothing about him cheating on her since that night she slept in the guest bedroom, and of course neither had he. They'd formed a somewhat uneasy truce, but he knew it wouldn't last.

Bruce wished he could feel differently, but he just couldn't help how his body reacted to her. At this point he wasn't sure if plastic surgery would help. He knew that disease lurked in her breast, and perhaps grew elsewhere in her body. Maybe that made him an awful person, but he couldn't control his true feelings any more than he could control the receding hairline that had led him to eventually start shaving his head.

Any way he looked at it, asking for a divorce would hurt his family. In spite of Susan expressing her suspicions to him, he knew it would break her heart to learn that he really did seek fulfillment elsewhere. He also wanted to protect his children against coming from, as it used to be called, "a broken home." Sure, divorce was the only way to go when it came to truly warring spouses, but he and Susan got along fine. They did all their arguing behind closed doors, and they both worked hard to keep Quentin and Alyssa in the dark about the true state of their marriage. Even when Susan stormed out that time and went to sleep in the guest bedroom, she returned to their bed before Quentin and Alyssa awakened. Their welfare mattered as much to her as it did to him. On the surface they were a happy family, but that was as deep as it got.

He suddenly realized Shay was speaking and his ears sprang to attention.

"Sure you do. But not enough to divorce your wife."

He hedged. "Shay, you know I love you. But I also care about my wife . . . our family. I'm afraid I can't make you any promises."

"Then I think you should leave."

Without a word, Bruce slid to the side of the bed, where he'd carelessly dropped his clothes in his haste to make love to Shay. It sounded like she'd made a decision, and he had no argument. Maybe it was best to let her go. She had a right to make her dream of a family come true, preferably with someone closer to her own age. And he had no right to try to take that from her.

As he drove home, he realized he was going to have to make a decision.

He knew Susan well enough to know that surface happiness wouldn't be enough for her, at least not for any length of time.

Just like it wasn't enough for him.

Chapter 35

Early June
Chicago

Grace was stretched out on the down-filled chaise lounge in her bedroom, her favorite place for curling up with a good book, when the phone rang. She reached for the extension that she deliberately kept on the side table so she wouldn't have to get up every time the phone rang. She was enjoying her book and wasn't thrilled about being interrupted, but Pat's name appeared in the caller ID box. "Hey, what's up?"

"Hi," Pat said. "Do you have a few minutes to talk, or is Eric there?"

"No, I got rid of him first thing this morning."

"I need your advice about something."

"Sure, go ahead. You know me . . . Dear Abby. Is everything all right with you and Andy?"

"Fine. Maybe a little *too* fine."

Grace rolled her eyes. How could anything possibly be *too* fine? If she knew Pat, she was probably upset about something silly.

"When we were in L.A. he said a couple of things that made it sound like he plans on being around for a while."

Grace felt a pang of envy in the pit of her stomach. First Susan snared probably the only black millionaire in Wisconsin, in Kenosha of all places; and now Pat had snagged herself a rich white dude. All right, so she'd had Danny, and he'd been no slouch in either looks or money, but that marriage had ended years ago. Wasn't it time for her to meet another man who had more than two nickels?

She quickly put her feelings aside to answer her friend's question. As she suspected, Pat had gotten all worked up over something that was just plain dumb. "Would that be so awful? I'd grab him if I were you, Pat. Eligible men the right age, and with money to court you . . . They don't grow on trees. Most of the single ones with decent jobs are struggling to pay their kids' college tuition and don't have much left over."

"I know. It's just that I've kept telling myself nothing would come of it. Even though I lost my head and slept with him that first night we had dinner."

Grace made a choking sound. "You didn't tell me *that*."

"I didn't think you'd believe it."

"Believe me, I'm having trouble with it. Pat Maxwell, giving it up on the first date?"

"The bad part is that it wasn't even a date, not really. We were just meeting to have dinner and catch up. But I've always had a crush on him, Grace. He looked real good when he was in his twenties, and he's aged extremely well. I mean, he's not like Mel Gibson, who looks every year of his age. Andy barely looks forty."

Grace shrugged. Andy did look pretty good for a fellow his age, but she didn't know about barely looking forty. "Do you think he's had plastic surgery?" Hell, most white folks aged badly, unless they'd been blessed with good skin and had the brains to not smoke or stay in the sun. Sometimes she couldn't believe some of the celebs who were her own age. Either they looked all wrinkly or they'd had everything pulled so tight they could hardly smile.

"Of course not. He's always been a health nut. Anyway, when he told me I always looked good to him, even back in the day, well, I decided there wasn't any point in waiting any longer. It's already been nearly twenty-five years."

"You and your white men. One of these days I'll have to try me one." She'd had Ricky, of course. But he wasn't white . . . at least most white people wouldn't say so.

"That's what I'm calling to talk to you about. He already mentioned introducing me to his daughters."

"He has?"

Pat chuckled. Grace sounded so surprised. "I know. It took me off guard, too. But if I meet his family, it's only fair that he meet mine. And you know my parents."

"That I do. Pat, what happened to all that talk about standing up to your parents if you and Ricky got back together? Why would that apply to Ricky and not to Andy?" She paused. "You're still in love with Ricky, aren't you?"

"No, of course not. That would be silly."

"You might *say* it's silly, Pat, but everything you do or say suggests it's the truth. You wouldn't let your parents' feelings interfere if you had a second chance, but with Andy you're hesitant. And then there's the way you interrogated me about what he said that night when Stephanie and I went to Nirvana. Like it could possibly matter after all this time."

"I was just curious—"

"Bullshit. Listen, I hate to be blunt, but if you're still afraid of your parents at this point in your life, you *deserve* to lose Andy. Your brothers, rest their souls, have both been gone a long time now. Maybe you were in a tricky spot thirty years ago, but there's no need to tiptoe around a sensitive issue for your parents, not now."

Grace had always felt that Pat should have asked Ricky for another year before going public with their engagement. Her parents' wounds were still too raw from losing their son Melvin. The timing was all wrong. If she'd done that, everything probably would have worked out, even if her parents still weren't thrilled about the match. By the time the Maxwells's oldest child, Clarence, took his fatal heroin overdose three years later, Pat and Ricky could have been married. Instead, Mr. and Mrs. Maxwell grabbed at her like she was their lifeline. No child should have to bear the responsibility of all his or her parents' hopes and dreams. "It's your damn life," she added.

"I know, Grace, but—"

"No. I don't even want to hear the excuses, Pat. I've heard

them all before. You've got a good thing going. Hell, if you don't want Andy, maybe *I'll* take him."

"Thanks, Grace. And I did hear everything you said."

"I hope so."

Grace hung up, shaking her head. What the hell was wrong with Pat? Didn't she know to jump on a good thing when she saw one?

She certainly hadn't hesitated the day she read that article in the *Tribune* about Enrique "Ricky" Suárez, Chicago's rising new restaurateur. She started planning right away to show up at his restaurant and renew old acquaintances. There was the sticky matter of what to say when he inevitably asked about Pat, but she quickly decided to tell him she was unavailable.

He'd hugged her hello as an amazed Stephanie from the gym looked on, then sat down beside her in the booth, and in conversation mentioned his recent divorce. She quickly told him that her marriage to her second husband was officially over. "How's Pat?" he asked, almost too casually.

Grace hadn't been fooled. Ricky still carried a torch for Pat, after all these years. It was only natural to start wondering about old flames when a marriage ended. Lord knew she didn't have much to say to Jimmy, her first husband, whenever he came to Chicago to visit his mother and Shavonne, while she was married to Danny. But once Danny and she broke up, she didn't hesitate to hit the sheets with Jimmy during his visits for some good, unencumbered sex. She forgot all about Jimmy after he returned home, and she knew the nonfeelings were mutual. It angered her that all Ricky could think about was Pat, especially when she just told him *she* was available. So what if he and Jimmy had been friends, and if she and Pat were still friends. Hell, high school was eons ago. Jimmy was long gone, and as for Pat, well, she didn't want Ricky enough to tell her parents to stay out of her business, so how could she complain if *she* took him?

Grace heard herself saying, "Oh, she's fine. She's seeing someone, and I'm waiting for those wedding bells to start ringing."

She got even angrier at the sight of Ricky's crestfallen expression. "I should have known," he said sadly.

Sure, like he really thought anything would have changed in twenty years, Grace thought with annoyance. The moment Pat told her parents she was seeing Ricky again, they would have told her that she should forget about him and find herself a nice black man. And Pat would be too afraid of disappointing them to go against their advice.

Pat hadn't been seeing anyone, of course. Grace justified the lie by telling herself that she'd saved Ricky additional heartbreak against the inevitable—Pat choosing her parents over him a second time—if he resumed their old romance.

Moving quickly, Grace excused herself to Stephanie, stood up and linked her arm through his as she steered him out of Stephanie's earshot. "Tell you what," she suggested. "You and I both have the postdivorce blues. What say we have a nice buddies' dinner at my new condo? I'll even cook, and we can drown our sorrows together, with the understanding that come morning, we leave all those woe-is-me feelings behind us."

Ricky had grinned. "Sure, why not? I think you've got a point there. Get all that self-pity out of the way all at once."

She quickly pinned him down to coming that Friday night, by which time she knew she had him. How wonderful life would be. Grace imagined stopping in at Nirvana to have dinner with him nightly at their reserved table, making suggestions for new dishes, having her photo taken with celebrities whenever someone took over the private room upstairs for a function . . . The only fly in the ointment was how Pat would take the news. Even after twenty years, Grace knew she still carried a torch for her first love. If you asked her, it was silly. Pat knew damn well that she'd never defy her parents, and her parents—especially her father—were bullheaded enough to rather see her alone than with Ricky Suárez, just because he wasn't black. The irony was, no one would consider him white. He was certainly darker than Susan, nearly as brown as Pat herself.

She could readily understand why women deemed him so attractive. He'd been blessed with his mother's good looks: soulful brown eyes, thick black hair. He'd been an all-around athlete in high school, participating in most sports the school offered: football in the fall, basketball over the winter, and baseball in the spring. That old conditioning from high school and college—he had gone to the University of Arkansas on a baseball scholarship—had likely remained with him, judging from his toned abs.

But in the end theirs was nothing more than a quick fling of wild sex. That was all it was *supposed* to be, at least in Ricky's mind, but Grace hoped he would want to keep her in his life. Instead, after a scant two weeks together, he told her that he just didn't feel right about sleeping with her when she was supposed to be Pat's best friend.

"I *am* Pat's best friend, and what you're saying doesn't make a lick of sense," she'd protested. "If you and Pat were together now, we wouldn't be sleeping together. I'm certainly not the type of woman to cheat with my friends' men behind their backs." In her indignation, she conveniently forgot all about how she'd lied about Pat being in a serious relationship. "But all that happened over twenty years ago, Ricky. It was nothing more than kid stuff."

"Pat and I might have been kids, but we were truly in love, and something like that you never forget. Do you regard Jimmy as kid stuff, Grace?"

She bristled at the mention of her first husband. "We were kids," she said. "Kids who got caught. I love my daughter, but my being pregnant was the only reason Jimmy and I got married in the first place."

"Well, I'm sorry you don't harbor any special feelings for Jimmy, but the fact remains that I'll always have good memories of being with Pat."

"Yeah, and when she had to choose between you and her parents, she dropped you like you had a contagious disease."

She hoped that would rile him, bring him to his senses, but Ricky merely shrugged.

"That devastated me, but she did the only thing she could have done. One of her brothers had just been killed, and the other one had become a junkie. In hindsight, the timing wasn't right for us to get engaged. Her parents transferred all the hope they had left into her future. And it wasn't all about my being Mexican. No one would mistake me for white, and I've known as much discrimination as you have. I think they would have felt a lot better about our being engaged if I wasn't poor. Mr. and Mrs. Maxwell were afraid Pat would waste her life on me."

"And she didn't have faith in you to believe that you'd make something of yourself one day. Such devotion," Grace said sarcastically.

He shook his head, not speaking, but not giving in, either.

She lost her temper. "Too bad you didn't knock her up. Then you two could have gotten married—the Maxwells wouldn't have wanted Pat to have a baby out of wedlock any more than my parents did—and your memories of her would be as fond as mine are of Jimmy," she snapped.

"Grace, we need to admit we made a mistake."

His calm demeanor infuriated her. He made breaking up with her sound no more complex than deciding which wine to drink with dinner. It hurt for her to face the truth: He never even considered her as a serious love interest. Instead he saw her as no more than someone to jump in the sack with while he adjusted to the life of a single man after separating from his wife.

He was no better than Douglas Valentine, a damn cocaine addict whose life was going nowhere fast. She'd gone after Douglas after Susan quit him, thinking she might be able to keep him under control and get him back into the NBA. She'd still been low on the career totem pole back then, and life in the NBA seemed so exciting. Besides, she had to be on the lookout for a successful man. Her mama had warned her that men didn't like it when women had more education or made more money than they did, and pro athletes made plenty of money.

Within two dates she knew Douglas was hopeless and left him alone. Susan would never know what she'd done, but Grace doubted she would have cared. At least Douglas didn't hold on to any stupid romantic notions about Susan and her being friends . . . or that he and Jimmy were buddies as well. She and Jimmy were on the rocks by then, anyway, and Grace knew Jimmy was messing around.

She sighed and picked up her book, but her thoughts didn't allow her to concentrate on it. So her plan to make Ricky her third husband hadn't worked. For once Pat was seeing someone with real promise while she stood on the sidelines, listening to Pat talk about all the expensive places Andy took her while she and Eric went to the movies and places like Chili's and Panera Bread. Grace didn't like being the one out in the cold. She was the only one of her longtime friends lacking a suitable partner.

Susan was married, of course. But look at poor Elyse, with a deathly ill husband. Medical science had made great strides in recent years, but pancreatic cancer still represented a real hurdle. Pat had asked her to ride up to Lake County to call on Elyse last weekend, and Grace was secretly glad when Elyse asked them to make it another time because her parents were visiting from Tennessee. Grace wasn't good at handling these types of situations; she never knew what to say. They must have gotten the pathology results by now. Grace could only hope the news had been good. Surely if it hadn't been, Pat would have mentioned it. It seemed that all she talked about these days was Andy.

Grace was glad Pat had found someone she liked, but she thought Pat a fool for worrying. She clearly hadn't learned a thing from all that uproar with Ricky. Plus, she was getting way ahead of herself. Andy might not mind letting his kids know he was seeing a black woman, for kids today tended to be more broadminded about these things, but he might be just as reluctant to introduce her to his parents as Pat was to present him to hers.

It was ridiculous for Pat to allow her parents to call the shots. If she'd played her cards right, she would be happily married to Ricky Suárez today. And Ricky wouldn't have made a bad husband.

That's why she'd tried so hard to get him for herself.

Chapter 36

Elyse, her arm linked through Franklin's, waved jauntily at a passing neighbor. She and Franklin had taken to walking around the neighborhood after dinner. She wanted everyone to see Franklin up and about, to quell any rumors about his imminent demise. Elyse knew how people gossiped, even though she knew it came out of concern. After fifteen years in this house, she and Franklin had gotten to know their neighbors fairly well. They looked out for each other's children and property. Several people had brought covered dishes over while Franklin was hospitalized, just to make things easier for her.

They'd deliberately been close-mouthed about his illness, mentioning the word "cancer" but not its origin. Pancreatic cancer had such a negative connotation to it; she didn't want anyone starting a death watch. For all their neighbors knew, Franklin had merely had a patch of skin cancer removed although she'd heard that some skin cancers could be particularly grueling and require all kinds of treatment.

It was wonderful to see Franklin back to his old self. His hair was growing out, and he had regained much of his strength. They were even making love again.

"Oh, look, here's the ice-cream truck," he said. "I feel like a good old-fashioned chocolate fudge cake ice-cream bar."

"Do you really?"

He patted his midsection. "Ice cream will help me pick up some of the weight I've lost."

Elyse squeezed his arm. "Come on, let's go get it. We can get a couple, and we'll put them in the freezer. Hell, I'll buy him out."

"Elyse, I know you're trying to fatten me up. I've never eaten so much fried food in my life. You've even been frying broccoli, for crying out loud."

She shrugged. "I like fried zucchini and you don't. But broccoli florets work in the batter just as well."

"I'm not complaining. But don't get carried away, okay? No point in going into remission if you're going to clog my arteries."

"All right. But let's catch the truck before it drives off." It delighted her that he wanted to eat dessert. He was usually too full after dinner. Of course, she'd been cooking a lot of high-calorie foods, like mashed potatoes and gravy and macaroni and cheese, along with the usual meat and vegetables.

Franklin's recovery helped him develop an optimistic outlook about his future, and that in turn raised her own spirits. Frankie and Rebecca weren't hovering around as much as they used to, thank God. Elyse doubted that she could ever look at her stepchildren the same way after the contemptible way they'd questioned her. How dare they think she would take less than optimum care of Franklin!

As her life slowly returned to normal, Elyse didn't see as much of her old friends anymore. Pat, Susan, and Grace had come to spend a few hours with her when she needed them the most, and of course there'd been Kevin.

She'd felt so guilty after he kissed her. Why had he done that? Although their phone chats had slowed down to a crawl as Franklin recovered, she still looked forward to lunching with him, but his inappropriate behavior had put a stop to that. She sent him an e-mail that same day and told him that she didn't feel that they should see each other anymore. He wrote back telling her how sorry he was. He asked her not to blame him because he found her attractive. She reminded him that his action had been unsuitable and suggested that they limit their future correspondence to an occasional e-mail.

Elyse did appreciate his being there and helping her through a difficult time, though, and she sent him a gift card to have lunch on her.

As for Pat, Grace, and Susan, she knew they were all busy with their own lives. Susan's husband had taken the family up to Lake Geneva over Memorial Day, Pat had flown to L.A. for a long weekend with her new boyfriend, and Grace . . . Well, maybe she'd gotten as far as the Oak Street Beach.

Elyse chided herself for being so petty, but she was annoyed at Grace. When she'd mentioned how caring and concerned Kevin had been during Franklin's diagnosis, Grace had promptly asked what he did for a living. Grace then nicknamed Kevin "The Orkin Man," which Elyse thought was just plain mean. She knew it had to be eating Grace up inside that Pat had captured the attention, perhaps even the heart, of a rich man, while Grace was stuck with that Wade kid. He really couldn't be called a kid, but he was younger than them by four or five years. Grace's way of not liking anyone to achieve more than she did was well known by anyone who knew her.

But Elyse was truly happy for Pat. She'd done the only thing her conscience would allow at a tragic time for her family and given up the man she loved to help ease her parents' pain. But thirty years later she was still alone. Maybe this thing with the fellow she'd first met in law school would really turn into something.

Chapter 37

Late July
Pleasant Prairie, Wisconsin, Illinois

Susan awakened on the morning of her fiftieth birthday feeling better than she had in a long time. Quentin and Alyssa presented her with orange juice and a pink grapefruit on a tray that held fresh flowers in a small vase and a newspaper . . . at eight in the morning, with Bruce bringing up the rear.

"Oh," she said groggily, propping herself up on her elbows. "How sweet, kids. But it's awfully early, don't you think?"

"You're usually up by now, Mom," Quentin said. "You and Daddy must have had soooome celebration last night."

Susan met Bruce's eyes. Last night he'd taken her to dinner and dancing on a boat out on Lake Michigan, after which they came home, sent the babysitter on her way, and made love. But all Bruce's preparations and attempts to make her feel special left her feeling strangely empty. He'd made romantic gestures, like kissing the back of her hand; and he even managed to squeeze her left breast, although he still avoided the right one, from which the cancer had been removed. Susan didn't see the action as building up toward where they had been before her surgery; she saw it as a valiant attempt to recapture something they'd lost, an attempt she now knew could never be successful. She also couldn't help wondering what was behind Bruce's sudden change of heart.

But as she fell asleep with Bruce's arm wrapped around her, all she could think of was Charles.

She'd driven down to Chicago twice more during the kids' last week of school. Since then, seeing him had been more of a challenge. Susan had a housekeeper come in every Wednesday, and she often ran errands during that time, leaving the woman in the house with Quentin and Alyssa. On other days when she needed to go out she asked a fourteen-year-old girl from the neighborhood to stay with Quentin and Alyssa. The problem was that most of the time she actually did have errands to run: the bank, the supermarket, the dry cleaner. She'd managed to see Charles just once, meeting him at a small Italian restaurant in nearby Zion, across the Illinois border.

She'd already acknowledged with sadness that it wouldn't be possible to see him on her actual birthday. Since it was a Sunday, Bruce was home. They were all going to dinner in Kenosha: she and Bruce, the kids, her long-divorced parents, and Sherry and her family. Charles accepted the situation, but she could tell he didn't like it much.

Susan suggested to Charles that they meet for lunch Monday in Zion, under the guise of a shopping trip. She knew Bruce wouldn't be suspicious, for he always gave her money for her birthday; and the kids hated going shopping and preferred to stay at home. Charles agreed to this. Already she couldn't wait to see him.

Funny. She used to feel guilty for cheating on Bruce . . . But now being intimate with Bruce made her feel like she was cheating on *Charles*.

Susan rushed into the garage at 11:45 Monday morning, car keys in hand. She activated the garage door opener, then began backing out. A telltale *thump-thump-thump* made her heart stand still. She shifted into PARK and jumped out to inspect her tires.

The tire on the rear driver's side was completely flat.

She cursed under her breath, then got back into the car to get her cell phone. She punched in Charles's number. No way could she meet him at noon; it would probably take an hour for the auto club to get here and repair her tire.

He answered. "I'm about a block away from the restaurant. Are you there already?"

"No. I'm afraid there's a problem." She told him about the tire.

"I'll come get you."

"Charles, you can't. Someone might see you. My kids might see you and ask questions. I can't risk that."

"I didn't plan on ringing the doorbell, Susan. Just walk down the street. Your kids will never know the difference. They think you've left already, don't they? Now, you're near the lake, so that tells me I should keep going north across the state line and then head east?"

"Uh . . . yes."

He hung up before she could protest. She didn't bother to call him back. Charles could be awfully stubborn sometimes. Instead she went to the front of the garage and stood in the corner near the opened garage door. The kids never came into the garage, so they wouldn't notice the car still there. Her neighbors, though, were another matter.

She saw no activity on the other side of the street. Her neighbors were probably preparing lunch or relaxing in their yards. Still, she could see only one side of the street, the opposite side. For all she knew someone on this side of the street could be out tending to his or her front yard. It would look mighty suspicious if she started walking down the street carrying her purse, like she was going somewhere on foot. It would look worse if someone spotted her getting into a Blazer with Illinois plates. Someone with a flair for the dramatic might think she was being abducted and call the police.

An idea occurred to her. She went back to the car, opened the trunk with her remote, and dropped her purse inside, retaining only her cell phone and keys. If she went for a walk, better to do it without a purse. She'd look more like someone just out for exercise.

At the garage door she paused once more, then walked halfway down the driveway and glanced up and down the street, which appeared quiet. Maybe she had nothing to worry about after all.

Her cell phone rang, and she retreated toward the garage to take Charles's call. "Are you here?"

"I'm on Lake Shore Drive. Any farther east and I'd be in the damn lake. What number is your house?"

She told him.

"All right. Looks like I'm going the right way. I should be there in about two minutes."

"Okay. I'm coming out now. Just keep driving." She hurriedly broke the connection, stuffed the cell phone back in the pocket of her capri pants, speed-walked out of the garage, and closed it with the remote she kept on the ring with her car keys. All she had to do now was prevent anyone from seeing her get into Charles's truck, and she'd be fine.

She'd barely gotten to the curb when she spotted his Blazer approaching. He pulled over between her house and her neighbor's, and she hastily got in.

"That was fast," she said. To her despair, he made no move to drive on.

"This is some house," he said. "Is *this* where you live?"

"Be it ever so humble," she said, feeling slightly embarrassed.

"Humble, my ass. It's a damn McMansion! It's practically a castle. Is that a whatchamacallit . . . a *turret?*"

"Yes. Let's go, Charles. I really don't want my kids to come running outside and see me with you."

"Oh, sure." He started to drive, but slowly, his eyes focused on her house rather than the road. "Damn!" he exclaimed. "I knew your husband made good money, but it didn't occur to me that y'all lived like *this.*"

"Business is good," she said matter-of-factly. "People will always use credit cards. Somebody has to process all those transactions." She shrugged.

"I didn't realize that credit card processing paid so well," he remarked dryly after he'd resumed a normal residential speed. "How many rooms does that house have?"

"Four bedrooms, a home office, a bonus room, a family room, and three and a half baths."

Charles whistled. "And it's right on the lake. I suppose you've got a beach on your property?"

"Yes. Bruce provides quite nicely for us. I'm not bragging, Charles. I'm just stating a fact."

"No wonder you're so reluctant to leave him."

She looked at him through eyes suddenly gone narrow. "That has nothing to do with anything. I'm not happy with him."

"And no wonder you were so skeptical when I said I could take care of you."

She looked straight ahead and sighed. Maybe this outing hadn't been such a good idea. She didn't want to think about how a radical change in living environment would affect Quinton and Alyssa, nor her desperate need for medical insurance. She'd just turned fifty and was living in comfortable but miserable circumstances . . . and she was too frightened of an uncertain future to do anything about it. Charles being so freaked out at the sight of her house did nothing to help. Didn't he understand it wasn't merely about how much money he had?

"I thought today was supposed to be about my birthday," she reminded him gently.

"You're right. So, how'd the big day go?"

"Nice," she admitted. "We all went out to dinner. My mom, my sister, her husband, their kids . . . even my father. Getting everyone together at once doesn't happen too often, and I'm happy to report that no one got hurt."

"You celebrated turning fifty by going out to dinner? That seems kind of ordinary for such a milestone."

"Bruce offered me a trip out of town, but truth be told, I didn't feel all that much like celebrating. Dinner with the family meant a lot to me. Plus, Bruce and I went out Saturday night. We went on one of those dinner cruises on Lake Michigan."

"Did you have a nice time?"

She turned to him, exasperated and knowing that he really didn't want to hear about her night out with Bruce any more than she wanted to talk about it. Charles didn't know that she and Bruce occasionally still had sex; she'd deliberately given him the impression that Bruce was so turned off by her post-lumpectomy body that he didn't come near her. She knew it was wrong to mislead him, but she also knew that if Charles knew the truth he would insist she leave Bruce right away. She couldn't blame him. What man wanted to feel like he was sharing his woman? And what kind of woman would consent to being shared?

The kind of woman Ann Valentine said I was.

Charles's mother would have a field day if she knew what was going on. Susan tried to chase the thought away, but it stuck like peanut butter to her palate. Her life had become so complicated. She never would have believed she'd ever find herself in such a pickle.

"Why are we even talking about this, Charles?" she asked.

"I asked a simple question. I don't see a need for all the fuss."

"No," Susan said forcefully. "I tried not to show it, but I *didn't* have a good time. I wanted to be with you. All right? Do you feel better now?"

He braked for a stop light, then swiftly leaned over, his palm bringing the back of her head closer, and kissed her hard. It felt too good for her to be concerned about who might recognize her. She moaned approval, the familiar tingling coming over her body.

Charles broke away from her. "*That* makes me feel better."

"It only makes me want more," she said softly.

They had reached the main street, Sheridan Road. Charles turned right. "Charles, you're going the wrong way," she said. "Zion is that way." She pointed to the left.

"But my hotel is this way."

"Your hotel?"

He grinned at her. "I didn't want to spring this on you until after lunch, but I'm going to stay up here for a couple of days. I could stand some time away from home, and maybe you'll be able to drop in if I'm not too far away."

"But I won't have a whole lot of time, Charles. What'll you do all day?"

"Oh, maybe take a tour of the Jelly Belly factory, or do some shopping at the outlet mall."

She laughed. "Are we going to the mall now?"

"I'm sure they've got restaurants around there."

"Let's see what your room looks like first. I'm hungry, but not for food."

He took his hand off the wheel long enough to squeeze hers. "I like your thinking."

* * *

Susan got home at four-thirty. She carried bags from Chico's and from Bass Shoes, having stopped at the outlet mall after lunch, walking arm in arm with Charles. She felt happy, fulfilled, and satiated.

It surprised her when Bruce arrived home at a little past six. That meant he'd left work on time. Come to think of it, he really hadn't been late for some time now, probably from around the same time she first started sleeping with Charles. He usually got in by seven at the latest, which, considering that it took him an hour to get home, didn't leave him much time for play.

The four of them sat down to dinner together, and when they finished Susan moved quickly to put away the pork chops she'd made, load the dishwasher, and wipe down the table and counters. Even as she did this she caught Bruce eyeing her long legs, and instinct told her he wanted sex tonight, of all nights.

After she swept the kitchen floor, the dishwasher already humming through its cycle, she went upstairs to shower. Eyes closed, she thought of the blissful afternoon with Charles as she scrubbed away all traces of his touch. She even washed her hair, towel-drying it and leaving the hand towel on her head, wrapped turban-style.

Susan was changing into her sleepwear—a pair of pretty if not particularly sexy shorty pajamas she'd bought earlier—when Bruce entered their bedroom as she was bending to put on the panty bottoms. She held her breath. He rarely came into their bedroom so early.

Relax, she told herself. *If he seems amorous, you know how to kill the mood. Just take off your top and parade around topless.*

"What's that?" he asked.

"What's what?"

"That thing sticking out of your underwear." He moved closer.

Susan went rigid. Was there something on her panties that would give away what she'd done this afternoon?

Bruce closed the distance between them with a few strides. "Oh, it's a tag. You've got on your panties inside out."

She laughed nervously as her fingers closed around the tag,

then moved to the side and felt inverted seams. "Well, *that's* a first," she said. She pulled them down, flipped them right side out, and then pulled them up with a furious yank. Her movements seemed slow and clumsy to her, and she cursed herself for not moving faster.

"Hey, what's your hurry?" Bruce's hand poked inside her waistband, first cupping her behind and then poking his finger the last place she wanted it.

She stiffened. She *couldn't* have sex with Bruce tonight, not after being intimate with Charles just a few hours ago. Taking a shower didn't make her feel better about having sex with two men within the space of a few hours' time. She wasn't a slut, and she had an unpleasant vision of Ann Valentine shaking her finger in her face and saying, *"What kind of woman sleeps with both a man and his brother?"*

"I thought I'd go to bed a little early tonight, Bruce. My throat feels a little sore." Her throat felt fine. It was her head that was throbbing, but she didn't want to give that as an excuse. The old, "Not tonight dear, I've got a headache" pretext sounded so lame. Headaches had long since become synonymous with evading sex, even when it was a legitimate complaint.

Bruce moved behind her and ran his hands over her slightly soft and rounded belly. "You might be older, Susan, but you still look good," he whispered, nuzzling at her neck.

Oh, God. It had been agony to have sex with him since Charles had been in her life. Before that she would have welcomed his advances. But everything had changed.

"I'm sorry you don't feel well. Go ahead and get in bed. Can I fix you a cup of tea?"

"No, thanks. I swallowed a spoonful of honey and gargled with some saltwater. I'll probably be fine tomorrow. All I need is a good night's sleep."

"Sure, go ahead." He landed a noisy kiss on her cheek, and she tried not to wince. "Let me know if you need anything."

Susan felt a thousand years old as she climbed between the cool sheets of their king-sized bed. She didn't know what to make of Bruce's behavior. It hadn't been fair for him to starve her of his affections for so long, then all of a sudden start acting like it was old times. She had breast cancer. She felt lucky to be able to keep her breast. It wasn't right for Bruce to act like she had a contagious disease. Did he have the vaguest idea of how much he'd hurt her by acting like her breasts didn't exist? It wasn't her problem he couldn't accept her body; it was his.

She was still the same person, and he was supposed to love her no matter what. Now, after she gave in and received such tenderness from Charles, here came Bruce, as considerate and thoughtful as he'd been in the early days of their courtship. But even as he held her from behind and nuzzled her, he still hadn't touched her chest. Maybe he was feeling guilty about not showing her affection.

She didn't want to continue living with a husband who cared about her but wasn't attracted to her. But what was the alternative? Divorce? That came with its own set of hurdles. For one, it would mean the end of her health insurance. As a breast cancer patient, she couldn't afford to be without good coverage. The only way she could get coverage would be if she had a full-time job. No way could she get insurance on her own, not with the state of her health. She represented too great a risk to insurance companies as someone who would actually need to *use* her health insurance, not merely pay premiums and file claims only occasionally.

Susan wondered how much money she could earn as a working woman. She held an accounting degree, but things had certainly changed in eleven years. She feared the business world wouldn't view her as an asset because of her long absence. She'd be considered more of a novice. What kind of life could she provide for Quentin and Alyssa on the salary of a recent college graduate? She could probably get Bruce to willingly contribute alimony, as well as child support, but if she married Charles the alimony would stop. Quentin and Alyssa would have to live in whatever surroundings she and Charles could afford to provide, which would be much less elegant than the large house on the banks of Lake Michigan they were accustomed to. That alone could cause problems. The kids might even say they wanted to stay with Bruce! Bruce, of course, would love that. He'd hire a live-in nanny and go about his business.

Where would she and Charles even settle? It couldn't be

Chicago; there was school to consider. They'd have to live in a good district, like Buffalo Grove or Lake Forest.

She leaned backward, her face raised and eyes closed. There was so much to consider when starting a new life. No wonder so many women chose to stay in unfulfilling marriages rather than go through all the changes. But just because she'd fended off Charles today didn't mean the subject wouldn't come up again.

She blinked. Wait a minute. She didn't have to do *everything* at once, did she? Why couldn't she start slowly, by getting a job? That way she could tell what kind of updating her skills needed. At least she did remember the basics of accounting; those would never change. She could look for something part-time. Surely Bruce wouldn't object to that.

She brought up the subject the next night at dinner, after Quentin and Alyssa were granted permission to leave the table. "Bruce, I think I'd like to go back to work," she said as she set down a second helping of pork chops and fried potatoes before him.

"I don't know, Susan. The kids are still kind of young. I know Quentin is almost eleven, but Alyssa just turned eight. We agreed before that you would be here for them until they're in junior high. That's still four years away for Alyssa. So why the change?"

"I just don't feel like I'm doing enough with my life, Bruce. And I wasn't thinking about working full-time. Just something part-time that I can do while they're in school."

"What about school holidays and summer vacation?"

"Oh." She hadn't thought of that. "Maybe the kids can go to day camp or something. After all these years of being a stay-at-home mom, I'm feeling a little bored." Then she played her trump card, her one shot at keeping at bay any suspicions Bruce might have about her motives. "I find the more idle I am, the more I worry about what the future holds." She hated to use her illness as a cover for her desire to get on her feet, and she wondered if God would punish her for it.

The list of reprehensible things she'd done was getting longer by the week.

She certainly wasn't getting any sympathy from Bruce. "I understand that, Susan," he said. "But I don't want the kids in day care. We agreed a long time ago that you would be home at the end of the school day. I think it's important for mothers to be home when their kids get out of school."

"My mother wasn't, and my sister and I turned out all right."

"Out of necessity. Your mother had to work because your father drank up so much of his paycheck."

All she could do was shrug. She'd held nothing back from Bruce about her home life. He wasn't rubbing it in her face; he was merely pointing out a fact.

"But I always envisioned that you would stay home with the kids until they were older, and then go back to work and add to their college funds. We can afford for you not to work. I understand that you feel a little anxious about your health, but I'd advise that you do volunteer work at a hospital or a nursing home. It'll keep you busy, it should be rewarding, and best of all, you can go in when it's convenient for you."

She sighed. That wasn't the solution she was looking for, but she'd opened the door, saying she sought fulfillment. What else could she say? *"I can't work for free, Bruce! I need to sharpen my skills so I can increase my earnings potential and live decently after I leave you,"* just wouldn't work. She didn't want him to know about her plans until she was good and ready for him to know. From the time she gave up her job just before Quentin's birth, Bruce had taken care of her, paid all her bills, kept the roof over her head and food in her mouth. He'd never been bad with money, certainly never denied her anything she wanted, but of course what she wanted now wouldn't go over too well. Instinct told her not to spill the beans until she absolutely had to.

The same instinct told her he wouldn't budge from his stance about her working.

And she also instinctively knew that Charles wouldn't be patient for very much longer.

Never before had she felt so hemmed in.

Chapter 38

Late July
Chicago

Pat decided that Andy must have told his daughters about her being black. Neither Lauren nor Kaitlyn blinked when he brought them to his Hyde Park town house to meet her. She could discern no signs of discomfort or even evasion. They spoke to her normally, like their father brought home black girlfriends all the time.

She didn't know what to make of it. None of the men she'd dated had ever introduced her to any of their family members. Maybe it really wasn't a big deal. Or maybe Andy would be served with papers denying him visitation from his ex-wife when the girls told her about their daddy's new girlfriend.

They lounged on Andy's deck, with her close to the town house's back wall, safely under the retractable awning. This was the warmest time of year in Chicago, and Pat liked to stay out of the sun. She wondered if it would be this hot on the Riviera.

"Where's Daddy?" Lauren asked.

"He took a phone call."

"But it's Saturday."

Pat smiled. She wanted to tell the teenager that money never slept, but she didn't want to sound jaded. Funny how kids today took their expensive possessions for granted. Did Lauren have any idea that all the kids in America didn't have a car of their own, or split their time between the Hyde Park town house of their father and the suburban estate of their mother and stepfather, who was a publishing executive?

"He's always on the phone," Lauren complained. "I'd hoped he'd spend more time with us, since we go on vacation next week."

"Oh? Where're you going?" Pat asked.

"To Maui," Kaitlyn replied. "I'm going to get better at surfing this year."

Pat nodded. "You've been there before."

"A couple of times," Kaitlyn said breezily. "Haven't you?"

"Well, yes," Pat admitted. "But I only went once, and it was a while ago. I'm going on vacation next week, too. I'm going to cruise the Mediterranean." She couldn't keep the pride out of her voice.

"We went on that cruise two years ago, before my mother and stepfather got married," Kaitlyn said. "It was a lot of fun. We went on a Disney ship."

"If this is your first time, you'll love Cannes," Lauren added confidently.

Pat's eyebrows shot up. Had these kids been *everywhere?*

The patio door opened, and Andy came outside. "Sorry about that. How're all my girls?"

The dark lenses of the sunglasses he wore hid his eyes, but Pat sensed he was looking dead at her.

"I'm hungry, Daddy," Lauren said. "Are we going to dinner?"

"You're amazing. You've been nibbling on those hamburgers I cooked ever since lunchtime."

"I'm a growing girl," she said with a shrug.

"You keep eating like that and you'll be as wide as you are tall."

"I wish I could eat like Lauren," Kaitlyn said, "but I gain weight."

"Yes, my dear, you take after your daddy," Andy said, giving his youngest daughter an affectionate hug. He glanced at his watch. "It's six-thirty. I made a reservation for seven-thirty, so you might want to get dressed. You can't wear shorts."

"Where're we going?" Pat asked.

"A place where I had lunch with a client last week. I think you'll enjoy it. It's called Nirvana."

Chapter 39

Late July
Chicago

Grace was awakened from dozing by the jerking of Eric's chest, as well as the loud cry that came from his mouth. Her eyes fixed on the TV screen. Someone must have scored a knockout, if his reaction was any indicator.

Sure enough, one of the boxers was struggling to his feet as the referee in his trademark black and white striped shirt performed a countdown. Grace wasn't a boxing fan, but even she could tell that the boxer wasn't going to make it.

"It's over!" one of the commentators shouted.

"Damn, that was a good fight," Eric said.

"I missed most of it."

"I know. I heard you snoring."

"I don't snore!" she said indignantly.

"Baby, you can't hear yourself when you sleep. Trust me, you snore like a buzz saw." He laughed. "Get up, will you? It's not hot in here, but you're soaked. What're you doing, flashing?"

"Of course not," she lied. "I get periods every month, as you well know."

"Well, you're sweating like a convict on a chain gang. Must be part of getting old."

Grace sat up. From the very beginning, Eric occasionally said something that could be construed as nasty about her age, or her education, or her condo, or even her car. She thought it was his way of coping with the fact that she made so much more money than he did. Lately, though, the comments were coming more often.

That was one reason why she preferred coming here to his place rather than having him come to hers, so she could get up and leave first thing in the morning. Another reason was his smoking.

The first time he'd seen her floor-through condo, he knew she was no secretary. "You said you ran things in a department, but it looks more like you run the damn company," he'd said.

Grace recognized the slight accusatory nature of his tone and immediately recognized that he felt threatened. They'd both grown up during a time when men brought home the bacon and paid the bills while women cooked and cleaned, when a woman out-earning a man was unheard of. This was what her mother feared, that she'd earned her way out of the marriage market.

"How many bills a place like this go for?" he'd asked, and she watched his features harden as she explained it wasn't a rental, it was a condo unit.

She'd seen that look many times before. She took a moment to be grateful that she'd hidden away her sculptures and other evidence of worldwide travel. It was a real pain packing them away and then taking them out again after he left, but she saw no need to rub her success in his face.

"What kinda car you drive?" was Eric's next question.

"I've got a little Mercedes. Eric, is something wrong?" The question had been a mere formality . . . She already knew exactly what bothered him.

"I'm not used to all this. A condo in Lincoln Park, a Mercedes. Tell me what you do again?"

That was how their relationship had started. After that she began suggesting that she come to his place. Eric lived in an apartment above the office on the property of the moving and storage unit he managed on the far South Side. He was a neat freak, perhaps in reaction to the squalor of his family's apartment in Dreiser. Grace thought his apartment was cleaner than her condo. He kept it aired out, too—the only sign of his smoking habit was the few butts in his frequently emptied ashtrays.

Another thing she liked about his place was that it was well secured, with a keypad-controlled gate. She could spend the night there without worrying about her car being broken into.

"So when do you leave for your big, fancy trip again?" he asked.

"We fly out Wednesday night. We come back a week from Monday."

"A week and a half?"

"Well, the actual cruise is ten days. Part of the time is spent flying to Madrid and back."

"That's pretty cool. I'll bet you take a trip like that every year. Maybe you ought to think about bringing me with you. I've never been out of the country, except to Canada once."

She stiffened. By "bring me with you," she knew that Eric expected her to pay his way.

"How much that trip cost, anyway?"

"What difference does it make?"

"Whoa! You sound a little sharp there, Grace."

She knew he was right and tried to soften her tone. "I didn't mean to."

"Hey, I know I got a rich old lady. I got no problem with it."

"Eric, I'd appreciate it if you'd stop calling me old. Fifty is the new forty, remember?"

He shrugged. "You're just being overly sensitive. So while you're on this Carnival cruise, you want me to take care of your car and your place?"

She didn't bother to point out that she wasn't sailing on the cruise line he named. "I've already told my neighbors that I'm going away. They'll keep an eye on my place for me."

"What about your car?"

"I always park it at one of the lots outside O'Hare. There's someone on duty twenty-four hours a day, so it's safe."

"I'll bet that costs a pretty penny, especially with you gone so long."

"Pat splits it with me, so it's not bad." If he thought she was going to give him free rein of her condo and her Mercedes while she was out of the country, he had another thought coming. He couldn't even hide the hopefulness in his voice. "But I appreciate your offer just the same."

He shrugged, then grabbed her left breast, squeezing it through her blouse. Then he undid the buttons, revealing a floral-print bra trimmed in beige lace. "I'll bet your panties match," he said softly. "You wear some pretty underwear. I like how everything matches. I never seen that before."

Grace was tempted to ask what kind of women he'd been dating over the years. A visual memory of Eric talking with Stacey Noe at Junior's flashed before her eyes. The guys used to say that "Stacey Noe never says no." Things like matching underwear probably meant little to somebody like Stacey, whom Grace was certain had had an affair with Eric at one point, and probably whenever Eric wanted some from her. Did she and the other women he'd been involved with wear plain white underwear? Or did they pair pink bras with yellow panties? She couldn't imagine wearing mismatched underwear. Even if no one would see what she wore beneath her clothes, she wanted to feel pretty, inside and out.

Eric's hands were roaming over her body, and his breathing had become audible. Grace knew he enjoyed her body as much as she enjoyed his. She suspected that she had a better figure than other women he'd known, at least since he'd gotten older and women in his age group were inclined to be heavier.

He started pulling at her clothes. "Get 'em off," he ordered as he moved away to undress himself.

Grace's excitement rose as she stripped, throwing her clothes on the floor. They'd had sex on his brown leather-like couch before, and it looked like they were about to do it again. The two matching hassocks gave them the extra width they needed to be comfortable. Eric might have some uncultured ways about him, but he did know how to get her motor running.

The moment she had her underwear off he pushed her back onto the sofa and dove between her thighs. She moaned, then reached down to cradle his head with her palms and pull him closer. Her left foot couldn't quite reach the edge of the cushion, but she didn't care. She could cope with a little discomfort in her thigh muscle as she held her leg in midair. She knew that he'd be anxious to get inside her before too long.

He slid back. "Turn over," he whispered.

She knew how he wanted it. She flipped over on her stomach and held her hips in the air, backing up so that her knees were close to the edge of the hassock. They both gasped when Eric slid his rigid penis into her, and he began pumping furiously, with Grace meeting him thrust for thrust. The level of excitement was too high, and they both reached climax quickly.

In Grace's opinion, love was the best thing that could happen to a person.

But good sex was the next-best thing.

Chapter 40

Late July
Chicago

Pat tried to calm herself as she entered Nirvana with Andy, Lauren, and Kaitlyn, but her stomach suddenly decided it wanted to be a gymnast. It was Saturday night, the busiest of the week in the hospitality business, so she had little doubt Ricky would be on the premises. By showing up at his place of business with Andy, Ricky would probably think she was trying to get back at him for bringing his wife to the reunion luncheon, which of course wasn't the case. She knew she shouldn't care, but she did. It mattered terribly, and that was why her stomach wouldn't relax.

The restaurant was bustling with activity, so she began to feel better. If Ricky was here—and she felt certain he was—maybe he wouldn't even see her.

The maître d' showed them to their reserved table. Pat found it amusing that Lauren nearly fell off her chair as she leaned to the side to watch trays holding plates of hors d'oeuvres and entrees go by. She knew how the seventeen-year-old felt. She hadn't been particularly hungry when they left Andy's, but now she was ravenous.

"I think I'll have something with shrimp in it," Pat said.

"Me, too," Andy echoed. "Those things look huge, don't they?"

They had placed their orders and were munching on an appetizer sampler when someone approached them from behind.

"Hello, I'm Ricky Suárez, the owner. Just checking to make sure you're pleased with our service and our food."

He smiled at the group, and his expression changed from jovial to quizzical in an almost-humorous manner when he recognized Pat. The shock on his face was comical—he clearly was taken off guard by the race of her companions—and Pat had to hold back a laugh.

He recovered quickly and spoke in a gracious tone. "Pat! I didn't know you were coming down tonight. You should have called me. I would have given you a better table." He bent to give her a friendly embrace as a stunned Andy looked on.

"You two know each other?" he asked.

"All our lives. Our families were neighbors growing up." Ricky made no mention of Dreiser, purposely, Pat thought. He couldn't know whether or not she'd told Andy about having grown up in the projects and didn't want to give anything away that might embarrass her. How considerate . . .

Ricky held out his hand, and Andy shook it while remaining seated. "Andy Keindl. Pat and I went to law school together."

Pat suppressed a smile. Had this chance meeting—at least *she* knew it was purely accidental, even if Ricky didn't—evolved into a turf war? First Ricky told Andy that they grew up together, and now Andy told Ricky that they, too, went back a long way. She wondered if Andy had guessed Ricky was the Mexican her parents forbade her to marry.

"My daughters, Lauren and Kaitlyn," Andy continued.

"So where's the better table?" Kaitlyn asked.

"Kaitlyn, I think this table is just fine," Pat said hastily.

"No point in moving now," Andy agreed. "But thanks."

"You folks enjoy your meal." Ricky placed his palm on Pat's shoulder for what felt like an eternity before moving on.

Feeling strangely ill at ease, she nervously reached for a mozzarella stick and dipped it in the marinara sauce, conscious of Andy's eagle eyes on her. He was a criminal attorney and a damn good one; he made excellent observations and understood body language.

Suddenly Pat could stand it no longer. She felt like her entire body was trembling. Why did Ricky still affect her this way? Any psychiatrist would tell her she needed to move on. She swallowed the last of the appetizer, wiped her hands on her napkin, and announced that she was going to the ladies' room. She needed to splash some cold water on her face, wash her hands, anything to steady herself.

To her dismay, Kaitlyn said she would go with her.

Once inside the lounge, Pat went directly to the sink, and Kaitlyn made no move to use a stall, either. "Pat, I was hoping you'd be able to help me with something."

"If I can. What is it, Kaitlyn?"

The teen spoke in a low voice. "Well, there's this boy at school. Giles Henry."

"Giles? Is he British?"

"No. He's black."

Pat's curiosity soared. She knew that a handful of well-off blacks lived in the monied suburbs of Cook and Lake counties, and if this kid's name was any clue, his family had a few bucks . . . unless he came from a line of butlers. Her curiosity stemmed from Kaitlyn's connection to him. *Lord, please don't let her ask if I know his family, like every black person in the country is supposed to know each other.* Then again, Kaitlyn was fifteen years old and lived in a wealthy suburb. Pat had seen enough legal cases stemming from improperly supervised teenagers getting into trouble to know that it wasn't uncommon among the affluent. What if she'd slept with him already, willingly? Good grief, what if she was pregnant by him and afraid to tell her parents?

"He's really cute. All the girls like him. He's on the basketball team, and he plays baseball, and he's real smart, too. So many of the girls want to take Melanie's place. That's his old girlfriend," Kaitlyn explained. "I was hoping you might be able to help me stand out. Give me some pointers on how to catch his eye."

It relieved Pat to know Kaitlyn's issue was a mere crush rather than something more serious, but she still didn't know how to proceed. She had little experience with young people. Helping high school kids decide on careers was one thing. Helping them in the social graces was something else. This Giles seemed like a heck of a good catch for any girl, but the racial issue made it even more complicated. Just because Andy was dating her didn't mean he wouldn't object to Kaitlyn dating a black student, and, of course, she didn't know Kaitlyn's mother at all. She could hear Andy's ex telling him, "This is all *your* fault. Kaitlyn sees you with a black girlfriend, and now she wants to start dating a black kid."

"Um . . . Kaitlyn, this brings back memories of when I was in high school. Of course, it was a hundred years ago," she said with a laugh. "I'm afraid I can't really make any suggestions other than to just be yourself. Uh . . . Do you think that Giles being black might . . ." No, that wasn't how she wanted to say it. "I would suggest that you make sure that . . . that your parents won't object to your dating Giles, if everything works out for you."

"You mean because he's African-American?"

God, she hated that expression. Everybody was a damn hyphenate these days. Andy was considered a German-American, Ricky a Mexican-American, and they hadn't been born in Germany or Mexico any more than she had been born in Africa. Why did social culture insist on all these stupid labels?

"I'm just asking that you think about it," Pat said, trying to tread delicately.

"But you're Pop's girlfriend. Why would he be upset if I start going out with Giles?"

Pat chose her words diplomatically. "When I was growing up, my mother used to tell me, 'Don't do as I do, do as I *tell* you to do.' In other words, parents don't always want their children to emulate them." She patted Kaitlyn's arm. "I'm sure it'll be fine." She turned on the tap and splashed cool water on her eyes. "I'm feeling a little tired. This should be a nice pick-me-up."

"Pat, did Mr. Suárez used to be your boyfriend?"

Her hand, reaching for a paper towel, froze. "What makes you ask that?"

"You had a weird look on your face when he was talking to us, and you've seemed kind of nervous ever since."

"Did I? I think you were imagining things, Kaitlyn." Pat grabbed a paper towel from the dispenser and dabbed at her eyes, feeling more edgy than ever.

If Kaitlyn had noticed the change in her demeanor, then Andy certainly had. He was bound to ask her about it. But how could she explain it to him when she didn't understand it herself?

Chapter 41

Back at Andy's town house, the girls went upstairs to their room. Andy poured two glasses of wine, and he and Pat went to sit out on the lighted patio.

His movements seemed a little stiff to her, but she wondered if she was imagining it.

"Your daughters are charming, Andy, just like you said," she said, meaning it. She felt foolish for worrying. She wanted to ask if he'd introduced them to many of the women in his life since his divorce, but she didn't know how she could phrase the question without sounding nosy. And she wasn't about to bring up the subject of Kaitlyn's crush.

"They're my two sweethearts. I think their mother and I did a great job raising them."

"You've been divorced for a long time, haven't you?"

"About seven years, which is half of Kaitlyn's life."

"How do you feel about your ex's second husband?"

"Uh, he's all right."

He didn't seem to want to say anything else, so Pat didn't press the issue. For a few moments they sat companionably, enjoying the lights of the city on this clear summer night. Finally, Andy spoke.

"That was him, wasn't it?"

Pat decided against pretending she didn't know what he meant. "Ricky and I used to date back in high school. He wanted to marry me."

"And your parents broke it up when you were nineteen."

"Yes."

"Thirty years ago."

He had an almost mocking look in his eye that made her uncomfortable. "How did you know it was him?"

"The shock in his eyes when he saw you. The way you got so jumpy. I can understand his being caught off guard at seeing you with me. A long time ago, your parents made it clear to him that they wanted you to settle down with a black man. He probably didn't think you'd ever go against their wishes and get involved with someone like me. But I don't understand why you couldn't carry on a simple conversation without being so nervous. It makes me think it's not over, at least not for you, even after all this time."

"That's ridiculous. It ended years ago, and that was that." She watched as he took a slug of his wine, not acknowledging her denial, and a sinking stomach told her something was terribly wrong. "Andy?" she prompted. "Are you okay?"

"I don't know, Pat. I saw you react with a lot more feeling than you should have for a love affair that ended such a long time ago." He drained his glass. "Why don't I take you home? I know you've got a lot to do before your trip. We'll talk about it when you get back."

She swallowed hard. When she got *back?* She wasn't leaving until Wednesday, and she'd be gone for a week and a half. Did he mean he didn't intend to have any contact with her until she returned?

Or was he breaking up with her, all because he felt she showed too much emotion when Ricky stopped by their table? How foolish was that? She'd been nervous, that's all. She feared Ricky would think she was flaunting her relationship with Andy in front of him out of spite.

Her glass was only half empty, but she pushed away from the table and stood up. "I'll just get my purse," she said coldly.

She might feel like her life was falling apart, but she'd be damned if she'd let him see her despair.

Chapter 42

Grace woke up early, as she usually did. She felt like she'd been caught in a stampede. Every part of her body ached.

Eric snored beside her, his feet hanging over the queen-sized bed. *Sleep, you bastard,* she thought as she remembered why her skin felt so tender.

After the short but exciting sex-capade in his living room, they went to his bedroom and started again, but this time Eric had been uncharacteristically rough, slapping her ass with brute force and pushing into her like he expected to strike oil. The little love bites he usually planted on her nipples felt instead like he was tickling them with razor blades, and while she gave him head he grabbed her hair and bobbed her head up and down until his penis practically tickled her tonsils. It was as if he was expressing all his frustrations during sex.

And she had a good idea of what had him so bothered. Her job. Her car. Her condo. Her travels. And, most of all, her unwillingness to share with him what he perceived as her good fortune, rather than the fruits of years of hard work.

The future for their relationship didn't look promising.

Grace returned from vacation on Monday and went back to work on Wednesday. She could have used another day off, but she'd already used the bulk of her vacation time for the cruise, which had been every bit as fantastic as she'd hoped. Hopefully, she wouldn't have to deal with anything other than catching up on her e-mail.

As she entered the building she saw a shadow in the glass behind her, and she held the door open. It pleased her to see that the shadow was the muscular form of Calvin Pendleton.

She'd seen him only occasionally since first meeting him two months earlier. Grace usually started coming in to work earlier after Memorial Day so she could wrap up her workday earlier and take advantage of the extended daylight hours. While she would welcome the opportunity to get to know Calvin better—especially now that Eric was losing his luster—she hadn't been willing to sacrifice the summer season to do it. Summers in Chicago were way too short. She saw no reason why Calvin wouldn't still be around in the fall.

Seeing him in midsummer was like a gift. "Good morning!" she said cheerfully.

"Morning." His eyes swept over her body appreciatively. "I haven't seen you in the gym lately," he said, "but obviously you've been going."

"Thanks." Unlike Eric's first assessment of her at Junior's Bar, Calvin looked her over in a subtle, complimentary manner that made her feel all warm and tingly, rather than like a stripper. They fell into step together as they both headed for the cafeteria. "I usually try to get in earlier between June and August. I'm late this morning, but I've been on vacation the last two weeks and it's my first day back."

"I thought you looked a little tanned. Where'd you go?"

"On a cruise through the Mediterranean."

"Nice."

"Are you still working out regularly?"

"Absolutely. I'm usually out of there by five, though."

In the cafeteria she headed for the fruit bar, while he walked toward the grill, where the eggs and meats were on display. They called out friendly farewells.

Grace glimpsed him on the cashier line a few people ahead of her. She watched as he joked with the cashier. God, he was handsome. Maybe she should stay a little later tonight and get to the gym while he was there.

Grace was working in her office when her administrative assistant, Carla, tapped on her door. "Something's come up, Grace."

Shit. She'd been hoping for a nice, quiet day of catch-up. "What is it?"

"It's serious. There's trouble brewing in Brazil. A patient taking our new antihypertensive died, and his lawyer is charging that his death is a direct result of the medication. Jeff Post is putting together a meeting at noon to discuss the matter, and Marlon wants to see you this afternoon at three."

Jeff Post was the global head of the hypertension division, and Marlon—no last name necessary—was Marlon Kellerman, the president of the company. So much for her quiet day. A public relations nightmare was unfolding in the Southern Hemisphere.

She glanced at her watch. It was already eleven-twenty. "I guess I'd better get some lunch now, if I want to eat."

"They're having the meeting catered. It's scheduled to run until two."

"All right. I'd better see what I can find out about what's going on down there."

Carla took this as her cue to leave, thoughtfully closing the office door.

Grace arrived at the conference room at two minutes before twelve, just as the previous group using the room filed out. She joined in the conversation of the other early arrivals, discussing the possible ramifications of the customer's death if it turned out to be linked to their product. Of course, the drug had undergone the same rigorous testing as any to be approved by the FDA, but it was still brand new. Anything could go wrong.

A white-smocked fortyish woman from Catering arrived, her petite size belying the weight of the two three-tiered carts she'd wheeled over from the cafeteria, pushing one and pulling the other. The sandwiches, salads, and desserts probably didn't weigh much, but the canned sodas and bottled water had to be hefty.

The people closest to the door began to go inside. She smiled when she saw Calvin approaching. She'd forgotten that he was a member of the hypertension team. It would be nice to work with him on this.

"Long time, no see," she joked with a smile. "Are you in this meeting, too?"

He looked a little embarrassed. "Uh . . . no."

At the moment Grace noticed Calvin wasn't carrying a notepad, the Catering employee asked him, "Are you the person who's going to help me set up?"

"Excuse me," Calvin said to Grace. He turned to the petite woman. "Yes. We have to hurry. It's a closed-door meeting, so they can't begin until we're out of here."

Grace watched, dumbfounded, as Calvin and the woman disappeared inside the meeting room with the carts.

"I appreciate this," the woman was saying to Calvin. "Normally for an order this large they send two of us, but it's our busiest time downstairs, and we couldn't spare anyone else."

"I understand. This all came up at the last minute," Calvin said.

Grace took a deep breath. The man she'd planned to replace Eric with was an *administrative assistant?* She felt like someone had sucked all the air out of her.

Nevertheless, she had a job to do. Certain that her facial expression gave nothing away, she walked in the room and took a seat at the large conference table.

When Grace got home she dialed Eric. She'd called him when she got in from the airport on Monday, but she deliberately kept that conversation short, making a date to meet him at Panera Bread on Saturday for lunch. She knew he was expecting to go to her place or his afterward for a sex-filled afternoon, but after the way he worked her over the last time she saw him, she'd decided to break it off with him. Pat was right. Better to be by herself than with someone who resented what she'd worked long and hard to accomplish. Now, because of the developments in São Paolo, she'd have to postpone the inevitable another week. She'd been looking forward to making a clean break and wasn't happy about the delay, but it couldn't be helped.

"Hi, Eric," she said when he answered.

"Hey, baby! What's up? I know—you decided you can't wait until Saturday to see me and you want me to come over now."

She cringed, grateful he couldn't see her face. "Actually, I wanted to let you know that I won't be able to see you this weekend. I have to go to Brazil."

"Brazil? But you just got back from vacation."

"This isn't vacation; it's work. We've got a major problem going on down there, and the company president wants me down there. I leave tomorrow."

"Damn." Eric paused. "You been there before?"

"Yes."

"Where *haven't* you been, Grace?"

She said the first thing that came to her mind. "Antarctica."

"Yeah, well, I hear they've got a lousy climate. I didn't know you speak Spanish."

Grace had a fleeting thought of Danny and his relocation to San Juan. "I don't. But they speak *Portuguese* in Brazil."

"Whatever. They gonna be having Carnival down there, people dancing in the streets and shit?"

"Eric, Carnival is before Lent. Just like Mardi Gras in New Orleans." Good Lord, did he not know *anything?* São Paolo was hardly a picnic. The last time she went she was transported to and from her hotel in a bulletproof vehicle. "Anyway, I just wanted you to know. I've got to get packed. I'll see you when I get back, okay?"

"When will that be?"

"Tuesday."

"All right. I guess you still don't need me to keep an eye on your place and your car while you're gone, huh?"

"No, I'll be doing the same as I did when I went away." The company was providing airport transfers via limousine, as it always did for staff who traveled, but she doubted Eric knew enough about corporate culture to know that. Her car would stay in the garage.

"Grace, do you have somethin' you want to say to me?"

She frowned. "Something like what?"

"You've been gone for almost two weeks. Now you call and say that you're goin' out of town again. On a day's notice. Who the hell does that? Then you act like you don't want me anywhere near your house or your car. And you're always throwing all this shit about your travels up in my face."

"This is legit, Eric. If I wanted to dump you I would come out and tell you." Grace viewed his outburst as a way to try to shame her into giving him a spare set of keys to her condo and Mercedes. How could he say she threw her travels in his face when she downplayed it by hiding the artwork she'd purchased abroad before he came to her place?

"Yeah, well, I've got a bad feeling about it."

"Well, I'm sorry to hear that," she said coldly. "But right now it's most pressing for me to get ready for my trip. I'll call you when I get back." She hung up.

As Grace packed, she asked herself why she hadn't just broken it off with him on the phone. Did she really feel he deserved a face to face after the things he did to her in bed that night? Sure, she'd felt better after she took a hot shower, which soothed her muscles. There were no marks anywhere on her skin, but she felt like she'd been mildly assaulted just the same. He'd stopped just short of biting her damn clit.

Of course, now that she'd learned that Calvin's job was even more low ranking than Eric's, she had no prospects at all. But Pat's refusal to date anyone not on a similar economic plane with her had paid off in the form of Andy Keindl.

Grace could only hope she would be as fortunate.

Chapter 43

Mid-August
Kenosha, Wisconsin

Susan snuggled up to Charles. Everything was going beautifully. She'd enrolled Quentin and Alyssa in a two-week day camp, which kept them occupied until five-thirty. Charles had rented a room in an extended-stay hotel just a few minutes north of her home. She'd spent every day with him, and it saddened her to think that it would all end today.

But she'd made progress in her plan. She'd been offered the bookkeeping position she applied for, and she accepted it. She would work four hours a day, from ten until two. She would start a week from Monday, which was the kids' first day of school. Bruce hadn't objected to the schedule, for she would be at work while the kids were in school. She'd already gotten permission from the owner about taking off on single-day school holidays, like Labor Day, Columbus Day, and even two days for Thanksgiving. Christmas break was something else, lasting up to a week and a half, but Susan assured the owner that wouldn't be a problem. She could get one of the older neighborhood kids to stay with Quentin and Alyssa while she went in. She so looked forward to working again and gaining some experience.

"Guess what?" she murmured to Charles.

"I know. It's time for you to go."

"The past two weeks have been wonderful."

He pulled her closer. "For me, too."

"Are you going back right away?"

"I'll probably wait until the morning, since I'm paid up through tomorrow. If I leave early I shouldn't run into traffic. I'll go out and get something to eat and bring it back."

"I think I'll take the kids out. Bruce already told me he'll be late." Susan sighed. After getting home relatively early for weeks, Bruce had returned to late hours. She wanted so badly to just throw in the towel on her marriage, but she had to resist the urge to spontaneously blurt out her intentions to Bruce. "Tomorrow's Quentin's birthday, so we might as well get an early start on our celebration."

"What is he, eleven?"

She nodded. "It's going to be a busy week. I've got to take the kids shopping for school clothes, and Elyse and I are having lunch . . . And I moved up my appointment for my one-year cancer screening so I don't have to take time off from work." Her body went rigid, as it always did as the time for her screening approached. She couldn't help feeling nervous. Its results would help determine her future . . . whether she lived or died.

"I can tell you're worried," Charles said. "Would you like me to go with you?"

His concern made her want to cry. Bruce had made no such offer when she told him about the appointment. It gave her the uncomfortable feeling that he secretly hoped her cancer would claim her life, just to make things easy for him.

"I'd like that, Charles. But I don't think I should. Bruce hasn't said anything about coming along, but I think he might do it at the last minute."

"If he doesn't, you call me."

She shut her eyes, overcome with emotion. She knew how difficult it was for Charles to volunteer to be second. He truly did love her. She couldn't wait to be with him openly. "Thank you," she whispered.

Chapter 44

Mid-August
Milwaukee

Bruce left his office five minutes before Shay got off work and waited by her car, leaning against the driver's-side door. Five minutes later she came out of the building, crossing her arms in front of her chest when she saw him. "Not a good idea, Bruce."

The words rushed out of him. "Shay, I can't stand being without you. I promise you, by the end of the year my divorce will be in motion. I've already spoken to a lawyer."

"Really. And have you spoken to your wife?"

"Not yet. We're working on our strategy. I don't want to spring it on her until we've got everything worked out. I'm not looking to screw her out of anything, but I don't want her to get half of what I've got, either." He didn't want to mention that he also wanted to wait for the results of Susan's workup. Shay had already accused him of hiding behind his wife's health, but it did play a role. As much as he wanted Shay, he knew he wouldn't be able to bring himself to ask Susan for a divorce while she fought cancer. He only prayed her remission would continue. He couldn't reclaim his passion for her—Lord knew he'd tried—and he suspected she had grown weary of his halfhearted attempts. All he could think about was Shay.

"So you're hiding your assets."

He began to feel foolish. He'd hoped that the moment Shay heard about his consulting an attorney she'd rush into his arms.

Instead she still stood several feet away from him, not relaxing her stance one bit.

"I've put the wheels in motion," he corrected. In a softer tone, he said, "Come on, Shay. It hasn't been that long. Surely you haven't been able to replace me already."

She dropped her arms and stared at him uncertainly. "Bruce, if you're stringing me along. . . ."

He looked her dead in her eye so she could see the truth in his. "I've always been honest with you, Shay, from the very beginning. I told you I was married and had a family. When you decided you couldn't wait for me to get my life together, I walked out of your life without objection or even hesitation. And now I'm telling you that I'm in the process of divorcing my wife, that I want you in my life. No, Shay, I'm not stringing you along. I'd never want to deny you anything you want, and certainly not something you want so badly."

She hesitated. "I just can't get too excited about this. Not until it actually happens, and too much can go wrong."

"Why don't we go to dinner, and we can talk some more?" Bruce stepped forward and held out his hand. He breathed a sigh of relief when she took it.

This was the first step toward being happy again.

Chapter 45

Mid-August
Pleasant Prairie, Wisconsin

Susan listened as the person at the register repeated their order. "That's right," she said. The cashier stated the total and instructed them to drive to the pickup window.

"You kids are really giving me a break," she remarked as she drove. "I never thought you would have wanted Culver's."

"I wanted a hamburger," Quentin said, "and theirs are the best."

Susan had to agree. The chain, located predominantly in the Midwest, had the best burgers she'd ever tasted, whether in a fast-food or more elegant setting. She'd ordered hers with mushrooms and Swiss cheese.

She pulled up to the window, a twenty all ready to hand over to the cashier.

"Oh, the gentleman in front of you paid for your order, miss," the cashier informed her.

Susan's neck jerked as she peered at the car at the second window. An aqua Blazer with Illinois plates. It had to be Charles. Of all times for him to go out to get something to eat. What the hell was he thinking, paying for her order? He'd obviously seen her pull up behind him—she hadn't noticed him—but hadn't he noticed Quentin sitting in the front seat next to her? Okay, so he wasn't tall enough for his head to extend beyond the seat. But every two minutes he stuck his head between the front seats to say something to Alyssa.

Susan leaned out of the window and spoke to the cashier softly. "In that case, can you break this twenty for me? Two tens would be fine."

"But, ma'am, I can't open my register without making a sale."

"Get your manager," she hissed. The last thing she wanted was for Quentin to ask why they didn't have to pay. He sat right beside her, and he missed nothing.

"What's going on, Mom?" he asked now.

"Nothing. Everything's fine." She turned her head to face the cashier, putting the index finger of her left hand to her lips.

The cashier took the cue and said softly, "I'm going to get someone to bring this bill up front for me and break it for you, since I can't leave the window."

"Fine," Susan said tersely. She cursed herself for not recognizing Charles's car in front of her, but even if she had, she never thought he'd pull a stunt like this. How was she supposed to explain a stranger buying their dinner to her children?

Just wait til she got hold of him.

The change was given to her shortly, and she replaced it in her wallet and pulled forward. Their food had already been bagged up. Charles had pulled into a parking space in the front of the building. If he expected her to stop and introduce him to her kids, he really was nuts, Susan thought.

She drove by without so much as slowing down.

After she got home, she dialed Charles's cell from the privacy of her bedroom. He answered on the second ring. "What do you mean, paying for my kids' food? Don't you think that's going to make them curious about who you are and why you're doing that? They might even mention it to their father. What am I supposed to tell them, Charles?"

"What *did* you tell them?"

"Fortunately, I didn't have to tell them anything. The cashier told me that you'd paid, but she spoke softly enough that no one but me heard her. I already had my money out, and my son was sitting right next to me, so I covered by asking the cashier to give me change for a twenty."

"So everything worked out."

"Don't sound so disappointed. I want to know what it is you're up to, Charles Valentine."

"All right. You deserve to know the truth. I'm getting a little tired of having the woman I love be some other man's wife. I want you to get a divorce, Susan, so you can marry me. We've already lost twenty-five years because of a bunch of foolishness. I don't want any more delays."

Not this again. He hadn't mentioned it once during the two weeks he'd been staying at the extended-stay hotel. His offer to go with her to her cancer screening if Bruce didn't had probably gotten him thinking about how much he disliked having her go home to Bruce every time they were together. Now she regretted having brought it up.

"Where are you now?" She decided that the seriousness of his action called for a face-to-face confrontation, not a telephone call.

"On my way home. I'm driving through Waukegan, I think."

That was too far for her to travel; he was already halfway to Cook County. "All right. Monday I'm coming down. Can you meet me? We need to have a talk."

"Just tell me where."

Over the weekend Susan arranged for a sitter. She drove to the station and boarded a southbound train. After a scenic ride that lasted nearly an hour and a half, she arrived at the Ogilvie Transportation Center. She easily found the restaurant where Charles had suggested they meet. The lunch rush hadn't started yet, and she had an attentive waiter.

Charles rushed in after just under ten minutes. "Sorry," he said. "Metra's running a little behind schedule."

"That's all right. They haven't started looking at me funny yet."

They placed their orders, and then he said, "I know you're angry at me for what I did Friday."

She sighed. "I've gotten over it. I know you won't do it again. But Charles, you have to be patient. Things can't move as fast as you want them to."

"I'm not some stranger you just met, Susan. I wanted to marry you years ago, but you said no because of Douglas and my mother."

"That's *another* problem," she muttered.

"That's my point. There don't have to be *any* problems. Don't make everything more complicated than it has to be."

"You know I'm trying to get things in place, Charles. You know I start working part-time next week. I'd rather get in at the school board because they pay better, but they said they wouldn't consider me if I only want to work part-time."

"Why don't you work full-time, then?"

"Because Bruce will never go for it. Alyssa is just going into third grade. Even though I feel she's too young not to have me at home after school, I do not want to put all that responsibility on Quentin. Someone could knock on the door pretending to be the mailman. Quentin might open it. . . ." She raised her chin defiantly. "I won't put my children in that position."

"I wouldn't want you to," he said. "But are you actually telling me that Bruce will refuse you alimony so you can stay at home?"

"Alimony will end the moment I remarry."

"*I* want to marry you. I've told you that a half dozen times. I don't expect Bruce to support you forever. That's supposed to be *my* job. This is just for an interim period."

"Trust me, the minute he finds out about you he'll fight for custody of the kids. I don't want that to happen, either."

She watched his expression harden just as if someone had slid a veil over his face and magically turned him into stone.

"So, more hiding?" he asked with narrowed eyes. "Tell me, Susan, do you ever anticipate being able to walk down the street holding my hand? Or do you intend to keep me hidden away forever, like a crazy uncle in the attic?"

"What I'm trying to do," she hissed, "is come up with a way that will allow me to keep my children and be with you openly. *And* maintain my health insurance, since once I'm divorced,

Bruce can't legally cover me. I've got a health issue, in case you've forgotten."

"Of course I haven't forgotten. But there's COBRA."

"COBRA is expensive. Besides, you can't keep it indefinitely. The only way I can be covered is if I've got a job. I don't know how I can get that to work out, Charles. I wish you'd help me come up with some ideas instead of giving me a hard time."

"Susan, if you marry me I'll put you on my insurance. We can get married as soon as you're free, the day after, if we can arrange it that fast. You won't be without coverage at any time. I really think you're making too much of this. Divorce Bruce, marry me. If you want to work part-time so you can be there when your kids get home from school you can do it." He looked at her through eyes that suddenly had gone suspicious. "I'm wondering if there's something you're not telling me."

She sighed, not wanting to say anything that would hurt his feelings. "I have to consider my kids' feelings, Charles. You haven't even met them yet."

"Under the circumstances that would be a little awkward, don't you think?"

"Of course it would. That's why I was so upset when I thought Quentin had seen you. The divorce is going to come as a huge shock to them. They might not cotton so well to seeing me with a new partner."

"We'll work it out. Maybe you haven't noticed, but I can be pretty charming when I want to."

She wished he would give the situation the serious consideration it merited. "It might not be as simple as you expect. Then there's the economics. It's going to be a hard adjustment for them. You've seen the house they live in now. They don't want for anything. That wonderful lifestyle they enjoy is provided by Bruce, who's a millionaire several times over. You and I won't be able to afford to keep them in that fashion. Trust me, that's the first thing Bruce will pounce on when he finds out I'm seeing you."

He nodded thoughtfully, then looked at her with a cautious expression she'd never seen on him before. "Are you sure it's only the *kids'* adjustment you're concerned about, Susan?"

She didn't know where he was headed, but she didn't like it. "What's *that* supposed to mean?"

"Exactly what it sounds like," he snapped. "How do *you* feel about living a middle-class lifestyle after being married to a millionaire?"

She glared at him, knowing he wouldn't have asked this question if he hadn't insisted on coming to pick her up that time she had the flat tire. But because he'd seen her house, he had doubts. "You know better than to ask me that, Charles, after all I've been through."

"It's a valid question."

"I grew up in the Theodore Dreiser Projects, just like you did. And if there's one thing I've learned in my life, it's that I'd rather be happy and middle class than wealthy and undesired." Her eyes dampened with tears. She was trying so hard. How could he say such a cruel thing to her?

"Susan, you're being hesitant. What other conclusion can I come to, other than you don't want to leave that lifestyle Bruce provides for you?"

Her fury strengthened like a hurricane. Only their public setting kept her from screaming at him. "How dare you say that to me. The first time we met to talk, you told me I'd never been a shallow person. But now you accuse me of staying in an empty marriage just because I like living in a large house and being a stay-at-home mother. It's like you didn't hear a word I said when I told you how unhappy I was, or how I'm trying to get back into the workforce so I can support myself and my children."

"Susan." He looked like he was ready to apologize, but she wasn't having it.

"Your answer to everything is that we'll work it out, that everything's so simple. But you've never once explained where we'll live or what will happen if my remission ends. You have a one-bedroom apartment, and your job's insurance company might not take kindly to your marrying a cancer patient. For all I know, you're expecting my children to move into your apartment and sleep on the kitchen table and in the bathtub. So don't sit there and tell me that money doesn't count, or accuse me of being overly concerned about it. Bruce pays for everything for the kids and me, and I don't work at all. If I get sick I wouldn't have to go to some crummy hospital on the verge of losing its accreditation. Will *you* be able to do all that on a teacher's salary?"

Charles slid back his chair abruptly. "I see this wasn't such a good idea. Tell the waiter I changed my mind."

"That makes two of us," she said, waving her hand. "But you go first."

She sat there, seething, long enough to wait for the waiter to return and tell him that they wouldn't be staying. Then she went to the ladies' room, forced herself to calm down, and headed for the train station and home.

Chapter 46

Late August
Chicago

"Oh, it's good to be home again," Grace said as she did a full-body stretch. "I can't remember the last time I walked on the weekends."

"Believe it or not, I've been walking while you were away," Pat said.

"I believe it. You look good. Your chest even looks like it's gone down a little. You'd better be careful with that. Andy might not like it."

"I haven't seen Andy since I've been back."

Grace's head jerked. "You haven't seen him? But what happened?"

"I'll tell you about it while we're walking. Let's go."

Grace quickly tied her shoelace. She stuck a twenty in the pocket of her shorts and grabbed her keys and sun visor. "All right, I'm ready."

They'd barely gotten to the sidewalk when Pat began. "I guess I should have told you about it sooner, but I didn't want to talk about it. Everything was going so well, and I was fool enough to think it could last. I should have known better. My relationships *never* last."

"Pat, what the hell happened?"

"The Saturday before we left. He had me come over and meet his daughters."

Grace drew in her breath. "Don't tell me that they—"

"No, they were fine. One of them even asked for advice about a black kid at school she's got a crush on. The problem was that Andy brought us to dinner at Nirvana."

"So what? I would have been tickled if I had a chance to show off my new boyfriend to my old one, even years later. Ricky didn't have any problem bringing that wife of his to the Soul Queen, did he?"

"That's not the point, Grace. I'm not into all that kid stuff, showing off. Anyway, Ricky was there. He was stopping by the diners' tables to chat, and when he saw me with Andy and Andy's daughters he looked like he'd seen Martians sitting there."

"He doesn't know your dating habits, Pat. It had to come as a shock to him, because of your father putting his foot down."

"I know that. But the whole situation made me uncomfortable. Andy commented on it afterward. He said I showed too much nervousness for Ricky to be someone who meant nothing to me."

Grace groaned. She'd always felt that Pat still harbored feelings for Ricky. "And I'll bet you denied it."

"Of course I denied it. Ricky and I ended a long time ago, Grace."

"And you've never gotten over it. Don't deny it, Pat. You might not admit it to yourself, but it shows."

"Shows how?"

Grace didn't have to think for long. "There was that time a couple of months ago when you met that girl Stephanie at the pub. She mentioned that she and I had eaten dinner at Nirvana, and you pounced on me like a mouse on a hunk of cheese, asking me if Ricky had been there, and if he'd asked about you, even though I'd already said that it happened years ago. You know that he's remarried now and that it couldn't possibly make any difference, but still you insisted upon knowing every detail. Details I couldn't even remember."

"I was just curious. What's wrong with that?"

"I'll tell you what's wrong with it, Pat. I didn't see it as curiosity; I saw it as a woman who hasn't been able to move on, even after thirty years. I'm sure Andy saw your reaction the same way. Maybe instead of denying it to Andy you should have admitted you still have a soft spot for him. You could have told him that you were just caught off guard at seeing your old boyfriend and you felt a little weird. He could live with that if you assured him he's the only man in your life. Having Ricky come between the most promising relationship you've had in years would be a real shame."

"I think it's too late for that. He's the one who dismissed us when we got back to his house after dinner. He said something along the lines of it being just as well I was going away for nearly two weeks. In other words, he wanted to make the break more gradual."

"But you've been back nearly a month. You haven't heard from him?"

"No. And I'm not calling him, either."

"Pat, you sound like a little kid. You were wrong, and if you admit it, you might still be able to salvage your relationship."

"It's too late, Grace."

Grace sighed. Pat looked so resigned. This was silly. Did she really think she'd be able to meet another man like Andy just like that? He might well be her last chance. Grace wished she could talk Pat into reversing her decision not to contact Ricky and admit that she hadn't been truthful about her feelings for him, that she had realized how asinine it was.

Suddenly a way to accomplish this occurred to Grace, but she wasn't sure it would be the right thing to do. It involved confessing something she never wanted Pat to know, and she didn't know if she was really willing to live with the consequences.

She decided to think on it while they walked. It wasn't the type of thing she could discuss with Pat while they were on the street, anyway.

By the time they wrapped up their three-mile walk and were back at Grace's condo, Grace had decided to go for it. If she didn't speak up, Pat and Andy might not ever get back together. She'd become convinced that the two of them belonged together. Pat had never looked as happy as she had since she started dating him. Maybe it wasn't meant for them to grow old together, but

Pat simply couldn't afford to walk away from a perfectly good man just out of stubbornness and denial.

Grace knew that coming clean might mean the end of her friendship with Pat. She hoped her confession would help Pat see how foolish she'd been where Ricky was concerned. Surely trying to get Pat back with Andy was the right thing to do.

Pat sat on the edge of an upholstered chair, mindful of her sweaty body. She sipped the last of the raspberry smoothie they stopped to get in the home stretch. "That hit the spot."

"Yeah, it felt good to walk again."

"So what are you doing the rest of the day? I guess you're going out with Eric."

"No." Grace decided to share her news. "I broke up with him."

"You didn't! When did this happen?"

"Between the time I got home from the cruise and my trip to São Paolo, I called to tell him I couldn't see him because I had to travel for work. He accused me of making everything up just to try to get rid of him."

"But that was a serious situation your company had down there."

"Of course it was. But Eric docsn't understand about things like that, Pat. We had some words about it, and the next day I decided to break it off. I wanted to do it in person, but after I got back I didn't see the point, so I called him and told him."

"How'd he take it?"

"Not well," Grace admitted. "He said he should have known that, and I quote, 'a rich bitch like me would get tired of him,' and he said that the next time I'm horny I'd better use my fingers before I call him again."

Pat made a face. "That was low-down, but it's what I'd expect from him."

"It convinced me I'd done the right thing. He was becoming really frustrated with my job, making nasty comments all over the place, things like that." She didn't tell Pat that Eric had begun to give her physical pain during sex, like he was punishing her for being successful. "But back to you and Andy and Ricky . . ."

Pat sighed. "I thought we finished talking about that."

"Pat, I've got to tell you something. I'm pretty sure you're going to be angry at me, but it's one of those for-your-own-good things."

Pat smiled. "Why do I suddenly feel like I'm ten years old again, and my mother is about to teach me a lesson?"

"Seriously, Pat. It has to do with Ricky." Pat's expression changed immediately, as Grace had known it would. "After Stephanie and I had dinner at Nirvana, he called me. He was in the midst of a divorce, and I was already divorced."

"Wait a minute, Grace. You said before that you were still married to Danny when you went to Nirvana."

Grace cursed under her breath. She'd forgotten about that. She just needed to put a stop to all these lies. It all happened such a long time ago. Surely it couldn't matter now. And if it did . . . Well, she'd have to learn to live with it.

"No, I was divorced," she said. "I remember, because I'd just moved into my condo. I gave him my card at the restaurant. We got together one night, and one thing led to another—"

Pat jumped to her feet. "My God, you had an affair! With *Ricky? My* Ricky?"

Grace forced her breathing to remain even. She had to struggle, for Pat had suddenly gone as green as the Chicago River on St. Patrick's Day.

"You had an affair," Pat repeated in an accusatory tone, "even though you knew how I felt about him."

"Pat, this happened a long time ago, but even then it had been more than twenty years since you and Ricky broke up. You'd made no move to get back together with him. The man was hurting, and so was I."

"You could have told me about it. If I'd known he was hurting, I would have gone to him. But you didn't, and I know why. The minute he told you he was getting divorced you decided you wanted him for yourself." Pat shook her head. "Just like you and Douglas Valentine when he was in the NBA, after Susan dumped him. You knew he'd been her boyfriend, her first love, but you went after him anyway, just because you saw dollar signs."

Grace drew in her breath. "Who told you that?"

"Never mind who told me. I just know that if he'd been interested, you would have unloaded poor Jimmy like last year's capri pants, even though he and Douglas were friends. Why be poor and live on the South Side of Chicago when you could be living in luxury with an NBA player?"

"I'm not going there, Pat. This is about you and Andy. I hoped that my telling you this would make you realize how silly it is to hang on to something you lost a long time ago. Ricky has been married twice. He's moved on, and you're getting all tongue-tied, concerned because he might get the wrong impression from you showing up at Nirvana with your date. If that isn't pining for somebody, I don't know what is. No wonder Andy's feelings were hurt. Now, *there's* a man who truly cares about you, Pat. Letting him go would be a mistake."

"I'm leaving." Pat picked up her shoulder bag from the floor in front of the coffee table. "I can't even stand to look at you, Grace. You're supposed to be my best friend, and you tell me that you slept with the one man I ever truly loved." She spun around and ran toward the door, letting it slam shut behind her as she exited.

Grace leaned forward, her hands cradling her forehead. Then she dropped her hands and sank back into the sofa cushions. "*That* went well," she said aloud.

Chapter 47

Mid-October
Lake Forest, Illinois

Ever since Franklin's diagnosis Elyse had gone into panic mode whenever he felt less than chipper. If he complained of having a headache, she wondered about brain metastasis. If he had indigestion, she wondered about his stomach. She'd been wrong, and eventually she'd learned to calm down.

But three weeks ago, when he'd left his office early and told her he just didn't feel well, she had bad vibes. She'd insisted he see the doctor and he'd undergone a battery of tests.

On the way to the appointment with Dr. LeBlond, Franklin insisted that it wasn't necessary to tell anyone, at least not right away, if the news was bad . . . But they both knew in their hearts that it would be. Once they sat down in Dr. LeBlond's office, he told them that Franklin's cancer had returned, this time having spread to his liver, stomach, and bone.

Franklin asked about the prognosis.

"It's what we call 'guarded,'" the physician replied.

"Well, *that* doesn't sound very promising," Franklin pointed out, and Elyse picked up on the sharpness to his tone.

"I'm afraid it isn't. We have to talk about treatment."

"No treatment," Franklin said. "I went through hell that last time, and it only helped me for three and a half lousy months."

"Franklin!" Elyse exclaimed.

"I'm sorry, baby. I know I should have shared this with you, but I knew it would only upset you. Besides, I hoped it wouldn't come up again this soon. I can't go through that again. What are the odds that it'll really prolong my life by any substantial length—and I'm not talking three months here—anyway?"

They both looked at Dr. LeBlond, whose solemn expression only served to prove Franklin's point.

For a horrifying moment Franklin seemed to shrivel before her eyes, slumping in his chair. Then he straightened up and calmly said, "I guess that's that."

Nevertheless, Elyse tried to change his mind the moment they left the doctor's office. Only when he looked her directly in the eye and said quietly, "Elyse, my mind's made up," did she know that he really meant it.

She felt numb. Franklin, her husband of twenty-six years, was going to die. How could she tell Todd and Brontë? And what about Frankie and Rebecca?

This time there would be no rebound. She could tell just by looking at Franklin. He'd been either listless or visibly uncomfortable since the day he'd left work at two o'clock. He hadn't been back, and she knew he would never return.

Things would be different in another way, too. Franklin *would* have a caregiver, whether he wanted one or not. If the way he looked was any indication, Elyse couldn't imagine him objecting. She'd talk to her boss about cutting back on her hours. Even a few hours would give her more time to spend with Franklin, especially while the sitter became acclimated. A sitter would do for now. She'd bring in home hospice as a supplement when the time came. And if any of them knew what was good for them, they wouldn't question her judgment. *She* was calling the shots, damn it. Franklin would be comfortable and well cared for, and that was all that mattered.

Elyse opened the bedroom door a few inches, then closed it when she saw Franklin sleeping peacefully. She returned to the living room, walking like a zombie. But strangely, she couldn't cry. The tears just wouldn't come.

Just as Elyse had when he was first diagnosed, she wished she could talk to one of her friends, but there was no one to talk to.

She and Kevin had whittled down to no contact at all, and her girlfriends all had a lot on their plates. Susan was adapting to being back in the workforce part-time and was busy with her family on the weekends . . . or so she said. She'd begged off the last two times Elyse suggested they meet for lunch, leading Elyse to suspect she had something else on her mind. At any rate, Elyse wasn't going to ask her again. If Susan really wanted to keep in touch, let *her* make a move.

Grace had broken up with Eric Wade and seemed a little broken in spirit, like she'd given up on ever finding the right man. And Pat had made up with Andy after having a big fight about, of all things, Ricky Suárez. Ironically, Grace had been the catalyst for getting them back together by confessing that she'd had a secret affair with Ricky after both their divorces. Grace's confession helped Pat realize how foolish she'd been to carry a torch for Ricky all these years and that she shouldn't let the best thing that had happened to her in years get away. Andy loved Pat, and she loved him. But she had yet to introduce him to her parents, and Elyse knew she was frightened.

Elyse knew from talking with both women that Grace had apologized to Pat and they'd formed a truce, but only on the surface. They hadn't even seen each other since making up.

Elyse saw on her calendar that they were all supposed to meet for dinner next Saturday, the first get-together for the Twenty-Two Club since the reunion; and she wondered who would be the first to cancel. Too bad. One should really never leave bad feelings to fester. You never knew what the future might hold for you. Did Franklin have any olive branches to offer? she wondered. And what would *she* do if she was told she was going to die? Was there anyone she would want to make peace with?

A childhood memory flashed through her brain. *Yes,* she thought, *there was.*

Chapter 48

K evin was waiting at a bench just inside the front door when Elyse arrived. He immediately got to his feet and held out his arms. "How about a hug for old time's sake?"

Elyse felt a flash of discomfort only for a second. After all, the whole point of her calling him was to put the kissing incident behind them and to show she had no hard feelings. She stepped into his arms and out of them within seconds.

"Thanks for meeting me," she said.

"Thanks for calling me. I was beginning to think I'd lost an old friend."

They followed the hostess to a booth. "That's the reason I called," Elyse explained when they were seated. "I didn't think it was right to let one bad impulse put a damper on our friendship. I wanted to make things right."

"I can't tell you how glad that makes me feel, Elyse. I'd pretty much given up on your ever talking to me again. Tell me, how's Franklin?"

"He's . . . he's not good." She lowered her gaze. She'd spoken to her children about Franklin's prognosis, to her parents, and to her manager at work, but it still hurt to put it into words.

The waitress appeared, all perky and bright. "Hi. Are you ready to order?"

"Yes," Elyse said, glad for the interruption. "I'll have the chicken quesadillas."

"You can bring me a roast beef sandwich with the sauce," Kevin said.

The waitress repeated the order and left.

"Now, what were you saying about Franklin?" he asked. "Is he still working?"

"No. We saw his oncologist last week. There's cancer in Franklin's liver and stomach, even in his bones."

"Oh. Elyse, I don't know what to say. I'm sorry."

A sob caught in her throat, and she covered her face with her hands, unable to hold back the tears. It had been such a difficult week.

Elyse had tried to be stoic, and while her posture showed no weakness, she sat there with uncontrollable tears running down her cheeks in rivulets. The worst that could possibly happen had just happened.

She found it inconceivable that he might not be alive a year from now, that this might be his last fall and winter on earth. Talking about his condition drove home the reality, and she sobbed harder, her tears wetting both her palms and her face.

She felt movement beside her. Kevin had slid into the booth. He rested her head on his shoulder. "Elyse," he said simply.

"My husband is dying, Kevin. What am I supposed to do without him?"

"You'll do what every woman who loses her husband does. You'll find the strength to go on. The important thing is that he's still here now, Elyse. Take advantage of that."

She nodded, then dabbed at her eyes with the corner of her cloth napkin. She took a deep breath. "I didn't mean to do that. We just found out last week. I haven't even told my friends yet. It hurts just to talk about it, to think about it. And I can't think of anything else."

"I guess you can't. So this is why you called me?"

"I just got to thinking that if I were to leave this earth, I wouldn't want to leave behind any unfinished business. You've always been a good friend to me, Kevin." She laughed. "Remember the time I had to pee on the way home from school when we were in the fourth grade?"

He chuckled. "You didn't even want to wait for your friends. You thought you could get home, but you wet your pants halfway there."

"And you never told anybody. I've always appreciated that." She'd always felt a special bond with Kevin because he'd kept her secret.

"I never understood why you didn't go before you left school."

"Because I'd just gotten a special pass from the teacher to use the bathroom like, an hour before. I found out later that I had a UTI—that's a urinary tract infection. One of the symptoms is having to go frequently." She laughed. "Thanks a lot, Kevin. I feel a lot better. If I can laugh now, I guess I'll still be able to laugh when . . . after . . ." She couldn't bring herself to put it into words.

He gave her arm a squeeze. "Are you sure you're all right, Elyse?"

Once more she nodded. She looked up and glanced at the people at surrounding tables, many of whom had been looking at her and quickly averted their eyes. "Okay. That's enough of that. I see I've already attracted unwanted attention."

"I wish there was something I could do for you, Elyse."

"I know. You're doing more than you know, just by keeping me company."

"All right. I guess I'll move back to my side of the table." With an arm around her, he gave her eyes one last dab with the napkin.

"Hello, Elyse."

The stinging tone of the female voice signaled trouble. But nothing could have prepared Elyse for the sight of her stepdaughter, Rebecca, glaring at her.

"Rebecca!" she exclaimed, realizing too late that she should have taken a more subdued approach. Her shocked tone gave the impression that she'd just been caught doing something illicit, which, of course, she hadn't. But that look on Rebecca's face certainly gave away *her* thoughts.

This had all the makings of a disaster.

"Yes, it's me. I guess I'm just about the last person you expected to see . . . since my father is helpless at home."

"Rebecca—"

Kevin quickly removed his arm from around Elyse's shoulder and stood up.

"Don't move on my account," Rebecca said coldly.

Oh, fine, Elyse thought. She and Franklin's kids had already had it out over his care. Now Rebecca was jumping to conclusions as casually as little girls jumped rope double Dutch.

"I was just getting up," Kevin said easily. "Your stepmother was having a difficult moment, and I went to comfort her. You of all people have a better idea than most of what she's been going through." He held out his hand. "Kevin Nash."

Rebecca shook his hand limply. "Rebecca Reavis."

"I'm an old friend of Elyse's," Kevin explained. Elyse silently blessed him for trying to smooth things over. "We went all through school together. We haven't seen each other in years, and then a couple of months ago they had a reunion for people who used to live in the projects where we grew up."

"And you were able to reconnect." Rebecca met Elyse's worried gaze. "I guess that will make it easier for you, won't it? Just remember, you're not single *yet.*" She gave Kevin a scathing glance and moved on.

Elyse leaned back in her seat. "Great. Just what I needed."

"I gather you and your stepdaughter don't get along too well," Kevin guessed as he took a seat on the opposite side of the booth.

"We used to, in spite of her mother not being too happy about Franklin's remarrying and having a new family. She and her brother were still pretty young back then, and I won them over. But I've been butting heads with her and her brother ever since Franklin first went into the hospital. They feel like they have to have someone to blame for his illness, and I'm the one they chose. She'll get over it." She touched her tear-streaked face with her fingertips. "Excuse me, Kevin. I'm going to go wash my face before our food comes."

"Sure, go ahead. I'll take this call." His cell phone was ringing, the ringtone being the "1812 Overture."

He flipped open the phone as Elyse walked away. "Hello. Hey, man!" He listened as his would-be business partner explained that he'd won the baseball pool at work and had gotten a little closer to his goal. "That's great news. Congrats!" He paused as his friend asked him a question. "Yeah, I think I might be getting closer to that golden number myself. I just came into a stroke of good luck. You can say I've got to wait until somebody's out of the picture, but it shouldn't take long. Maybe a couple of months."

Chapter 49

Late October
Lake Forest, Illinois

Elyse entered her home, which looked as it always did. This time Franklin had not objected when she insisted that he have someone in the house to assist him, and they'd interviewed several candidates before deciding on a black woman in her early sixties named Winnie. Part of Winnie's duties included light housework, and she seemed to be doing a good job. Elyse noticed fresh vacuum tracks in the carpet, and the scent of furniture polish suggested that Winnie had also dusted. That was part of the reason why she and Franklin had decided to hire an older person; they tended to take more pride in their work. There wasn't much money in being a sitter, but caring for those unable to do for themselves was a vital position just the same. Winnie worked to supplement her pension from her bank teller job.

"Hello, Mrs. Reavis," Winnie greeted. "I was just giving Mr. Reavis his pain pills."

Elyse winced. Franklin was in such pain, and chances were that it would only get worse. "Hello, Winnie. Were there any calls today?"

"Yes. Your Number One son called this afternoon."

Elyse's shoulders grew tense. Winnie distinguished Todd and Brontë from their older half siblings by designating them as

Number Two son and daughter. Number One son meant Frankie. "He did? Did the call seem to upset Mr. Reavis?"

"Not that I could tell. Of course, I left the room right after I told him his son was calling."

"I see. Well, thank you, Winnie."

"If there's nothing else I'll be on my way."

"That's fine. Good night, Winnie."

Elyse wearily walked toward the master bedroom, the stress of the afternoon hitting her all of a sudden like a tidal wave. She paused at the entrance to knock on the open door. Franklin had been dozing.

"Well, what do you know," he said. "I'm surprised you came back."

She walked toward the bed. "And why would that be?"

"Why be bothered with a sick old man when you can have someone ten years younger who's in perfect health?"

"I see Rebecca called you."

"Actually, it was Frankie who called. Rebecca told him about your lunch partner."

"Franklin, that wasn't anyone but Kevin Nash. I've known him since kindergarten."

"Is that supposed to present some kind of obstacle? 'I can't possibly be having an affair with him. I've known him since kindergarten.'"

"I'm *not* having an affair with Kevin or anyone else," she said, more sharply than she intended. "I ran into Kevin at the Dreiser reunion. You would have met him if you'd come with me."

He flinched, and she immediately regretted her choice of words. "I'm sorry. I shouldn't have said that. Of course you didn't come with me. You were ill, you just didn't know it yet. I'm just trying to tell you not to let anyone make you believe that I'm stepping out on you, Franklin."

He turned away.

She sat on the edge of the bed. Franklin didn't turn over again, but nor did he say anything.

"My God, Franklin, what did Frankie tell you? All I was

doing was having lunch with a friend." Maybe that was it—Rebecca talked to Frankie, and then Frankie talked to Franklin. Things often got miscommunicated when passed through multiple channels.

"On the same side of the booth."

"Yes, on the same side. But that was only temporary. I had sort of a meltdown—over you, I might add—and he came to sit on my side to calm me down."

"Yeah, right. It was all my fault."

"Franklin, are you saying you don't believe me? This is asinine! We've been married twenty-six years. If I tell you there was nothing to it, there was nothing to it. And quite frankly, I expect you to believe me, not some information you received thirdhand from Frankie."

He glared at her. "Couldn't even wait until I was cold."

That did it. She jumped up from the bed as if it had just burst into flames. "I don't deserve to be treated this way. Don't say another word to me unless it's an apology." She left the room, slamming the door behind her.

The moment the door was closed she choked on the sob that rose from her throat. Damn Frankie and Rebecca for upsetting their father this way. What a couple of instigators they were.

Well, she wouldn't cry. That would mean they'd won, and she wasn't about to give up. If her stepchildren wanted to play dirty, she'd show them how tough she could be.

She stood still, listening for sounds of activity from the bedroom. Franklin might be calling out to her right now, ready to say that he was sorry and that of course he believed her.

Seconds ticked by. With a heavy heart she realized he had nothing to say to her. She turned around and placed her hand on the doorknob, but something stopped her from turning it. Franklin's health was failing, but he wasn't an invalid. He spent a good part of the day seated in a recliner. She'd look in on him in a half hour. If he wanted something that badly before then, let him get it himself. In the meantime, a little cool-off time wouldn't be a bad idea . . . for both of them.

Elyse glanced at her watch as she went to the kitchen. She

browsed in the refrigerator before deciding she really didn't want anything to eat.

As far as something to drink, that was another matter entirely. She reached for a bottle of Chardonnay and after carefully removing the cork, poured herself a glass. Then she cut off a block of cream cheese and stirred some of the spicy roasted red pepper dip she always kept on hand into it. Using one hand to cup her glass and the other to hold the bowl of dip, while grasping a bag of pretzel sticks with her fingers, she plodded into the family room and placed it all on the table. Then she dug out the novel she was reading from her tote bag, kicked off her shoes, and settled down sideways on the cushy tan sofa, her sock-clad feet resting on the opposite end. Smooth jazz, courtesy of the cable radio station, would complete the scenario, and she didn't even have to get up to turn it on. All it took was a flick of the remote. If she wasn't so lazy she'd get a fire going in the fireplace. Franklin always used to do that. . . .

Elyse bit her lip. She wasn't supposed to think about Franklin, at least not for the next half hour. No matter how she tried to convince herself, she would never leave him to fend for himself when he was ill. She kept hoping he'd come out and tell her he'd been wrong. But by now the pain medication Winnie had given him had probably put him to sleep.

She picked up her book and quickly became engrossed in it. She could relate to the character who'd lost her husband suddenly in a freak accident, but this poor woman found herself in a financial pinch. Thank God that wouldn't be her after Franklin was gone. . . .

Elyse looked up. What was she thinking? Franklin was dying, yes. Dr. LeBlond told them to plan only for short-term survival, twelve to eighteen months at the most, and very possibly much less than that. Just this afternoon she'd cried when she told Kevin about it. Now, after one argument with Franklin, she could accept his impending death as matter-of-factly as the knowledge that they were almost out of green tea.

Franklin had never once complained about his fate. Instead he accepted it readily, feeling blessed because he had been cho-

sen for death while she and all four of his children remained
healthy. But he wasn't a saint. What she'd just seen a few minutes ago was his striking back against his misfortune, aided by
the equally bitter Frankie. They all felt cheated by Franklin's
disease and—Frankie, Rebecca, and Franklin himself—were
taking it out on her. And that sucked.

Elyse had been reading for barely twenty minutes when she
heard the chime of the door alarm. Someone with a key had entered the house.

She put the book down eagerly. Todd and Brontë had said
they would drive up from Champaign early Saturday morning,
but maybe they'd decided to surprise her and Franklin by coming up tonight. She rushed toward the front door. "Todd?
Brontë? Is that you?"

A female figure stood with her back turned as she put the
latch on the door. Elyse froze when she turned around.

"What are you doing here, Rebecca?" she demanded.

"I came to see Dad. He didn't tell you?"

"No." The word came out as a whisper. Franklin had known
all along that his daughter was coming. No wonder he didn't
come out of their bedroom and apologize.

Rebecca shrugged. "It sounds like you two have a failure to
communicate. But that's not my problem." She began walking
toward the master bedroom.

"No, it's just your responsibility."

Rebecca paused. "What's that supposed to mean?"

"I mean that this morning when I left the house, everything
was fine with Franklin and me. But you and your brother decided
to fill his head with a lot of nonsense about me having an affair,
and now we're not talking."

"It wasn't nonsense, Elyse. I know what I saw, and so do you.
It's Dad I'm thinking of."

"Horseshit. I told you why Kevin was sitting on my side of
the booth. He was just about to move back when you pounced
on us. I've got a feeling that part was left out of your account of
what you saw." She grunted. "I don't understand why you
would even want to rush to tell your father when you know it
would only upset him."

"I talked it over with Frankie, and we both feel that Pop deserves to know, Elyse."

A possible reason for Rebecca and Frankie's behavior occurred to Elyse, and she looked at her stepdaughter through narrowed eyes. "Are you trying to get him to cut me out of his will?" If this was their goal, she had no doubt that their mother, Carolyn, was behind it. Carolyn had made a few catty remarks about how well off Elyse would be when she visited Franklin earlier in the year, which Elyse had simply dismissed as jealousy at the time. Now she considered that Carolyn had urged her children to manipulate Franklin.

"That's preposterous."

Rebecca sounded just like Johnnie Cochran, Elyse thought. That had been a favorite phrase of the famed criminal defense attorney. Annoyed, she turned away.

Elyse had resumed reading when Rebecca came storming into the family room. "I'm glad I came over. My daddy is in his room, hungry and thirsty, and here you are, reading a book!"

Startled, she quickly sat up. "What the hell are you talking about?"

"Dad's hungry. You didn't even go to see if he wanted anything. He told me you just stormed out and told him to fend for himself."

"He said *what?*"

Rebecca glared at her. "You heard me."

"Now, listen here, Rebecca. I won't have you taking that tone with me in my house. You either speak to me with a civil tone, or you can leave."

"This is my father's house, and I have just as much right to be here as *your* children."

Elyse gasped. She had never differentiated between her children and her stepchildren. Frankie and Rebecca always had a key to their home, so they could come by as they wished. The rule of "Please call before you come" was followed by all four offspring, just for the sake of privacy. It always stood for Frankie and Rebecca, who had never actually lived here; and it went into effect for Todd and Brontë when they left for college.

"If you'll excuse me," Rebecca said coldly, "I have to take care of my father." She turned and walked to the adjacent kitchen.

Elyse was so angry she felt there might be smoke coming out of her ears. Her first thought was to run to her room, throw a few clothing changes into a bag, and go check into a hotel. Just as quickly as the idea formed she vetoed it. Rebecca and Frankie would say she'd abandoned Franklin. If they were looking to increase the size of their inheritances by reducing hers, that would be all the ammunition they needed.

No, the best thing she could do was to stay right here. When she was ready to go to bed, she'd just go up and get on the left side, just like she always did. The king-sized mattress was large enough so she and Franklin could stay out of each other's way, yet she'd be there if he needed her.

Tomorrow would be better.

Elyse wasn't surprised to see Rebecca still around the next morning. Well, that was fine. Todd and Brontë were probably on their way up right now. At least she'd have someone on *her* side.

"Mom, what does Rebecca mean, you aren't taking care of Daddy?" Brontë asked, a frown marring her pretty face. A worried-looking Todd stood behind her.

Elyse sighed wearily. She hadn't expected it to take long for Rebecca to spread more gloom and doom. "Sit down, kids, and I'll tell you what's going on."

She related yesterday's incident, including her clashes with their father and older sister, then sat back expectantly, waiting for them to express indignation.

Todd looked puzzled. "Mom . . . I don't get it. Who is this guy, anyway?"

Elyse's mouth fell open. This wasn't the response she'd anticipated. Hadn't Todd heard what she just said about the terrible things that had been said to her, or had he been unable to get past her having lunch with a male friend? "I told you, an old friend. We were kids together. It's always nice to have someone to tell your troubles to."

"But why not Annie?" Brontë asked, shaking her head, referring to the nurse who was Elyse's closest friend at work. "Or one of your friends from the projects whom you grew up with, like Miss Susan?"

Elyse tried not to show her disappointment. Her own children were acting like she had done something wrong.

"Because," she said testily, "my friends are busy with their own families, and besides, sometimes even very good friends can act strangely when illness hits close to home." Neither statement was one hundred percent true. Only Susan had young children, and only Grace sounded a little stiff and unnatural when she called to offer assistance, like she really didn't mean it; Pat expressed genuine concern and support. Elyse had no doubt that they would react the same way when they learned of Franklin's relapse. But she needed support and had to give as many valid reasons as possible, since Todd and Brontë couldn't get past this man/woman thing.

"And because Kevin suggested we have lunch together," she continued. "He wanted to try to cheer me up. What was I supposed to do, turn him down and keep trying to manage by myself just because of his gender? My having lunch with him is no different than if I ate with Susan, Pat, or Annie." She grunted. "I'll bet Rebecca wouldn't have been on the phone to Frankie if that had been *Susan* sitting on the same side of the booth with me trying to get me to stop crying."

Elyse watched as Todd and Brontë looked at each other. "Mom's right," Brontë said. "You and I are down at school. She should be able to lean on any of her friends who's available, even if it's a man."

"Answer this question for me," Elyse commanded. "Do you honestly believe that I would cheat on your father with anyone?"

"No, Mom," Todd said. "And I think Dad was wrong to say those things to you. Rebecca, too."

"Let's go in and talk to him now, Todd," Brontë suggested. "Come on. We'll see Rebecca as soon as she gets up."

Relief flooded through Elyse. This was more like it. She needed a show of support. Maybe the kids could make Franklin see how silly he was being. "Why don't I make us all a nice breakfast? I'll get it started while you two are in with your father."

As Elyse mixed pancake batter, her thoughts kept going back to the half-truths she'd just told. She'd gotten Todd and Brontë over to her side of the issue, but she'd done it under not entirely accurate circumstances. It didn't feel good.

As she heated the electric griddle, she decided to confide in her friends when she saw them next week, provided anybody showed up.

Chapter 50

Late October
Skokie, Illinois

"This was smart, to meet at three o'clock," Susan remarked as she glanced around the restaurant with its empty tables. It's too late for lunch, and too early for dinner, so we avoided the crowd and they won't rush us out of here."

"At least not until the dinner rush starts," Grace said.

"This is what we'll do," Pat suggested. "Whenever we notice the waiter looking at us funny, somebody order another drink. They won't ask us to leave if we're still spending money."

"But they will if we get drunk," Elyse said with a laugh.

In the end they ordered a bottle of Merlot. Elyse hoped the liquor would help everyone relax. She could practically reach out and feel the tension in the air.

The waiter filled their glasses. "I propose a toast," Susan said, holding up her glass. "Here's to almost fifty years of friendship. May we always be there for each other, through ups and downs, good times and bad. . . ."

They clicked glasses and drank. "All right," Pat began, "I know that you two know that Grace and I were on the outs, but we had a good talk on the drive up here, and we'll be all right. Won't we, Grace?"

"You betcha. I'm just glad that everything worked out with you and Andy."

"Yeah, it did. I'm feeling very happy these days."

"Do I hear wedding bells?" Susan asked, her voice ringing with excitement.

"No. But we're in love and we're happy. It's been too long since I've been able to say that." Pat looked at Elyse. "And how's everything with you? How's Franklin?"

Elyse swallowed. She didn't want to put a pall over their luncheon. "He's not doing too well. The cancer has spread, and it doesn't look good." She stopped to listen to the sympathetic murmurings she'd known would come.

"You seem like you're dealing with it pretty well," Grace commented.

"I think it helps that after his first diagnosis Franklin and I did a lot of talking about what we would do if this happened. But he didn't tell me then that he wouldn't want to undergo more treatment because he didn't want me to get upset."

"I guess it would be different if his remission had lasted longer," Pat said cautiously.

"I think so, too. But he was never cancer free. There was always a possibility that it would show up elsewhere in his body."

"Why didn't you tell us sooner?" Pat asked.

"Is there anything we can do?" Susan asked.

"I'm still trying to come to terms with it. And, yes, there is something you can do. I'd like your take on something that happened the other day. I was having lunch with Kevin, and when I told him about Franklin's prognosis I broke down. He came to sit on my side of the booth to comfort me, and at that moment in walks my stepdaughter. She told her brother, and he told Franklin, and Franklin's been mad at me ever since. He said some pretty nasty things to me."

"I'm a little surprised that you told Kevin about Franklin before you told any of us," Pat said. "Are you two really all that close?"

"No, not really. We'd actually had a disagreement. After Franklin's diagnosis, I asked myself if my own life was tied up in a neat little bundle if I were to die suddenly, and I decided to make up with him."

"What happened with you and Kevin?" This from Grace.

"It wasn't really a disagreement," Elyse clarified. "We'd just finished having lunch, and he walked me to my car. Before I got in he suddenly grabbed me and . . . kissed me."

Susan's jaw dropped. "He *kissed* you?"

"Yes."

"From the guilty look on your face, I guess it was no quick peck on the lips."

Elyse didn't back down. "I won't lie to you. It felt real good."

Susan shrugged. "I'm sure, but it wasn't appropriate behavior, feeding you his tongue in a parking lot. Did he have the decency to apologize?"

"Yes. Well, sort of." She recounted what Kevin had said to her.

"So you made up," Pat said. "That's a good thing, but you don't plan on seeing him again, do you? It seems like he caused a lot of trouble in your household, even if it was indirectly. And I agree with Susan. He had no business kissing you."

"Why shouldn't I see him again? Kevin showed me affection. He showed me that he thinks I'm attractive. You have no idea how wonderful that sounds to me after having to put up with all Franklin's insults. If I try to get him to eat something he'll say things like, 'You're a lousy cook,' or, 'I wouldn't put it past you to poison me so you can be the merry widow.' " She grabbed a napkin and furiously dabbed at her eyes; it hurt just to repeat the things that came out of Franklin's mouth.

Susan took a deep breath. "Elyse, I'm so sorry. It isn't fair for Franklin to say those things to you. It's verbal abuse, and I'm sure it hurts almost as much as if he'd physically slapped you. But if you continue to see Kevin, you might do something you'll regret."

That thought had occurred to Elyse, but she didn't want to admit it. Instead she fixated on Grace. "Grace, you've been awfully quiet. What do you think?"

"Are you sure he's not after something?" Grace asked bluntly.

Elyse's eyes narrowed. "Listen, Grace. I might not work out like you do, and I admit I need to lose some weight, but it's still a stretch for you to say that the only way a man will find me attractive is if there's something in it for him."

"That's not what I meant, so don't get your nipple in a knot. I'm just saying that men often have ulterior motives, and that Kevin is no different from anyone else. Trust me, Elyse. I've been out there in the dating world a long time."

"Kevin doesn't know anything about what I have or don't have. I don't wear designer duds or tool around town in a Maserati."

"No, but think about it. He knows what you do for a living. Physical therapists make good money, Elyse. I'm sure he also knows that Franklin is a software developer. I'm sure the fact that you live in Lake Forest has come up. Elyse, there are no poor folks living in Lake Forest, just people like Michael Jordan and Lovie Smith."

Elyse looked taken aback, realizing that Grace had a point. "Those guys are millionaires. Franklin and I are hardly in their league," she finally said.

"So you don't have a thirty-room mansion. You still live in one of the nicest suburbs in Lake County. Plus, I'm sure you mentioned that both your children live in campus housing down in Champaign," Grace concluded. "A person doesn't have to be a rocket scientist to figure out that you're no pauper. Kevin is an exterminator. You have to consider that his kissing you all of a sudden might be related to the fact that you're well off and your husband is in failing health."

Pat slammed her palm down on the table. "Grace, do you have to be so damn blunt?"

"No, Pat, it's all right," Elyse said quietly. She hoped that her two friends' truce wasn't about to go out the window, for she couldn't deny that Grace had a valid point. "It's something I have to consider."

"You'd be nuts not to," Grace said, casually buttering a roll.

"Do you get that a lot, Grace?" Elyse asked. "Guys with ulterior motives for dating you?"

"Yes, Grace, do you get that a lot?" Pat asked with a smile.

Grace's suddenly stiff body language relayed that she didn't enjoy having the focus shift to her. "Yes, it's been a problem before," she admitted. "As you well know," she added, her eyes fixated on Pat, "that's why I broke up with Eric. If he wasn't asking for the keys to my car and my house so he could 'watch' them for me while I'm traveling, he was making really cutting remarks about my job." She bit into her roll. "I just decided he wasn't worth it anymore."

"I think you made the right decision," Elyse said gently. She felt rather sorry for Grace, who, with her two failed marriages and countless affairs, brought new meaning to the expression "unlucky in love."

"He's really no different than the rest. They all feel threatened by my education and my income." She shrugged. "It's hard to find suitable black men out there to go out with."

"You've just outgrown him, that's all," Pat said. "You know, you can always see Glenn Arterbridge. He asked me about you just last week."

Grace rolled her eyes. "Not that again. He's a nice man, good-looking and all that, but there's no sex appeal. And without that, why bother?"

Susan watched the exchange curiously. "Maybe you ought to lower your standards just a little bit, Grace. Where there's good looks there's *always* sex appeal."

"Yeah, somewhere in that fifty-inch waistline."

Susan blinked. *Fifty-inch waistline? Ugh.* "Oh." She turned to Pat. "Pat, I know you've got a boyfriend, but did you have as much difficulty as Grace trying to find good dates?"

"No, not really. But I never went out as much as Grace. I decided I'd rather be by myself than be with somebody just for the sake of being with them."

"Well, la-de-da," Grace said. "Elyse, Pat's no different from me. She just goes out with white guys instead of black ones."

"That's not true, Grace," Pat protested. "You make it sound like I date white men exclusively. I can't help it if I have more in common with the white guys I come across. All the successful black guys are married. And I won't go out with guys who don't have a level of education and success that's reasonably comparable with mine."

"In other words, no moving-and-storage guys," Grace said knowingly. "And no Orkin men, either."

"I hate to sound like a snob, and I wish that wasn't the way it is, but it's a rare man who can handle having a woman who's more successful than he is. I would have loved to have fallen in love with a nice black man, at least before I hooked up with Andy."

"I'd love to be a fly on the wall when you finally bring him home to meet your mama and daddy," Grace said. She caught Susan's eye. "See what you're missing out on by being happily married, Susan? All this men drama."

"Um . . . Maybe I'm not so happily married."

Three voices spoke a single syllable in unison. *"What?"*

"There're some things going on in my life that you don't know about, but I decided it's time to talk to someone," Susan said. She told her friends about how breast cancer had destroyed the passion in her marriage, and how she reached out to Charles Valentine and fell in love all over again. As she expected, her friends at first expressed shock at learning she was a cancer patient. It warmed Susan's heart when they assured her how wonderful she looked.

"Thanks. I feel good. I just try to take it six months at a time." But she didn't want to focus on her illness, not with what Elyse was going through with Franklin. Instead she recounted how she and Charles had broken up after he continually pressed her to leave Bruce for him, and how she lost her temper and asked how he intended to support her and her children.

"Ouch," Elyse said. "That's probably the worst thing you can do to a man. Attack him in the pocketbook."

"I couldn't help it, Elyse. It wasn't fair for him to nag me about leaving Bruce when he had no plans for what would happen after that."

Elyse nodded. "True."

"I can't believe you've been having an affair," Grace said. "You'd leave Bruce for Charles? You said it yourself, Susan. No way can he provide for you the way Bruce can."

"And *you* said it yourself, Grace. You've got to have sex appeal to have a happy relationship. As far as my husband is concerned, I don't have any."

"Susan, it seems to me that you're being hypocritical," Elyse said. "You tell me not to have an affair with Kevin, but you slept with Charles."

"And now that it's over, I feel worse than ever. And Elyse, I truly believe that if you sleep with Kevin or anyone else while Franklin is on his deathbed, you'll never forgive yourself. I think it will haunt you always. Nothing makes cheating right."

"That's easy for *you* to say. You're not the one being criticized all the time." Her head was bent, and tears flowed freely down her cheeks.

"Elyse, if you sleep with Kevin, you'll only be doing it to soothe your pride. You'll hate yourself afterward. And you'll always regret cheating on Franklin."

"Yeah, well, did *you* regret cheating on Bruce?"

"No," Susan admitted. "But I know he has someone else. Franklin is coping with a serious illness. That's different. I know how that feels, too, and I think it's even more difficult for men." She tried a different tack. "Listen, I'm not saying not to have an affair with Kevin. I'm just saying don't do it now, while Franklin is still your husband. At least wait until he's gone."

Elyse blew her nose. "I understand what you mean. I truly do love my husband. But lately I don't like him at all."

"I wish there was something I could do," Grace said. "I'm in complete shock. I thought you two both had great marriages. And I never dreamed that you were ill, Susan. Why didn't you tell anyone?"

"Because I wanted to keep it personal." She wanted to smack Grace. Even as Grace had spoken, her eyes kept going to Susan's chest, like she was thinking, *Now, which one was it again?* And Grace had the nerve to ask why she'd kept her condition secret?

"Franklin is the same way," Elyse said. "I understand how you feel, Susan."

"But what are you going to do?" Pat asked. "Will you just keep on living with Bruce?"

"No. I decided that if I can't have a hundred percent of the man I'm with, I'd rather not have him at all, even it means being out there by myself. I was hoping you might be able to give me some pointers, Pat."

"Divorce isn't my specialty, Susan," Pat began. "But have you considered talking to Bruce? You say there's no real acrimony between you. Maybe the two of you can work out something between you without getting the court involved."

"Of course, when I was married to Jimmy we didn't have the proverbial pot," Grace said, "but my divorce from Danny was amicable. We sold the condo, split the proceeds, and I bought the one I live in now."

"You and Danny didn't have kids together," Susan pointed out. "And you make a lot more money than I do. I'm an experienced accountant, but I lost eleven years. This job I have now only brings in pin money. I'd have a lot of trouble trying to run a household unless I could bring in a lot more cash."

"Susan, do you really think that Bruce would allow you and the kids to live hand to mouth?" Elyse asked.

"That's just it; I don't know. Bruce has always been generous with money, but once I tell him I want a divorce his whole attitude might change. For all I know, he might want custody of Quentin and Alyssa, just to be spiteful."

"Wisconsin is a community property state, isn't it?" Pat pondered.

"Yes, it is. That means Bruce risks half of everything he has in a divorce."

"In that case, don't tell him you're divorcing him until the very last minute," Grace said. "You don't want to give him time to hide assets. And don't tell him about Charles. Even if it's over between the two of you, he might use that against you."

Elyse looked sad, and Susan knew she was thinking about the state of her own marriage. "I like to think that Susan and Bruce can end their marriage in a dignified manner," she said quietly.

Grace plunged on, ignoring Elyse's suggestion. "And if you think he's cheating, Susan, get a PI to follow him and make a report."

"Grace has a point, Susan," Pat said reluctantly. "If you can prove Bruce is cheating on you, it'll be great leverage for you in a settlement. He's less likely to fight for custody of the kids or try to screw you out of your fair share. And since you're not seeing Charles anymore, even if he has you followed, nothing will turn up that he can use against you."

"I say tell the PI to carry a camera and catch the mother-fucker in the act," Grace said, pounding the tabletop for emphasis. "Then confront him about it with copies of the photos and take him for half of everything he's got."

"Grace, are you all right?" Susan asked. She didn't know what to make of Grace's vehemence.

"No, I'm pissed. I'm fifty years old and I can't get a damn date."

Susan tried to think of something positive to say. "You look great, Grace. Fifty really agrees with you."

"Gee, thanks, Susan."

Elyse frowned. Didn't Grace realize Susan had just paid her a compliment? "I don't know why you're acting like Susan told you you've got bad breath or something. Hell, we'll all be fifty by the end of the year."

"Yeah, but I'm fifty *now.*"

"Consider the alternative," Susan snapped.

"Yeah, you're right." Grace smiled. "But since you and Charles broke up because you were afraid to get a divorce, and now you've decided to get one, maybe you two can get back together again."

Elyse and Pat both looked on, hope in their faces. But Susan shook her head. "I haven't heard from him at all since I lashed out at him. I know he's very upset with me. And don't forget, this is the second time I broke things off with him. And nothing was solved about where or how we'd live. Charles kept saying he could take care of my kids and me, but frankly, I don't see how. He's lived in that one-bedroom apartment in his mother's house for decades, and even if his place were big enough, Quentin and Alyssa aren't really city kids. I think they'd hate living in Chicago."

"Maybe his mother will trade places with him. She doesn't need all those rooms anymore," Pat said.

"And Hyde Park is considerably nicer than Dreiser," Elyse remarked.

"First, Ann Valentine hates me, so she's not about to go out of her way to accommodate me. Second, Hyde Park is still the city. Hell, just a few months ago Carol Mosely Braun got attacked at her front door by a man with a knife who'd been hiding in the bushes."

"I hope you can work it out," Elyse said. "That man loves you, Susan. I could see it in his eyes that night at Junior's Bar."

"I love a happy ending," Grace said dreamily. "I still hope I'll get to have one."

A silence fell over the table as each woman thought about what would make her happy:

I wish that Franklin will recover, that things could be like they used to be. . . .

I wish that my parents will accept Andy, and that Grace had left Ricky alone. . . .

I wish I could get my divorce, keep my kids, and be with Charles . . . if he still wants me. . . .

I wish I had a nice man to settle down with. . . .

Chapter 51

A familiar feeling of dread came over Elyse as she turned onto the street where she lived. She hated coming home these days, since Franklin had started acting so badly. She'd heard people in unhappy marriages say that, but she never expected to be one of them.

She got out of her car without hesitation. Her unhappiness with his attitude aside, it was her responsibility to take care of Franklin. Brontë and Todd were at home with him, but she wanted to check on him as well. Maybe he'd finally gotten over this foolishness. It had been a week already, the worst week of her life.

Seeing her friends had helped her spirits tremendously. At least she knew that there were people who cared. Between the coldness of Franklin and her stepchildren and her own children's bewilderment, she needed to know she had allies. And it was best for any warm, tingly feelings to come from her girlfriends rather than from Kevin.

Elyse knew Susan had been right to warn her to stay away from Kevin. They had done nothing wrong, well, other than that kiss. Rebecca witnessed a perfectly innocent scene at lunch. Elyse felt falsely accused, but she knew, because of the impression they'd given, it would be foolish to spend additional time with him.

As Elyse walked into the living room Brontë looked up from the book she was reading. "How was lunch, Mom?"

"It was a lot of fun. How's Daddy?"

"He's okay. Todd is in there with him."

"Did he eat?"

"Not a whole lot."

Elyse's heart sank. The more weight Franklin lost, the more strength went with it. He'd gotten so thin.

She entered the bedroom. "Hi, there! I'm back."

"Hi, Mom," Todd said. "Did you have fun?"

"Yes, I did. It was good to see the girls."

Franklin merely grunted.

She laid down her purse and hung up her jacket before sitting on the bed. Franklin and Todd sat in the two matching recliners with a table between them. "Brontë tells me you didn't eat much, Franklin. Can I fix something for you? You've got to eat to keep your strength up."

"Too bad you can't give me some of that extra fat you're carting around."

She drew in her breath. "Franklin! What an awful thing to say."

Even Todd looked startled.

"There'd still be plenty left over for your boyfriend."

"Dad—" Todd began.

"Stay out of this, Todd."

"Damn it, Franklin, how many times do I have to tell you that I'm not cheating on you?" Elyse was near tears. She hadn't been in the house five minutes and he was starting in on her already.

He looked at her coldly. "I guess he likes his women fat."

A defiant Elyse returned the stare, determined that he wouldn't see her crumble. "All right, then, don't eat. Waste away to nothing! See if I care."

"Mom!"

She turned on her heel and left, slamming the door shut behind her. Already she regretted what she'd said, but damn it, she couldn't help it. What was she supposed to do, collapse in a crying heap and beg him not to say such cruel things? Damn Franklin for bringing out the worst in her.

She whizzed through the living room and up the stairs, too upset to respond to Brontë's urgent, repeated question about what was wrong. In the privacy of the guest bedroom she fell across the bed, sobbing.

She'd been praying for strength ever since Franklin's diagnosis. His terminal condition after such a promising start had nonetheless come as a shock, in spite of her having had months to consider the possibility. But why was he giving her such a hard time? Did he have no confidence in her love for him at all? She'd been so sure all these years that they had a strong marriage. Now he was dying, and she feared he would go to his grave and leave her nothing but cruel taunts to remember him by. Of course she had many happy memories of their twenty-six years together, but the bad ones had a way of taking center stage, especially if they were the most recent.

Someone knocked at the door, followed by the sound of the door opening. "Mom, I'm sorry," Todd said.

Brontë, on his heels, sat on the edge of the mattress to the double bed. "Are you all right, Mom?"

Elyse struggled to control her tears. "I'm all right. And you have nothing to be sorry for, Todd. It's your father who's behaving badly."

"I couldn't believe the things he said to you. I don't want him to die, Mom, but it's not right for him to take out his frustration on you."

She absorbed his words. "Do you think that's what it is? That he's angry at dying and is taking it out on me?"

"Mom, there's no way Dad can believe you're cheating on him. I don't know what else it can be. Has he been this way since that incident last weekend?"

She nodded.

"I think Rebecca should have kept her mouth shut," Brontë said.

"Are you going to stay up here tonight?" Todd asked.

She sighed. "I was thinking about it. But I don't want to be

too far away from your father. He might need . . . something."
She'd almost said, "me." That was silly. She was the last person
he'd need.

"I can stay in the room with him tonight. I think you deserve
a break. As it is, I feel awful about having to leave tomorrow.
But maybe I can talk some sense into him before we go."

"I wish we could take off the rest of the semester," Brontë
said wistfully.

"No more talk about missing school, young lady. Todd, I'll
take this break you're offering, at least for a few hours, but
don't you two go worrying about me."

Elyse had planned on spending only a few hours in the tran-
quility of the guest room, but she fell asleep while watching a
movie on one of the Lifetime channels, and when she awoke it
was after nine o'clock. She went downstairs to check on Franklin. Todd and Brontë were watching a premiere of a made-for-
cable movie in the living room. If the dark setting was any
indication, it was a scary movie, the kind where Elyse would
grip Franklin's upper arm and squeeze it at the most tense moments, and he would laugh and loosen her grip on him. . . .

"How is he?" she asked.

"I checked on him about fifteen minutes ago," Brontë said.
"He was asleep."

"We made some hamburgers, if you're hungry," Todd added.
"And you feel free to go back upstairs and relax. I meant what I
said about taking care of Dad until Brontë and I have to drive
back tomorrow."

"That's sweet of both of you, but taking care of your father is
really my responsibility. I'll take over from here." Elyse yawned.
In spite of the good nap she'd had, she was still tired. Emotion-
ally worn out was more like it. "I guess I'll go in now. I'll use my
night-light to read."

"Mom, I hate to think of him saying something else hateful
to you," Todd said.

"I'll be all right. You two have taken care of him since early
this afternoon. Don't worry. I'm not going to crumble again."

Elyse quietly slipped into the bedroom. A dim night-light at the base of the lamp shone. She took a quick shower, then slid underneath the covers and looked at her sleeping husband. He looked so peaceful in repose. His face had gotten thin—he'd lost nearly forty pounds. Her heart swelled . . . six months from now she might not have him to look at anymore.

Elyse's book remained on her nightstand. She didn't really want to read. All she wanted to do was look at Franklin. She wanted to move close to him and snuggle, but she didn't dare. All she could do was look at him from a safe distance that the other side of their king-sized bed provided.

Her thoughts went back to the way he'd been behaving for the past week. From the beginning of this ordeal she'd tried to be as good a wife to Franklin as she ever had been. Why was he so convinced that she was having an affair, or even about to have one? Were Frankie and Rebecca feeding his paranoia?

Reluctantly she allowed herself to consider the part her own actions might have played in contributing to his fears. She knew it had hurt him deeply when she called him an old fart, and maybe even alarmed him when she went out those times and left him home, first to have dinner with Pat and Grace, second to the reunion, and last, that night at Junior's Bar with Susan.

If only she'd realized he was really ill. If he'd constantly said he felt listless, she would have gotten him to the doctor sooner. But he had no problem going out to play cards or getting to the driving range to practice his golf swing. He'd mentioned an ailment only when he canceled plans that involved her.

She turned out the light and moved toward him, resting her palm on the curve of his hip. If he told her to move, then she would, but she couldn't bear another night of sleeping so far away from him on the same mattress.

As she was starting to fall asleep, her hand fell forward, stretching across his stomach. But she was aware enough to notice when he made a sighing sound in his sleep and covered her hand with his.

Then she fell asleep, confident that it would be all right.

Chapter 52

Early November
Chicago

Pat cleared the table, assisted, as always when her parents were over for dinner, by her mother. She liked to have them come over every now and again. They enjoyed visiting her condo, which was only a few miles from their apartment on 67th Street.

"You're a good cook, Pat," Moses said appreciatively, patting his protruding belly.

"Thanks, Daddy."

"I wish I could take credit for your skills in the kitchen," Cleotha said. "Those stuffed pork chops are fabulous. Of course, when you kids were coming up, pork chops were for special occasions, like birthdays. And we could never afford chops thick enough to be stuffed."

"You taught me the basics, Mama. That's where good cooking starts. I just expanded on it a little."

"You're so sweet, Pat."

Cleotha straightened up after stacking plates in the dishwasher. The hand she placed on her lower back told Pat she shouldn't have been doing that, but she'd insisted, and Pat knew how futile it would be to argue with her.

Still, she thought about the bending required to shelve books at the library. How tired her mother must be. And how like her never to complain. "Mama, I can take it from here. Why don't you sit down?"

Cleotha didn't disagree. After she returned to her seat she said, "Pat, Daddy and I were hoping your friend would be here today so we could meet him."

"Yes, your new boyfriend I've heard so much about. The one with the deep pockets, who brings you to expensive restaurants where the bill comes to more than I used to pay for my car," Moses echoed. "Where's he hiding today, anyway? Surely he's not afraid to meet your old man." He smiled as he talked, as if he enjoyed the idea of still being threatening to Pat's suitors.

"Of course not, Daddy. This is his weekend with his daughters."

"He's divorced?" Cleotha asked.

All Cleotha and Moses knew about Andy was that he was a partner in a law firm and that he'd brought her to Galena and then to L.A. for the weekend. They only knew that much because she'd left town and felt they should know about it in case of an emergency. She'd deliberately left them in the dark for the most part, but the time had come to tell them about him, including his race. "Yes. He has two daughters in their teens. It's not an unusual background for an unmarried person almost fifty. *I'm* the odd one out, having never been married and not having any children." She watched as her parents exchanged glances. "You don't think I'd be involved with someone who's married, do you?"

"No, that's not it," Cleotha said. "Come sit down, Pat. Your daddy and I want to tell you something."

Pat dried her hands on a paper towel and tossed it in the trash before sitting down at the casual square laminate-topped table, which she always dressed up with a tablecloth and candlesticks when she had guests. "Is everything all right?" she asked. She felt fortunate to be nearly fifty years old and still have both her parents alive and well. Grace had lost both her folks, Elyse's father was ailing down there in Tennessee, and Susan's father, a recovering alcoholic, had plenty of bad days. Her parents had been a little younger than those of her friends, but age didn't determine how long a person would live.

"Nothing's wrong. Your mama and I were talking, and we decided there's something we need to tell you," Moses said.

Pat still felt uneasy. Her father had suddenly gone ill at ease, continually shifting in his chair, as if he couldn't get comfortable.

Cleotha took over. "I told Daddy about my little talk with Miriam at the luncheon, Pat. How triumphant she sounded as she talked about Ricky, and that smug smile on her face when she asked about you."

Pat's shoulders stiffened, and her throat felt constricted. She'd done her best to lock the past away and toss the key like a gum wrapper, but she still hated to be reminded of what happened with her and Ricky. Grace confessing her affair with him had hurt and would probably sting for some time to come, but at least it helped Pat see how futile it was to harbor feelings for him after all this time.

She thought that after her mother's report about her encounter with Miriam at the luncheon she'd never have to hear Ricky's name again. Andy was her present and her immediate future, and it was him she wanted to talk about, but for some ungodly reason both her parents felt they needed to discuss Ricky and his mother again. Would she ever be free of their long shadow?

"I can't imagine what Ricky and his mother have to do with anything now," she said slowly.

"Patty-cake," her father said, using the pet name he'd given her as a child, "your mama and I decided a long time ago that we were wrong. We knew about Ricky, about how he'd made good. The *Tribune* did an article on him some time back, when he opened his place downtown. It said how he already had a little lunch counter by the factories and how his move into a more upscale market seemed to be working. We talked about how he could have been our son-in-law and the father of our grandchildren."

Her old resentment embraced her like the welcoming arms of an old friend. "And I'm sure you talked about my still being single as well."

"Pat, please don't be angry with us," Cleotha pleaded. "We thought we were saving you heartache. And we were so afraid."

"You never even told me about the article."

"We didn't want to open an old wound that we hoped had healed," Moses admitted.

"When we lost Melvin"—Cleotha stopped speaking for several moments to compose herself—"it brought back so many old memories of Jacob."

"Mama, it wasn't the same thing. White men didn't kill Melvin. He was killed by street punks."

"I know. But when you're grieving, your emotions don't always make sense." Cleotha looked down for a moment. "I'm afraid we wanted to blame someone, anyone, for what happened to Melvin."

Moses spoke up. "But there's no relieving your pain, no matter what. Even that prison sentence that gang member got for shooting your brother didn't help. Nothing would, short of bringing Melvin back."

"We're so proud of you, Pat," Cleotha said. "But I'm afraid we did you a disservice by sending Ricky away. I felt we ought to tell you as much."

"But we did it for your own good," Moses said, citing a well-worn parental refrain. "To tell you the truth, we always thought you'd meet another young man, fall in love again, and get married."

Pat shrugged. Her parents' long-overdue apology did make her feel better about what they'd done. She hadn't realized how much of her resentment stemmed from their never saying another word about the part they'd played in changing the direction of her life. "I thought so, too," she said quietly. "But it never happened, did it?"

"But we're so excited that you've met someone special," Cleotha said. "We're looking forward to meeting him."

"So he has teenage daughters," Moses said. "Do they live here in the city, too?"

"No, they live with their mother up in Buffalo Grove." Pat

began to feel better. After her parents' apology, they'd have a hard time refusing to accept Andy.

Moses whistled. "I always knew there were more and more black folks with money all the time, but I never thought I'd have anything to do with them."

Pat took a deep breath. The time had come to let the proverbial cat out of the bag. She opened her mouth.

"What's his name, Pat?" her mother asked.

"Andrew Keindl. I call him Andy."

Cleotha nodded approval. "A nice, sturdy, biblical name. I like that."

"I knew some Kendalls that lived out in the west suburbs," Moses said. "I did handy work for them years ago. Nice people. Could they be a relation?"

Pat hadn't expected this reaction. She thought that once her parents heard Andy's last name they would realize he wasn't black. She'd forgotten that in the Anglicized pronunciation Andy favored it could easily be confused with a similar, more American-sounding name.

"No," she said. "Andy's last name is spelled 'K-e-i-n-d-l' and technically pronounced 'Kindill.' The first syllable rhymes with 'mine.' "

"That's an odd name," Cleotha said. "Is he—what do they call it now?—biracial?"

"No, Mama," she said quietly. "He's American, but his background is German."

Moses looked stricken. "He's *white?*" he finally sputtered.

"Yes, Daddy, he is."

"What's with you, Pat? Don't you ever come in contact with any black men?"

"Plenty. And many of them want to get closer to me. The problem is, they're all married."

"It's all right, Pat," Cleotha said quickly, although her eyes were on Moses. "We just weren't expecting that. You can't blame us for being a little surprised. *Can* she, Moses?" Her question held a warning.

"A German," Moses repeated. "I don't believe it. Do you know what the Germans said about the black athletes at the

Berlin Olympics back in '36? Then Jesse Owens took to the track and shut them all up. But I swear to God, if they'd won the war we'd all still be working in the cotton fields."

"Daddy, that whole Aryan-supremacy thing came from the Nazis. Not every German was a Nazi. Many of them were victims."

"Is his family Jewish?" Cleotha asked.

Pat found her mother's hesitant expression almost laughable. She could accept her daughter dating a German man as long as he was a Protestant. "No, Mama, they're not."

Moses sneered. "What do you know about how his parents feel about black people? Have you ever met them?"

"Well, no, but—"

"But nothing. You haven't met them because he's got no intention of presenting his black girlfriend to his parents."

Tears pooled in her lower lids. "Daddy, that's not fair. And it's a complete turnaround from your saying you're sorry you stopped me from marrying Ricky."

"That was different, Pat. We knew Ricky. A fine boy he was, ambitious and hardworking. I admired him for that. Many times I wished your brother Clarence had Ricky's ways instead of getting hooked on smack the way he did. Plus, we knew Miriam. And she knew you, from the time you were an infant in your carriage. She always thought highly of you. . . ."

Pat's lower lip dropped. Was this actually her father speaking, the man who'd called Ricky a "burrito boy" way back when? Now he made him sound like he'd been the catch of the fucking day. What a hypocrite.

Moses continued his rant. "But these people, strangers, and Germans to boot! They'll think it's bad enough you're black, but once they learn you grew up in the projects they'll raise a real ruckus." He shook his head. "Cleotha, I think we can forget about this new relationship of hers amounting to anything. This Andy dude may be giving her the rush, but eventually he'll get tired and move on."

That ripped it. Pat turned angrily on her father. "Daddy, I'll thank you not to talk about me like I'm not here."

Again Cleotha jumped into the breach. "Daddy didn't mean

it. I can't say I'm not concerned myself, Pat. I don't want you to get hurt. What if his people don't approve of you?"

"You mean, just like you didn't want me to get hurt if I married Ricky, and just like *you* didn't approve of *him.*"

"I didn't think Ricky would hurt you, Pat. I know he loved you. We were worried about the discrimination you would face as an interracial couple, plus the hard life you might have if Ricky's dreams of owning a successful restaurant didn't come to pass. There might be mixed-race couples all over the place now, but you didn't see a whole lot of them thirty years ago."

"Susan Bennett's parents lived right there in Dreiser."

"Yes, and her father became a drunk. I heard he came from a good family who disowned him when he married Frances, and he couldn't get back into their good graces afterward, which sent him down the road paved with gin."

"That was just gossip, Mama. David Bennett's family might have disowned him, but they didn't have a whole lot of money. Susan told me that herself. I think Minnie Johnson started that rumor because it made for a good story."

Moses spoke up again. "Yeah, well, the Bennett family might not have had a lot of money, but I'll bet none of them lived in the projects."

"Enough about the Bennetts. We're not talking about them; we're talking about Andy and me." Pat cleared her throat. "Mama . . . Daddy, I'm going to do now what I should have done thirty years ago and was too weak to. I'm sorry about what happened to our family. I don't think there was anything you could have done to prevent it. You always said it was no crime to be poor as long as you did your best. We're not the only family to have lost members to gang violence and drugs.

"And I don't know what's going to happen with Andy and me. We might break up next week. And it's true, his parents might not like his getting involved with a black woman. But I can tell you this: This is a happy time for me. For years I've dreamed of being courted the way I am now. And regardless of what you say, Daddy, I know that Andy genuinely cares about me. I'm not just a bed partner to him." The more she spoke, the stronger she felt. "I'm going to see this thing through, wherever it takes me. If it goes all the way—and I'm not saying it will— and the thought of having a white son-in-law doesn't sit well with you, well, I'm very sorry. I'll have to work it so that I see you alone." Her speech over, she folded her hands in front of her on the table, enjoying the rush of exhilaration. She felt almost serene. God, why hadn't she said this years ago?

"Like I said, I don't think you have to worry about it getting that far," her father said, stubborn to the end.

"We respect your wishes, Pat," Cleotha assured her. "The last thing Daddy and I want is to interfere with your happiness a second time. If you and this Andy get serious about each other, Daddy and I will learn to live with it."

"I appreciate that." She didn't bother to point out that she and Andy were already serious. Instead she pulled her clasped hands apart and patted the tabletop with her palm and flashed her sunniest smile. "Now, anybody for pound cake?"

After her parents left Pat thought about what she'd said. Funny, in hindsight it had seemed so easy to hold her ground. Thirty years ago, though, everything had been different. She'd been a nineteen-year-old desperate to make her parents happy after the tragic murder of their youngest child. Because Clarence had already gone down the wrong path, Pat knew that she alone represented her parents' dreams of success.

They hadn't steered her wrong. Her father had taken on a second job as an extra hand on a moving crew to earn extra money to help her pay for what her scholarship didn't cover. Her mother had registered to do some weekend housecleaning. Pat had always been a good student, but she wasn't as smart as Grace, who'd been awarded a full scholarship. Pat remembered protesting when Cleotha insisted that she learn to type back in high school. "I don't want to be a secretary, Mama," she'd said. "I want to go to college. I'm gonna be a lawyer."

"And you *will* go to college, Pat. But it's going to take a long time to get your law degree. It won't hurt for you to have a back-up skill."

Cleotha had been right. Not only did Pat, who typed ninety words a minute, make a nice amount of money typing up term papers for her fellow students, but she did temporary office work during school vacations.

Pat knew her parents loved her and wanted the best for her, but Grace was right. It was time to let them know they weren't the engineers of her life.

Chapter 53

Late November
Pleasant Prairie, Wisconsin

Susan looked up when Bruce returned. "Anything wrong?"
"Yes. There's a problem at the office. I'm afraid I've got to get up there."

"But it's a holiday," Frances McMillan protested.

"I know, Miss Frances. But people are always using their credit cards. Money never sleeps. I'll try to get back. Y'all just go ahead and watch the movie without me."

Susan's father, sister, and brother-in-law expressed regrets that he had to leave, but Susan said nothing. She didn't believe it.

It certainly hadn't taken Bruce long to find another sweetie to cuddle up with. Susan deduced that the time Bruce spent at home last summer happened only because he and his flame of the moment had broken up. The one he'd replaced her with must be plenty demanding, for he spent more time than ever away from home. She didn't think he'd have the nerve to leave on Thanksgiving when they were hosting her entire family, but here he was, leaving again. *Work, my ass.*

Bruce still hadn't returned by the time the family had their dessert and went home, all except for Frances, who was staying with them so she and Susan could hit the stores before daylight the next morning. Frances went to bed early, and Quentin and Alyssa stayed up watching TV. Susan retired to her bedroom and tried to read, but her thoughts kept going to Charles. How had he spent the holiday? Did he and Douglas call a truce long enough for them to sit down to dinner with their mother and Douglas's wife and daughter? Most important, had he been thinking of her?

No, that's not right. He shouldn't *be thinking of me. He's supposed to move on, find himself a nice girl, and settle down.* Their romance simply wasn't meant to be. The first time she'd walked out on Charles, and now he'd walked out on her after she said something that he no doubt interpreted as an attack on his ability to provide. At least, she thought sadly, they were even.

Susan's plan called for her to start looking for full-time work in March. She wanted six months of recent experience on her resume to convince prospective employers that she knew how accounting was handled in today's market. At that time she'd tell Bruce that she wanted a divorce.

The timing would work out perfectly. She was due for her next six-month cancer screening in March. If she received another clean bill of health, she'd move on. If she didn't, well, she wasn't exactly stuck, but there seemed little point in starting a new life if not much time remained.

Chapter 54

Pat went into Andy's kitchen to get matches for the candles. She and Andy were hosting their first joint get-together: a postdinner Thanksgiving cocktail party at his town house. She'd eaten with her parents, and he with his, but their situations differed in that Kurt and Renate Keindl had come to their party, while only Cleotha represented the Maxwells.

Pat had brought her mother herself after Moses flatly refused to attend. He seemed shocked by Cleotha's insistence; she had deferred to his wishes throughout most of their long marriage.

"Your father is just being stubborn, Pat," she said on the ride over. "He'll come around. Don't worry."

Pat was glad to have her mother present. She'd been a little worried about meeting the senior Keindls for the first time. In addition, Andy's ex-wife and her husband had driven down from Buffalo Grove to drop off his daughters, who would spend the rest of the weekend with him, and stopped in to have a drink.

The swinging door opened as Pat rummaged through the drawer. "Hey, you all right in here?"

"Oh, yeah. I just want to light the candles." She held up a grill lighter. "Voilà!"

"I just wanted to make sure nothing's wrong."

She knew he was referring to her father's absence, plus unexpectedly having to meet his ex-wife face-to-face. "You are so thoughtful. No wonder I love you so much."

He bent to kiss her, then spontaneously pulled her into his arms for a quick embrace. "I'll go with you when you bring your mother home. Then I'm expecting you to spend the night with me."

"But Lauren and Kaitlyn are here. I figured I'd just go home."

"I'm tired of doing that. My daughters aren't babies, Pat. They know the facts of life. I don't think we have to tiptoe around protocol."

She shrugged. "If you're sure it's all right . . . okay." She really didn't think it was a big deal, but she wasn't a parent and was prepared to defer to his judgment where his children were concerned. She'd once mishandled a similar situation, disagreeing with a date's rules for his kids in front of the youngsters, which put the relationship on a downward slide from which it never recovered. She didn't want to repeat that error with Andy.

It amazed her how happy she was, now that she'd gotten rid of her baggage and given her full emotions free rein to love Andy. She still remembered what he'd said the night he brought her home after their disastrous dinner at Nirvana: "I'm in love with you, Pat. It really hurt me to see you reduced to a quivering mass of Jell-O because you saw an old boyfriend, especially one from such a long time ago. Maybe you don't feel the same way about me. I could try to win you over, but experience has taught me that if a woman is hung up on another man there's no point in going on. I know you're denying it, but the way you reacted shows you're still hung up on him." Then he'd kissed her cheek. "When you get over him, give me a call. Maybe I'll still be around."

He'd been so honest with her, and yet she was unable to admit that she still had feelings for Ricky. Her instinct told her that Andy was telling her the truth when he said he was in love with her, and as happy as that made her, she'd nonetheless held back on committing her heart to him, and she didn't understand why.

When Grace confessed to her that she'd had an affair with

Ricky, Pat had her answer. In the deepest recesses of her heart she'd still hoped for the happy ending with Ricky. His acquiring of two wives wasn't even enough to get her to drop a notion that anyone with half a brain would recognize as ridiculous, but learning that he'd slept with Grace did the trick.

Pat then shared the details with Elyse, who'd been the one to tell her years ago that she'd seen Grace at the movies with Douglas Valentine. This happened after Susan broke up with him, but Elyse didn't know whether she should tell Susan or not. She'd called Pat to seek advice. Neither of them felt it was right for Grace to date Susan's ex. In the end they decided to tell Susan about it, and they were surprised when Susan didn't seem fazed.

Like Grace, Elyse had also urged Pat to make up with Andy. "He cares about you very much, and no man wants to feel that the object of his affection is pining for someone else."

She was awfully wise, that Elyse. Pat hoped she would make it down to the party. Franklin's condition had deteriorated, and Elyse had said that he might not even live out the year. *Thank God Elyse is getting moral support from her children, Susan, and me.* Even Grace tried to spend more time with her, heading off to Lake Forest after work.

Pat hoped Elyse would heed Susan's advice and stay away from Kevin Nash. She had nothing against Kevin, but he'd done so little with his life, and Elyse had accumulated so much. It just seemed like an ill-fated match, whether Franklin was alive or not.

Susan had told Pat she wouldn't be able to make it to the get-together, but Grace was coming. Pat couldn't wait. She had a surprise for her.

In the living room, Pat stopped to chat with a few of their guests. She noticed her mother talking with the Keindls and Glenn Arterbridge, and Andy's ex and her husband talking with some of his friends, and Andy with one of her fellow prosecutors. They'd assembled an eclectic mix of people, and it seemed to be working. Lauren and Kaitlyn passed hors d'oeuvres to the guests. A mixture of jazz and standards played in the background on CDs that had been specially downloaded through a paid service. Pat smiled as Glenn and her mother began to dance to Nnenna Freelon's cover of "If I Had You." The party was on. Grace, as usual, was late.

Cleotha cornered Pat a half hour later. "Congratulations, dear. It's a lovely party. And your boyfriend is a delight. He's paid special attention to me and really makes me feel special."

"You *are* special, Mama."

"And his parents seem like nice people. Of course, I don't know what they'll say to each other privately—"

"Oh, Mama, look. Grace is finally here." Pat said a silent prayer of thanks for Grace's well-timed arrival.

Grace handed her coat to Kaitlyn and nodded to people she passed as she made her way to Pat. As usual, she looked lovely, today in an angora sweater dress belted at the waist and suede boots. "Hi! Sorry I'm late."

"I know you wouldn't have it any other way," Pat said affectionately as Grace embraced Cleotha.

"Where's Mr. Maxwell?" she asked, glancing about.

"He's at home. But there are some other people I'd like you to meet," Pat said quickly before Grace could ask any more questions.

"Oh. Sure!"

"Will you excuse us, Mama?"

"Go ahead. I'm going to flag down the girls for another one of those celery sticks. I love the filling."

Pat introduced Grace to the friends of hers and Andy's whom she hadn't met. Out of the corner of her eye she saw Glenn approaching.

"Hello, Grace."

Pat was supposed to be following the conversation, but she couldn't resist sneaking a look at Grace's expression when she saw Glenn. The judge had increasingly lost weight over the past year and had reduced considerably. He was still a large man and probably would never be lighter than two-fifty, but he had lost the rotund center that Grace had found so unappealing.

Grace, as Pat expected, didn't hide her shock. Her eyes grew wide, and her jaw dropped. "Glenn! I almost didn't recognize you. You've lost quite a bit of weight, haven't you?"

"Well, I was having difficulty getting a date, and I had a feeling it had to do with my physique." He held out his hand. "Dance with me, and I'll tell you all about it."

She took his hand and he led her to a cleared area of the room.

Andy appeared at Pat's side and poked her waist with his elbow. "They look good together."

"I was thinking the same thing."

"Do I sense a little matchmaking in play here?"

"Glenn had been asking me about Grace. I thought it might do her good to get a look at his 'after' self, since she wasn't interested when he was so heavy." She gave his arm an affectionate squeeze. "Can you blame me for wanting everyone to be as happy as I am?"

"Hi, Pat. I made it."

She looked up to see Elyse, but her face froze when she recognized Elyse's companion.

Kevin Nash.

Chapter 55

Elyse thanked Kevin as she reached for the drink he'd prepared for her. She spoke with Cleotha Maxwell, accepting her good wishes for Franklin's health and explaining that his daughter Rebecca was sitting with him. Cleotha seemed sincere, but her eyes kept going over to Kevin, who was charming another group. Elyse knew Pat's mother wondered who this man was who'd escorted her. "I don't know if you remember Kevin Nash. He went to school with all of us."

Cleotha frowned. "I can't say that I do. Did his family live in Dreiser?"

"No. They had a house a block from where I moved when we left the projects. Anyway, he's been very helpful to me since Franklin has been ill. He's helped me understand illness from a man's perspective."

"I see. Elyse, would you mind terribly if I went to sit down? I'm getting a little woozy. It must be the wine." She chuckled.

"Not at all. You go right ahead." Elyse caught Pat's eye and saw her cock her head toward the hallway. She'd been waiting for this. Pat wanted to know what was going on.

As Elyse entered Andy's home office at the front of the town house, she saw that Grace also wanted to know, for both of her friends sat in wait.

Elyse had barely closed the door behind her for privacy when Pat began. "Elyse, is everything all right?"

"Of course."

"You didn't leave Franklin by himself, did you?"

"Of course not. Rebecca is with him. My kids went to the movies with some friends. I had to get out of there. He was brutal to me." Her face contorted as she tried to hold back the tears. "I was starting to put it behind me until you brought it up. Thanks a lot, Pat."

"I'm sorry, Elyse. I'm just so shocked to see you here."

"Me, too," Grace echoed.

"I felt safer if Kevin was with me, so I called. He and his son were at his parents' house, but getting ready to leave."

"He has a son?" Grace asked.

"Yeah, with Lucy Key. He's grown now, in his late twenties."

Grace rolled her eyes. "Lucy, yeah. I think she's a great-grandmother by now."

"Grace, we all know that Lucy had her first baby at thirteen, but that's not what we're here to discuss," Pat said sternly. "The important thing is Elyse." She turned to their friend. "Is there anything we can do?"

"Nothing. I appreciate your asking, but if you'll excuse me, Kevin is probably starting to wonder where I've gone." She left the room.

Pat and Grace looked at each other. "My God, what do you suppose Franklin said to her?" Grace asked.

"I don't know, but it must have been pretty damn awful for her to run to Kevin."

"He's good-looking and charming, but there's something about him that bothers me, Pat."

"I feel the same way. But we've done all we could. It's up to Elyse now."

The party broke up around eleven. Andy and Pat walked out with the remainder of their guests—his parents and ex-wife had left quite some time earlier, and Cleotha was clearly ready to go home. Andy and Pat were driving her.

Elyse said good night to her friends. She tossed her car keys to Kevin. "You know how to get back to your apartment better than I do."

"So Pat's got herself a white boy, huh?" he remarked during the drive.

"Yes. They seem very happy."

"The brothers not good enough for her?"

"I don't think it's that, Kevin." She hoped he wouldn't say anything else; she really didn't feel like talking. Now that they'd left the party, melancholy had started to set in.

She couldn't remember a worse holiday. First of all, Frankie had asked if his mother, Carolyn, could join them for dinner. Elyse agreed, although less than thrilled with the idea. Normally Frankie, his family, and Rebecca dined with Carolyn, but because of Franklin's illness both of his older children wished to spend Thanksgiving with him.

He'd come to the table in elastic-waist drawstring pants and a long-sleeved polo shirt and ate next to nothing. Elyse sat seething on the opposite end of the table as Carolyn, who managed to seat herself on Franklin's left, fussed over him and fed him small bites of food.

After dinner Franklin sat up briefly, but eventually had to take a pill for his bone pain and went to bed. Shortly afterward, Brontë came to Elyse in tears. She and Todd wanted to go to the movies along with a group of their friends, and Rebecca had commented that their doing so suggested they didn't care about their father.

That bitch, Elyse thought. To Brontë she said, "You two run along. Don't you worry about Rebecca. I'll set her straight."

She waited until after the kids left before confronting her stepdaughter, who was sitting in the living room with Carolyn and had been jumping up every fifteen minutes to go check on Franklin. Rebecca had been annoying Elyse all afternoon with that dutiful-daughter routine, at one point even saying to Elyse, "I just checked on him, he's fine," when Elyse headed for the bedroom. She'd simply ignored her stepdaughter and the dramatic sharp intake of breath she knew had come from Carolyn.

Frankie and his family had already gone, headed to spend some time with his in-laws, by the time Todd and Brontë left. Elyse decided to speak in front of Carolyn. "Rebecca, Brontë told me what you said to her. I think it's despicable for you to say such a thing."

"Now, wait a minute, Elyse—"

"No, *you* wait a minute. How dare you suggest to Brontë that she and Todd don't care about their father because they wanted to see a movie. How many times have *you* been to a show on the days you don't get up here? Todd and Brontë have been here every single weekend for months now, all the way from Champaign; while you aren't able to make it all the time just from Evanston because you've got plans. So do you want to tell me again who's showing the most concern?"

"Elyse, is this really necessary?" Carolyn asked calmly.

"Keep out of this, Carolyn. Rebecca, you owe your sister and brother an apology."

Franklin's voice called out something from the bedroom.

"That's Pop," Rebecca said, halfway out of her chair.

"That's another thing. Stop trying to do my job. Franklin is my husband, and I'll take care of him. Don't you *ever* tell me not to go check on him." She turned and went to see after Franklin.

"What's all the fuss about?" he asked.

"There were a few problems I had to straighten out. I'm sorry if I woke you. I didn't think we were that loud."

"What problems?"

She told him what Rebecca had said to Brontë. "I also needed to straighten Rebecca out about trying to stop me from coming in to check on you." She turned at the sound of the bedroom door opening and gasped. Not only had Rebecca entered without knocking, but Carolyn was right behind her.

"Pop, Elyse is lying on me," Rebecca said. "She claims I said something mean to Brontë, but I didn't. I just suggested that she should spend as much time as she can with you."

"That's bullshit, and if you don't believe me, ask Brontë when she gets back."

"Franklin, you know our daughter doesn't lie," Carolyn said.

Elyse raised her chin defiantly. "Neither does ours."

"Brontë's a good girl, Franklin," Carolyn agreed, "but I doubt she's above exaggerating some to elicit sympathy. After all, Frankie and Rebecca tell me things have been pretty tense around here lately since you discovered Elyse spending her lunch hours trysting with another man."

Elyse stared at her, speechless. Even Rebecca looked startled.

Elyse looked to Franklin. "Either *you* say something to that, or so help me, *I* will."

"Carolyn, you always had a tendency to overdramatize. If you'll remember, that's why I left your ass."

"Franklin!" she exclaimed, her chin dropping.

"Pop, did you have to—" Rebecca began.

"Carolyn, will you please leave the three of us alone for a few minutes? We need to discuss our family business."

Carolyn had little choice but to leave. As she did so she glared at Elyse. "This isn't over."

"Just get the hell out of my bedroom."

"All right," Franklin said after she'd gone, "I don't know what's going on, but I want it to stop right now. Rebecca, I'll be talking with Brontë tomorrow. If you did say what Elyse told me, you were wrong, and you owe your sister an apology."

"I didn't mean it, Pop," she said quietly, a sob catching in her throat.

Elyse straightened her spine triumphantly. *Sounds like a confession to me.*

"All right. You can go."

Elyse remained at his bedside. When the two of them were alone she said, "That wasn't much of a defense you put up for me. If it'd been up to me, I would have told her to leave the house."

"Can I help it if everybody knows you're making a fool out of me?"

"I'm not making a fool out of you, Franklin. I broke down in a public place because I was sad about your cancer coming back. You won't make me feel guilty for that, no matter how hard you try to."

"Yeah, with some dude you went to school with. I'm sure he was more than willing to provide you with a shoulder to cry on. But I guess that's what I get. Everybody told me I was nuts to marry a girl from the projects."

She squared her shoulders. "I may have lived in the projects, but my family moved out long before I met you."

"Don't go putting on airs with me. Once from the projects, always from the projects. And you seemed so damn proud of it when you went down to that reunion. Probably couldn't wait to see what other project peeps you could take up with."

"I haven't taken up with anyone. And Kevin never lived in the projects. He was from the neighborhood, and we went to the same schools, but he never lived—"

"Who gives a shit where he lived? He went to that bar looking for somebody he could have an affair with. And there you were, having turned yourself into a lady, with your diamonds and your hair styled so perfectly. You might look like a lady, but you're just another ho from the hood."

Her eyes filled with stinging tears that she fought to keep from spilling out. "You don't mean that, Franklin."

"Why don't you go back to the South Side? Go live in the projects. It's where you belong. I gave you everything, a house in Lake Forest, but you'd rather be in the ghetto. So bring your ass on back there."

Abruptly Elyse left the room. She ran down the hall to the powder room, not wanting to stay in the same room as Franklin another second. She turned the cold water on full force and rinsed her face, the cold water from the faucet mixing with her warm, wet tears.

She could hardly believe these words were coming out of her husband's mouth. If he wasn't weak and sick she would give his shit right back to him. But he was dying, and she didn't have the heart to hurl such cruel words at him.

But that didn't mean she had to stay here. She needed to get out before she lost her temper and gave Franklin what he deserved.

Elyse grabbed her coat and purse and ran out into the night, ignoring Rebecca's pleas to know where she was going. So Rebecca felt she could take care of Franklin better than she could? Fine. Let her do it, at least until Todd and Brontë got home.

In the car she called Kevin. She'd already decided to drive

down to Pat's get-together in Lake Forest. She had scribbled down the information on the notepad she always carried in her purse, so she had the address. The navigation system in her dashboard would tell her how to get there. But she was a little apprehensive about parking and walking in the city after dark. Maybe Kevin would go with her, since he lived north of Andy Keindl's town house.

He answered and agreed to go to the party with her.

Elyse was glad she'd gone, but now that it was over she dreaded going home. A worried Todd had called her when he and Brontë got home and Rebecca informed them that she'd walked out without a word to anyone. Elyse told Todd that she was at a cocktail party given by her friend Pat—conveniently leaving out the fact that she'd stopped to pick up Kevin on the way. Todd didn't ask what had driven her out of the house in such a hurry. He probably already knew the answer.

Traffic was remarkably light from the South Side up through downtown and points north. Elyse attributed it to people going to bed early so they could hunt down bargains in the morning, when stores would open as early as 5 AM. They got to Rogers Park in no time, to her dismay. She'd been hoping for one of those traffic snarls that made the Dan Ryan Expressway so notorious. Damn it, it was just her luck to be out on one of the few nights of the year when everybody else was at home.

She wasn't ready to go home, back to more insults and ridicule.

Kevin easily pulled into a space on the street, just around the corner from the entrance to the three-story brick walk-up where he lived. He removed the keys from the ignition and handed them to her. "I don't know what's going on with you, Elyse, but something tells me you'd like to stay out a little longer before you go home."

She shrugged. "It's the same thing that's been going on for over a month. My husband is behaving beastly. If he wants to insult me all the time, let him get along without me."

"Why don't we talk about it?"

"It's too cold."

He chuckled. "You're right about that. Come up for a little while, or as long as you'd like." Without waiting for a reply, he opened the car door and got out.

Elyse did the same, trying not to think about his seemingly open-ended invitation. *Stay as long as you'd like.*

An invitation to trouble if she ever heard one. But she'd rather risk it than go home.

Chapter 56

Elyse entered the apartment, taking a look around as Kevin closed and locked the door. The faded-brown brick building looked dingy and old on the outside, but the apartment was clean and bright, courtesy of spotless white paint. It was furnished simply, if inexpensively, with a furry brown living room set and thin glass accent tables. The computer center looked new, but the entertainment center that held his TV, DVD player, speakers, and sound system had peeled in spots. Both pieces obviously came out of a box and had to be assembled, no doubt made of corkboard with wood strips pasted on the outside. Two crates full of albums flanked each side of the entertainment center. The sofa was against the wall, with the chair and loveseat facing each other in front of the sofa. A swirly print area rug lay neatly beneath the coffee table, filling most of the space in the seating area. Two windows were framed by checkered curtains, and to one side stood a black pole lamp. The apartment looked more like it belonged to a kid a few years out of college than to a middle-aged man, but she admired his neatness.

Kevin put on a Peter White CD, then went into the kitchen while Elyse took a seat, at his invitation. She chose the side chair rather than the sofa or loveseat. Best to keep some distance between them, and this way he wouldn't be able to sit next to her.

Kevin approached, holding two small blue-tinted stemmed glasses, the shape of which reminded Elyse of a small can of tomato paste.

"I thought you could use some wine," he said as he handed her the glass.

"Thanks. Your apartment is very comfortable."

"It's a dump. But I've lived here for over twenty years. It's clean, and it's cheap. Nothing like Pat's boyfriend's place, but then I'm not a big-bucks attorney. I'll move once I open my Laundromat. Once the money starts coming in I'll be able to afford it." He sat on the edge of the sofa and held up his glass, his eyes meeting hers. "Let's drink to . . . happiness."

"To happiness," she said softly, but she cast her eyes downward, even as she touched her glass to his. These days she didn't think she'd ever feel that emotion again.

"I feel real bad about what's happened, Elyse. If I hadn't moved to sit next to you at that exact moment your stepdaughter came in the restaurant, you wouldn't be having such a hard time now."

"It's not your fault, Kevin."

"I can tell you're stressed. You've lost weight."

"That's because I haven't had much appetite. It's hard to eat when you're continually being derided for, among other things, being too fat."

"On you it looks good. But try to understand that it's hard for a man when he becomes ill. We're raised to think that we have to be strong, that we have to be the providers. Being sick is, well, unmanly in the eyes of society. Unable to go out and make a living, to unscrew a tight lid on a jar, to perform sexually—"

Elyse broke in, not comfortable with the direction the conversation was heading. It was true that she and Franklin hadn't made love since shortly after his remission ended and probably would never do so again, but she wasn't about to discuss that with Kevin. "I spoke with Franklin's primary care doctor a few weeks ago. He explained that it's not all that unusual for both men and women to resent that the end of their lives is near and to take it out on those closest to them. Tonight Franklin was especially nasty to me, but he was also unpleasant to his daughter from his first marriage, and his first wife . . . although, in my opinion, *she* had it coming." Picturing the stunned look on Carolyn's face when Franklin reminded her of the reason for their divorce and again when he asked her to leave the room brought a rare smile to Elyse's face.

"Did the doctor make any recommendations?"

She made a face. "A support group, but that's not for me. I'm not much for sharing tales of woe with complete strangers. His other suggestion was counseling, but I'd prefer not to do that. It's pretty much the same thing, except the stranger is a professional."

"Hang in there, Elyse."

"Yeah. Dr. Obi said the same thing."

"Obi? What is he, Japanese?"

"No, he's from Nigeria. He's been Franklin's doctor for years."

Kevin put his glass on the coffee table and got up. Elyse thought he was going to change the CD, but when she felt strong hands on her shoulders, she knew he'd gone to stand behind her.

"You feel so tense. Relax." He repeated it, this time as a whisper. "Close your eyes and relax."

Elyse felt the stress start to drain out of her. "You're actually pretty good at massage."

"I used to work with a guy from Korea who was an expert. He showed me his technique. I'm glad it works for you."

Her eyes closed. His fingers felt wonderful, invigorating her flesh. Hell, she'd pay for a massage this good. She hadn't felt so alive since she'd seen a chiropractor a few years back, who did wonders with her spine. . . .

Her eyes flew open, and she drew in her breath with a loud sucking sound when she felt warm lips against her skin on the back of her neck. Kevin didn't miss a beat.

"Just relax," he repeated.

Elyse's breath came in short gasps. The gesture had been so unexpected, and she knew what it would lead to if she didn't stop him, but what was her alternative? Try to do the right thing and go home to her husband, who would no doubt berate her with taunts that grew more brutal with each passing week? Franklin had practically sent her here into Kevin's arms with his relent-less verbal attacks. He'd actually called her a whore.

She tensed at the memory, then allowed herself to relax once more. Maybe it was wrong for her to be here, but it felt so right. Kevin's hands continued to work their magic as his lips moved toward her throat and higher still. In an instant Elyse made up her mind. She'd moved her body forward when she first felt him nuzzling her, but now she leaned back again, her face lifted toward the ceiling.

It made it that much easier for him to kiss her.

Her mouth opened to draw in his tongue. When was the last time she'd been kissed with such tenderness? Kevin's palm cupped her chin, holding her in place, but if he was worried about her trying to get away, he had no need to.

Dear God, what have I done?

Elyse, lying naked on the way-too-soft mattress of Kevin's bed, inadvertently shivered.

"Are you all right?"

"I'm just thinking . . . I should probably go."

"Already?"

"It's after midnight, Kevin."

"I hoped you'd stay until morning."

She bit her lip. "As much as I'd like to, I do have responsibil-ities at home."

He moved on top of her, and this time, instead of arousal, she felt repulsion.

"I hope you enjoyed yourself as much as I did."

Elyse was able to get away with a sigh as he planted little kisses on her throat while squeezing one of her breasts.

Kevin moved his face opposite hers. "And I hope you'll slip down here to see me every chance you get."

An old R&B song immediately began playing in Elyse's head. She didn't even remember who sang it; she just remembered the refrain: *"Slip away . . . slip away . . . slip away-ay-ay-ay."* Kevin kissed her, and as he did she wondered how she'd be able to take a shower without anyone noticing. If she used the bathroom she shared with Franklin he would notice and would give her more grief than ever. If she used the one upstairs, the kids would notice.

Maybe she could slip down to the tiny shower stall in the basement. . . .

She felt his erection against her thigh. It would be so easy for him to slide it inside her for another session. She had to stop him, and not just because he didn't have a condom on.

"We can have one more quick one before you go," he murmured against her mouth.

"Kevin, I really do have to go. It'll take me a half hour to get home. My kids are probably frantic with worry." She'd left her cell phone in her purse in the living room.

"All right. I know you have to get back." He rolled off her.

Elyse lowered the window and waved good-bye to Kevin. She didn't want to honk her horn because of the late hour.

Her body felt satisfied—okay, more than satisfied—but her heart felt heavy. It was just like Susan had said it would be. She'd just committed adultery, and it didn't feel good. In fact, she felt lower than Death Valley. And now she had to go home and lie beside her husband, a husband she loved but who was making her miserable.

During the drive to Lake Forest she vacillated about whether to sleep in bed with Franklin or spend the remainder of the night in the spare room.

It was quiet in the car—she didn't even have the radio going—and Elyse jumped when her cell phone started ringing. Brontë had loaded it with songs from movie musicals as her ringtones, and the warbling of "Some Day My Prince Will Come" struck her as particularly ironic, given what she'd just done. She knew it had to be one of the kids. "Hello."

Todd's voice filled her ears. "Mom, I've been trying to call you for hours. Where've you been?"

"At Pat's party. I put my purse away, and my phone was in it. Sorry. Is everything all right?"

"Yeah. Dad's sleeping. I sent Brontë upstairs a couple of

hours ago. She's going to hit the electronics store for that predawn shopping tomorrow, so she has to get up in a few hours. I'm kind of dozing off myself."

"Was Daddy asking for me?"

"Every five minutes until he fell asleep. What'd he say to you, Mom?"

"He called me a whore."

Elyse's declaration met with shocked silence. After a few seconds' pause, Todd said, "I'm going to talk to him in the morning. This time he's gone too far."

"Todd, would you mind terribly sleeping down there tonight?"

"No, I'll stay here. I can't blame you for not wanting to sleep in the same bed as him."

"I'll check on him when I get home, which will be in about fifteen minutes. I hate to put his care in your hands, but I really do need to take a break."

"I understand. Did you have a good time at the party?"

"Oh . . . yes. It was wonderful." A faint vision of her and Kevin furiously making love appeared before her on the highway, and she blinked it away. "I'll see you in a few minutes."

With heavy steps, Elyse entered her bedroom. The dim nightlight helped her make out Franklin's form beneath the down quilt. She headed for the bathroom, confident that he was fast asleep.

"Elyse."

She froze, as if she'd been shot with a stun gun.

"Come here. Please."

Her eyebrows shot up. *Please?* That didn't sound like the Franklin who'd been lashing out at her every chance he got.

She turned around and approached the bed as he turned on the light. Her heart did a little somersault at the sight of him lying with the covers up to his chin. Only his head showed, propped up on two pillows.

"I didn't think you were coming back."

"If you don't want me here, Franklin, I don't have to be," she said wearily.

Someone—it had to be Todd—knocked on the door.

"Come in," she called.

Todd entered the room. "Just wanted to make sure everything's all right in here. But Dad, since you're awake, there's something I have to tell you." He cleared his throat. "Mom told me what you said to her. That was a terrible thing to say. How could you? You know she's always been here for you. We're the most important people in her life. You've treated her like a dog these last couple of months, and she still insisted that taking care of you is her responsibility. She doesn't deserve the terrible things you said. You know you've been the only man in her life for years, and that she'd never cheat on you. . . ."

Elyse swallowed and averted her eyes, wishing she could vanish into thin air. She felt like she was worth two cents as she listened to her son defend her against Franklin's endless verbal attacks, knowing that she was still carrying the scent of another man. And even now she felt torn—measuring physical pleasure and the emotional need to be desired against the wrongness of adultery.

Todd, clearly fueled by nervousness, finally concluded his speech. "I wouldn't be any kind of a man if I let you get away with talking to Mom like that."

Franklin closed his eyes and nodded. "You're right, Son. I said terrible things to your mother, especially this afternoon. I was afraid that she'd walked out for good, that I'd never see her again. I was just about to tell her how sorry I am and beg her to forgive me."

Elyse sat on the edge of the bed and took his hand in hers.

"I'm dying," Franklin stated simply. "I tried to accept it when I first found out I had cancer. I thought I'd been successful, but when it came back so quickly I felt angry. When Frankie told me that Rebecca had seen your mother and a man embracing on the same side of a restaurant booth, it hit me that I'd be dead and your mother would be seeing other men."

Elyse opened her mouth to protest, and he gestured for her to be quiet. "Don't deny it. You're still young and great-looking. I knew you weren't stepping out on me, and when you explained what happened I understood perfectly, but I know there'll come a time after I'm gone when you'll be seeing men and it won't be so innocent. That was too much for me."

"Dad, you shouldn't torture yourself with those types of thoughts," Todd said.

"I can't help what I think. I've got nothing but time to think about the future of my family, and how I won't be here to see it. I won't see Frankie's children grow up. I won't be here to walk Rebecca and Brontë down the aisle when they marry. I won't see you and Brontë graduate from college."

Tears ran down Elyse's cheeks, but she made no sound.

"I can accept my fate now. But I'd want to die right away, Elyse, if you left me. You mean the world to me."

She tried to speak without breaking down. "Everyone has a breaking point, Franklin, and you pushed me dangerously close to it with the things you said to me this afternoon. But I'm back, and I'm not going anywhere."

At that point Todd began backing toward the door. He slipped out of the room silently.

"Our son is quite a man, isn't he?" Franklin remarked.

She laid her head on his chest. "Yes, he is. I love you, Franklin. Don't you ever doubt that again."

He stroked her hair and her cheek. "I wish I could take it all back. I'll never forgive myself for hurting you the way I did. I love you, baby, now and always."

Elyse sat up. "I'm going to get ready for bed. I'll be with you in a few minutes, all right?"

He chuckled. "Where'm *I* going?"

As Elyse scrubbed herself during a quick shower, she kept thinking, *If only he had said this to me yesterday. If only he hadn't called me a ho tonight. If only I could take back my actions just like Franklin wanted to take back his words.* It sickened her that she couldn't even meet his sincere apology with a kiss, but instead could go no closer to him than his chest, because she hadn't had an opportunity to wash off the evidence of intimacy with another man.

One thing she knew for sure. She could never see Kevin Nash again. He was a living reminder of the most low-down action she'd ever taken in her life.

Chapter 57

Grace beamed across the table at Pat. "This is nice, isn't it? The two of us having a quick drink after work before our dates get here."

"It's nicer for some of us than others. *You'll* get a ride home in Glenn's car service."

"One of the perks of being a judge; you don't have to drive yourself to work. I think you've got a good shot at finding that out yourself one of these days. Pat, I can't thank you enough for inviting Glenn to the party you and Andy gave; otherwise I never would have known he'd lost so much weight."

"Part of me wanted to tell you last summer that he was becoming a shell of his former self, but something told me to wait until he'd reached a size I felt you could live with. And in the meantime I kept hoping you'd get rid of that Eric." Pat made a face. "As much as I felt him to be wrong for you, I didn't know if I'd feel comfortable with your dumping him just because someone better came along."

"Oh, yeah. That one was definitely headed down the wrong path." Grace shook her head. "But, you know, Eric would be considered a catch by a lot of women. He has a reasonably good job, he's handsome, has no children, and he knows how to hang up his clothes. He's no Oscar Madison. And he's great in bed."

"True, but you're not most women, Grace. I believe that

some relationships can work if the woman makes more money than the man, but it takes a special man to do it." Pat took a sip of her wine. "So tell me how things are going with you and Glenn."

"Real well. We went to dinner last Saturday and talked for hours."

"And then?"

"Then we went back to my place," Grace said innocently.

"And then? Did Miss Grace give it up on the first date?"

"Oh, hell. I've always been a pushover. Besides, I haven't had sex since I broke up with Eric, and that was months ago." Her mind indulged the memory of that night with Glenn, and the next thing she knew she was wearing a grin as wide as her face.

"I take it he curled your toenails."

"Well, I'm not one to kiss and tell, but I will say this . . . Glenn's a big man. *All* over."

They dissolved into a fit of giggles.

Chapter 58

Late December
Chicago

"Susan, you'll have to give me a refresher," Bruce said as they drove toward the church in Bronzeville where Franklin's funeral was being held. "I haven't seen your friends in a long time. Now, Elyse is the bereaved, right?"

"Yes. Her husband's name is . . . was Franklin."

"And Grace . . . Is that the one with the pointy chin?"

She laughed. "You'd better not let *her* hear you say that. The proper term is 'heart-shaped face.'"

"Maybe, but with that chin she could give the Wicked Witch of the West a run for her money."

"Bruce, you're awful."

"Sorry. Okay. Who did I leave out?"

"Pat. She's the one who knows everybody. She'll be there with her boyfriend. He's white."

"I guess I'll be able to spot her easily enough."

She gave his thigh an affectionate squeeze. He'd surprised her when he said he would go with her to Franklin Reavis's funeral. Sometimes it seemed like old times between them. She knew it would end the moment they got to their bedroom, but easygoing times like these made life a little more pleasant. She still had two months to go before she had enough recent experience to start looking for a full-time job, after which she'd sit him down and tell him she wanted her freedom. Even with that, she saw no reason for relations between them to be frosty.

"I guess there'll be a bunch of other folks you'll want to introduce me to," he remarked.

"No, I don't think so. Most of the people from the old neighborhood probably went to the wake last night so they won't have to miss work." While many people did take vacation time the week between Christmas and New Year's, many others did not. "This will be family, close friends, and coworkers, maybe some folks from church."

"Just as well. So the only names I have to remember are Elyse, Pat, and Grace."

"Yes. You know, I should probably warn you about Grace. She's on the lookout for a new husband, one who makes more than she does. She's seeing someone now, but he's just a judge. High on prestige, but not exactly pulling in the big bucks. If anything happens to me, she'll probably try to move in on you."

"That's ridiculous, Susan. She's your friend."

"Yes, but she's always felt that once a relationship is over she can try to wiggle her way in. She did that with my first boyfriend, and with one of Pat's as well."

"I think that's low-down."

"I just thought I'd warn you," she said loftily, before turning her face away and looking out at the passing scenery.

"Susan." Bruce said her name like it was a command. She turned her head to look at him.

"I know what you're thinking," he said. "I just have one word for you: Don't."

She feigned innocence. "Don't what?"

"Don't go thinking that the next funeral will be yours. You're not dying of cancer, Susan. You're *living* with it."

She blinked back tears. That was exactly what she'd thought the moment Pat had called her with the sad news of Franklin's passing the day after Christmas. Bruce knew her so well, better than anyone, even Charles. What a sweet thing for him to say.

At moments like this she felt blessed, in spite of the worry and unhappiness she lived with every day.

* * *

Pat held her breath as she and Andy entered the church. She wondered if her parents had arrived yet.

Her mother had suggested that they all drive up together, but then Pat told her that Andy was escorting her. "Your father won't like that," Cleotha said after a long pause.

She had responded without hesitation. "Then he might want to stay at home. You be sure to tell him that, all right? I have to go now." Then she'd hung up the phone. She hated to be rude, but she had to stick to her guns. She'd just turned fifty a few days ago. She wasn't some child who lived under his roof whom he kept fed and clothed, abiding by his rules in exchange for the privilege. Hell, for years now she'd been helping take care of *them*. She could be doing a whole lot with that two hundred dollars she gave her parents every month.

"You all right?" Andy asked. "Your arm went kind of stiff."

Pat quickly realized that she'd allowed her entire body to go rigid with all the tension she felt. "I'm fine," she said.

She knew that her parents had missed her over the holidays, but she'd eagerly accepted when Andy asked if she'd like to celebrate both Christmas and their fiftieth birthdays at the cabin of a friend of his in Breckenridge, Colorado. They'd been born the same week, he on the nineteenth and she on the twenty-second. They'd flown out on the eighteenth and returned two days ago. Pat knew that Franklin had little time left and had pleaded with Elyse to call her if she needed to talk, or if anything happened. Elyse called the evening of the twenty-sixth, as she and Andy were packing, to inform her that Franklin had passed away that afternoon.

Pat had spoken to Elyse since she'd been back, but she hadn't seen her yet. She knew from Elyse that Franklin's last weeks were happy ones, that the two of them had made up, and that Franklin got the entire family together to ask them to stop sniping at each other. Of course, he'd really been talking to his older children, both of whom had been trying to curry favor with him by criticizing their stepmother and younger siblings. Pat wished she could smack that Frankie and Rebecca for behaving so badly. She remembered how Elyse used to take them everywhere when they were kids, to the movies, to Six Flags, even once to the water parks at the Dells.

But at least Franklin had passed away with his wishes made clear, and with his relationship with Elyse intact.

Grace adjusted the face netting of her hat. She'd nicknamed it the I'm-so-sorry-for-your-loss hat because the only time she wore it was to funerals. She paired it with a tailored black suit and simple black slingbacks, and she had to admit she looked good. Once out of the car, she slipped her arm through Glenn's. He gave her a reassuring smile, and once more she thought to herself how glad she was to have him with her. How lucky for her that he'd taken vacation time this week. Pat had Andy, and Susan had Bruce, at least as an escort. She didn't want to be the only one to show up alone.

God knows that if she was still seeing Eric, he would balk at taking a day off to attend a funeral of someone he didn't know, the husband of someone he barely remembered. To get there, she would have had to dangle over his head the Mercedes he liked driving so much, possibly even tell him she needed someone to lean on if she got upset during the service. The likelihood of her getting that distressed was nonexistent, but that was beside the point.

But how nice it was to have someone she didn't have to bribe or cajole. Glenn helped her out of his Cadillac STS and took her arm. He'd insisted they leave in plenty of time before the service, much to Grace's annoyance. She doubted anyone would even be there yet.

The moment she got inside the church she craned her neck. "I don't see Pat." Then she spotted Ricky Suárez and his wife sitting in a rear pew, and she steered Glenn to the pew directly behind them. She wasn't surprised to see Ricky, for she knew that Pat had sent out e-mail notices about Franklin's passing to everyone who signed the guest book at the Dreiser reunion luncheon.

Ricky turned at the sound of movement behind him. "Grace, hey!" He leaned forward to give her a quick hug, then shook hands with Glenn, introducing himself before Grace could do it, and presenting his wife, Miranda.

"Hello, Miranda. I remember you from the reunion luncheon last spring. Nice to see you again." Grace beamed at Ricky's wife, who in spite of her beauty looked rather dowdy in a long-sleeved black dress with a white collar. Then Grace introduced Glenn.

"Pardon me for not getting up," Miranda said, patting her stomach. "It's getting more difficult these days."

Grace stared at Miranda's midsection. She was pregnant. No wonder she looked so drab.

"Well, congratulations to you both," Glenn said. Grace managed a big smile.

"Thanks. Four more months to go."

"There's Susan," Ricky said. "And Pat's with her."

Grace turned to see the Dillahunts pausing to sign the guest book while Pat and Andy waited their turn. They stepped aside to let someone pass, Andy placing his hands casually on Pat's shoulders to move her out of the aisle. Grace stole a glance at Ricky. The surprise in his eyes told Grace he recognized Andy as Pat's date from last summer. Did he figure she'd be alone and he could flaunt his pregnant wife in front of her? Grace wondered.

She waved Susan over. Susan said something to Pat, who was now signing the guest book, before walking over with Bruce. Introductions followed. Grace was surprised that Bruce remembered her name. Wow, was he good-looking. And fit. *And* rich. Too bad he was such a prick. Imagine avoiding your spouse because of his or her medical condition. Didn't he know that marriage was supposed to be for life?

Grace wasn't dismissing her own two failed marriages, but they ended because both parties were unhappy. That made it a little different. Susan would have been happy to spend the rest of her life with Bruce if he'd handled her illness like a man instead of a cowardly lion.

Pat and Andy joined them. Time for another round of hellos, how've-you-beens, and introductions. Grace noticed that Pat didn't seem the least surprised at seeing Ricky, nor did his being there seem to cause her any dismay. Grace considered that maybe she just didn't care. *Good for you, Pat. It's about time.*

Finally someone got around to the point about why they were all there.

Pat glanced at her watch. "The service isn't scheduled to start for another ten minutes. Since we're all here, why don't we go up and offer condolences to Elyse?"

"I think that's a good idea," Susan said.

"I think I should stay here, Susan," Bruce told her. "This isn't the time for renewing old acquaintances. I'll get to speak with her after the service."

"I'll wait here, too," Glenn added.

Grace rose to her feet. "Well, all who's coming, let's go." She led the entourage of Pat, Susan, and Ricky.

The organ music seemed louder in the front of the church. A rich-looking mahogany casket was on a stand just opposite where Elyse sat, flanked by Todd and Brontë. A black hat with a large brim obscured much of Elyse's face.

Grace's eyes automatically went to the casket. She stood in front of it for a moment and gazed down at Franklin. His face looked thinner than she remembered and older than his sixty-three years, but didn't look particularly weathered. She wondered if the funeral director had puffed it up somehow, like he'd clearly done to Franklin's chest.

She bowed her head and said a prayer, then gracefully turned to Elyse.

What could she possibly say to comfort a woman who'd just lost her husband of twenty-six years?

Susan waited for Grace and Pat to finish viewing Franklin's casket. She considered going over to Elyse while the others prayed with bowed heads, but felt she should pay her respects to Franklin first, so she merely waited. She could tell from the redness of Elyse's eyes that she'd been crying. "This is going to be difficult," she said to Ricky.

"I know. I never know the right thing to say to people at a time like this."

After Pat and Grace turned to Elyse, Susan and Ricky took their places in front of the casket. Susan bowed her head and said a prayer. She opened her eyes and looked at Ricky, whose eyes were closed and whose lips were moving. She turned to face him as he crossed himself, and her eyes went to the man waiting to the left.

It was Charles.

She swallowed, then quickly looked away. What the devil was Charles doing here? She thought he'd have been among those attending only the wake last night.

The answer came to her just as quickly. The schools were closed for the holiday break. She'd had to engage a sitter to stay with Quentin and Alyssa.

She hadn't seen him since their last ill-fated meeting downtown last summer, but he crept into her thoughts often, especially at night.

Charles had probably decided to come to the service rather than the wake because he knew she'd be here. She didn't know if he wanted to try to convince her to renew their affair, or if he wanted to make the break official and tell her no hard feelings. No doubt he expected she'd be alone. The fact that Bruce was here complicated matters for both of them. What was she going to do? How could she act naturally with Bruce when Charles was so near?

Ricky, unaware that his friend from the old neighborhood stood just a few feet away, took her arm, and together they went to speak to Elyse.

Elyse's face was wet with tears, and Susan's heart broke for her. Brontë, too, had obviously been crying, while Todd tried to be stoic and move into his place as the man of the family. Also in the front pew sat Elyse's stepdaughter and her stepson and his family. Pat and Grace had moved back a few pews to converse with Elyse's parents, the Hugheses.

As Susan feared, Charles caught up with Ricky, who invited him to sit with them for the service. Her spirits dipped. How was she supposed to introduce her lover to her husband?

Pat said good-bye to Mr. and Mrs. Hughes, having assured them that she would do what she could to comfort Elyse in making the difficult adjustment from wife to widow. She then headed for the pew where Andy waited, looking straight ahead and smiling when he saw her approaching.

"Pat!"

She stopped at the stage whisper, knowing who had spoken. Her mother moved to the end of the pew, her father right behind her.

"Hi Mama, Daddy. I didn't know you were here."

"We arrived just a minute ago. We saw you up front." Moses's eyes darted around the room, probably trying to pick out which of the numerous white men present was Andy.

"Where are you sitting?" Cleotha asked.

"Andy and I are near the back, with Susan and Grace and their . . . companions. Ricky is here, too, with his wife." Just a few months ago having Ricky show up with his wife on his arm would have devastated her. Funny what love could do for a person. Sure, the sight of Miranda Suárez's swollen abdomen made her heart wrench a bit. She would have loved to have had children. She knew her time for that had passed. Soon she'd be getting those hot flashes Grace complained about. But she had no feelings for Ricky, other than goodwill. She hoped he would always be happy.

"I'm surprised. I figured he'd be working the lunch rush," Moses remarked.

"Daddy, Ricky *owns* Nirvana. I'm sure he has a manager working for him to handle the more mundane aspects of day-to-day business." She deliberately glanced toward the front. The organ music had suddenly gotten louder, and the minister had appeared and was speaking with Elyse. "It looks like they're about to start. I'll see you outside after the service." She punctuated her statement with a little wave and quickly headed back to Andy, knowing that both of their gazes followed.

Susan stopped to say hello to Mr. and Mrs. Maxwell. It appeared the service would begin at any moment, and she hoped to delay her return to Bruce until she could introduce him to Charles or, better yet, let Ricky do it. She watched as Ricky passed the pew with no more than a polite nod to the people who were so against his marrying their daughter. Charles did the same. He, along with nearly everyone else who lived in Dreiser at the time, knew how the Maxwells had interfered in Ricky's relationship with Pat. Naturally, Charles didn't want to put his friend on the spot.

Susan and Bruce had done little exchanging of their romantic histories before they married—she hadn't even told him that she'd once been Douglas Valentine's girl—so he would have no idea that Charles was a former boyfriend, much less suspect that many of her "errands" were spent in his arms. Still, she'd prefer for Ricky to introduce him, so it would appear as if he were no more than a friend from their old neighborhood.

And she prayed that nothing in Charles's expression would make Bruce suspicious.

Grace found, to her surprise, that she was shedding real tears during the service, but it was quite moving. Franklin Jr. addressed the congregation with fond memories of his father, telling everyone how Franklin taught him the ways of a man. His sister, Rebecca, while not quite as composed as her older brother, managed to share her own memories of being a "daddy's girl." For Grace, it brought back memories of her own parents, who loved her and wanted the best for her. She still remembered how difficult it had been to tell them she was pregnant, how disappointed they'd been. Her father hadn't lived to see her success, just like Franklin wouldn't see whatever Brontë did with her life.

A sob caught in her throat, and Glenn put a comforting arm around her, encouraging her to rest her head on his shoulder.

Suddenly she was very glad to have him here with her, and it had nothing to do with the fact that Pat had Andy and Susan had Bruce.

Outside the church, the mourners formed little pockets of people. Bruce stood with Ricky's wife and watched as Susan, along with Pat, Grace, Ricky, and that other guy, Charles, exchanged words with an older couple he presumed were Elyse's parents.

"I guess they know a lot of people here," Miranda Suárez remarked.

"I do feel a little like a Johnny-come-lately. Hey, it looks like congratulations are in order," Bruce said, noticing her swollen belly for the first time.

"Thank you," she said, patting her midsection. "I'm due Valentine's Day. We're having a little girl. Ricky's glad about that. He says he's too old to get out and play ball with a son."

"Is this your first?"

"*My* first," Miranda answered. "Ricky has a sixteen-year-old daughter." She smiled as Ricky joined them. "I was just talking about you."

"Whatever she told you, Bruce, it's not true," Ricky said with a laugh.

Miranda playfully slapped his arm. Then she sighed. "I can't believe this. I actually have to use the restroom again, or I'll never make it home. I'll be right back."

"I'll be right here," Ricky said with a loving smile.

Her departure gave Bruce an opportunity to indulge his curiosity. He knew that Ricky was the same age as Susan; they'd gone through school together. And Miranda was about Shay's age. "I give you a lot of credit, Ricky, for starting over at this point in your life. I've always been curious about men who become fathers late in life."

Ricky shrugged. "Between you and me, Bruce, I would have been content if it was Miranda and me from now on. But she wanted a child. I've heard of men who marry younger women and get their wives to sign contracts promising not to have kids, and don't think I didn't consider it. But I couldn't clear it with my conscience. My daughter has brought a lot of joy to my life. I didn't feel it was fair to Miranda to ask her not to have children just because my daughter is almost grown and I'm old enough to be a grandfather."

"Yeah, I can see that." Bruce nodded, thinking of Shay.

"I'm fourteen years older than she is," Ricky continued. "I'll probably die before her, and even if she's taken care of financially she'd still be alone."

Bruce swallowed. He'd never thought about *that*. . . .

"So we agreed to have just one." Ricky grinned. "Come on, I know you and Susan aren't thinking about having another baby."

"No, of course not." He laughed to cover his nervousness.

"I'm just starting to notice a lot of older men with younger wives and small children . . . And I wonder how they really feel about fatherhood past fifty. I didn't mean to get into your business."

"Don't worry about it. I don't believe in telling my business. We're just talking, that's all."

Bruce observed Susan and her girlfriends, plus Charles, talking among themselves. "Did you know Franklin well?"

"I never even met him. But Elyse is my girl. We've been friends all our lives. Pat Maxwell put together a network of e-mail addresses and current phone numbers of people from the old neighborhood. She said that a lot of people who used to live in the projects came last night to pay their respects."

"I'm sure that was a big comfort to Elyse. Are you and Miranda going to the cemetery?"

"No, I'm going to bring Miranda home, change, and head up to Waukegan. I'm opening another restaurant up there."

"Really?"

"Yes, in about two more months. I took over the lease on an Arby's that closed. It's a change of pace for me. My place on the South Side is a luncheonette, even though we expanded a couple of years ago. My place downtown is upscale. This is a sit-down, casual restaurant, like McDonald's."

"Why Waukegan?"

"Demographics. The city is nearly half Hispanic."

"That's not too far from Susan and me."

"In that case, take one of my cards. And think of me the next time you've got a hankering for Mexican food."

Susan tried not to look nervous as she talked with Grace and Pat. Bruce was talking to Glenn, who, along with Andy, had stopped to speak with someone he knew from the courthouse. She began to feel hopeful. Maybe she and Bruce could get out of here without Bruce and Charles having any contact at all.

"Poor Elyse, she's just heartbroken," Grace said. "I feel for the kids, too. I've never had a spouse die on me, but I do know how it feels to lose your father."

"She handled the funeral better than I thought she would," Pat said. "She was very upset at the wake last night, and Franklin's son told me she broke down when they went to view the body the first time. We should probably make a special effort to spend time with her," she suggested. "I think she really needs us now."

"I'm surprised I didn't see Kevin Nash here," Susan remarked. "I know Elyse has been in touch with him since Franklin's been ill. They had lunch a few times. Kevin helped provide a man's perspective on illness for her. She found him a great help."

Pat and Grace exchanged glances. "He's here," Pat said. "He came in late and sat in the back. Oh. Here come my parents. I know my father wants to meet Andy. Excuse me."

Susan and Grace looked on as Pat tapped Andy on the shoulder and led him over to where her parents stood. "*This* should be interesting," Grace whispered. "Do you suppose Mr. Maxwell will try to punch Andy out?"

"That's silly, Grace. The man is probably seventy-five years old. He's not punching anybody out. But what's going on with Kevin that I don't know about?"

Grace filled her in on how Elyse showed up at Pat and Andy's party Thanksgiving night with Kevin, telling them that Franklin had gone too far in his cruelty and she'd walked out. "Elyse never said what happened with them after they left Andy's house, but she and Franklin made up right afterward, I think."

"She probably just brought him home, went home herself, and Franklin apologized. He had to know he'd crossed the line, and I'll bet he got the scare of his life when Elyse left the house and didn't come back for hours."

"Yeah, I guess you're right."

Glenn rejoined Grace. "They're bringing out the casket now," he said, nodding toward the church entrance. "I guess we'd better get in the car so we can be part of the procession."

"All right. See you guys later, huh?"

"Okay, Grace." Susan's mouth felt dry. She turned to Charles. "I guess I'd better get going myself."

"Susan, I—"

She spoke in a low voice. "Don't, Charles. My husband is standing three feet away, and I'm sure he's watching."

"I didn't think he'd be here."

"I know you didn't. He was worried about me. Franklin died of cancer, and he knows me well enough to know my fears."

"Are you all right?"

"Yes. I'm still cancer-free."

He let out his breath audibly, telling Susan he'd been holding it. "Will you be going back to Elyse's?" he asked.

"I don't know. Bruce said something about going in to work."

Charles's eyes looked in Bruce's direction. "Here he comes. Get him to drop you at Elyse's. I'll make sure you get home. I have to talk to you." Then he walked off.

"Everyone's getting in their cars, Susan," Bruce said. "I think they're giving out dashboard signs for the procession."

"Yes, let's go." Bruce followed her as she stopped to embrace Ricky and to say good-bye to Miranda—and then to Charles, who by that time was nearby, looking away as Bruce shook Charles's hand.

Pat breathed a lot easier now that the meeting she'd so dreaded had finally taken place. Andy had been more charming than ever, and of course he'd already won over her mother. Her father, at least, was on his best behavior, if guarded. Pat feared he would refuse to shake Andy's hand.

"Mr. and Mrs. Maxwell, did you know Franklin?" Andy asked politely.

"No, but Elyse is one of Pat's very best friends," Cleotha said. "I can't believe that she's been widowed so young."

"Very sad," Andy agreed.

"Moses and I also know Elyse's parents very well. We didn't have much of an opportunity to speak with them here, but I suppose we'll see them at the house."

"It looks like they'll be heading for the cemetery any minute now," Andy said as the pallbearers carried the casket outside. "Why don't you two ride with us? We'll be happy to bring you back here to pick up your car afterward."

Pat watched her mother look at her father uncertainly. "It really doesn't make sense for us to drive all the way to Lake Forest and back if Pat and Andy are going, too, does it, Moses?"

Pat turned a stricken gaze on Andy. What the hell was he doing, inviting her parents to ride with them? She struggled to come up with something to say, some reason why his suggestion wouldn't work. But she could think of nothing.

Moses gave a reluctant nod of approval, and they began walking toward the Jaguar, Pat and Andy leading the way. Andy unlocked the doors with his remote control. "Mr. Maxwell, you might be more comfortable if you sit behind Pat," he suggested. "My seat is pushed back farther because of my legs, but Pat's shorter than I am."

"All right," Moses said in gruff agreement, not sounding the least bit gracious.

When Andy opened the door for Cleotha to get in, Moses quickly moved to open Pat's door and do the same. She tried not to laugh out loud at this competition her father had allowed himself to get into. For much of her early life her father didn't own a car, and while he always unlocked Cleotha's door first, she'd never known him to actually seat her.

"What a lovely vehicle," Cleotha said when they were all inside. "I've never ridden in one of these before. Isn't this nice, Moses?"

Pat strained her ears, not wanting to miss her father's reply. Then she realized he hadn't made one.

She sighed. It was going to be a long drive.

At the cemetery, Cleotha pulled Pat aside and made one last comment. "Don't be fooled. Your daddy is impressed with Andy. I think he's in shock because Andy is so polite and respectful. He's really going out of his way to be charming."

Pat beamed more broadly than was appropriate, considering a burial service was about to commence. Could it be that her father could be won over?

At the Reavis's home, Pat and her mother were speaking with Mrs. Hughes when, out of the corner of her eye, Pat saw her father approach Andy at the buffet table and say something to him. Then the two men disappeared. She fought back a wild urge to follow them. She'd warned Andy about her father, so she was confident Andy could handle him.

She turned to see Kevin Nash looking around the house with an awestruck expression on his face. She felt like she'd been transported to an old movie where a thief or rapist "cases the joint" or checks out the lady of the house before returning to rob it blind or to attack the woman. She closed her eyes for a moment as she chuckled. Her imagination was in full play this afternoon.

Still, she wondered what her father could possibly be saying to Andy.

"Susan, I didn't want to stay here long," Bruce said. "I'd really hoped to get some work done today, and I didn't want to be too late getting home."

You mean, you really wanted to spend some time with your girlfriend today, she thought. Again she thought that this new chick must really have her mojo working on him.

"If it's all right with you, I'd like to stick around for a while," she said. "The train station is right up the street. I can get someone to drop me off, and then I'll just call a cab to get home." Today was the day the weekly housekeeper came in, and she was happy to accept extra hours for babysitting duties for Quentin and Alyssa. "I really think I can be of some help to Elyse."

Bruce absorbed this for a few moments. "I hate to leave you here."

"C'mon, Bruce. I'm a big girl, and I'm not exactly surrounded by strangers. I'm with people I've known all my life."

"How long is Dolores going to stay with the kids?"

"Until I get home. When she finishes her work she can just sit down and relax and still be on the clock, so she's thrilled."

Bruce hedged. "I still don't know. Are you sure you can get someone to bring you to the train station?"

"With both Pat and Grace here? Of course. We'll probably be among the last to leave." She saw his apprehension melt away and slipped her arm through his. "Come on, I'll walk out with you."

Charles stood outside, keeping Kevin company while he smoked a cigarette, when Susan and Bruce left the house, both wearing their coats. His pulse began to race, and then he noticed that Susan wasn't carrying a purse.

"Kevin? It was nice meeting you," Bruce said, extending his hand.

"You leaving, man?"

"Yeah, I've got to head up to work. Susan's going to stay a while longer. She'll get a ride to the train station with Grace or Pat."

"The North line is just a few blocks from here," Kevin offered. "You can see the trains from here when they pass. I'd be happy to run her over there myself."

Bruce grinned. "I guess with all these old friends around, I'm foolish to worry." He turned to Susan. "Be sure to call or go online to check the schedules. Those trains only run something like once an hour after rush hour, and I don't want you sitting there waiting that long."

"Good point. I'll take care of it."

Charles, listening to the exchange and watching their body language, sprang to life when Bruce held out his hand to him. "Nice meeting you, Bruce."

He continued watching as Susan crossed the street with her husband. He winced when Bruce leaned in and kissed her lightly on the mouth.

Kevin drowned his cigarette butt in a Styrofoam cup of water. He stared at the royal blue Thunderbird convertible Bruce drove. "He may have to get to work, but something tells me he doesn't have to worry about using a personal day."

"He's a business owner up in Milwaukee," Charles said absently, still watching the pair.

"That's what I want to be, so I can trade in my Cavalier for something with, uh, more style. Damn, you'd never know those girls ever lived in Dreiser. They sure got rich, didn't they?"

"Oh, I don't know that I'd describe them as rich," Charles said, one eye still on Susan. Bruce was in the car now, but he was saying something to her. *Hurry up and drive off, already.*

"Were you and I just in the same house?" Kevin asked incredulously. "The furniture alone must be worth 100K. Plus, look at those cars in the driveway. A Navigator and a Maxima. Susan's husband drives a two-seater sports car. Grace has a Mercedes. And Pat's boyfriend drives a damn Jag. Okay, so he's white."

Kevin was starting to get on Charles's nerves with all his whiny talk. If he'd wanted to accomplish something with his life, why didn't he prepare for it thirty years ago instead of making a career out of spraying homes and offices for insects? "Plenty of white people drive Fords and Chevys, you know."

"Oh, yeah. Believe me, I don't believe all white folks are rich. But these people are all living the good life." Kevin flashed a knowing smile. "I'm sure you're not doing too bad yourself, with that house in Hyde Park Douglas bought."

"That house belongs to my mother, not to me."

"Yeah, but I'll bet—"

"Maybe you'd better not say what you're about to say," Charles suggested, a warning in his tone.

Kevin shrugged. "Sure, man. I ain't lookin' to start no shit. I'd better get back in and see how Elyse is doing."

Sorry-ass Negro, Charles thought as Kevin returned to the house. He'd seen lots of people like him before. Always begrudging everyone else's good living, and acting like it came from good luck instead of hard work. And not respecting their property. He'd been out here earlier, needing to take a break from seeing Susan with Bruce, when Kevin came out for a smoke break, stubbing it out in the middle of the Reavis's well-kept lawn when he was through. Charles had suggested that he not leave it there, reminding him that a spark could start a fire that might burn down the entire house. The old crabs-in-a-barrel mentality: "If I can't have anything this nice, then neither should you." But you couldn't take people who had nothing and expose them to a different lifestyle.

He couldn't imagine where Kevin's sudden attachment to Elyse had come from. Surely Elyse could see he wasn't much more than a thug. Mr. and Mrs. Nash, if they were still alive, must be brokenhearted that their firstborn had amounted to so little. Charles would never forget how disappointed his own father had been when Douglas wrecked his once-bright future with substance abuse. Like many others, Charles believed that Douglas's arrest and jail sentence had induced their father's fatal heart attack.

He couldn't help smiling when he considered that if Kevin saw the house Susan lived in, he'd probably drop dead from shock. Or ask if Bruce was in the record business or some other dumb question.

Bruce had finally driven off. Charles stood where he was, not wanting to arouse Bruce's suspicions if he was looking in the rearview mirror by walking forward to meet her. Already Bruce might be wondering why he was still standing out here. He wished he'd known Susan was bringing Bruce. He disliked "midnight creepers"—men who made nice with the husbands of the women they were sleeping with; yet here he was doing just that. The whole thing made him want to go home and take a shower.

Susan looked beautiful, he thought. She wore a plain knit black dress with a roomy white coat belted at the waist over it. Her hair had grown out a little, and she wore it brushed back and caught at the nape of her neck. It really wasn't long enough to hang down in a ponytail; it just sat back there in a curly mass. Her cheeks were full of color. He prayed she was as healthy as she looked. He couldn't bear to be with her at last only to have her taken away.

He'd been too impatient, and he knew it. It hadn't been right for him to pressure her the way he had. No wonder she blew up at him. He should have shared his plans with her. But what she said about him not being able to take care of her still stung.

Unlike Kevin, who seemed consumed by jealousy, Charles could accept not being as successful as Bruce Dillahunt. The important thing was that he could provide a home for Susan and her children. In addition to his salary, he earned good money from tutoring, and he also profited from the ATM machines he owned.

In a way it hadn't been fair for him to cut Kevin off when he mentioned his mother's house. True, the house Douglas bought belonged to his mother, but her owning the home free and clear allowed Charles to amass impressive savings and investments for a high school teacher, holdings that would help him support a new family. He just didn't want to put up with Kevin standing there insinuating that he was living off his brother's former success.

"When do I get a chance to talk to you?" he asked when Susan was within hearing distance.

"You don't have to talk. I already know what you want to say, and it won't work."

"Susan—"

"You and I won't work out unless we wait until I ask Bruce for a divorce. I know that, and you know it, too."

"How long will that be?"

"Another three or four months."

"It's already been nearly six. It's been agony for me." He searched her face anxiously. "Plus, I'm not sure Bruce will make things so easy for you. The way he was acting, all concerned for your safety and reluctant to leave you here . . . I saw him kiss you good-bye. Those aren't the actions of a man who's ready to unload his wife."

"He cares about me, Charles. Just because he feels no sexual desire for me doesn't take away from that. That's why he came with me in the first place; he was afraid I'd fall into a depression because Franklin died of cancer. But as far as him still being in love with me the way a husband loves a wife, don't fall for that any more than you should for that line about him going to work. He's going to spend a few hours with his girlfriend."

Charles felt a lot better. Susan meant what she said. He didn't like that hard set to her jaw, and recognized the strain she was under, how difficult these last months had been for her.

He resolved not to do anything to make it harder for her.

Chapter 59

Late December
Pleasant Prairie, Wisconsin

Bruce felt an ache in the pit of his stomach. It wasn't the kind of ache that came from eating something that didn't agree with him; it came from having to do something he dreaded.

He'd been consulting with his lawyer for months now, and they'd worked out a settlement. He was set to move in with Shay on January 1 and then they'd start house hunting. All that remained was to tell Susan.

Shay was so excited. They'd marry as soon as the divorce was finalized, which his attorney told him would take four or five months, but could drag on longer if Susan objected to his proposed settlement.

He hated having to tell her he wanted a divorce just after Franklin Reavis's funeral, but he'd made a promise to Shay that he would have everything in motion by the end of the year, and tomorrow was New Year's Eve. Quentin and Alyssa were up at his mother's in Kenosha, and from there they would go spend a few days with their other grandmother, Frances, who lived just fifteen minutes away. If he was going to do this, this was the perfect time.

He found Susan in the kitchen. "I'm fixing a turkey sandwich. Can I make one for you?"

"No, thanks." She was as polite and considerate as she'd ever been. Theirs had to be the most cordial failed marriage ever. He knew he couldn't stand living like this another minute. After he told her, he would be free to be with Shay.

Thinking of that gave him the courage to tell her.

"No, but I wanted to talk to you about something, if you've got time."

She looked up from the toast she was spreading mayonnaise on. "Sounds serious."

"It is. But go on and make your sandwich. It can wait until you eat."

"No, tell me now. We can talk while I eat."

That made it a little easier, talking to her while she sliced a tomato and heated her turkey slices left over from Christmas dinner at her sister Sherry's. "Uh . . . Susan, there's no easy way for me to say this. I'm afraid I haven't been a very good husband to you. I know I've told you that I'm not cheating on you. . . ."

Her eyebrows shot up. "Sounds like a confession."

". . . but that was because I didn't want to hurt your feelings. I know it's not fair for me to have been affected by your lumpectomy the way I have, but I can't help it. Lord knows I've tried."

"That's a moot point now, wouldn't you agree?" she asked evenly, taking a bite out of her sandwich before she opened the refrigerator door and removed a jug of skim milk.

He gave a sheepish look and shrugged. "I suppose. Susan, the truth is that I've been seeing someone for the past year. A little more than that, I think."

"And . . . ?" She carried her plate and glass over to the nook, sitting on the stool the farthest away from him.

She sounded awfully calm. He wasn't sure if that was a good thing or a bad thing. He'd been standing near the nook, but now he sat down on the opposite end, leaving an empty stool between them and swiveling it so that he faced her profile. "And I don't think it's fair to either of us if we stay married. She wants to be with me, and I admit that I want to be with her." When she failed to say anything, he talked more rapidly. "I don't see the point in us staying married. Neither one of us is happy together. Wouldn't it be better to be free to pursue other relationships?"

"I guess."

At least she said *something*, he thought, even though he could have been asking her to pass the salt. "We'll work this out. I'm not about to leave you or our kids out in the cold. I want you to have the same lifestyle you've always had, including the house."

Her mouth fell open. "You're saying you'll give me the house?"

"Well, I was hoping that once the divorce is final you'll agree to sell it and get something smaller. But for now, I really do think it'll be less traumatic for Quentin and Alyssa if they continue to live in the same house. It's going to be difficult for them to adjust to our living apart as it is. Now that you've got some work experience, I thought you might want to work full-time. Of course, I'll provide you with alimony in either case," he hastily added. God forbid she think he wanted her to get a full-time job so he wouldn't have to pay her quite as much. Sure, he'd love if it she did work full-time—maintaining this house wouldn't be cheap—but he didn't want her to feel pressured.

"To tell you the truth, I was thinking that I'd like to work full-time. But who's going to take care of the kids?"

"I thought we could hire a nanny or a housekeeper to come in from two to six. She can pick up the kids from school, do some housework, even cook dinner for you. Offer the job to Dolores, if she's willing to work part-time."

Susan knew she appeared calm, eating her sandwich and drinking her milk while Bruce nervously related his plans—plans he'd obviously put a lot of thought into, probably for months—but she wanted to jump up and shout hallelujah. Bruce's girlfriend must have a greater hold on him than she'd ever imagined, if he was willing to call an end to what they had become: little more than polite strangers living under the same roof. She now had the freedom that she'd spent the last eight months dreaming about. The trapped feeling and the hopelessness that had nearly threatened to destroy her relationship with Charles no longer existed. Bruce wouldn't be asking for his freedom if he planned on staying in the house another night. She and Charles had no reason to remain apart. They could even bring in the new year together!

She did agree with Bruce's assessment to limit the sense of upheaval for Quentin and Alyssa, but it angered her that he assumed she would be alone. He wanted them both to be "free to pursue other relationships." He'd already admitted he'd done just that, so his comment referred to her alone. The bastard didn't even consider the possibility that she might already have someone who loved and wanted her, even with breast cancer that could come back at any time. She wanted to pick up the heavy decanter on the counter and throw it at him.

"Susan?" he asked. "You seem more surprised at getting to keep the house than you do at my asking for a divorce."

"I suppose I was. Bruce, I always knew you were having an affair." Her mind was reeling. She would introduce Charles to her children, make him a part of their lives.

"I'm sorry I lied to you. You probably won't believe this, Susan, but I do love you."

"I know you do. But the cold, hard truth is that you don't *want* me anymore, and you've killed the passion I had for you by rejecting me over and over again. That's the best reason for not staying together." The relieved look on his face made her wonder if she should have given him a harder time. He was getting off too damn easy. But what was the point? He'd already said he would move out and she could stay in the house, with him paying the mortgage every month until their divorce became final.

"I'll start taking my things out tonight. But I won't leave until the kids come home on New Year's Day. We probably need to discuss how we're going to tell them."

"I'm sure we can come to an agreement on everything," she said brightly.

"You seem to be taking this awfully well. Mind if I ask why?"

He looked more baffled than suspicious, Susan thought. She wasn't about to tell him she had a man she loved and wanted to marry any more than she would have told him that Charles had driven her all the way home from Lake Forest the night of Franklin's funeral; there was no train ride. "I've found that I've given up, Bruce. I've thought about getting out on my own and starting over. That's why I thought I probably should work fulltime. I haven't been happy, either."

"I knew you hadn't been. I know this sounds ridiculous, Susan, but I care what happens to you."

"And this sounds equally ridiculous, but I understand completely what you mean, and I wish you happiness. And I wish your girlfriend good health." God forbid she develop breast cancer down the line. Or uterine cancer, or anything affecting her sexual organs. She, too, would find herself cast aside for a healthier specimen.

But that was *her* problem. Susan's problems with being rejected were finally over. The hangdog look on Bruce's face told her he understood her meaning. "Uh, yeah."

"So," she said brightly, "I suppose that as of now, we're free to do whatever we wish. The kids won't be back until the day after tomorrow."

"We'll tell them together," he said. "I'm dreading it, but I know it has to be done."

"Your timing is curious, Bruce. Did you want to get your house in order before the first of the year?"

"Something like that." He looked at her quizzically as she put her plate and glass in the sink and fluffed up her hair. "Hey, are you going out?"

"Yes. You said what you wanted to say, didn't you?"

"Yeah, but . . . Susan, you're not going to do anything foolish, are you?"

He's such a fool. "Of course not. It's just that I've got places to go and people to see . . . starting right now. I would tell you not to wait up . . . but of course you won't be here, will you?"

In the privacy of Alyssa's yellow and white bedroom, Susan's fingers felt unsteady as she punched in Charles's home number on her cell phone. She'd try him at home because she didn't want to risk his being out and about while she poured out her heart to him. How could he possibly concentrate on her words if he was paying for groceries at Dominick's?

She knew she shouldn't have insinuated that he was lacking somehow and compared him to Bruce. But Charles was equally wrong to continually nag her about getting a divorce the way he did. Didn't he know how difficult it was for her to step out on her husband? Didn't he realize she'd never done such a thing before? Why should she bear the brunt of everyone's bad behavior? First, Bruce's inability to handle her breast surgery and his refusal to discuss the matter in counseling, which might have saved their marriage. Then, Charles's being too damn impatient and trying to rush her when she needed to take baby steps to reclaim her independence. She began to get annoyed all over again just from thinking about it, but now the phone was ringing. . . .

Chapter 60

Late December
Chicago

One of the nicest parts of living downstairs from his mother, Charles thought, was her eagerness to help him out. She enjoyed doing his laundry and ironing his shirts. Right now she was in the living room folding the clothes and linens she'd just washed and dried. Such activity kept her busy and probably helped her from missing his father so much. Charles Valentine Sr. had been dead for over twenty years now.

Charles, on a stepladder, carefully removed the oblong covering of the kitchen light, bent to place it on the counter, and then removed the fluorescent bulb inside. It had probably been over a year since the last time he had to change the bulb; these things really lasted.

His phone started to ring.

"I'll get it," his mother said.

"Thanks, Mom."

The kitchen extension was fairly close to him, but picking it up would be awkward while on the ladder. He picked up the new tube-shaped bulb. Charles knew his mother hoped to hear the voice of a woman on the other end. She wanted to see him married before she died. Even Douglas had gotten married to a South Side girl and had a daughter during one of his periods of life on the outside.

His first reaction was to tell her not to bother, that it wouldn't be a woman calling because he wasn't seeing anyone, but then he decided to let her have her fun. It was harmless.

Of course, when she found out about him and Susan she'd have a fit for sure, but she'd just have to get used to the idea. He and Susan had come close to losing each other a second time, and he wasn't going to let *anyone* come between them again.

He listened to his mother say, "This is Charles's mother. What's your name?"

That was curious, he thought. It sounded like the type of thing she'd say to a female caller. He snapped the bulb into place and descended the ladder, just in time to see his mother's smile turn into a vicious snarl.

"Oh, it's you? And what do *you* want? No, nothing happened to Charles. He's fine. It took him a long time, but he's gotten accustomed to the idea of you being out of his life."

Charles rushed into the living room, ready to take the phone from his mother. It had to be Susan calling. No one else could elicit such an uncompromising response in his mother. But why would she call? She'd been so adamant that they had to stay away from each other until she and Bruce no longer lived under the same roof. She said that otherwise they would fall back into the same habits, and someone would say something out of frustration that would hurt the other's feelings. He couldn't say she'd been wrong, but at times he didn't know if he could stand being apart from her.

Of all times for her to call, at the moment his mother brought down a fresh load of laundry and was folding it. But surely she wasn't calling just to say hello, not after laying down the law the way she had. Something must be wrong.

"Mom," he said gently. "Give me the phone."

But Ann held tight and continued her tirade.

"Susan, you've brought my boys nothing but grief. You broke my Douglas's heart when you quit him and took up with his brother. I don't have to tell you what kind of woman sleeps with a man and his brother, too. And my boys' relationship has never been the same since that fistfight they had over you."

Charles tried again, louder this time. "Mom. Give me the phone."

Once more she paid him no heed. She turned her back to him. "Charles was devastated when you left him the first time. Yeah, I'll bet you didn't know I knew about your most recent sordid little affair with my son. Douglas told me," she said triumphantly.

Charles gasped. His mother *knew* he and Susan had resumed their romance?

"Douglas was upset when he heard that after everything that happened so long ago you were sleeping with Charles again. He knew you'd hurt him, and you left him a second time. Douglas might even start using drugs again because he's so upset. You've got a husband. Why don't you leave my boys alone?"

Charles's large hands attempted to pry his mother's fingers from the phone. He couldn't believe he was practically wrestling with her for control of the receiver. She had surprising strength. "That's enough, Mom. This call is for me."

He could get the receiver away from her, of course, but he didn't want to knock her down to do it. The most she'd give him was turning the phone with its earpiece facing up so that they could both hear.

Susan was speaking. "How dare you place the blame for Douglas's substance abuse at my feet. He clearly has an addictive personality, if he's been unable to stop using after nearly thirty years. It didn't have a damn thing to do with me. If you ask me, you ought to stop kidding yourself.

"And everything between Douglas and me was over more than twenty-five years ago. As for Charles, there are things between him and me that you aren't privy to and don't understand."

Ann moved the receiver so she could speak into the mouthpiece. "I understand that you've got a husband, and I don't see where he fits into this pretty picture. He's probably why you broke it off with my boy again. I hear he's rich. You don't want to risk losing that money. Never mind that you've wrecked both my sons' lives. Charles would have been happily married to someone else if it weren't for you."

"If Charles wanted to be married, he would be married. And as for me, I may be married right now, but not for long. My husband and I are getting divorced. And I'm going to come back to

Charles, and if he'll have me I'll live with him the rest of my life."

She heard the sounds of a scuffle, heard Charles's voice say, "Mom! That's *enough*. I'd appreciate it if you let me talk to Susan in private. I'll be up in a few minutes. You and I have to talk." It dismayed him to take such a stern tone with his mother, but he couldn't risk her driving Susan away with her delusions. Susan had already expressed doubts about his family accepting her.

His mother didn't much care for what he said, for she threw the phone at him before turning to leave. He caught it easily. "Susan? I heard what you said. Is it true? You and Bruce are really getting a divorce?"

"Yes. He just came to me and said he thinks we ought to end it because neither of us is happy. The kids are up at his mother's, and I think Bruce is packing a few things. I'm free until the kids come home New Year's Day."

Charles's grin covered his whole face, like a character in those animated *Peanuts* cartoons. "Will you come down? I almost hate to ask you, but I think it would be disrespectful for me to come to your house."

"I agree. Just give me a few minutes to throw a few things together." She squeezed her shoulders together. "Charles, do you know what this means? No more waiting to be together."

"It's almost like a reward from God. He knew how much I wanted you, and that it would kill me to wait more months to see you. Hurry down, will you? In the meantime I'm going upstairs to talk to my mother."

"Did you know she knew about us?"

"No, she never said a word. And I don't know how she knew you and I had broken up. I guess she couldn't help but notice that I wasn't going out like I used to." He paused. "Susan . . . You do know it might be hard, don't you? She'll probably never come around. But I'm prepared to move out."

"Oh, I couldn't ask you to do that, Charles. I don't know if you realize how high rents are nowadays. Giving up an apartment where you don't pay much for rent will hurt you financially. I'll deal with it."

"That reminds me . . ."

That day at Franklin Reavis's funeral, when Susan told him it would be best if they had no contact until she was able to see him openly, he never did get a chance to tell her that his financial picture was a lot brighter than she knew. It wasn't the right setting. He knew Susan didn't want to be seen spending too much time alone with him, not with both the Maxwells and Elyse's parents, the Hugheses, present. He respected her wishes to keep their involvement a private matter, but since neither Pat nor Grace appeared surprised to see them reenter the house together, he wondered if Susan's friends knew about them. "We need to talk about my ideas for where we'll live after we're married."

For a moment she was silent. He was about to ask her if something was wrong when she said in a small voice, "You still want to marry me, Charles? You really do?"

The sudden way her life had changed in an afternoon had caught up with her, Charles knew. He couldn't blame her for being in such awe . . . He felt the same way. After a delay of two and a half decades, he would finally get to be with the woman he'd always loved. And he'd wipe away that hard edge that had invaded her personality, once and for all.

"Yes, I really do," he told her. "And what's more, I *will*."

Chapter 61

Mid-January
Evanston, Illinois

Elyse, wearing a heavy winter coat, took a moment to be grateful for the frigid January temperatures in Chicago as Kevin rose from the table and pulled her into an embrace at Wolfgang Puck Café. She couldn't stand for him to put his hands on her. She couldn't even stand to look at him. He was a living, breathing reminder that she'd been unfaithful to her husband while he was on his deathbed.

She wished he hadn't come to the funeral, and she'd been shocked when he showed up at her house afterward. The way he hovered over her, always eager to be of assistance; it was embarrassing. Elyse knew people wondered what was up with that. Her own mother pulled her aside and asked, "Who *is* that?" Elyse told her it was just a friend who was a little overzealous in his concern for how she was bearing up, to which Jeanette Hughes replied with characteristic bluntness, "He's acting like he expects to take Franklin's place."

Grace, too, pulled her aside. "Listen to me, Elyse. I don't know what's going on with you and The Orkin Man, but my gut tells me he's looking for more from you than just to be your new chum. For God's sake, be careful."

The tension arising from Kevin's presence only added to her stress load. Elyse witnessed Rebecca's frosty reaction to him, saw her stepdaughter whispering to her brother and mother. What was worse, Kevin acted like he didn't want to leave. He stayed as long as Grace and Susan, and longer than Pat, who left fairly early because her parents had ridden with her and Andy and no doubt were ready to leave. She had to tell him—speaking softly so no one else could hear—that he should probably be on his way, too, that she was tired.

In the weeks since he'd made several attempts to see her, but she'd put him off, saying she had personal business to attend to and simply wanted to rest before returning to work. He obviously felt their one-night encounter would resume now that Franklin had died, but she knew otherwise. She'd gone back to work Monday, and she knew the time had come to tell him that they'd never see each other again.

"You're looking well, Elyse. How're you holding up?" he asked now as she laid her coat over a spare chair and sat down opposite him.

Elyse shrugged. "One day at a time, as they say. Going back to work has actually helped me, if you can believe it."

"Have you made any plans? You know, to sell your house?"

"I'm going to stay in it. It feels a little large when I'm there alone, but the kids come home every couple of weeks. Besides, there's really no reason for me to sell it. The mortgage was paid off because of a life insurance policy Franklin and I had, if either of us passed away. It's my biggest asset, and I might need to tap into it in case Todd or Brontë decide to go to graduate school or something." She took a deep breath, trying to work up the courage to tell him that they would never see each other, much less sleep together, again. Sure, they both worked in Skokie, but she hadn't ever run into him in all these years, and she doubted she ever would. "Uh, Kevin, you know—"

"Well, I'm sure you've got more than just the house, don't you?"

Elyse shifted her hips in her chair. Franklin had taken care of her financially, but she wasn't about to discuss the details with Kevin. Still, she didn't want to hurt his feelings by telling him not to be nosy. "Let's just say that I won't go hungry and leave it at that," she suggested, hoping he would take the hint.

"Sure. I just thought you might be interested in doing a little investing."

"In your Laundromat?" she asked tentatively.

He shrugged. "It's going to be a real profit maker, Elyse. I've been putting aside every dime I could, but I'm still a couple of thousand short."

She just stared at him.

"Well, okay, seven and a half K."

Their waiter appeared. "Are you—"

Elyse held up a hand. "Give us a few minutes." After the young man discreetly disappeared, she said, "Are you kidding me, Kevin? You want me to give you seventy-five hundred dollars?"

"Well, not *give*. It would be a loan, that's all."

Her spine straightened. "Kevin, I want to be as polite about this as I can. I'm not loaning you any money."

His eyes narrowed. "Why not?"

"Because I don't believe in lending money to friends."

"I thought I was more than a friend."

She spoke softly. "We slept together once, Kevin. I was feeling very vulnerable because of all the friction in my marriage. In hindsight, it was a mistake."

Kevin's confident grin faded like daylight after sunset. "No, you don't mean that. We're just getting started. This was in the cards. I know you didn't mean to cheat on your husband, but . . . Well, it doesn't matter much now, does it?"

"Yes, it does, Kevin. I'm sorry you feel that our friendship was headed in that direction, but it never was, and it never will be. In fact, I wanted to have lunch with you today to tell you that we'll be going our separate ways."

He shook his head in disbelief. "You mean . . . We won't be seeing each other anymore?"

"No, Kevin. It won't work. You're a reminder of a painful time in my life. Having you around will only make me relive it. I'm sorry, but that's the way it is."

"Yeah, I get it," he said with a nod, his features suddenly gone hard. "You want to stay all secure in your rich little world in Lake Forest. You don't want to let a brother get in, give him a break."

Elyse put one hand on her coat, ready to grab it. "Before you start accusing me of being some sort of elitist, maybe you should ask yourself what your motives were for getting close to me in the first place." Her voice shook with emotion, but her hand was steady as she grabbed her coat. "Sorry. I'm not staying," she said to the bewildered-looking young waiter as she passed him.

She drove back to work, stopping at a fast-food drive-thru to pick up a salad. It saddened her that her friendship with Kevin had ended on such a sour note, and she also felt hurt. Grace had been right. He hadn't shown all that concern because of her; he merely wanted to get close to her because he saw an opportunity to get her to finance his damn Laundromat once Franklin was out of the picture. Knowing that she'd actually slept with him while Franklin was alive would haunt her the rest of her days.

One day she'd probably tell Grace she'd been right about Kevin's motives, but Elyse knew that she'd take the secret of their one-night stand to her own grave.

Chapter 62

"Well, here I am," Pat said, opening the door of the dressing room. "How do I look?"

Elyse caught her breath, and her palm went up to rest on her chest. "Oh, Pat. You're just beautiful."

"I've never seen you look prettier or happier," Susan said in agreement.

Grace shook her head. "I still can't believe you bought a wedding dress from Target."

Pat fingered the rayon-blend material of her simple white gown with spaghetti straps. "Listen, I'm only going to wear this once. I'm too practical to spend a thousand dollars on a dress I'll wear for just a few hours. It's not like I'll have a daughter I can pass it down to."

"Grace, stop being such a sourpuss," Elyse chided.

Susan flashed a devilish grin. "Could it be that our Miss Grace is feeling left out because she wants to be a bride and the center of attention instead of Pat and me?" They all knew that Grace's first marriage had taken place at City Hall and her second in Las Vegas. She'd been a wife to two men, but never a bride.

"No, because Grace *isn't* feeling left out," Grace said testily, her touchiness belying her claim. "Besides, you and Charles aren't having any guests, so there won't be anyone to fuss over you."

Now it was Susan's turn to shrug. "I've already done the big wedding thing. I would have done it again if that's what Charles wanted to, but he's not interested. After all, we're a mature couple getting married." With a panicked look Pat's way, she hastily added, "Of course, if we *were* having a ceremony and guests, it would be small and elegant, like this."

Pat knew Susan hadn't meant anything by the slight blunder. Instead she looked at herself in the three-part full-length mirror. The soft fabric of her gown created a natural draped neckline, and it also hugged her curves, which had been streamlined since taking up a regular exercise regimen. She hadn't looked this good at forty. "I can't believe I'm actually getting married for the first time at fifty."

"And I can't believe we're getting to be bridesmaids again," Grace replied. "It's been a long time between turns." When Elyse married Franklin twenty-seven years ago, they had all been bridesmaids, with one of Elyse's cousins serving as maid of honor. "But I guess that's what happens when your lives turn out something less than traditional."

"Oh, getting married at my age is definitely not traditional," Pat said. "That's why I just wanted the three of you as bridesmaids with no honor attendant, and why I wanted you to pick out your own dresses . . . as long as they were peach."

"I still think you should have gone with yellow," Grace said with a frown.

"No, Grace, because yellow makes me look all washed-out," Susan protested. "Why should I wear an unflattering color just because it looks nice with your complexion?"

"I like peach better on me, too," Elyse added.

Grace rolled her eyes.

Elyse dismissed Grace's complaint with a wave of her hand. "You've got yourself a wonderful man, Pat," she said. "You mark my words. You and Andy are going to be happy together the rest of your lives. June is a wonderful month for weddings. Franklin and I were married in June."

"I know, hon." Pat walked over to give Elyse a careful hug, barely pressing her cheek with her own for fear of mussing her makeup. Then she pulled back and clasped her friend's upper arms. "Are you sure you're all right?"

"Oh yes, I'm fine. But I do miss Franklin terribly. I'll always wish that things could have been better between us those last few months, but at least he died making sure I knew he loved me and he didn't really mean those terrible things he said."

"I heard what happened to Kevin," Susan said. "That's really too bad. Pat told me about it the other day."

Kevin had been arrested and charged with grand larceny, on suspicion of masterminding a burglary ring at the homes of some his former employer's clients. The police figured out that he had been in each home to handle ants, termites, and other pests before they were robbed of plasma televisions and other expensive items that were out in plain sight. He was being held at the Cook County Jail because his bond hadn't been paid. The senior Nashes clearly had their own reasons for not paying to have him sprung.

"Yes, I thought so, too," Elyse replied in a small voice. "He was desperate to raise the cash to make his dream come true. He even came to me after Franklin died for a loan."

"I knew it!" Grace slammed her hand down on the makeup table for emphasis. "What'd you do, Elyse?"

"I walked out of the restaurant and never looked back."

"Well, your new doctor friend seems very nice," Susan said graciously.

Elyse nodded. "He lost his wife nearly two years ago, so he knows how I feel."

"Have you two been seeing each other long?" Grace asked.

"Not long. He called me several weeks ago, just to inquire how I was doing. Then he called again a couple of weeks later and kind of tentatively suggested that maybe we could have brunch together one Sunday. We've been out a few times. I guess you can say we're friends." She looked pointedly at Grace. "And no, we haven't slept together. I'm not ready for that yet, and Isaac knows it. He's acknowledged that he's not going to try to push me into anything."

"How do Todd and Brontë feel about your dating?" Susan asked.

Pat knew Susan was thinking about her own situation. Her youngsters were having difficulty coping with both the divorce and seeing their parents with new partners.

"Pretty good, actually. I worried they might not like the fact that Isaac had been their father's doctor, but they said it was okay. Although Todd did call me at midnight when I was out with Isaac to make sure I'd gotten in safely." She laughed at the memory. "I'm surprised he didn't make that long drive up from Champaign just to check him out."

"Well, you're looking great these days," Pat said. "That weight loss looks great on you. You must have dropped a good twenty-five pounds."

"Yes, twenty-eight, to be exact."

Grace had been following the conversation eagerly and now spoke up. "Susan, how are *your* kids coping with the divorce and the remarriage plans?"

"I think they're baffled by it all. They really don't understand why their mommy and daddy don't live together anymore, why we've taken up with other people. We thought it was a good thing that we hadn't had any arguments in front of them. Now I'm not so sure. I'm afraid they might be left with security issues." She sighed. "Bruce and I have been trying to work it out. And they do like Charles."

"Well, I'm sorry I won't be there to watch you and Charles finally make it legal," Elyse said, "but know that I'll be thinking about you down there in Jamaica. I'm really happy for you both."

"I know you are. Thanks so much."

"I'm glad everything worked out for you, too, Susan," Grace said, and Susan knew she meant it. "I think the whole thing is very romantic, reuniting with your first love after so many years. And it was really sweet of Charles to agree to leave Chicago and move up to Kenosha."

"Well, houses are cheaper up there, and the kids will be closer to Bruce and both grandmothers. Hopefully, Charles will find a teaching job in Kenosha soon so he won't have to make the commute for long, and of course, I'll be able to stay where I am." Susan had gotten a full-time accounting position at one of Kenosha's largest employers.

Someone knocked at the door.

"It's probably the photographer," Pat said.

"I'm ready for my close-up," Grace quipped.

The women walked down the aisle in height order. Elyse went first, holding her bouquet tightly and looking straight ahead. Unlike Grace, she disliked knowing that people were looking at her. But the looks were all admiring, not critical. She did look good these days. The dress she'd chosen, with a lacy fitted bodice and a full skirt ending just above her ankles, showed off her slimmed-down figure to best advantage.

She allowed her gaze to go to the left, where she knew Isaac would be sitting. He winked at her, and she winked back, breaking into a beauty-contestant smile.

Her heart still belonged to Franklin, and part of it probably always would, but nevertheless, life was good.

Grace moved easily to the music, moving her head from left to right and smiling at the eighty guests. She knew that she could easily have been sitting in one of the rows of chairs, or that she didn't have to be here at all. She felt grateful that Pat had forgiven her completely for having that affair with Ricky. If she hadn't confessed, would Pat and Andy even be getting married?

She caught sight of Glenn staring at her from his seat. He stood out in a crowd, with his six-feet-three height and his still-broad build. The look in his eyes suggested that he'd like to slip away to some quiet place and make love to her at the first opportunity. Her vaginal muscles twitched just thinking about it. Although yellow was a better color for her than peach, she'd nonetheless found a flattering dress, which bared her shoulders just slightly and dipped to a wide V-neck in front. The bodice fit snugly, and, like Elyse's dress, the skirt flared to tea-length. She'd had her hair styled in an upsweep, with curls across the entire width of her head to balance her chin. She hated the way her chin came to a point but had long since learned the best styles for her. The smiles she received from the guests told her she'd been successful.

Grace vowed to be the one to catch Pat's bridal bouquet. She liked the idea of getting married at a trendy boutique hotel like the W. If she played her cards right with Glenn, maybe she'd get the chance.

In the meantime, they were having fun and plenty of great sex.

Who could ask for anything more?

Susan serenely strolled down the aisle. She'd chosen a dress with a nautical look, with an oversized collar and double-breasted buttons in matching fabric running from her breastbone to her waist. She'd thought about cutting her hair, but Charles said he liked it longer, so she'd pinned it into a French roll.

She saw him beaming at her and knew his thoughts mirrored hers . . . that in another month they would be the ones getting married—on a beach in Jamaica. They wouldn't have to travel to a honeymoon destination, like Pat and Andy, with that long flight to Acapulco in front of them.

When she and Charles got back they would move into their new house. They'd found a spacious Dutch Colonial in Kenosha, with three bedrooms, two baths, and a full finished basement. It was much smaller than what she and the kids were used to, but plenty roomy.

Bruce was building a large house with his girlfriend, soon-to-be wife. Susan hadn't met Shay yet, but Quentin and Alyssa had. She told them it was all right for them to like her, even love her, the same way it was all right for them to have special feelings for Charles.

It was a complex situation for children to deal with, but Susan felt confident that with time, Quentin and Alyssa would be all right. Best of all, she wouldn't have to see a lot of either Ann or Douglas down in Chicago. Ann had moved into Charles's old apartment, and Douglas and his wife and daughter lived upstairs. It was a perfect solution, for Ann had been complaining about the stairs to get to the front door, as well as the inside steps to her upstairs bedroom. And Douglas would have possession of the house he'd paid for.

Charles had taken an apartment in Pleasant Prairie so he could be near her while the divorce became final. The final decree was awarded last month, but Charles gallantly refused to sleep with her in the bed she'd shared with Bruce, in a house where Bruce still paid the mortgage. A purchase bid had been accepted on it, but Susan wanted to delay the closing on both the old and new houses until the weeks just before their trip to Jamaica.

She and Charles would at long last be married, like he'd wanted to do so many years ago.

Her smile got wider.

Pat smiled at her father before the wedding march began playing. She knew it was hard for him to hand her over to a man who wasn't black, but she was proud of him. That afternoon at Elyse's he'd quietly told Andy that he didn't care if he was ninety or even dead, if Andy ever mistreated Pat he would somehow find a way to make him pay for it. Andy understood and took the threat with a grain of salt.

"Ready, Patty-cake?" he asked, patting her hand.

"I'm ready. Let's go get me married off."

They moved into another room for the reception. Pat had plenty of pictures taken with her lifelong friends, and at one point she called for their dates to join them. Only Susan had a permanent relationship, but she hoped that whatever happened with Elyse and Isaac and Grace and Glenn, they would look back upon this day with fondness.

When they were all seated, Elyse made an announcement. "I've got something you've all got to see," she said, holding something behind her back. Amid cries of, "Let's see it!" she dramatically unveiled a blown-up photograph.

"Oh, my God! That's us!" Pat exclaimed.

Andy peered at the photo. "That must have been during the Blizzard of '67. I don't remember any other time when there was that much snow on the ground."

"My dad took a picture of us playing when the snow stopped. We were some of the first kids to get outside, and the snow was still fresh."

Grace and Susan got up to look at the photo over the shoulders of Pat and Andy. The projects at that time were just ten years old, but the playground had already fallen into disrepair, with broken swings and no netting on the basketball rims. That day, though, it looked like a snow-blanketed paradise. The snow practically came up to their waists. They were all bundled up and barely recognizable, but it was them, nine years old in that January, some forty-one years before.

"Gigi, is that really you?" Grace's grandson asked her. He'd served as ring bearer and called his grandmother "Gigi," for "Grandma Grace."

Grace pointed each of them out with a French-manicured finger. "That's me, and that's Aunt Pat, and this is Miss Susan and Miss Elyse."

"Wow."

"My mother sent this to me," Elyse said. "She thought you might enjoy seeing it. I had 8 x 10s made for all of us."

"That was so thoughtful, Elyse," Pat said. "Thank you."

Shavonne appeared, having been brought over by her son to see Grace's photo. "Y'all were so cute." Her one-year-old daughter, whom she held, made a cranky cry. "All right, Baby Girl. I'm going to change you now. Maybe then you'll go to sleep like a good girl."

"Hasn't she taken a nap yet?" Pat asked incredulously.

"No. I think she likes the music, Aunt Pat. She's afraid she's going to miss something, so she's fighting sleep."

"Try telling her a story," Pat suggested. "You can start off by saying, 'Once upon a time, there were four little girls who lived in the projects. . . .' "

ONCE UPON A PROJECT

BETTYE GRIFFIN

ABOUT THIS GUIDE

The questions and discussion topics that follow are
intended to enhance your group's reading of
this book.

DISCUSSION QUESTIONS

1) Pat gave Ricky up rather than defy her parents, conscious of their telling her, "You're all we have left" and not wanting to cause them more heartbreak. Should she have handled the situation differently? If so, how?

2) When Grace sought out Ricky after learning of his divorce, she reasoned that Pat didn't want him when she had him. Does this argument have any validity?

3) Grace, a highly paid professional, frequently dated men who, when compared with herself, earned considerably less money and had less familiarity with the world beyond the South Side. Pat, an attorney for county government, often stayed home dateless on weekends, refusing to accept invitations from men with blue-collar jobs because she felt it was futile to pursue such relationships. Who was wiser? Who was happier?

4) After her lumpectomy, Susan chose not to have the small but noticeable defect on her breast surgically repaired because she couldn't bear another surgical procedure. Do you think it would have made a difference in her marriage to Bruce?

5) With his unwillingness to look at Susan's breasts after her lumpectomy, most people would agree that Bruce Dillahunt was insensitive and even a bit cruel. Although he could afford counseling, he refused it, maintaining that *he* wasn't the problem; Susan's cancer was. Do you feel that men are more resistant to seeking psychological help? Why or why not?

6) Ann Valentine felt Susan was a whore to have slept with both of Ann's sons. Others felt the same way. What do *you* think?

7) Why do you suppose that Kevin, whose family were middle-class homeowners as opposed to project dwellers, did so little with his life?

8) How do you think Elyse handled Franklin's illness and his treatment of her?

9) Who was your favorite character in this book? Your least favorite character? Why?

10) Years ago, the average stay in public-housing projects was shorter than it is now: five, ten, perhaps fifteen years before moving on to better living conditions. But today's poor tend to live in these surroundings much longer. Why do you suppose this is?